PASSION'S DESTINY

"Do I have any choice?" Aimée asked, her hands pushing against his chest. She tried to ignore the treacherous leap of her pulse.

"None, my sweet, green-eyed wildcat. Neither of us has had a choice since the minute we laid eyes on one another," Sebastian replied. He captured both her hands in his, pulling her against the hard, lean length of him. "It's time, my *agigaue,* my beloved woman. Time to celebrate the joy between us."

Lifting her in his arms he carried her to the place where he had spread the bear furs in front of the blazing fire. He gazed down at her, devouring the sight of her alabaster skin against the ebony fur.

Aimée looked up at him, her jade gaze filled with wonder. "You saw me in a dream also," she whispered. "As I saw you."

"It was destined, you and I," Sebastian's voice was a velvet caress as he reached for her, pulling her down in his embrace to the enveloping softness of the fur.

The time for talking was over.

CAPTURE THE GLOW
OF ZEBRA'S HEARTFIRES

AUTUMN ECSTASY (3133, $4.25)
by Pamela K. Forrest

Philadelphia beauty Linsey McAdams had eluded her kidnappers but was now at the mercy of the ruggedly handsome frontiersman who owned the remote cabin where she had taken refuge. The two were snowbound until spring, and handsome Luc LeClerc soon fancied the green-eyed temptress would keep him warm through the long winter months. He said he would take her home at winter's end, but she knew that with one embrace, she might never want to leave!

BELOVED SAVAGE (3134, $4.25)
by Sandra Bishop

Susannah Jacobs would do anything to survive—even submit to the bronze-skinned warrior who held her captive. But the beautiful maiden vowed not to let the handsome Tonnewa capture her heart as well. Soon, though, she found herself longing for the scorching kisses and tender caresses of her raven-haired BELOVED SAVAGE.

CANADIAN KISS (3135, $4.25)
by Christine Carson

Golden-haired Sara Oliver was sent from London to Vancouver to marry a stranger three times her age—only to have her husband-to-be murdered on their wedding day. Sara vowed to track the murderer down, but he ambushed her and left her for dead. When she awoke, wounded and frightened, she was staring into the eyes of the handsome loner Tom Russel. As the rugged stranger nursed her to health, the flames of passion erupted, and their CANADIAN KISS threatened never to end!

Available wherever paperbacks are sold, or order direct from the Publisher. Send cover price plus 50¢ per copy for mailing and handling to Zebra Books, Dept. 3489, 475 Park Avenue South, New York, N.Y. 10016. Residents of New York, New Jersey and Pennsylvania must include sales tax. DO NOT SEND CASH.

DIANE GATES ROBINSON

DELTA DESIRE

ZEBRA BOOKS
KENSINGTON PUBLISHING CORP.

In loving memory of my Grandfather Stephen A. Gates, whose kind and gentle heart understood the Native American's reverence for Mother Earth and all her creatures. He took the time to show a little girl nature's beauty.

and

For my parents with love, and in fond remembrance of all the happy wilderness sojourns of my childhood.

ZEBRA BOOKS

are published by

Kensington Publishing Corp.
475 Park Avenue South
New York, NY 10016

Copyright © 1991 by Diane Gates Robinson

All rights reserved. No part of this book may be reproduced in any form or by any means without the prior written consent of the Publisher, excepting brief quotes used in reviews.

If you purchased this book without a cover you should be aware that this book is stolen property. It was reported as "unsold and destroyed" to the Publisher and neither the Author nor the Publisher has received any payment for this "stripped book."

First printing: August, 1991

Printed in the United States of America

Part One

Our destiny rules over us, even when we are not yet aware of it.

Nietzsche

Twice or thrice had I loved thee,
Before I knew thy face or name.

John Donne

Prologue

Was it a vision or a waking dream?

Keats

Chickasaw Bluff on the Mississippi River, 1782

The low moan of the wind through the cottonwood trees was the only sound to break the stillness of the hot, lonely night. A shaft of moonlight fell across the silver-gray trunks, turning them into ghostly sentinels guarding the dark rushing waters of the mighty river below. A low chanting joined the wind's voice as the Chickasaw youth began his song of invocation to the unseen powers about him.

Standing tall in front of the dream bower he had made from slender willow saplings, the handsome young man sang with deep emotion, "Oh, Great *Ababinili,* composite force of the Four Beloved Things Above, I come to you with open heart. My soul is given into your keeping. Grant me the dream to see my totem. Give me the power to allow my eyes to see a vision of the future. I seek the knowledge of myself and my destiny."

Light seemed to stream down from the full ivory moon upon the dark rushing water as the Indian youth stared up into the star-strewn sky, singing his song of faith as he sought guidance in his vision quest.

He had prepared long for this most sacred vigil. The holy man of the tribe known as the *Hopaye,* who was also his mother's uncle, had instructed him on how to make his heart clean. The rites of purification had begun when he reached the age of fifteen, and now he had finally achieved the rank of a "powered" one. A week ago he had bathed in cleansing waters in which his mother had mixed herbs. Next he began his journey to maturity, leaving the Chickasaw Old Fields villages behind. Alone, the boy traveled many days to the high bluffs above the mighty river known to his English father as the Mississippi, and to his mother's people as *Occochappo,* Ancient Waters, or *Mecassheba,* the King I am. Here in the sacred hunting ground of his mother's people he sought his vision quest. Without this experience where his destiny would be revealed to him, he could never be called warrior. When the visions did not come it was one of the great tragedies of life, for a boy was considered an earthly dolt unfit but for the most humble of work.

"Do not fail me, oh Great Mystery," prayed the tall, sinewy youth called Sebastian Macleod by his father, and One Who Walks Alone by his mother. Two days he had been fasting and chanting alone here by the river. He had taken the purges and emetics given him by his uncle, the holy man, but still he had experienced nothing.

It had to be this summer, for true to the bargain with his father, One Who Walks Alone was to travel back with his father to Robert Macleod's home in Charleston. In his father's fine house he would once more assume the identity of Sebastian Macleod, only son and heir to the Macleod fortune.

He could not leave his mother's people without his adult warrior name, the name that would come from his vision. His mother's clan was the *Minko,* the Chief clan. They were the clan of leaders and great warriors. He could not let them down.

The taunts of mixed blood had followed him in both his mother's and his father's world. They had not lasted long, for he soon silenced the boys who taunted him, but always there was the undercurrent, the looks that told him he didn't quite belong. No, he couldn't fail this greatest test of his young manhood.

Staring up into the heavens, he concentrated on the stars while he continued his invocation to the Four Beloved Things Above, which were the Sun, Clouds, Clear Sky, and He that Lives in the Clear Sky. Slowly, all became still, and he felt himself soaring up, up into the dark velvet night. He was one with the elements. The wind was part of him and he was the wind, he was the rushing water of the river, he was the trees twisted by the force of the seasons and of time. He was the earth below, and the sky above. No longer earthbound, but one with the stars in the Great Mystery Spirit of the universe.

Filled with exhilaration and a strange peace, the youth became aware of a shadowy figure moving along the bank of the bluff. He knew the beast, it was a creature who was as much a loner as he, a great sinewy panther. Burning eyes reflected the moon glow, as the huge cat lifted its great head and stared across the long grass at the young man. In the unearthly light of the shimmering moon on the vast water, he could see the long shadow of the beast, and it seemed to reach out to him.

I know you, he thought, *you are me, one who walks alone. Is this what you are telling me, that I shall always be apart from others? I shall be a strong, but a solitary hunter?*

Then as he drew nearer to the beast, unafraid because he felt such kinship, he saw another figure emerge from the dark forest. He caught his breath, for it was the figure of a beautiful woman, a woman of silver and glowing light. Waving hair of white-gold hung to her waist, as she seemed to glide without fear to the great, dark figure of the panther.

Turning toward him she smiled, and he saw her eyes green like a cat's. They were glowing with happiness and love. Placing a slender ivory arm about the beast's neck she stroked him with gentle caresses. The youth felt the great cat's joy and peace. He had found solace and love with this beautiful, loving woman who was also wise and all-seeing. He was no longer alone.

Suddenly, the boy knew that he had seen his vision of the future. Like the panther, he would walk the lonely road between two cultures, fierce and strong, but someday he would find his beloved woman, his *Agigaue,* and would be alone no longer.

The glowing figures faded, and the moon slipped lower in the sky, paling as the light of day rose in the east. Sebastian Macleod slipped inside his dream bower and found the deep sleep of those at peace. The quest had been successful, for he had seen his destiny. He could begin his journey back to his mother's people. He had his warrior's name, Shadow Panther.

Chapter One

New Orleans, Louisiana, December, 1794

"You will marry him, Aimée, because I say so." The aging, yet still attractive Leona Louvierre glared down at her stepdaughter in triumph. "Your father's will made me guardian of you and your sister Mignon, and that gives me the right."

"My father never knew what you really were, Leona, or he would never have done such a thing," the young woman spat out in contempt, flinging back her silver-blonde hair from her shoulders.

"It matters not how much of a fool your *père* was, my girl, for he is dead these two years. I am the one who decides your future as a good Creole stepmother should, and in my far greater wisdom have chosen Señor Rodrigo Hernandez as your husband." An evil smile curved the corners of Leona's mouth. She had waited a long time to get rid of this troublesome, entirely too beautiful stepdaughter. "It is not as if you had any other offers. You should be grateful some man wants you, what with Mignon's problem."

"What has he promised you, Leona?" Aimée asked

with scorn, trying to control the trembling that shook her voice, so filled was she with anger. How could her father have married this woman? But then she had always shown him a different face than that she had worn with Aimée and Mignon.

"Fabien will get a position with the government on your wedding day. I should think you would be happy to help your dear stepbrother advance his career," Leona answered stiffly.

"The only career that one has is seeing how much he can drink, or how many women he can chase," Aimée replied in disgust. Help her stepbrother? She would rather die. Just thinking of the man who had tried countless times to force himself on her until the night he broke into her room through the French door and climbed into her bed, made her feel ill. She had pulled the small dagger from the pillow and pressed it to his throat. Telling him if he ever touched her again she would kill him had brought back some feeling of control over her life. He had left her alone after that, for Fabien was lazy and a coward. Ever since that night his mere presence filled her with revulsion.

"I am through arguing, Aimée. Get dressed. You are going to the ball tonight, and you will smile when your engagement is announced to Señor Hernandez. If you don't obey then I shall suggest he take Mignon as his bride. 'Tis up to you." Leona gave an ugly laugh at the horrified expression on the young woman's face before sweeping in triumph from the room.

Aimée Louvierre stood stunned, realizing her stepmother had played her final card and the game was over. Leona had won. Stumbling to the long French door, she stared out at the ghostly fog that had crept into the courtyard from the river. It swirled about the second story gallery and added to her feeling of suffocation.

She was trapped with no way to run. Leona knew her only too well. She could not allow her delicate younger sister take her place in marriage with the old man they called *El Lobo*.

Mignon was barely fourteen, and out of touch with the world. Ever since she had seen their father die before her eyes in the fire that destroyed their plantation home, she had withdrawn from life. She spent her days with the gentle nuns at the Ursuline Convent, for they understood the speech impediment that made talking agony for Mignon, especially to strangers. From the day Cato, the butler, had saved her from the flames that had engulfed the mansion, killing her father, Mignon had had trouble speaking. At first she had said nothing for weeks. Then at the town house in New Orleans she had gradually regained her speech, but was left with a marked stutter and violent mood swings.

Many in New Orleans society thought Mignon crazy. They whispered about the Louvierre blood being tainted, that insanity might run in the family. Although Aimée had many friends and was considered a beauty, no young gentlemen came to court her.

Aimée sighed, turning away from the sight of the depressing winter afternoon to pace back and forth in the confines of her chamber. She was caught; there was naught to do but attend the ball at the Hernandez town house tonight. She had looked after her sister since they were both small, ever since their mother had died of the fever. Aimée had always been the stronger of the two; she could not fail Mignon. Tonight, she would become betrothed to the most hated man in all the city since the Spanish had taken over New Orleans. As a captain of police he had earned his reputation for brutality and corruption.

Standing in front of the fire, trying to warm the chill that had penetrated the marrow of her bones, her gaze fell on her easel in the corner. A half-finished portrait she had been working on earlier in the day stood there uncovered. She stared at the handsome male visage and felt a familiar wild pang of longing. Who was he, this man whose face haunted her dreams, till she drew him over and over? The high cheekbones, the raven hair, but she could never get the eyes quite right. It was as if he were standing just at the edge of a mist. She could barely make him out, for it was more that she felt his presence, a warm, wonderful feeling that was like an embrace. He was a stranger, yet she felt she knew him. Somewhere he was waiting for her. Ever since she could remember she had dreamed of his face, but she had never found him.

Now, she was to marry another, a man hated by the French of New Orleans for both his cruelty and as a member of the ruling Spanish government. Aimée shuddered, knowing that because of his reputation all other families had refused his offers for their daughters.

Pulling the cloth over the portrait, she knew she mustn't think of what lay ahead or her courage would fail. She would face one day at a time. Perhaps it would be a long engagement, and it was said Señor Hernandez might be ordered up river to command a fort high on a bluff in Indian country. Their marriage could be postponed till his return. Knowing it was wrong, but unable to help herself, Aimée imagined that an Indian arrow might take care of her troubles forever. Hastily, she made the sign of the cross, and begged God's pardon.

"Mam'zelle, is you ready to dress for the ball?" The soft voice of the housemaid Clarice interrupted Aimée's dark musings.

"Oui, come in, Clarice. I can't put it off any longer."

"Madame Louvierre says the carriage will be brought round at seven, and you must be ready by then," the maid informed her, her dark eyes full of pity. Everyone in the house had heard the quarrel earlier in the afternoon.

"Has Mignon returned from the convent, Clarice?" Aimée inquired, slipping off her day dress.

"Oui, mam'zelle. One of the good sisters accompany her home. Can't you hear the music the poor angel is playing?" Clarice shook her head in amazement as the faint trill of a flute floated down the gallery from Mignon's room.

Her sister was truly gifted with her instrument. Aimée guessed that much of Mignon's pain and frustration was eased when she played her lovely music. With the flute she was articulate once more.

After her bath, Aimée sat before the mirror for Clarice to dress her white-gold tresses high on her head. Two long ringlets fell gracefully over her shoulder. She stared at her reflection, noting the green eyes looking back at her with a haunted expression under winged, ash-blonde brows. Her high cheekbones gave her an almost feline look, but the full lower lip gave some balance, she decided. But what did it matter how she looked for the detested Captain Hernandez?

Dressed in the ivory silk gown with the silver lace over-skirt and deep lace ruffles at the elbow and low neckline, Aimée felt quite elegant till she realized why her stepmother had insisted she have a new ball gown made weeks ago. Leona had been planning this evening for a long time.

With her wine-red velvet cloak fastened tight against the chill, she joined her stepmother and brother in the carriage. Sitting as far away from Fabien as she could manage she stared out into the wet, dark night.

"Damnable weather, but what can one expect for December," Fabien drawled, trying to engage Aimée in conversation. He took a drink from the silver flask he carried with him everywhere.

Aimée knew he would be drunk before the ball was barely begun. How could her father have married into such a family, Aimée wondered, not for the first time. Étienne Louvierre had been lonely after her mother's death so many years before, and Leona had been attractive in a sensual, over-blown way, but what havoc his marriage had brought into his two daughters' lives.

"Tonight should be quite an experience, dear sister," Fabien continued. "Your engagement announcement, and a glimpse of real Indian chiefs dressed up just like they were white men." He gave a snort of laughter as his mother and step-sister stared at him.

"What are you talking about, Fabien? Indians, indeed," his mother snorted, pulling her cloak tighter, trying to ward off the damp chill that permeated the carriage.

"Baron de Carondelet is concerned the Americans will move in even greater numbers into Spanish territory. Those louts are restless and have itching trigger fingers. They have little love for the Spanish since the import tax was placed on all their produce deposited here in New Orleans for transshipment. That's where the Chickasaw and Creeks come into the picture. They can be a buffer between the American settlements and Spanish Louisiana. If the Americans are busy fighting off the Indians they will have little time to march on the Spanish Territory, so the government is courting the goodwill of the tribes. Chiefs of the Chickasaw were invited to the city to insure their cooperation when the fort is built this spring on the Chickasaw Bluffs. That's their hunting grounds, and considered sacred land to these heathens."

"Why, *chère,* I am so impressed," Leona gushed, beaming at her son. "See how important it is that Fabien secure his post with the government, Aimée. He is so knowledgeable."

Aimée shook her head in disbelief. Her stepbrother had most likely picked up the information in one of the many cafés he frequented, but Leona adored her son and would not hear a word against him.

"I do hope they keep a watch on these chiefs," Leona sniffed. "Why, those savages could kill us all. I do think inviting them to a ball is a bit much."

"Don't worry, *maman,* there will be plenty of the militia about. There is one strange fellow I heard about, who although a chief of the Chickasaw could pass for a white man. Some mixed-blood business. His father is a wealthy Charleston man and his mother a squaw. He prefers to live with those red devils when he has a lavish home in Charleston, can you imagine? Well, breeding does always show," Fabien drawled, lifting his flask to his lips.

"It certainly does," Aimée agreed dryly, staring at her stepbrother in disgust.

There was little time for more conversation as their carriage drew up in front of the Hernandez town house. Flaming torches, held by slaves, made a small golden circle of light in the swirling fog.

"Madame Louvierre, you are lovely as always," the

high shrill voice of Rodrigo Hernandez greeted them as they entered the elaborately decorated foyer. The short, rotund man bowed over Leona's hand, the light from the chandelier glistening on his bald head.

"Señor, you are too kind," Leona drawled, giving Aimée a sly glance. A smile hovered on her thin lips, for their host appeared almost comical in an elaborate uniform dripping in gold braid. He barely came to Leona's shoulder, and his stomach strained the material of his breeches. The wearing of wigs was now out of fashion, which was a pity for Señor Hernandez, his own hair being scant and exceedingly greasy.

Aimée couldn't control the shudder that went through her slender frame as he turned his vicious, porcine eyes upon her. As he lifted her hand to his mouth she felt his wet, hot lips on her skin. She tried to pull her hand away, for it was an insult for a man's mouth to touch the hand of an unmarried girl. He should have merely bowed over her hand. He is a pig, she thought with revulsion.

"Ah, my bride-to-be, how beautiful you are, and how happy you have made me," he lisped in a falsetto voice, allowing his mean little eyes to roam over her figure in a lascivious manner.

How can I marry this man, Aimée anguished in despair. His appearance might be comical, but she knew his personality was cruel and ruthless.

"Come, my children, we must not monopolize the Señor's time. There will be plenty of time later for you two to enjoy each other's company," Leona trilled, taking her stepdaughter's arm and leading her up the curving staircase to the ballroom.

Aimée's fury almost choked her as she pulled her arm out of Leona's grasp. Quickly, she walked ahead of her up the stairs and away from the revolting sight of the man she was to marry.

The ball was underway as she entered the long red and gold room lit by several huge crystal chandeliers. She welcomed the heat from the hundreds of candles and the many bodies of the guests. Nodding at acquaintances here and there, she could sense their curious eyes upon her. The news of her engagement was circling the room; she could tell by the shocked expressions on the faces of her father's old friends. She saw the pity in their eyes also, and suddenly her head ached with a throbbing she knew would only worsen as the night wore on.

Moving toward one of the long French doors that opened onto the gallery, she snapped open her ivory lace fan. Its vetiver sticks perfumed the air. Welcoming the refreshing fragrance that drifted up from the fan, she tried to put as much distance as possible between herself and Leona.

It was then she saw him, and the rest of the room melted away. He turned from his conversation with several men and their eyes locked across the dance floor of polished cypress. Her breath caught in her throat, for she could not believe what was happening. *Here on the worst night of her life she was seeing the man whose visage had haunted her dreams.* It was the face she had drawn a thousand times.

Lustrous eyes, dark as onyx, bore into her own, reaching deep within her to the very core of her being. There was recognition in that gaze, and something so compelling she wanted to cry out, *at last I have found you*. Those were the eyes she could never quite see, but now she drowned in them as her heart fluttered wildly in her breast.

He was tall, towering over the other men with whom he spoke. There was a sinewy grace to that lean muscular physique that made the others seem lesser men. Pride radiated from him, as did strength. Hair black as a raven's flowed back like a crest from a noble brow, then was caught in a simple queue. Dark, heavy brows slashed above those compelling eyes. The high cheekbones she had drawn a thousand times, the aquiline nose with flaring nostrils, the strong sensual lips, the firm chin—she recognized each feature with a joy she had never known. His bronze skin glowed with vitality and health, making his companions appear pale and sickly. It was he! Her heart sang with excitement as she observed his air of authority and sense of isolation. He was a man who was alone, out of mood and temperament, not needing the approval of others.

How long they stood there lost in each other she did not know. Time seemed to stop, and she was unaware of anything or anybody but him. Then he came toward her, and she knew it was right. Aimée moved to meet him, impelled involuntarily by some force of passion she didn't understand, knowing only this was meant to be. She had been waiting for this moment all her life.

"Is it you, green eyes?" he asked, reaching her as others around them stared, so obvious was the attraction between them.

A quiver surged through her veins as their eyes locked, their breathing in unison. She murmured, "*Oui*. I am here."

Chapter Two

"Dance with me," he ordered, his voice a deep, sensual command. His hand was extended toward her. She placed her trembling fingers in his warm tapered ones, and she felt his hand, strong, firm, and protective, close over hers.

The music was swirling around them, but Aimée was aware only of this man whom she had thought existed only in her dreams. The warmth of his hand holding hers as they executed the steps of the quadrille made her feel as if she were floating She couldn't tear her gaze from his arresting, arrogant visage. There was a sense of leashed, dangerous power about him that was fascinating.

"What is your name?" he questioned, as the steps of the dance brought them close for a moment. He stared down at her with mesmerizing eyes.

"Aimée Louvierre," She whispered.

"Aimée—beloved in French," he stated as if to himself. Suddenly, for the first time, he smiled, and it softened his hard features.

"You are not French, m'sieur," She stated quietly, though he had spoken to her in that language with an accent that was flawless. He shook his elegant head no, as the dance once more separated them, making conversation difficult.

When the music came to an end he led her off the floor toward the door. She was aware of the other guests watching them intently. Her hand on his arm, she felt a flicker of apprehension run up her spine. What was she doing? She didn't even know his name.

"I must be alone with you, Green Eyes," he told her, his deep voice rough with barely checked emotion. He gazed down at her with a savage inner fire that reflected her own aroused hunger.

"Oui, I know," she answered softly, her jade eyes luminous with understanding.

"My dear Aimée, I have been looking for you. It is time for our announcement." The shrill, falsetto voice of Rodrigo Hernandez broke the spell of enchantment.

She felt the screams of frustration tear at the back of her throat. No, it couldn't be happening. She had just found him, and knew with a sickening ache in her heart that she was about to lose him.

He looked down at her in puzzlement as she dropped his arm, her face gone white, her eyes huge with pain and grief. A glazed look of despair began to spread over her face as she stepped back and away from him.

"What is it?" He flung the question at her as his eyes narrowed and hardened. A change came over him, he was wary, every nerve alert like some cunning, predatory, beast that sensed danger.

"Please . . . please. I am sorry," Aimée sighed, then gave a resigned shrug as Rodrigo placed his arm about her waist.

"I see, Macleod, you have met my fiancée," Hernandez smirked.

A murderous scowl darkened Sebastian Macleod's haughty features. It was an expression many of his foes knew only too well. "What did you say?"

"Aimée Louvierre, may I present Sebastian Macleod, known also as Shadow Panther, chief of the Chickasaw. Señor Macleod, my future bride," Rodrigo grinned, delighting in the situation. "Perhaps you already know one another?"

Aimée was assailed by a terrible sense of bitterness as she watched the cold fury on Sebastian's face. She was trapped by the circumstances of her life and could see no way out. Her future had appeared bleak before, but now that she had glimpsed this man of her dreams the thought of marriage with Rodrigo seemed a hidcous obscenity.

"Is this true, Aimée? You are going to marry this man?" He spoke to her in a tightly controlled, yet gentle voice. He stared at her intently as if he could probe into her heart and see the truth.

"Oui, it is true," Aimée whispered, closing her eyes against his gaze that saw too much.

"You want this man as your husband, Green Eyes?" he continued in a low, composed voice that those who knew him recognized as an effort to control the deadly anger that ate at him like a cancer.

She could not answer him, for the pain in her heart had become a sick and fiery gnawing. Rodrigo's fingers dug cruelly into her side, but she stood silent, hcr hands tight fists at her sides.

"Answer him, *querida.* Tell him of the joy your family feels about our marriage. Tell him how well I shall help you care for your sister Mignon. Tell him!" Rodrigo ground out in an ugly growl.

The large room had grown silent. The musicians

ceased their playing as all stood waiting, listening to the confrontation between their host and the handsome, elegant stranger who was known to be an Indian chief.

Then, in the stillness that was full of tension, they heard the cries from outside the French doors and the frantic ringing of the cathedral bells. *Fire! Fire!* The words flew about the room invoking memories of that day eight years before when almost all the city had burned to the ground.

Men opened the doors leading out to the gallery and shouted down to the street below, as everyone crowded to the open French doors to hear what was happening.

Rodrigo dropped Aimée's arm and turned to one of his men. "Find out what is going on, for God's sake."

Sebastian took her arm and quickly led her away from the pompous Hernandez. "Come, while no one is looking. We must get out of here."

"My cape is downstairs," she managed to say as she followed him down the staircase. What she was doing was mad, but she didn't care.

Taking her cape from a maidservant, Aimée pulled the hood down low over her face, and with Sebastian at her side similarly cloaked, hurried out into the cold, damp night.

"This way," Sebastian told her, holding firm to her arm and leading her to where a nervous stallion pulled at the hitching post to which he was tied.

There was a choking smell to the air. Aimée felt the smoke tickle the back of her throat as Sebastian helped her mount the horse, then got up behind her.

"Better head for the river!" a man in the crowd shouted. "The fire started on Royal and it's heading this way!"

"I must go home. My sister is alone except for the

servants." Aimée turned to look up at him with fear-stricken eyes.

Pulling her tight against his chest as he took the reins, he nodded, asking, "Which way?"

"Down Royal, that way!" Aimée sobbed, pointing to the left.

"Good God!" he muttered, urging the skittish horse down Royal street.

The fire was at their back, a great cloud of black smoke nipping at their heels. Women, wrapped in blankets soaked in water, holding their children and pets, clogged the road as they headed toward the safety of the waterfront. Dogs and cats, freed by their owners, dashed between the frantic people as they too sought sanctuary from the racing flames.

Aimée tried to close her ears to the horrible sounds of weeping women and children. Long plumes of black, billowing smoke engulfed them as clots of ash fell like rain from the sky.

"Here!" she screamed above the commotion of the panic-stricken people as they reached her home.

Driving the horse down the tunneled passageway called a *porte cochère,* Sebastian brought him to a stop in the deserted courtyard. Helping Aimée to the ground, he tied the rearing animal to a branch of a magnolia tree, then followed her up the outside stair way to a second floor gallery.

"Mignon! Mignon!" Aimée called frantically, running from room to room in the deserted house. Then she heard it, the faint high sounds of a flute above the roar of the rapidly approaching fire. Following the sound, she came to her own chamber.

There, huddled on her bed, sat Mignon, terrified eyes huge in her pale face, the silver flute to her lips as she tried to drown out the sounds of the street coming from the window. She gave no sign of recognition as Aimée approached the bed, Sebastian right behind her.

"Come, *chère,* we must leave the house," Aimée said softly holding out her hand.

Mignon stared at her with the frightened gaze of a trapped animal, holding the flute to her lips. Slowly she shook her head, the honey-gold hair rippling down her back. Pale blue eyes continued to look at them, but now with a mad cunning. Suddenly, she began to play louder and louder as if the music would keep the terrified shouts of the crowd below from the chamber.

"She is frightened of fire; she saw our father killed in one. What can we do? I know her, she will never leave here," Aimée moaned to Sebastian. Expensive panes of glass, imported from Europe, began exploding from the heat of the fire as it spread from house to house like a scarlet-orange wave.

Stepping to the bed, to Aimée's horror, Sebastian hit Mignon squarely in the jaw, knocking her unconscious. Wrapping her in the counterpane, he picked her up in his arms. "Follow me, we don't have much time" he ordered tersely.

Her eyes tearing from the smoke, her throat raw from coughing, Aimée nodded, grabbing Mignon's flute from the bed.

She followed Sebastian down to the courtyard. Plants and trees were smoldering as she mounted the horse and held Mignon's limp body in front of her.

Sebastian led the horse out into the street where there were fewer people than before, most having escaped onto other streets. The horse, nervous with the smoke clogging its lungs, tried to pull loose, but Sebastian held on, leading it through the hell that was New Orleans.

The streets became more crowded as people surged toward the river. The elderly and sick were fainting from asphyxiation as the air became foul with smoke and ash. Aimée clung to her sister and the saddle, her mind numb with the horror all around her. Bodies lay in doorways either dead or gasping for air. Horses let loose from a stable plunged through the crowd, eyes wild, their mouths frothing, trampling the frantic citizens that didn't manage to get out of the way. The din was awful with people crying out for lost loved ones, the hysterical moans, the curses of men. Through it all strode Sebastian, tall, proud, and strong. His commanding air of assurance made a path for the horse as he continued to lead them to safety.

Nearing the waterfront, after what seemed an eternity, they crossed the dry grass of the Place d'Armes. Ahead lay the levee and the Mississippi River. They struggled through throngs of people with eyes blank with shock, faces dirty with soot, their voices wild like animals. Aimée turned from the sight of a woman, skin blistered, carrying a dead child, crooning a lullaby as she rocked it in her arms.

Staring down at the back of Sebastian, she fixed her eyes on his tall, regal figure. He was her deliverance from this inferno, and her hold on sanity.

Reaching the levee, Sebastian saw that many of the warehouses were ablaze and the ships that had been at dock had sailed out into the middle of the river. He knew if he could follow the levee far enough he would reach the boundaries of the city and the swamp. It was their best chance, for the levee was teeming with people and when Mignon regained consciousness their anxiety would set her off.

"We will follow the levee till we come to the city boundary. I think we will do better out in the country," he told Aimée. He stood beside her, holding tightly to the reins of the horse. Looking up at her pale, dirt-streaked visage he reached up to wipe a tear from her cheek. She held her sister's limp body against her own.

"I . . . I agree," she replied, staring down at him. "If we can get out to Bayou St. John I know a place we can find shelter. It's obvious there will be very little left in New Orleans."

"Good, you are thinking, my brave green eyes. I know the path, 'tis one used for portage. If one drags a canoe a mile up this path, one is able to reach a navigable stream. It is called the back door to the city. We shall find this trail. Do not fear—I shall get us out of this hell." Strength shone from his dark, intense gaze. A shaft of light from the raging fire that was devouring the city gleamed across his bronzed cheekbones, showing an implacable face that didn't know the word defeat.

"I know, *mon coeur,* I never doubted it," she responded, smiling down at him with love and trust radiating from her tired green eyes. If anyone could do it, it would be Sebastian.

Through the crowd of dazed, sobbing survivors on the embankment, they headed for the path out of the city. The river below them was crowded with those who would only feel safe in the muddy water. Aimée flinched as behind them they heard the arsenal blow up, sending a deafening roar out across the river. Huge balls of fire shot skyward, showering sparks on the frightened people battling to climb the muddy levee. She made the sign of the cross, then turned away from the sight of the city she loved.

Leaving the burning city behind, they plodded down the narrow path that led into the swamps that surrounded New Orleans. They were not alone, for others had thought of the same escape route. No one spoke as they moved down the raised earthen pathway that was the only way through the marshy land on either side. As they left the heat of the fire behind, a cold damp surrounded them, seeping in with the fog from the swamp.

Aimée could see but a few inches in front of her. She wondered how Sebastian could move so sure-footedly through the fog. Others had stopped, too exhausted or too confused to move on. The fleeing citizens sat by the side of the trail and thanked God they had been spared. Staring at the stalwart, masculine figure moving forward with such assurance, Aimée suddenly remembered Rodrigo's words of introduction. Sebastian Macleod was a Chickasaw Indian chief.

Oui, she thought, shivering in her cape that now seemed as thin as gossamer he walked with that straight, silent walk she had seen among the Indians at the market. She moved uneasily in the saddle, shifting Mignon's inert body to a more comfortable position. It didn't seem possible this dashing, commanding man could be part Indian. Indians were ignorant savages, weren't they? How could the man she had dreamed about all her life be an Indian? She shuddered inwardly at the thought. No, she must have been mistaken, for after such a night how could she remember ballroom conversation?

Suddenly Mignon groaned, stirring in her arms. Her sister mustn't awaken yet.

Sebastian turned at the sound. "Is she coming around?"

"I am afraid she is," Aimée sighed, trying to hold the thrashing Mignon.

"Here, we must take her off the horse," he told her, tying the animal to a tree and then reaching up for her sister. Lifting her easily in his arms, he carried her to the base of the giant oak, placing her against the trunk. "Come, hold her so she can see you are with her."

Aimée scrambled from the horse, the flute still in her hand, and hurried to Mignon's side, cradling her head in her lap. The girl was thrashing and moaning, pushing with her hands as if to keep something at bay.

"It's, going to be all right, *petite chère,"* Aimée crooned to her sister, pulling the strands of damp hair from her cheeks.

"A . . . A . . . Aimée" Mignon stuttered, opening her pale eyes to stare up at her sister.

"You are just fine. We are safe," Aimée reassured her, as terror once more shadowed her sister's lovely face.

"Here, let me speak with her," Sebastian said softly, taking Mignon's trembling hands. "Look at me, Mignon, look into my eyes. You can see me by the light of the moon. See, the fog has blown away and the night has become fine and still."

The trembling girl clung to his hands and nodded, struggling to sit up. To Aimée's amazement her eyes didn't leave his face.

"Good, very good, little one. My name is Sebastian, and I am here to take care of you. Do you understand?" He spoke in a firm, quiet voice, holding her hands in his own warm, strong ones. The moon shone down through the branches of the oak turning his dark eyes into luminous black pools.

Mignon nodded her head and even managed a thin smile as she leaned toward him. Aimée watched, spellbound, as her sister grew calm and still, her gaze never leaving his face.

"We have a way to go before we will be home, but you are going to be a good girl and ride with your sister. See, she even has your flute. I know your head must ache a bit, but that will go away with time. I will be right beside you, so you know you will be safe. Come, now you will get back on the horse, and I will walk beside you." Slowly, he rose to his feet, lifting her up till she stood beside him. He motioned for Aimée to follow.

Never had she seen Mignon react so to anyone. It was a miracle, for often the doctor had to be summoned when her sister worked herself into a state. He usually gave her a heavy dose of laudanum that caused her to fall into a deep sleep. Sebastian had calmed her with a few words and a gentle touch. It was miraculous, indeed, she thought as she mounted behind her sister, who gave a gentle smile over her shoulder at Aimée.

Who was Sebastian Macleod? He had walked into her life when she needed him the most, and he continued to amaze her. Was she awake, or was this some fantastic dream?

Chapter Three

"How much further will we be going, green eyes?" Sebastian asked, taking the reins in his hand and starting once more down the narrow path between the arched boughs of the great oaks. The moon shone between the branches, casting long shadows.

"With the fog gone I can tell where we are. The Boussard place is to our right and the Dubois next. Our land is after that." Aimée paused as she realized for the first time that she was taking them back to the plantation where their father had died in the terrible fire that had caused Mignon's problems. "The house is gone, but the kitchen house and barns are still there. I thought we could stay in the kitchen house where there is a fireplace."

Sebastian looked up at her as if sensing there was more to it then she was saying. "The plantation is no longer worked?"

"My stepmother sold it off after . . . after the fire. No one wanted the land where the ruins of the house and buildings were located. The slaves were sold off so there was no need for the quarters."

"How long since you have been back?" he asked

gently, understanding in his depthless, onyx gaze.

"Not for over a year. We thought if Mignon visited it again the nightmares would stop." Aimée's words trailed off as her sister turned and looked at her. "It didn't work."

"Mignon knows that she can't be hurt by the past. It is over, and we are with her. Nothing can hurt her now," he smiled up at the young girl.

"A . . . a . . . all right, S . . . Sebastian," Mignon finished, returning his smile.

With a jerk on the reins they were off, walking toward their shelter for the night. Aimée's thoughts were in a whirl. This man's mere presence had the most unusual effect on her sister. He had such assurance that it communicated to others. She no longer felt alone in her battle for survival for herself and Mignon.

A great weariness washed over her as they rode on through the cold moonlit night. It seemed they had been riding for hours when finally she saw the brick pillars that marked the beginning of the avenue up to the ruins of the old house.

"We are here," she called out to Sebastian. He guided the horse up the long, crushed white shell drive glowing in the unearthly light of the moon glow. At the end of the avenue four pillars soared to the dark sky, holding up nothing but memories as they kept their ghostly vigil. Aimée clutched her sister tightly, and then realized with relief Mignon had fallen asleep, her head resting on her chest.

With his heightened awareness of her feelings, Sebastian guided the horse away from the ruins of the mansion, through the overgrown tangle of a garden to a small brick structure that had served as the kitchen house. Having tied the horse to the spreading branches of a giant oak, he carried Mignon like a child in his arms as Aimée pushed open the door of the small cottage.

"I know there used to be quarters up above for the cook," Aimée whispered to him as they stood on the threshold, moonlight streaming in through the windows showing a small, narrow staircase.

"See if there are any Lucifer sticks above the mantel in that tin box," he told her as his eyes peered into the dark, deserted house. The moon shone across the fireplace from a small window highlighting that part of the room.

With stiff, cold fingers Aimée opened the lid and felt inside. "I think, *oui* there are, although how good they will be after all this time . . ." her voice trailed off as she struck one against the fireplace and a small golden flame sprang to life.

"There is a candle in a holder next to the box," Sebastian pointed out.

Quickly lighting the candle before the stick sputtered out, Aimée felt flushed with triumph. Moving to the sconces on the walls she soon had several more candles lit and the room did not seem so forebidding.

"Light my way up the stairs and see if there is some type of pallet up there for your sister. She is exhausted."

They found a crude bed with a thin mattress stuffed with Spanish moss, as well as several dusty quilts in a chest. He put the sleeping Mignon to bed, wrapped tightly against the cold. Aimée left a candle burning on the small table beside the bed, for she knew her sister feared the dark.

Returning downstairs, she found Sebastian had made a roaring fire in the huge fireplace that took up one wall. Holding her hands to the flames, she basked in the warmth.

"I never thought a few hours ago I would seek the heat of a fire," she sighed, staring down at her mud stained cloak.

"It will soon be warm in here. That fireplace is enormous for this small house. The warmth from the chimney will even heat the room upstairs. Do not worry, your sister will not take a chill." Sebastian rose to his feet and made sure there was plenty of wood to keep the fire roaring.

"You were wonderful with Mignon. I never saw anything like it," Aimée said softly, aware they were finally alone together. Her heart fluttered in her chest like a caged hummingbird as she looked up at him.

"A wise old man taught me how to commune with wild creatures who are hurting. Mignon is a wounded bird who only needs understanding and reassurance to find her way back to peace of mind," he replied, his voice husky, his gaze steady on the pale flower that was her face. Lightly, he brushed a silver tendril of hair from her cheek as his dark compelling eyes seemed to reach out to her and touch some deep buried part of her.

"I wish I knew your magic," Aimée breathed, her cheeks crimson under the intensity of his gaze. The mere touch of his hand on her skin had sent a wild yearning through her veins. His nearness was overwhelming, for he stood so close she could feel the heat from his body. She knew with a pang of embarrassment that she wanted to touch that masculine warmth, to experience his touch in return.

"We have what is left of the night," he whispered, cupping her chin with his firm, tapered fingers and brushing her mouth with his teasing, firm lips. "But first I must see to the horse. Then we will become better acquainted, my lovely moon flower."

Aimée stood staring after him, touching her lips with her fingertips. Who was this man who could move her so with just a look, or the briefest kiss? The room seemed so warm that she pulled her cape from her shoulders. She must pull herself together and stop acting like a silly child. While Sebastian was seeing to the stallion she would see if she could find anything to eat. Looking around for the first time she saw that there was a smaller second room through an open doorway. Taking a candle, she walked into what appeared to be a large pantry. The shelves were still stocked with simple crockery plates and cups, as well as jars of apple sauce, beans and corn. It wasn't much, she thought with a sigh, and they had been there for almost two years. Then looking further, she saw several dusty green bottles of wine, what her father would have called *vin ordinaire,* but wine nevertheless.

Taking several jars of the canned food, and a bottle of wine, as well as two plates, two cups and a dented fork and knife, Aimée put them on a rickety table she moved closer to the fire. It was wonderfully warm in the kitchen house now, and she realized she was ravenous. Pulling two straight-back chairs with sagging rush seats to the table, she was placing the plates on the scarred pine surface when Sebastian walked in carrying his saddlebags and the rifle that had been tied to them.

The draft of cold air flickered the candles and caused Aimée to shudder. Glancing down, she saw that her ball gown was stained and the lace over skirt ripped and sagging. Lifting her hand to her tresses that were tumbling over her shoulders, she knew with a pang she must look awful. "I must look a sight," she murmured, giving him a rueful smile.

"You are a beautiful sight," he replied huskily, a smoldering flame growing in his black, mesmerizing eyes. "Your hair should always be free like that. It is like captured moonlight."

"I found some wine," Aimée said both excited and frightened at the expression on his bold features. He wanted her in the way a man wants a woman, and innocent though she was, some primal extinct told her he would not take no for an answer. "Some food also, but it has been here for almost two years."

"There is food in my saddlebag and furs for our bed," he informed her, opening the leather satchels and placing a leather bag on the table. Untying what appeared to be a roll of skins she saw it was two bear skins with lush black fur. "The food will seem strange to you, but it will fill the empty places. At first light I shall go out and bring us back some game. We will rest a few days before we begin our journey."

Aimée stared at him as he opened the wine, and then placed strips of some type of dried meat and broke off pieces of something that looked like a kind of congealed fruit and nuts. The food looked like nothing she had ever seen before.

"Sit, eat," he ordered, pointing to her plate.

Sitting on the rickety chair, she gingerly picked up the meat and stoically chewed what tasted like leather. Liberal sips of wine helped the taste, she discovered, and soon she had consumed several mugs full.

"You have quite a thirst," Sebastian murmured, one heavy black brow arched in amusement. "The venison is rather dry, I must admit."

"Do you always carry food with you?" Aimée asked

through the warm, lazy haze that was settling over her with each sip from the mug.

"My people have learned never to venture from their homes without being prepared." He was watching her so intently that Aimée was becoming uncomfortable. He was waiting for a certain reaction, and she didn't know what he wanted that to be.

"This is better," she said picking up the nut and berry mixture. It had a sweet taste that she decided was honey. "Who exactly are your people, your family, I mean?" She quickly placed her hand over her mouth as she gave a rude yawn. The wine was catching up with her.

"My clan is the *Minko,* the Chief clan. My people are the Chickasaw." He stated each word with quiet emphasis, obsidian eyes ringed with thick lashes capturing hers, analyzing her reaction.

"But your name is Macleod," she protested, laying her fork back on the plate. Rodrigo had said something at the ball, what was it? She tried to remember through the fog of fatigue and wine.

"My father was a Scot named Robert Macleod. He still lives in Charleston. My mother was called Starfire. She is gone." Sebastian's visage had become a mask of stone as he regarded her with a remote cold gaze.

"Then you . . . you are a mixed-blood," she finished in a half whisper, embarrassed at her bluntness.

"Quite," he answered tersely, his lips twisted into a cynical smile that didn't touch his cold, hard eyes.

"I am sorry. I didn't mean to be rude. It is just that I have never known a . . . a gentleman of Indian blood before," Aimée apologized primly.

"Of course not, Mademoiselle Louvierre. Young ladies such as yourself only meet the finest people. Señor Rodrigo Hernandez, is he one of these fine people? Excuse me, I forgot, he is your fiancé, is he not?" He taunted her in a harsh, raw voice that made her stiffen, momentarily abashed.

Glaring at him, she drank the rest of her wine in one long gulp. What did he want from her? She had never even met an Indian before, only having heard stories of what they did to white people. They murdered and tortured them. She ought to get up, leave the table, go upstairs and get in bed with Mignon. In the morning she would straighten this all out.

"Thank you for your help tonight. You saved my sister and me. I shall always be grateful. Now, I think I shall retire, for I am quite exhausted," Aimée announced formally, struggling to her feet. Her dignity was rather impaired because of the wine, but she tried to hold herself like a lady even if she did stagger.

"You shall always be grateful," he mocked her, rising to his feet. "Yes, you will show your gratitude, my dear lady, and tonight." Pushing the table aside, he crossed to her side as lithe and quick as a stalking panther closing in on its prey. He pulled her roughly, almost violently, to him.

"What do you mean?" She glared up at him, her green eyes blazing. The memory of Fabien trying to force himself upon her triggered a violent reaction of fury. If only she had her dagger with her she would show him no man took her against her will. "Let me go, half-breed," she spat, seething with anger and humiliation, throwing the words at him like stones.

Pulling Aimée's struggling body closer to him he molded her against his lean sinewy form. With one hand he grabbed her long silky hair, spilling like silver moonlight over her back, and tilted her head up so she stared into his eyes that burned like the black fires of hell.

"Who are you saving yourself for, cat eyes—that fat bastard Hernandez?" He growled, taking her mouth with a savage hunger that caused her senses to whirl.

Trembling under his assault, she clenched her teeth trying to fight him, and to fight her own dangerous emotions. Holding her hands in fists at her sides she refused to touch him.

Sebastian tightened his grip on her hair, forcing her head back. "Let me taste you, little wild cat," he muttered against her quivering lips. "I want the feel of you on my tongue. We belong together, you and I. You know it, you feel it in the marrow of your bones, as do I." His hot lips slid down to the hollow of her slender throat, placing butterfly kisses against the satin of her skin. Finding the place above her delicate collarbone where her pulse beat madly like a tiny, trapped bird, he traced sensuous circles with his tongue. Moving back up to her trembling mouth he whispered huskily, "Do not fight me, little green eyes, for this between us was destined."

Aimée shuddered at his words, for she knew the truth of what he was saying. From the first meeting of their eyes across the ballroom, she had recognized him as someone she had always known, and was now returned to her. With a small sigh of defeat, she surrendered to him as his burning mouth sought hers, opening her soft lips to his insistent, demanding will.

Releasing her hair from his fingers, he pressed her to him, his tongue exploring the moist coral cavern of her mouth, gently probing, thrusting, teasing her lovingly. She tentatively touched him with the tip of her own tongue, delighting in his moan of pleasure.

Her arms stole around his neck as she yielded to him, enjoying the feel of his embrace. It was a revelation to her that a man could be tender, gentle, yet still communicate his passionate hunger to her. Her mind soared as she realized she could relish a man's touch. Fabien and his sordid fumblings had not destroyed her ability to respond to a man.

Moving his mouth from hers to trace the curve of her ear, he murmured, "I am going to make love to you. I have waited so long." His voice, thick with desire, allowed no resistance.

"Please . . . please, I don't think . . . not yet," Aimée protested, trying to push him away. She loved the feel of his kisses, his embrace, but it was too new. How would she respond to a more intense invasion of her being? *No,* she thought, *I am not ready for anything more than this.*

"Yes, now," his voice was a velvet murmur that simmered with his barely controlled passion, sending a thrill of frightening anticipation through Aimée. "I am a patient man, cat eyes, but you have driven me beyond waiting, for I have been waiting for you all my life. I am not asking. I am telling you how it will be between us tonight."

Chapter Four

"Have I no choice?" Aimée gasped in dazed exasperation, her tiny hands pushing against his chest. She tried to ignore the treacherous leap of her pulse at the warm feel of his sinewy muscle through the fabric of his shirt.

"None, my sweet, green-eyed wild cat. Neither of us has had a choice since the minute we laid eyes on one another," Sebastian replied, capturing both her hands in his, pulling her against the hard, lean length of him.

I must be mad, she thought hazily, then his mouth came down on hers and she knew she was lost. Reclaiming her lips, he crushed her tighter to him. Gently, with knowing persuasion he forced response after response from her awakened body.

Tracing the soft fullness of her mouth with his tongue, he felt her resistance fall apart. Slowly he let go of her hands, rejoicing as they fastened about his neck and her slender body involuntarily arched up to him. Her shy but passionate reaction forced a moan from deep within his being. He almost savagely explored the inner surfaces of her moist, trembling mouth with erotic swirls and thrusts of his tongue. His hands could not get enough of the feel of her sweet, slender form. Long masculine fingers traced her supple spine down to the voluptuous delight of her softly rounded buttocks, cupping them to press her sensually against his erect, throbbing manhood.

Desire won over her shyness and fear, driving Aimée to actually seek to learn the strange new contours of a man's body. Hesitating at first, then growing bolder with her aroused need, she caressed his broad shoulders to the strength of his back. He felt so good, so right. Was she wanton to want to touch skin not covered by his shirt?

Sebastian experienced a pang of desire so fierce it was like pain as she tentatively touched him. She grew more bold, showing him her complete acceptance of their lovemaking. He understood her innocence, and treasured the gift she was giving him, her trust, her complete love.

Brushing his lips across her ear he whispered, "It is time my *agigaue,* my beloved woman. Do not fear, it is right to celebrate the joy between us, for it comes rarely." Slowly, almost with reverence, he took the clothes from her body. As she put her hands in an age-old gesture to hide those most intimate parts of her being, he gently stopped her, taking her hands and first kissing the palms, then bending and kissing each breast. Lifting her in his arms he carried her the few steps to where he had spread the bear furs in front of the blazing fire. Tenderly, he laid her on them, staring down at her, devouring the sight of her alabaster skin against the ebony fur.

She lay enjoying the sensuous touch of the soft fur on her bare skin. The knowledge that she was displayed for him to see strangely didn't bother her, for the expression on his strong, bold features made her proud that she could do that to him. For the first time since the horror of Fabien's indecent fumblings she experienced pride in her body. A rush of gratitude surged through her for this sensitive, caring, passionate man who had given her back her femininity.

With slow deliberation Sebastian shed his garments till he stood before her—tall, lean, a bronzed god magnificent in his nude splendor. He stood unmoving as he watched the emerald jewels that were her eyes travel over him, not flinching when he heard her startled gasp.

Aimée sat up, holding out her hand to him. "What is on your chest?" she asked.

"My markings that show I am a Chickasaw warrior, a chief of my people," he answered her softly, sitting down beside her on the fur taking her hand and placing it on his chest.

The firelight made the muscled planes glow copper as she traced the intricate lines of blue-black tattooing, not concealed by any body hair. Her slender finger followed the graceful lines of a panther as it stalked across his skin under a moon, stars, a virtual map of the heavens. She winced, knowing how painful it must have been to endure as the artist worked, and it had been an artist indeed who drew these strange pictures, for they were beautifully done.

"What does this mean?" Aimée asked quietly, tracing once more the outline of the graceful feline.

"It is my personal totem, or dream animal. He is my protector, and will forewarn me of danger, and extricate me from difficulty. I saw him on my vision quest. Thus I am known among my people as Shadow Panther."

"And these?" Her finger traced the celestial

bodies and the moon in its several phases.

"My mother's totem was the shooting star that streaks across the heavens. One fell to earth on the night I was born. She always told me it was an omen of good fortune. The moon is a symbol of a figure I saw walking with my totem, a beautiful maid of silver moonbeams, and green cat eyes. She was a glimpse of my future, showing how she would come to me as my *agigaue,* my beloved woman, and enter my soul. We would then be as one."

Aimée looked up at him with expectation, and understanding. Her jade gaze was filled with wonder. "You saw me in a dream also," she breathed. "I drew your face over and over, not knowing why. Sometimes in those first few moments when I would awake it was as if I remembered you, but always it would vanish with the day.

"It was destined then, you and I." Sebastian's voice was a velvet caress as he reached for her, pulling her down in his embrace to the enveloping softness of the fur. The time for talking was over.

She trembled at the ecstasy of her nude body being held against his bronzed, heated flesh. Then his mouth was everywhere, licking the corners of her lips, then down to the hollow of her throat, and down further still to circle her breasts. He flicked with his tongue the beauty mark on her left ivory mound, trailing light, teasing kisses to the taut nipple. A moan rose deep in the base of her throat as he caressed the peak with his teeth and tongue, sucking it lightly, kindling the fire that rose in the center of her loins. Arching unashamedly under his masterful awakening of her innermost desires as a woman, her fingers dug into his back as she revelled in the feel, the taste, the musky male scent of him.

Her touch on his body, her sounds of pleasure, excited Sebastian to the point where he wanted to hold nothing back. He wanted to plunge wildly into her heated, honey sweetness, but he knew this first time he must deny the frantic urgings of his body until she was ready to follow him to that ecstasy of joining where they would truly be one.

Trailing soft kisses down to the soft mound of her ivory belly, he caressed her thighs insistently till they parted under his skilled touch. Long, tapered fingers wound the silky ash-blonde curls of her venus mound, moving gently to open the petals of her woman's rose seeking the tiny bud of desire.

Her eyes were a luminous green sea of ecstasy as she experienced a wave of passion wash over her. She couldn't stop the yearning movement of her hips or the moans of pleasure that poured out of her in a song of love.

"Now, we shall join together," his voice a husky rasp as he rose above her. "There will be a brief pain, my sweet Aimée, that I wish I could spare you, but it has been part of man and woman since the beginning of time." With a groan of fierce pleasure he slowly entered her, pausing for a moment as she gasped in pain, then buried his throbbing, swollen manhood deep within her.

He lay still, kissing her deeply, allowing her to accustom herself to his passionate invasion. It was agony for him not to move, but he wanted her to reach the pinnacle with him. He lay embedded within her, till she tentatively moved against him, her tongue meeting his, sucking it lightly as he had shown her.

At first she had wanted to pull away, for the size of him seemed too large, and she was frightened. Then, as she found her body stretching to accommodate his passionate intrusion, she experienced an overwhelming hunger that she could not control. Her hands slid over his back and down to the sinewy buttocks, reveling in the feel of him and the joy he gave her. She arched up and thrust against him again and again.

Aware that she was reaching her crest for her hips were moving in the age-old dance that told him of her pleasure, he joined her and they moved together, the tempo growing as they moved in circles of delight.

"Sebastian!" the cry was torn from the very center of her being as the world exploded into a million glowing stars of ecstasy. She felt the long shudder run through him as he joined her, and together they reached the fulfillment he had promised.

Unwilling to part, they lay entwined on the bear fur, the firelight casting long shadows across their faces. They continued to kiss, soft gentle kisses now, the frantic urgency gone. Finally, easing his sinewy form from her, Sebastian gathered her into his arms, her silver-blonde hair streaming across his chest as she lay against his heart.

"We will stay here a few days to allow Mignon to rest before beginning our journey to my people," he murmured into her hair, stroking its silky length with his fingers, allowing it to fall through them like water.

"Your people, the . . . Indians?" she stammered, trying not to show her dismay. Tracing the cruel-looking tattoos with the tip of her finger, she wondered how she could convince him that it would be impossible for her to live with savages.

"They are not what you think, Green Eyes. I know

you have heard stories, some maybe true, but there is a simplicity to their life that is a balm to the soul."

"Do you not miss your life in Charleston with your father, your friends?" she questioned hopefully. "Did you go to school there?"

"Oui, I went to school in Charleston, and to college at William and Mary in Williamsburg. I studied law in Virginia, and came to understand how my mother's people had been cheated by the laws and treaties of the white man." His voice was bitter.

He had been the object of curiosity at the college, a mixed-blood who was studying for the law. There had only been one man he had considered a friend. Thomas Berkely had helped him fight off those who challenged him to a fight every time they entered the Market Square Tavern, and it was through Thomas that he had met the fair Lydia. Lydia, whom he had thought for a moment to be his moon maiden with her blonde hair and gray-green eyes. Lydia, Thomas's sister, who had led him on and laughed in his face when he had asked her to marry him. He might have a fine house in Charleston, a plantation on the Ashley river, even a law degree, but he still was a mixed-blood. He had left Williamsburg and Charleston society the next day for his mother's people, the Chickasaw.

"Is something wrong?" Aimée asked with concern, for they were so close she could sense his mood. He had not spoken, and seemed to withdraw from her to some distant place she could not follow.

"No, sweeting, it is only late and we are both tired. Let us sleep," he reassured her, trying to throw off his dark mood. Pulling the other bear skin over them fur side in, he clasped her to his chest and she was soon deep in slumber.

Sleep didn't come so easily to Sebastian. He could sense Aimée was frightened of his people. He had to be fair, she had every right. The Chickasaw had a reputation as one of the fiercest tribes. They could be unmerciful to their enemies. What would a gently reared woman like Aimée do with the other women of the tribe? He should have explained he had a plantation called *Eagles' Roost* near the Indian village, that it was a two story house with precious glass windows and furniture brought from England via Charleston. Was he testing her? Did he want to make sure he had not met another Lydia Berkely? He knew in his heart that was exactly what he was doing, but he couldn't stop himself. If Aimée were willing to travel with him to the Chickasaw Old Fields, believing this would be her home with him, then he could be sure this was his chosen moon maiden. Hating himself for testing her, he still knew he could not change. Closing his eyes, he willed himself to sleep.

Aimée stirred, trying not to wake up for the fatigue was overwhelming, but something was rousing her. Opening one heavy eyelid, she realized she was alone. The warm fur had moved enough that there was a draft. Rolling over and looking about the room, shadowy with the pearl-gray light of early morning, she saw that Sebastian was nowhere in the small structure.

Sitting up, she felt the pangs of hunger and recognized the smell of coffee from a battered kettle hanging on a hook inside the fireplace. He had made coffee, which evidently he had carried in his saddlebags. Yawning, she knew she should get up. Sebastian was most likely out seeing to his horse and would soon return. A cup of coffee would be delicious, she decided.

Rising to her feet, she looked for her clothes and saw

that he had placed them over the back of a chair. On the table stood a pail of water and a rag of a dish cloth. He had thought of everything. She gave a tender smile, for she felt grimy and with a pang of embarrassment, noticed the smudge of blood on her thighs.

Shivering, she quickly made a wash although there was nothing but a sliver of old pantry soap. It had been used for the dish washing and was made of lye, stinging her tender skin. At least she was clean, she thought as she pulled on her crumpled chemise, then awkwardly laced her stays, slipping on the stained ball gown with a grimace of distaste. She had to search for a moment to find her rumpled, snagged, silk stockings and silver garters. As she slipped on the satin dancing slippers blackened beyond repair from the fire she heard the moan from upstairs. Mignon had awakened from her slumber.

Hurrying up the narrow stair, she found her sister sitting up in bed rubbing her jaw. There was a nasty bruise from where Sebastian had rendered her unconscious. What would her sister remember, she thought with a pang of anxiety.

"W . . . w . . . where is S . . . Sebastian?" Mignon asked, brushing her honey tresses from her eyes.

"He is out seeing to his horse, he will be back soon. Would you like to come downstairs and have something to eat?" Aimée smiled at her sister, thanking God once more for the gentle, determined man who had come into their lives. Her sister had remembered everything, but was curiously not frightened.

Mignon slid from the quilts and, slipping on her shoes that stood beside the bed, she followed her sister down the narrow stair.

"We are in the kitchen house of the old plantation,"

Aimée informed her as she took two chipped mugs from the pantry.

"I k . . . k . . . know. P . . . p . . . played here with . . . with *T . . . T . . . Tante* L . . . Lulu cooking," Mignon finished with an effort, giving a wan smile as she glanced about the room.

"Oui, Tante Lulu would always give me a taste of what ever wonderful dish she was baking," Aimée reminisced with her sister about the large African slave who had been their cook. She had never liked New Orleans after they moved there and had died a few months later.

Drinking the hot coffee and eating some of the berry, nut and honey mixture, the two sisters warmed themselves in front of the fire. Aimée wondered how she would explain her relationship with Sebastian to Mignon. She decided to say nothing for the moment. Her little sister lived much of the time in a world of her own; she might not notice for quite a while. Mignon seemed to accept that Sebastian was now part of their lives.

The room was growing colder, for the fire had died down. Aimée saw her sister shiver. Where was Sebastian? He had been gone a long time, long enough to feed and water the horse. Sighing, Aimée reached for her cloak. She would have to go outside to the woodpile and fetch more wood for the fire.

The morning was gray with a damp cold that seemed to go right through her cape as she started around the kitchen house for the wood shed. Suddenly, she heard the sound of horses coming from where the slave quarters and barn were located. They had visitors, probably refugees from the fire in New Orleans.

Starting down the overgrown path to the stable, Aimée halted as the riders came into view. A flicker of apprehension started at the base of her spine, for she recognized the heavy-set man that was leading the others. He was Pierre Lopez, a half-French half-Spanish bully who worked for Rodrigo Hernandez and his police. Señor Lopez was the head of an organization called the *Santa Hermandad,* the Holy Brotherhood. Their duty was to maintain law and order in the smaller settlements and rural districts. They had a frightening reputation, for when they captured a culprit they acted as both judge and executioner.

"Bon jour, Mademoiselle Louvierre, you have given us quite a chase. I trust you have recovered from your ordeal in the fire. Many others have sought sanctuary along Bayou St. John. Thankfully, they recognized you last night, and were so helpful this morning as we came to fetch you," Señor Lopez informed her, getting down from his horse, giving her a smile that didn't reach his cold, gray eyes.

"What do you want?" Aimée asked coolly, trying to still her trembling hands by clasping them tight together.

"Why, to return you to Captain Hernandez, of course. He would have come himself, but as one of the commissaries of police he has been busy getting the terrible fire under control. Even, in the midst of his duties he had time to send me after you last night. I did lose you when you left the city, but as I said some of the other citizens who sought refuge along the Bayou remembered the lady with the silver-blonde hair."

"My sister and I are fine where we are, and plan on staying here till the city has had time to return to normal," Aimée replied with hauteur, but her heart was in her throat. Rodrigo had had her followed. Even in the midst of the disaster he had remembered to send someone after her. Would she never be free of him?

". . . So thank you for your concern, gentlemen, but you may return to Captain Hernandez and tell him we will be staying here a few more days."

"That we can't do, Mademoiselle Louvierre. We have our orders. They say you and your sister will return with us to New Orleans. And, if I might inform you, that does not include Señor Macleod." Señor Lopez smirked at her and she saw the other men were grinning as well.

"What do you mean?" Aimée stared up at him, icy fear twisting around her heart.

"Señor Macleod is hunting on foot. We have been observing him for quite some time. He has happened upon a man, one of ours naturally, who wishes him to help with a broken wagon. Now, that will take some time, but if you delay too long he shall return and we will be forced to kill him. If you want him to live, Mademoiselle Louvierre, then I suggest you come quietly. If not then I am afraid he must die, and you will still come with us. You see, his life is up to you."

A suffocating sensation tightened her throat. She knew she was defeated. Her misery was so acute it felt like a physical pain. She was trapped. "We will come with you," she replied in a low, tormented voice in which all hope had vanished.

"Excellent, Captain Hernandez does not wish to lose the Chickasaws' good will by killing their chief, but if necessary he will do it," Señor Lopez drawled, menace in every word. Aimée was under no illusion that he would not do just as he said.

Mignon rose to her feet, fear coming over her delicate visage like a cloud as they entered the room. "S . . . S . . . Sebastian," she gasped, looking at her sister.

"It will be all right *chère,* we must return to New Orleans for a while without Sebastian. He . . . he will join us there," Aimée said with her heart breaking, managing a wan smile for her sister.

"My sister is delicate, Señor Lopez. Please treat her gently," Aimée pleaded.

"Si, she is *loco.* Captain Hernandez told me," he answered in a bored tone.

"She is *not* crazy," Aimée protested, putting her arm protectively around Mignon's thin shoulders.

"That is not my concern. Hurry if you don't want your lover dead. Oh, Captain Hernandez wants you to leave a note telling Señor Macleod it is all over. You don't want him to come after you. It would be such an embarrassment for the Captain's bride-to-be to have some other man hanging around her."

"I will not!"

"No matter, then I leave a man to kill him." Señor Lopez shrugged, putting away the inkwell, quill pen, as well as the paper he had taken from a pouch at his waist.

"Non! I will write the note," Aimée agreed, feeling the nauseating sinking feel of despair come over her in a wave.

She wrote, telling him that she had decided to return to New Orleans for she knew that she could never live as a Chickasaw. Tears rose in her throat to choke her. She continued writing some nonsense that it had not been written in the stars for them after all, that they came from two different worlds. Asking him to not follow her, that she preferred to keep their time together as a memory, she signed her name through the mist of her tears. They fell from her cheeks on to the paper smudging her signature.

"Good, just the right touch of regret, but determination. It will be very believable," Señor Lopez murmured, stroking his thick mustache.

"Pig!" she whispered, her voice full of loathing, her eyes emerald fire.

"Slut!" he replied, jerking her to her feet by her long silver-gold hair. "Behave, or I shall take the greatest pleasure in hurting you."

They left the plantation, the two sisters riding on Sebastian's horse. He had not returned. Señor Lopez's ruse to keep him from the house had worked.

Aimée held the sobbing Mignon in her arms as they rode next to Lopez. Never in her young life had she felt such an acute sense of loss. The anguish scared her heart, as she wondered how she would face the future that lay in front of her so devoid of any hope of happiness.

Part Two

Of all affliction taught a lover yet,
'Tis sure the hardest science to forget.

Alexander Pope

We hate some persons because we do not know them; and we will not know them because we hate them.

Charles Caleb Colton

Chapter Five

Fort San Fernando de las Barrancas
Fourth Chickasaw Bluff, Tennessee Territory,
June, 1795

The ochre-brown waters of the Mississippi River lapped the prow of the Spanish galleon as the mighty ship made its way up the broad, serpentine waterway that led from New Orleans to Indian territory. Aimée stood at the rail with her sister Mignon beside her, as she had done for days, watching the dense primeval forest of the shore on either side. She saw towering cypress trees that rose one hundred and fifty feet into the air, looking as if they could touch the sky. Graceful river birch dipped their green boughs into the water, and here and there the ivory blossom of a giant magnolia shone in the sunlight, but she saw no people. The sense of isolation from the civilized world was total.

"We should reach the fort today." The kind voice of one of the young sailors interrupted Aimée's somber musings. He had often taken time to describe the flora and fauna to them.

"It is so vast and empty," Aimée replied as she stared

at the passing shoreline.

"It is vast indeed, but not as empty as you would think. There are Chickasaw out there. You can't see them, but they are watching us. This is their sacred hunting ground," the young man informed her. His blue eyes scanned the heavily forested bank.

A bittersweet pang of remembrance tore through Aimée at the mention of the Chickasaw. They had been Sebastian's people. Her memories of him were pure and clear. She shivered with vivid recollection of his plan to bring them to the Indian's land. She could not have imagined such a thing, yet now, barely six months later, she was traveling to that wild land as the fiancée of Captain Rodrigo Hernandez, the commandant of the Fort *San Fernando de las Barrancas*. They were to be married on her arrival.

During the months since Señor Lopez had taken them back to New Orleans she had been only half alive. The city had been considerably damaged by the fire, and many citizens were forced to live in tents on the Place d'Armes while waiting for their houses to be rebuilt. Leona had told her continually how lucky they were to stay with Captain Hernandez. She and Mignon had shared a bed chamber so there had been little opportunity for her future husband to bother her, if he had had the time. She had been relieved his duties in helping rebuild the city had kept him gone morning till night. After the beginning of the new year, he had been ordered to the fourth Chickasaw Bluff to oversee the construction of a fort. He had left without marrying her for the cathedral had been damaged and was undergoing repair.

A twisted wry smile crossed her lips as she stared down into the muddy waters of the river. He had wanted a magnificent display for a wedding when he returned in the late spring to impress the haughty French who had looked down their noses at him for so long. Fate, however, had intervened. The governor had decided he would stay at *San Fernando de las Barrancas* as its commander. The Spanish were sending settlers to try to contain the Americans who were pouring into the Tennessee territory.

"You will have to sail upriver to the fort and be married there. Captain Hernandez's letter states a priest resides in the compound. It will be a symbol to the Americans, your marriage, that the Spanish intend on staying," Leona had told her with vicious satisfaction on her face. She had been married herself the week before to an elderly Spanish count who had come to New Orleans on royal business. She was glad to wash her hands of her two stepdaughters. "It is so kind of the Captain to allow Mignon to accompany you and share your home. You really must be grateful to him, *chère* Aimée."

"I am sure the large dowry my father put in the bank for my wedding day will be ample gratitude," she had snapped at her stepmother. It had been written in her father's will that her dowry was to be handled by Leona. Aimée had had no control over her own inheritance. He had given her stepmother the right to give her the dowry only if she agreed to the choice of bridegroom.

A cold shiver came over her as she realized the voyage would soon be over and with its termination she would become Rodrigo's bride. The only light that shone down the dark tunnel of her life was the thought that she would be living in the land of the Chickasaw, and perhaps someone would have word if Sebastian had ever made it back to his people. She had to know if he lived, if Señor Lopez had kept his bargain.

"Look, mademoiselles, the bluffs." The friendly sailor drew the two sisters' attention to up river on the right where high forested bluffs rose overlooking the Mississippi.

Aimée marveled at their colors of white, red, yellow, blue and gray with streaks of black and brown. "What wonderful colors in the earth. I have never seen anything like it."

"It is the clay, mademoiselle. The Chickasaw come here to fetch the pigments they use in their paints. They make pots out of it also. Some are quite pretty for the work of savages," the sailor commented.

"You think the Chickasaw are savages, *m'sieur?"*

"That they are. The Chickasaw warrior is the most warlike of all the tribes in this part of the country. They have a strength of endurance you would not believe, and can run for miles without stopping. But you don't want them to capture you, mademoiselle, for they are the cruelest of all the tribes to prisoners, and that is saying something."

"Merci, m'sieur, we shall certainly endeavor not to be captured," Aimée stated dryly, thinking of Sebastian.

"If you stay close to the fort, mademoiselles, you won't have any worry. I must see to my duties, ladies, for we will be docking soon." Giving an awkward bow, he left them engrossed in the scene before them.

"S . . . S . . . Sebastian, he will c . . . c . . . come," Mignon suddenly stammered to Aimée's surprise. It had not been a question, but a statement of fact. She looked at her sister's face and saw a calm on those delicate features she had not seen in a long time.

Disembarking from the ship, the sisters Louvierre

were greeted by the sight of a temporary Indian village at the base of the high Bluff. Bare-breasted women dressed in short skirts that reached halfway down the thigh stood watching out of lustrous black eyes. Many held children on their hips, or on strange wooden boards where only the babies' heads were visible. Tall, well built warriors—some with long, black hair like the women, and others that shaved the sides and wore feathers stuck in the hair that was left—stood watching as well. The crests of raven black hair shone in the sun from the bear grease they had used as a pomade.

Aimée felt their eyes staring unabashedly at them as they were helped up the steep bank by the Spanish soldiers. The going was hard, for the land was full of blackberry bushes whose branches caught at their long skirts. Aimée understood why the Indian women's skirts were so brief.

Reaching the top of the steep path, they saw that the fort's palisade walls formed a square, with a bastion in each corner. There were Spanish soldiers and horses everywhere. *The fort is a place of great activity,* thought Aimée as they entered through the open doors that could be latched and fortified in case of attack.

"*Mademoiselles* Louvierre, welcome to *San Fernando de las Barrancas.*" A tall, handsome man in Spanish uniform came out of what appeared to be the commandant's headquarters to greet them as they entered the compound. "I am sorry to have to tell you that Captain Hernandez is gone. There has been some trouble with one faction of the Chickasaw. He has gone to try and make peace with them. I fear he will be gone a few days, at least. Allow me, however, to be at your service. I am Lieutenant Luis de Vargas." He gave them a charming smile, and bowed gallantly over each of the sister's hands.

"Merci, Lieutenant Vargas, that will be fine," Aimée replied, feeling a slight lift in her mood. She would not have to see Rodrigo for several days; it was a gift.

"Let me show you to the Commander's house, ladies." The Lieutenant held out his arm to each of the sisters and proceeded to guide them across the compound.

There were Indians inside the fort, Aimée noticed, and some were in obvious states of intoxication. They sprawled in front of a building with a sign proclaiming *Firm of Panton and Leslie General Commissary.* Stacks of animal skins lay in a pile on the front veranda. One warrior was deep in an alcoholic stupor with his head on a black bear skin. Aimée turned from the sight, painful memories of another fur skin surfacing to haunt her.

"I apologize, mademoiselles, for those disgusting savages. They have no tolerance for alcohol – it's really amazing. It is a sight I am afraid you will see all too often now that Wolf's Friend's people are camped about the fort," the lieutenant explained, turning them in the direction of a substantial two-story house that stood against the wall of the' fort that overlooked the river.

"Then why are they given the whiskey, Lieutenant?" Aimée asked, not able to put the Indians from her mind.

"They have allowed us to build our fort here in their sacred hunting ground, and bring many valuable skins to the traders. It is their payment, for they have no conception of money. The whiskey is cheap stuff easily brought up from New Orleans. This is a rich, fertile country just ripe for the Spanish government. Captain

Hernandez will do well for himself here."

"I am sure he will, Lieutenant de Vargas," Aimée retorted in cold sarcasm. Her escort gave a look of surprise at her tone, then shrugged, sure he had misinterpreted her response.

The Commander's house was a surprise, for it had large rooms with high ceilings, comfortable in the muggy heat. The furnishings were luxurious, obviously brought up from New Orleans. Even the walls were plastered and whitewashed, hung with paintings and tapestry.

Yes, thought Aimée, Rodrigo was managing to do well for himself already. She took off her hat in the airy chamber that was hers, across the hall from Mignon. She wondered how many Indians lay drunk in the compound square from trading pelts that would earn her future husband a fortune in New Orleans. All they had cost him was some cheap whiskey. She gazed about the chamber in despair. How was she going to live with this man?

The first few days passed quickly as Aimée and Mignon became acquainted with their new surroundings. The men were gallant, even the most slovenly. They were the first white women to arrive in the Spanish settlement; the other nearest Spanish ladies were up river in New Madrid. Another ship with settlers, including women, was to arrive from New Orleans in a few weeks. It was the topic of constant discussion.

Aimée had gotten used to the sight of drunken warriors sprawled in front of the entrance to the store. It always made her feel sad that such stalwart men could be brought so low, but the constant sight began to cause the shock to wear off, till they became part of the scene. This was the saddest thing of all—that one could get used to such a pathetic display.

"Good morning, John." Aimée greeted the manager of the commissary, John Forbes, as she entered the well-stocked store. It had been an amazing surprise to find such an establishment so far from any civilization. She had come to buy pieces of the licorice candy the Indian children liked so much. Mignon had been surprisingly calm since their arrival, delighting the Chickasaw children who wandered into the compound with the music of her flute. Aimée had been sketching the scene, and had found they would willingly pose for her with the inducement of a treat.

"Good morning, Mademoiselle Louvierre." The pleasant English voice of John Forbes greeted her as he came from the stockroom carrying a bundle of luxurious fox furs. "How are you settling in?"

"Very well, thank you. Captain Hernandez's Indian servant takes care of the house so well I have nothing to do. In fact, I think he resents me a little," Aimée said ruefully, examining several bolts of new calico cloth. "He is a bit different from the other Indian men I have seen about the fort—his dress I mean, more like the women." She looked up at John Forbes before he could mask his emotion, clearly seeing the pity in his kind, gray eyes.

"Aye, well, he is different, Mademoiselle . . ." John's voice trailed off, and he looked very uncomfortable.

"Please, call me Aimée. I have noticed the frontier is much more informal. What do you know about this man?"

"He is what is called by the Chickasaw a woman-man. I . . . I think you may have had gentlemen of his persuasion in New Orleans. They are completely accepted as part of Indian society, and allowed if they wish to take the part of women . . . in all aspects," John Forbes struggled through, his voice troubled as he regarded her with sympathy.

Startled by his explanation and the picture it painted of Rodrigo's personal life, Aimée stood frozen. "Does he serve in this capacity for Captain Hernandez?" she asked quietly.

"We thought you knew, Miss . . . Aimée. I like you, anyone can tell you are a lady, so perhaps it is better you know. Like you said, everything is more informal on the frontier, it is hard to keep secrets here in this small community." He told her softly, his voice full of compassion. "Please call me John, and if I can ever be a help to you, all you have to do is ask."

"Merci, John, thank you for being so frank with me. I now understand much that I was confused about before. If you will excuse me, I think I need some time alone." Aimée gave him a wan smile, then turned and left the store.

Leaving the commissary, she stepped over several sleeping Indians far gone with drink, and then stopped, unsure where to go. She saw Mignon sitting with a group of children enthralled with the tune she was playing, her silver flute flashing in the sunlight. Lieutenant de Vargas watching with a gentle smile on his handsome face. He had been so kind and attentive to Mignon, and with him she stuttered less then usual. No, she couldn't go over there, her sister would sense something was wrong. The thought of returning to the house was equally distasteful. She had to be alone and have time to think of this latest development. The open door of the fort beckoned. Lieutenant de Vargas had cautioned her to not walk outside the enclosure alone, but she didn't want any company. She had to get outside where she didn't feel trapped. Looking around, making sure no one was observing her, she made quickly for the open door and freedom.

Leaving the fort behind, she walked along the Bluff staring down at the fast moving water of the Mississippi. From where she stood high above, the water sparkled a silver-blue in the morning sunlight. Here and there she passed settlers' cabins where English and American men lived with their Indian wives and children.

On and on she walked, finally leaving even the settlers' cabins behind, till she came to the mouth of a river that fed into the Mississippi. The French called it *Margot,* the Spanish *Lascasas,* the Americans *The Wolf.* Black willow trees, river birch, and sycamore all shaded her path as she walked, lifting her long skirts from the briars of numerous bushes that reached across the narrow trail.

Forced to stop because of a pain in her side, she sat under the spreading branches of an oak and stared down where the two rivers met. She now understood why Rodrigo had never touched her those weeks she stayed at his house after the fire. It was also clear why his suit was never considered by any other fathers of daughters in New Orleans, where his reputation was known. Had Leona known? Aimée realized she probably had, and did not care. A question went round and round in her brain; *why does he want to marry me?*

Suddenly, staring down at the river, she remembered what a lawyer had revealed when he told her of the clause in her father's will that gave Leona the power to choose her husband. In addition to a substantial dowry, she would inherit another sum when she had been married a year. Thus her husband would have to stay married to her for at least a year—he would not take her dowry and leave. By then, her father was sure, her husband would realize how lucky he was in his choice of a bride. *Oh father,* she sighed, *how foolish you were, for thinking Leona would pick a worthy man.* He had believed a young girl could be swayed by fortune hunters, never realizing Leona could as well if there was something in it for her. Her mouth twisted into a bitter smile, for what her father had feared is exactly what had happened. Rodrigo would marry her for her money. It was why he had not been put off, as had others, by Mignon's mental problems. He had no intention of being a proper husband to her or of having a family. The money was all that was important. What would happen to Mignon and her once the money was his? They were here on the frontier where any number of accidents could happen. Who would question if they met an early death?

Aimée began to tremble as the fearful images built in her mind. What was she to do? What could she do? Putting her hands to her face she tried to still the sobs of anger and fright. It was then that she heard a crackling noise behind her. Turning, the tears still wet on her cheeks, she saw two horrifying faces painted in a gruesome mix of red and black. Almost at the same instant she was seized by both hands. Quickly strips of rawhide bound them together at her wrists. It happened so fast she was barely able to struggle before she was dragged off by one warrior, as the other bound her mouth with a piece of calico.

All the warnings of the lieutenant and John Forbes surged through her brain. She was being kidnapped by Indians. Fear, stark and vivid, glittered in her eyes as she was half carried, half dragged, down the Bluff toward the river the Americans called The Wolf.

She was thrown into a canoe which one of the warriors dragged from where it had been concealed in the bushes. Lying on the bottom of the craft, she stared up at the frightening figure that loomed over her. He wore only a breechclout, belt, and moccasins, but his entire body was painted red and black. Reaching down, he held a knife to her throat, his black eyes savage like an animal. Then, with a guttural laugh, he sat down and picked up a paddle, dipping it gracefully into the brown waters of the Wolf River.

The canoe travelled over the river for what seemed like hours, the sun beating down on Aimée till her face and neck were covered in rivulets of sweat. Her hands were tied in front of her, so she was unable to wipe her face or swat away the stinging mosquitoes that were making an agony of every inch of uncovered flesh. Her lips became dry and cracked from lack of water and the calico strip that bit into her mouth.

When she thought she could stand it no longer, wishing only that she might die so the misery would end, she felt the canoe veer toward what must be shore. As the craft slid up on the muddy bank she was jerked to her feet. Unable to stand, she felt the dark trees swirling about her, the red setting sun burning into her brain as she fainted into a dark and welcome oblivion.

A splash of cool water thrown across her face brought her back to consciousness. Opening her eyes she realized she was lying under the shade of a large oak. The gag was removed, but her hands were still tied in front of her. Copper, feminine hands were holding a gourd full of water to her lips. Gratefully, she drank till she could drink no more. Laughter and expressions of amazement filled her ears as she felt women and children's hands touching and stroking her hair.

Suddenly they all moved away from her as two warriors lifted her to her feet. Holding her arms they dragged her forward to what appeared to be a small village under the shelter of the tall trees. A crowd of women, children, and a few dogs clustered on either side avidly discussing her. The hum of their voices was like the hum of bees, Aimée thought through her exhaustion.

She saw little of the village, for the people pushed so close she could see nothing but their curious faces and could only feel their hands as they reached out to touch the silver-gold tresses that flowed down her back in a tangle. Then the crowd parted, and she was thrust inside a rectangular house partitioned into two rooms with attached porches. The walls were covered with woven mat grass hangings and the high gabled roof was covered in grass thatch. She would later learn this was a Chickasaw summer house, but for the moment she was transfixed as her escorts threw her at the feet of a tall, bronzed man with raven black hair flowing down his back. He was dressed only in a breechclout and moccasins. The memory of being held against that strong, sinewy body cut through her like a knife. His name echoed in the black stillness of her soul as she stared up into burning, ebony coals that impaled her. *Sebastian! Sebastian lives!* Her heart sang his name in silent joy.

She stared up at him, her joy turning to shock as she realized there was no welcome on that handsome, bronze visage. He stared at her with a cold, controlled anger, and a flicker of hatred in his dark gaze. Her stomach knotted and she stiffened under his withering glare. Trying to hide her inner misery from his probing stare she attempted to get to her feet, but fell down once more on the dirt floor.

"Untie my hands," she demanded, glaring up at him, shock yielding to fury as she struggled to her knees.

"No, I think not. I have waited so long to see you on your knees to this ignorant savage, Green Eyes," his voice, though quiet, had an ominous quality.

How could this cold, avenging stranger be Sebastian, the man who had taught her about love. This man, this arrogant warrior, seemed to know only hate.

Chapter Six

"Who are you? I thought I knew you, but obviously I was wrong," Aimée spat out with contempt. Her voice shaking with the force of her anger. Kneeling in front of him on the dirt floor, her hands tied in front of her, she was still proud. There was nothing submissive in her erect shoulders, the lift of her chin, or the blaze of her jade eyes that clawed out at him like talons.

"As was I about you," he replied with a bitter edge to his words.

"Then why am I here?" she retorted, continuing her withering stare, not flinching from his gaze.

"Because I wish it. Your cold, mercenary heart may repulse me, but I find I still hunger for that lovely face and delicious body," he replied, his voice cracking with a sardonic weariness. Bending down slightly, he traced her full, trembling lips with his finger. Ebony eyes smoldering with both desire and dislike studied her pale visage intently. "This weakness makes me ashamed. Perhaps in time it will wear itself out; however until then you will stay with me."

Tears of frustration filled her eyes as her anger rose in her throat to choke her. Helpless to move away from him she retaliated in the only way left to her. As his finger traced her full lower lip in a display of ownership she bit him, hard.

"Ah, the kitten is a wildcat," he muttered, pulling his finger from her mouth. Anger flashed across his arrogant features, but also a grudging respect.

"Let me go," she ground out through clenched teeth, her breath coming raggedly in impotent fury.

"That, Green Eyes, I can not do. You won't escape me, not here. There is nothing but miles of dense woods between us and the fort. You might as well reconcile yourself to it. You might even enjoy it. Remember how it was between us?" His strong, tapered fingers clamped her chin, tilting her head up as his other hand jerked her to her feet.

As a moan escape her lips, his mouth claimed hers in a savage attempt at conquest. She twisted in his arms trying to escape his hot searching lips, but it only made her more aware of the touch of his warm, bare skin against her hands still tied in front of her. His tongue moved over her lips seeking entry into the portal she held tightly closed against his invasion. Determined in his assault, he used his teeth to press open her mouth. A small whimper, more like a sigh, came from deep within her being as he moved his tongue over hers with rough, hungry thrusts.

Sebastian was obsessed with possessing her once again. The memory of her slender ivory body had burned in his brain till he thought he would go mad with longing. He hated her, he loved her, he had to have her once more.

Aimée felt his hand tear what was left of her tattered gown from her back as his lips blazed a trail of liquid fire down the throbbing cord of her throat. The pressure of his mouth on her sunburn skin caused both pain and ecstasy.

"Sebastian!" she gasped, as he bent her back over the sinewy band of his arm seeking the soft velvet of her breasts exposed now to his touch through the thin linen of her chemise.

"I want to see all of you, Green Eyes, every ivory inch," he told her, his voice a harsh rasp of barely controlled hunger. Lifting her upright, he made quick work of her corset, throwing it to the floor. Her chemise followed torn from her body for he had left her hands tied. She stood in front of him in her stockings, garters and battered shoes. Aimée was unbowed, her head held high, her eyes green fire in her flushed visage.

It was then that he noticed how sunburned was her skin, a fiery red contrasting with the alabaster that had been clothed. She had not cried out, or asked for mercy because of it, although he knew it must have been painful to his touch. She could have been a Chickasaw, so stoic had been her endurance of her discomfort. They were reared to endure the greatest of physical hardship without any outward display. She had not been trained since childhood in such self discipline, but her pride had not allowed her to cry out. His respect for her courage grew, as did his hunger to possess her body and soul.

"And these, are they to be removed also?" she asked, holding out her bound hands. "I am unclothed – I will not leave this hut in such a manner."

"You are a strong woman, Aimée Louvierre, most others would have cowered in embarrassment to be seen in such a state by a man, a savage at that. But you, you stand proud like a goddess in all your glory." Amber flames danced in his eyes, as he took a knife from the belt at his waist and with one swift motion cut the rawhide cords that held her hands.

"Thank you," she said coolly, rubbing the circulation back into her wrists.

"Always so poised, such hauteur, like a true aristocrat, Green Eyes, but such should be the attitude of the Chief's woman. Allow me." He reached out and gently took her wrists in his hands lifting them to his lips. Slowly, with exquisite tenderness, he kissed the red marks on her skin from the rawhide.

"Am I to be your woman?" She stared down at the sleek, black satin of his hair, fighting the desire to reach out and stroke it.

"Yes. It was destined between us long ago. You know this, but you fight it. Don't fight it any longer. Allow it to happen, my lovely Moon Flower," his voice was a low seductive lure beckoning to her, breaking down her defenses. He traced the vein in her wrist with his tongue up to the hollow of her palm, setting her blood aflame.

This was Sebastian, her heart reminded her, the man she had waited for all her young life. His face she had drawn a hundred times not knowing if he even existed. Then like a miracle he had come to her that one night and had taught her the wonder that could exist between a man and a woman.

When she had thought she had lost him, he had continued to haunt her dreams. The memory of his strong body inside her, bringing her a rapture she had not known existed, had driven her mad with longing. She would have given anything on those long lonely nights to have experienced his touch once more.

He had treated her brutally when they were finally reunited her brain cautioned. Her humiliation had brought him satisfaction – that was obvious. Did she really know this strange half-savage man or had she, in her loneliness, only imagined he was the lover she had been waiting for all her life? The battle raged within her until suddenly he lifted her up in his arms, and she knew the decision had been made for her.

"Come, the time for talk is over. We speak now with our bodies," he whispered into the silk of her hair, carrying her to a raised platform covered in soft doeskin.

The hut was full of shadows now that twilight had fallen across the village. A faint, golden shaft of light fell across the room from a lantern hung from a cross beam. The Indians must have gotten it from a trader, Aimée mused through a haze of passion, for she had seen many like it at the commissary.

As Sebastian laid her down on the doeskin, she heard the faint sound of the others in the village going about their chores for the evening, but they seemed far away. There was only she, alone with the man who had taught her about love, together in this forest hut that smelled of cedar, herbs, and the fecund earth.

The skin was soft and cool as she lay against it, staring up into the obsidian eyes that had haunted her these last months. In her fantasy she had imagined being alone with her warrior lover in some deserted forest glen. They had only been the day dreams of a lonely woman sure she would never again see the fascinating stranger she had fallen in love with at first glance. *This is real,* she had to keep telling herself, for it all had the aspect of a dream.

"Am I awake, or are you some vision I have conjured up to comfort me in my solitary existence?" she whispered.

"I am real, beloved one. We have both dreamed of the other and of our joining. Tonight is no fantasy, but a reunion. It is what is meant to be."

With a swift, graceful gesture he discarded the breechclout. Standing nude before her in the magnificent splendor of his masculinity Aimée realized that a man could be beautiful. It was a beauty of strong, sinewy muscle, long, lean line, pride and power barely leashed. The bronzed skin glistened in the lamplight. She had to use all her force of will to keep from touching him. Oh, how she wanted to feel him, to stroke those hard, firm thighs, those broad shoulders, the taut buttocks, his manhood erect and pulsating his need for her. Her face flushed at the wantonness of her thoughts and desires. Shame flooded her being, and she turned her head away from his virile presence.

"Nay, do not turn away, Green Eyes. Do not be ashamed to enjoy the sight of your lover's body. These are false ideas that such things are somehow wrong. The Chickasaw man and woman understand that looking, touching, feeling with the eyes as well as the hands are part of true joining."

She felt the weight of his body as he lay down beside her on the doeskin-covered bench. His fingers, cool and smooth against her sunburned skin, cupped her chin, turning her face back toward him.

"Never let shame appear between us again. It has no place in our time together."

Tentatively, she raised her eyes to his dark gaze that studied her, awaiting her answer. A shy ghost of a smile hovered on her lips as she nodded her agreement.

"Good. Now you must rest while I see to your skin. It is red as flame," he muttered, staring at her skin which grew ever more painful with the effects of the sunburn.

He rose from the primitive bed and strode across the hard dirt floor of the hut to where a large deerskin bag hung from a hook. Returning to her side, he took a small clay jar from the bag and lifted off the lid that was shaped like a small bear. A pungent, yet not unpleasant aroma drifted to Aimée's nostrils on the warm, humid air.

"What is it?" she asked, as he dipped his fingers into the jar and began to stroke a paste on her burning arm. It felt cool and surprisingly, relieved some of the fiery pain.

"A healing ointment given me by a wise old woman of our tribe. It takes the sting from the sun's touch," he explained as he applied the balm to her other arm, then gently to the delicate contours of her face. "It is good for the skin, all of the skin." His voice was husky.

His hand moved down to her breasts stroking them with a caressing touch that made her heart flutter wildly. The peaks of her soft ivory mounds became taut and hard with desire. They seemed to throb with a sensuous will of their own.

"I have no sunburn there," she protested weakly, unable to stifle the moan of desire that escaped her lips.

"Ah, but I so enjoy the feel of you," he murmured. His hand took more of the balm from the jar and began to apply it to her thighs with a light touch that unfurled streamers of sensation.

The soft sounds of her moans filled the hut as she writhed on the doeskin, her body throbbing with arousal. His hands reached under her, lifting the globes of her bottom as he pressed his face to her belly, slowly circling her navel with his tongue. Every sense was vibrating at its peak of arousal as she arched up to his heated mouth.

"How I have hungered for the honey taste of you," he breathed against the satin of her skin. His strong, knowing fingers stroking, kneading the soft mounds of her buttocks as he gently ravaged her with his mouth.

Her hands reached out and clutched his sinewy shoulders as if to push him away, but as if obeying a more primal command they pressed him closer, her long fingernails cutting into his skin. The reality of him was far more overwhelming than she had conjured in her lonely nights of fantasy. She reveled in the warmth of his passionate, strong body seeking hers with a hunger she matched touch for touch, movement for movement.

His fingers slid down to part her quivering thighs as he sought to explore and excite the very center of her womanhood. Arching up to meet his touch, her hands clung to his muscular strength as she moved in circles of ecstasy. She was lost in the rapture only he could give her, all thoughts of right or wrong drowned in the surge of pure sensual emotion that swept through her being.

This was the moment Sebastian had ached for every sleepless night since he had returned to the kitchen house that cold Louisiana morning and found her gone. He had imagined it, every detail of how he would take her, violently, brutality, make her pay for the anguish he had felt that bleak day. Over and over he had played the scenario in his mind as he tossed and turned on his bed of furs, unable to find any peace. He had known he would have to have her one more time, just once more to drive her from his blood.

She lay in his arms now, more beautiful than his poor mind had remembered. A groan tore from deep in his throat as he thrust himself into her waiting honey depths. He could wait no longer as her tightness surrounded him with ecstasy, draining the hate, the anger from him. Slowly at first, savoring each thrust, he began to move inside her, leading her to that peak of sensual arousal they both craved with every fiber of their being.

"You are mine, now, always," he muttered thickly as his mouth came down, savagely claiming hers. He moved faster, plunging into her with frantic thrusts that she met, arching against him. Reaching the pinnacle of rapture he was aware with heartbreaking certainty that he, the captor, was in actuality the captive. Then all thought stopped, and there was only the ecstasy of release—the complete shared fulfillment of true lovers.

Darkness filled the hut as they lay entwined on the doeskin, not speaking. Aimée was aware of each of her senses in a way she had never experienced. It was as if she had been awakened. The rest of her life had been merely a dream till this moment when she was more intensely alive then ever before. Her nostrils quivered with the scent of the salve on her skin. Tonight it seemed like the finest of French perfumes. The sound of the night creatures of the forest, the crickets, the peeper frogs, the hoot of an owl, all were a symphony celebrating such a wonderful early summer's night.

"What are you thinking, beloved one?" Sebastian murmured against her tangled curls hearing her sigh.

"Only how very happy I am on this splendid night," she replied, stretching sensually against him, unaware of how like a contented cat she moved. He had awakened a sensuality in her that had been hidden, but now burst forth with a ripeness that was breathtaking to him.

"Ah, Green Eyes, there will be many such nights. On the morrow we will leave for Long Town, called *Chukafalaya* by my people. Tonight I have taken you for my wife in the sight of the Great Spirit. When we Chickasaw love in our hearts, as we did tonight, knowing that it is forever, we are man and wife. 'Tis all that is necessary, but when we reach Long Town I want to marry you again in a formal ceremony in front of all the People. There you will become a chief's wife and take your rightful place beside your husband. I want them to all know you as the wife of Chief Shadow Panther. You will be a fine example to the other women once you have learned our ways, and what is expected of a Chief's woman."

At his words, she stiffened. She felt the joy drain from her heart. What magic could this man work upon her that she could forget Mignon, her own sister? When she was with him she became some wanton creature of the forest, a primeval woman who acted like a savage intent only on seeking her mate. Shame flooded her as she thought of her fragile sister left back at the fort in the care of Rodrigo Hernandez.

So attuned to her, Sebastian sensed her change of mood, and pulled her tighter to him in a gesture of possession. Cupping her chin in a firm hand, he searched her upturned face. "What is it?"

"I cannot go with you. You must return me to the fort," she answered, her mouth dry and dusty as her heart broke slowly in two at the expression she saw in his dark, intense eyes. "What you want for us is not possible. I must go back. You must take me back."

"Never!" His fingers tightened on her pale visage till she winched in pain. "You do not give orders here. When we reach Long Town you will be known as my wife, the wife of the chief. It does not matter what you want. You will do as I say." There was a cold menace to his voice that caused her mood to veer sharply to anger.

"Savage! You ignorant savage, why would I want to

live like an animal in the middle of some forest? You must be mad!" Her growing fury was choking her, causing her to say the first thing that came to mind. Jerking her chin from his hand she sat up on the bed, too angry to explain the reason for her insistence on returning to the fort. He was treating her like a piece of property with no feelings, no desires of her own. It was a feeling she was all too familiar with from her childhood. First her father, then Leona, now this arrogant man she barely knew, all thought they had the right to decided her future for her without her consent.

"I will not be your Indian wife and live like a savage in some squalid hut. Never!" She ground out the words, flashing him a look of disdain as she rose from their bed. She would not tell him the real reason, for she would not lower herself to beg. Perversely, she knew she wanted to hurt him, for she had felt intense disappointment that the tender lover who could bring her such ecstasy could also be such a stubborn, pigheaded man. If he had really loved her he should have remembered Mignon, he should care more about her feelings. Deep within she knew she was being foolish for no one could read another's mind, but stubbornly, like a disappointed child she would not give in and explain. If he was the man of her dreams, shouldn't he understand her completely without the need for words?

"So be it, if you will not be my wife you will be my slave. Remember this, my haughty mademoiselle, you will not leave me till I say you can leave," his voice was quiet, yet held an undertone of cold contempt as he rose from the bench. "And, I say you will stay with me forever, in any capacity that I choose. You may live as my wife, or as my slave, but you are *mine.* My destiny and yours are one and the same, regardless of what you think you might want."

"Batard! Bastard!" she hissed, backing away from his tall, towering presence.

"Perhaps, but now your master," he muttered, grabbing her hand as she raised it to strike him. "My every wish will be a command for you to obey as my slave. Remember that, Cat Eyes. Perhaps the thought of being my wife is not so distasteful when you consider the alternative." Dropping her hand, he strode swiftly to the entrance of the hut lost in the shadows.

"Where are you going?" she cried out, anxiety cooling her fury as she realized she would be alone in the hut in the midst of the Chickasaw village. There was no reply as Sebastian vanished into the night.

Chapter Seven

An oppressive silence surrounded Aimée as she stood alone, her words echoing in the half-light of the Indian lodge. Choking back another agonized cry of his name, she tried to control the spasmodic trembling that shook her slender frame. Her anger had turned to anxiety as the full knowledge of her situation slowly sank into her tired mind. Although warm in the hut she felt a chill, her nudity only seeming to demonstrate her vulnerability. She couldn't even try to follow Sebastian, let alone escape, unclothed.

Slowly, she made her way back to the doeskin covered bench to search the ground for her garments. Each step was an effort as a great weariness washed over her. The day's events had taken their toll, leaving her fighting a total exhaustion.

She found the dirt floor was as hard as clay as she picked up the remnants of material that had been her chemise, petticoats, and gown. They were all torn from top to bottom. Only her stays were wearable and they hardly constituted an appropriate costume. Holding her shredded chemise in her hands, she sank down on the bed that just a few moments before had been the scene of such passionate delight. Tears of desolation rolled down her sunburned cheeks as she covered her face with the soft material and gave vent to the agony of despair.

Suddenly, through her sobs, she heard a rustling from the front of the hut near where she thought the door was located. Quickly wiping her tears away, she draped what was left of the chemise across her breasts and hips, waiting to see who was entering through the portal.

Two slender young Indian women, followed by Sebastian, approached her carrying clay pots and a large basket. They glanced up at her from lustrous black eyes then promptly looked away as she stared back at them. They wore only a brief skirt, leaving their firm, round breasts bare. It made her press her tattered chemise even closer to her own nude body.

"They bring you food and drink, as well as clothing," Sebastian announced, his coolly impersonal tone breaking the tension that hung so heavily in the air.

The fragrance of roasted meat reminded Aimée of how long it had been since she had eaten. She watched as the two Indian women unpacked their baskets and spread pottery bowls decorated in deep earth colors of ochre-brown, gold, muted rust-red, and purple-black on the woven mats they placed on the ground. The aroma of venison, rabbit, and several vegetable dishes drove all thought from Aimée's mind but that of her all consuming hunger.

"Eat!" Sebastian commanded, standing a few feet away, his sinewy arms akimbo, his black eyes watching her with an unwavering stare.

She wanted to refuse. He had ordered her as if she were a slave who needed his permission before she could attend to the most basic functions of life. Hunger, however, overcame pride. Wrapping the torn chemise about her body, she joined the two Indian women sitting quietly near the woven mats spread with the bowls of delicious smelling food.

"Are you going to eat?" Aimée inquired stiffly, as she looked for the table utensils. There were none.

"No. Among our people the men always eat first," he replied, watching her as intently as a hawk its prey. "You must use your fingers. It seemed wise not to provide you with a knife, or even a spoon, since you seem so eager to leave our village. They can be used as weapons."

Aimée glared at him, seeing his full sensuous lips twitch into a smile for a brief moment. The expression vanished so quickly she couldn't be sure she hadn't imagined it. There was now only a cold, implacable mask on that arresting visage. It was unnerving.

Aimée helped herself clumsily to a piece of venison but soon lost her embarrassment in the sheer delight of savoring the first food she had eaten all day. To her surprise the food was delicious, with a flavoring of wild herbs she had never tasted. If Sebastian thought to make her uncomfortable with his presence she was just as determined to ignore him. Once she had eaten and regained her strength she would deal with him, she thought with a perverse pleasure, scooping up a portion of rabbit.

"Good. I am heartened to see you eat with such a healthy appetite," he commented dryly. "There is corn drink in the jug. I believe you will find it refreshing."

She lifted the clay jar to her lips and found he was right. The liquid was cool and sweet. Finishing, she motioned for the two silent Indian women to partake of some of the dishes she had not touched, but they shook their heads keeping their eyes lowered.

"Why do they never look up at me?" Aimée questioned, her curiosity getting the better of her resolve to ignore Sebastian.

"They are behaving properly, for a Chickasaw never stares into a stranger's eyes. It would be showing great disrespect."

"You certainly do your share of staring," she huffed, boldly meeting his gaze.

"But, then I am only a half-breed. Isn't that what you called me, Cat Eyes, back in Louisiana?"

"Well, you are, aren't you?" Aimée asked with a shrug. "I didn't mean to insult you, but what else would you call someone of mixed blood?"

"Perhaps husband," he said softly, coming to sit beside her with that graceful tread which made no sound.

It was now she who lowered her gaze in confusion, for his nearness was disturbing and very exciting. Lifting the jug of corn drink to her lips she took a long drink, trying to conquer her involuntary reaction to his compelling presence.

"Why are they here if they will not eat?" she asked, changing the subject from the too-intimate tone of their relationship, gesturing to the women.

"They are waiting my dismissal. I am their chief—not of their village, but of the Chickasaw nation. They show me great respect. If you are finished they will take away the food and show you the garments they have brought for you, unless you prefer to wear that chemise wrapped about your lovely body."

"I hope 'tis more then they are wearing," she replied, a blush like a shadow tinting her cheeks, not looking at the barely clothed women.

"Aye, a bit more."

"Well, I should think so. Perhaps they could show me what they brought," she conceded, with a slight smile of defiance. She had heard the amusement and challenge in his voice. Pride made her accept his dare, for she wouldn't give him the satisfaction of thinking she was cowed by him.

Speaking a few words in a language she didn't recognize, Sebastian had the young women quickly on their feet. With a few graceful movements they opened yet another basket and placed a short skirt of soft tan doeskin, a brief, low-cut bodice made of a bright blue calico, and moccasins also of deer hide decorated with tiny blue beads.

"Is that all?" Aimée questioned, her lips parted in surprise. She might as well keep the chemise draped around her, it covered more. Sebastian couldn't expect her to appear in front of the tribe dressed in that scanty costume.

"It will be more than most wear, although now that our women have seen the clothes of the white women they do favor a bodice if they can trade for the calico. They are doing me a great honor by giving you, my woman, clothes that are greatly prized."

"I see," Aimée said stiffly, realizing what he told her was the truth. "Thank them for me." She tried to give the graceful young women a smile of appreciation, but they kept their eyes properly downcast.

The two women nodded their understanding at Sebastian's words of Chickasaw, and rose to leave after gathering up the food baskets. One of them, a lovely young Indian woman who looked to Aimée like a gentle doe, turned and handed her a beautiful beaded band, then left the hut before she could thank her.

"It is worn about the forehead to keep your hair from

your eyes," Sebastian explained at her baffled expression.

"They were so kind and hospitable. It is so hard to believe," Aimée murmured in amazement as she examined the intricate bead work.

"Hard to believe of savages?" There was a cold, sarcastic tone to his voice.

"One hears such horrible stories of what they do to white people," Aimée tried to explain. She turned to face him sitting beside her.

"There has been bad treatment on both sides. The white man has lied, cheated, and stolen from my people. He wonders why, after all of this, when he pushes the Indians they fight back. They are men and this is their land. Why shouldn't they fight to keep what is theirs?"

"But your father was a white man. You said you were reared in his world as well as that of your mother's people. Does this not make it easier to understand their point of view?" She spoke quietly, wanting to know this fascinating man with whom she seemed to share some mysterious bond that held them both captive.

"Aye, I understand what they want and it makes me fear for my people, Green Eyes." Sebastian spoke with a weary cynicism as he rose to his feet. "Come, enough of this. We should be abed for we must be off at first light. The distance to Long Town is great."

"I . . . I need to answer nature's call," Aimée stammered. "Where is the chamber pot?" She was glad of the semi-darkness that hid the flush in her cheeks. "And some water to wash."

"We do not use them. Come, we will go outside and you may have your bath. You will find that the people bathe in the morning when we greet the day, but tonight will be an exception." His dark eyes were kind and gentle as he motioned for her to follow him out of the hut.

Aimée hung back, clutching the ragged chemise about her form. Where was he taking her? How could she let the others, such as the fierce warrior who had captured her, see her almost naked? A shudder ran through her slender form as she remembered those cold, merciless eyes.

"There is nothing to fear, Green Eyes. I am their chief. You are under my protection, and they will not harm you." He stood waiting at the entrance holding a bag he had taken from a peg on one of the support posts.

With hesitant steps she followed him out of the hut, her torn chemise clasped tightly about her. Night had fallen and the village was quiet, but a full moon cast a silvery glow, making it easy to see the many huts clustered about them. The smell of food hung in the soft, warm air. A huge fire burned in the center of the square, casting long shadows on the bark and thatched grass walls of the numerous structures. Dogs barked, and here and there Aimée could hear the low hum of conversation in an unfamiliar tongue.

Sebastian followed a trail through the towering trees, leaving the village behind. Aimée tread on his heels hurrying after him, afraid of the dark forest that surrounded them. The ground beneath her bare feet was rough and she feared she would step upon some slivery creature of the night. She wished she had thought to slip on her scuffed shoes or even the soft moccasins.

"Here is your bathing chamber, mademoiselle," Sebastian announced as they rounded a turn and walked into a glade drenched in moonglow. A creek cascaded down through several large boulders to form a small pond before continuing on its way toward the river.

Aimée caught her breath, for if ever there was an enchanted place it was this lagoon, shimmering in the light of the moon. The water was silver, and the air was perfumed with the heavy scent of the wild honeysuckle that covered the banks and wound its vines up several of the oaks and sycamores. An enormous magnolia tree seemed to grow out of the rocky outcroppings where the creek fell in a small waterfall into the pond. The alabaster blossoms of the tree glowed like candles in the luminescent night.

"It is lovely," she breathed.

"Aye. We will be undisturbed here, for the people come only in the light of day. They fear the spirits of the night in such a place."

"But you are not afraid?" she questioned softly, gazing at his proud profile in the moonlight.

"I am a half-breed, remember?" he chided her with a teasing tone. "You may attend to nature's call behind that rock. Here, you may want this." He handed her some soft, fine moss.

Feeling the flush of embarrassment stain her cheeks she accepted the moss and hurried behind the enormous boulder. As she attended to her needs she heard a splash in the pond. Coming from behind the rock, she saw Sebastian's breechclout and moccasins on the bank. Looking up she saw his long lean figure cutting a swath through the water.

She dropped her chemise beside the hide bag he had left next to his moccasins, and ran lightly into the cool, silvery water. The touch was heaven to her sunburned skin. She turned over on her back, letting the spring water soothe and refresh her tired spirit as she gazed up into the starlit night sky.

Sebastian dove deep into the lagoon, trying to control the fierce hunger that had overtaken him as he watched her run into the water. She had been breathtaking in the moonglow – her nude body as exquisite as one of the magnolia blooms that seemed too perfect to be real. He wanted to wrap her white-gold tresses around his hands, feel those soft ivory breasts against his chest. The need to possess her once again was compelling, the urgency a growing fire in his loins that wouldn't be denied.

Suddenly, there was a movement underneath Aimée, but as she tried to turn over to swim away from what ever it was her long slender legs were clasped in strong hands. With a swift gesture, Sebastian pulled her limbs about his waist as he rose in front of her from the dark pond. She had drifted into shallower water for he stood holding her against him for a brief moment before pulling her up from the lagoon.

"You are a night spirit sent to enchant me, to drive me wild with longing," his husky whisper sent a delicious shudder of warmth throughout her body.

His hands caught her wet tangled tresses pulling back her head so his lips could explore the ivory column of her throat. Her breasts, the nipples taut with the cool wind that dried the water from her skin, were an offering to his burning mouth as he savored the taste of her, trailing slow kisses down to the erect peaks.

Her toes dug into the soft sand of the bottom of the pond as her hips arched against his, the throbbing shaft of his manhood pressing into the soft mound of her belly. Her tapered fingers delved into his sinewy back as her moans of desire shattered the stillness of the night.

Then his hands were at her waist. Lifting his dark, sleek head, obsidian eyes wild with desire impaled the sifting emerald lights of her gaze as he thrust with a fierce fluid movement of possession into her warm depths. The cool water caressed her bottom as his body plunged again and again into her with a desperate, tender savagery. Aimée had never felt so alive, every sense fine tuned to the highest pitch of arousal. She wanted him with a hunger that erased all other thoughts. It was so right to feel him deep within her, moving, thrusting, leading her to heights of ecstasy that she knew only with him. They were one with each other and with the air, the water, the glorious night. This is what they had been destined for, this complete joining of body and soul.

Higher and higher they soared, Sebastian embedded deep with her, burning mouth on burning mouth, hips moving in circles of passionate abandon. Then as a cry of ecstasy was torn from her throat, she felt him give a shudder of release. Together they reached the pinnacle and soared into an infinity of exquisite rapture.

Slowly, Aimée came back from that splendid realm of passionate fulfillment. She realized that Sebastian had carried her out of the water. He placed her gently on a bank covered with moss and honeysuckle. The sweet fragrance floated on the soft night air as her slender form crushed the tiny white flowers, releasing their heavenly perfume.

"I shall always remember you lying like that in your bed of flowers. My beloved Moon Flower of the Night. When we are old and have our children, and their children, gathered around us I shall savor the memory of my beautiful forest spirit who filled my heart to overflowing." He picked an ivory magnolia blossom from a gnarled branch that hung over the water. Tenderly he tucked it behind her ear in her damp hair. "We call them moon flowers, for they glow so in the light of the moon. It is your flower now, Green Eyes. It is both your name and your totem with the people."

Tears filled her eyes, choking her voice and glistening on her pale face as they coursed down her cheeks. If only it could be so, if tonight she could begin a new life with this man she feared she loved with every fiber of her being. A flash of wild grief tore through her. It could not be as he said in that deep husky voice she loved so much. She couldn't build her happiness on the knowledge that she had forsaken her sister. Mignon couldn't be allowed to take her place as Rodrigo's bride.

"Do not cry, my beloved one, unless these are tears of joy. I misjudged you before when I returned to the kitchen house in New Orleans. I understand you were only frightened and exhausted by the events of the fire. You can see you have nothing to fear from the people, not as my wife, the wife of the Chief Shadow Panther," he crooned softly as if to a frightened child.

"It cannot be, my love, no matter how much I wish it so," Aimée whispered with a sob in her voice. "I must return to the fort, for I cannot leave Mignon alone with Rodrigo Hernandez. She is not strong enough to cope with him. You remember how fragile is her mind, her spirit. Please take me back," she implored in a low, tormented voice, her eyes dark emerald with pain.

"Nay, 'tis not possible," his voice hardened ruthlessly as he moved away from her. Quickly he slipped on his moccasins and tied the breechclout about his slender hips. "They will be on alert at the fort since your abduction. I would be leading my warriors into a trap. You must come with me." There was a finality to his words.

"You wouldn't have to take me all the way to the fort—just part way. Give me a boat, and I can sail the rest of the way alone," she begged.

"You are mine, that is my final word. Come wrap yourself in this doeskin. It is time to return to camp." His jaw was clenched, his eyes slightly narrowed as he stared at her with a watchful cold anger upon his strong features.

His tone aroused and infuriated her as she realized he had no intention of returning her to the fort and her sister. It was all to be his way, what he wanted. He claimed to love her, but he cared not what she felt or wanted. His love was merely lust, she decided with a sickening pang. How dare he speak to her of love when he wanted only her body?

Rising stiffly, she took the soft doeskin from him and wrapped it around her body. "I have no desire to be your wife. You may take me to your village as an unwilling captive, but I shall never consent to be your wife," she countered with shards of ice in her voice, taut with anger and frustration.

"A few days as a slave in my lodge will change your mind, my proud Cat Eyes. How I shall enjoy it when you come and beg on your knees to be the wife of a chief," he gave a nasty chuckle, picking up the bag of hide.

"That you will never see," she ground out between clenched teeth flashing him a look of disdain.

"You are a foolish woman, Cat Eyes. I hope you are equal to the test of your courage, for believe me this strong will of yours will be tested. You may count on it." His voice was cold and lashing. He reached out and clasped her wrist tightly, causing her to wince. Without another word, or even a glance, he pulled her roughly along beside him on the trail back to camp.

Chapter Eight

Like a deep hum, the low sound of a chant caused Aimée to open her eyes, the lids still heavy with sleep. For a brief moment everything was disoriented and she experienced a sense of panic. The smoky scent of the hut brought back the memories of the preceding day. Struggling to sit up, she was jerked back against the moss-filled doeskin used as a bed. Her mood of confusion veered sharply to anger as she remembered a long rawhide thong was tied about her left wrist. It was connected to one of the sturdy wood supports of the lodge.

"I can't trust you, little wild cat, even though I sleep beside you," Sebastian had told her bluntly as he lashed her wrist to the pole. "It will not be the most comfortable way to slumber, but I think you are tired enough so it shouldn't matter too much. It would be most foolish to try and escape—you would only bring about your own end out there alone in the forest. However, like most women you will have your way whatever I say, thus the need to help you stay here with me as you should."

"I hate you," she had hissed.

"Be that as it may, you will remain tied, and you will

share my bed," he murmured, giving a sigh of exasperation as he stripped off his few articles of clothing and lay down beside her.

She had been infuriated when within a few minutes she could tell he was fast asleep. Exhaustion had taken its toll on her and soon she too found the oblivion of slumber.

The sound of the chanting had brought her fully awake and she saw that she was alone in the bed. A shaft of early morning light streamed through the opening on the east wall of the hut. It was there she saw Sebastian sitting cross legged, completely nude, facing the beam of sun light that shone into the lodge. The sound of his chanting had been what awakened her.

In spite of her anger she couldn't help admiring the beauty of his sinewy body glowing bronze in the sun. His blue-black hair hung loose below his shoulders and shone like a raven's wing.

Suddenly, she was filled with confusion and shock as she realized she still wanted him with a fierce hunger that caused a hot ache in the center of her being. How could she feel this way, she wondered. A shudder of humiliation ran through her.

"Good, you are awake. It is time we are off, the sun is up." He walked toward her carrying a jar and a bowl.

"What were you doing?" she asked, trying to avert her eyes from his manhood that hung in all its nude splendor.

"I was greeting the morning and asking Grandmother Sun to smile on my soul and show me the right path on my journey through life today."

"Do you do that every morning?" she inquired, her curiosity aroused. This man continued to amaze her.

"Aye, it is important at the beginning of each day to

think of your place in nature, to listen to the voice of your inner spirit. A wise man of my tribe told me you must try to keep your life in balance so your soul will be light as a feather."

She watched as he untied her wrist then calmly slipped on his moccasins and breechclout. Pulling his hair back in a queue he tied it with a thong made of animal hide. The last item was a large pouch ornamented with elaborated bead work which he wore at his side. Aimée wanted to ask what it was for, but she didn't want to appear too eager to know about Chickasaw customs.

"Dress in the clothes you were given last night. There is food and drink in the containers. Eat your fill, for we won't be stopping till the sun is high. Standing Fawn and Running Squirrel are coming to help you dress. I will return after speaking to the warriors who will accompany us."

Aimée watched as he strode away with dignified carriage, moving with a graceful swiftness that exhibited the arrogant, independent air that was so much a part of him. Minutes after he left, the two Indian women from the previous evening entered the lodge.

Sitting apart from her with downcast eyes, they waited till she had eaten the corn mush flavored with honey and drunk the corn drink before motioning she was to wash in a bowl of water fragrant with honeysuckle blooms. With giggles they showed her how to use a weed that, once in the water, lathered like soap.

After bathing, Aimée felt more like her old self, for at least she was clean. Slipping on the moccasins she marveled at how soft they felt on her feet. The skirt the women placed about her waist felt embarrassingly brief, as did the low-cut blue calico bodice that laced tightly over her breasts. It didn't reach her waist allowing several inches of her midriff to show.

From what was left of her dress Aimée took a brooch. She pinned it to the top of the bodice, trying to pull it higher, but to no avail. Ivory mounds, the nipples barely covered, rose almost spilling outside the confines of the material. She held the brooch for a moment in her hand before fastening it, for inside was a miniature painting of Mignon on one side and she on the other. Her sister had a matching brooch.

Gentle hands pushed her to sit down on the bed so the two women could attend to her hair. A bone comb was slowly pulled through her tangled tresses, as they exclaimed over the color in awed tones. At least that's what Aimée thought they were saying, for she couldn't understand a word. When all the snarls were gone each woman braided one half of her hair till it lay in two neat plaits on either breast. The final touches were done when thin copper wires holding freshwater pearls were threaded in her pierced ears and the blue beaded headband was tied about her forehead.

Aimée stopped them, however, when they tried to paint the part in her hair with red dye as they each wore. She shook her head and pushed their hands away. Her clothes might be Chickasaw, but she wouldn't go as far as to paint up like one of them. She didn't care what Sebastian thought, secretly hoping it would anger him. Perversely she wanted to hurt him, yet at the same time she wanted him to admire her beauty, so on display in the skimpy costume.

The two women finished with her hair and motioned for her to follow them out of the lodge. Hesitant at first, Aimée decided at least it was an opportunity to get some fresh air. It was soon obvious where they were taking her, and why. A few yards from the camp was a secluded spot where several other women and children were attending to the call of nature. Quickly she followed suit behind a low bush, taking the moss they handed her.

Following the women once more back toward camp Aimée was surprised when instead of returning to the hut she was taken to the bank of the river. Sebastian motioned for her to join him where he stood next to a long canoe that appeared to be hollowed out of one immense log. Several other fierce-looking warriors stood beside other canoes. She shuddered as she saw the cold-eyed brave who had captured her on the bluff.

"Get in. We are ready to leave," Sebastian said tersely, but his dark eyes smoldered as they swept over her in the dress of an Indian maiden. He was not as unmoved by her appearance as he acted, she thought with delighted malice.

"Do you approve?" she asked with a saucy tilt to her chin, giving a graceful turn so he could view her front and back.

"Aye," he muttered through clenched teeth, "and so do they. A chief's wife doesn't make a spectacle of herself."

"But I am not a chief's wife. I am only a slave being taken against her will," she reminded him with a light bitterness.

"Get in the pirogue before I throw you in." He grabbed her arm, his nostrils flared with fury, the corner of his mouth twisted with exasperation.

"Wait, I must go back for my clothes," she begged.

"They are not fit to wear. The women have disposed of them. You will not need them at Long Town." He lifted her up before she realized what he was doing and placed her none too gently in the canoe, then pushed it out into the water.

"No, I won't go," Aimée heard the panic in her voice as she stood up in the rocking pirogue.

"Hell's bells, woman, sit down!" Sebastian cried, pulling the craft back up on shore while the braves watched silently.

Pushing her back into the canoe till she fell in a half sitting position, he grabbed her hands in front of her. Pulling a length of hide from the bag at his side he lashed her hands together, then roughly pulling her feet out from under her tied them at the ankles. Pulling her up till she sat in the front of the boat facing him, he growled, "If you say one more word I will gag you. If you move and upset the canoe you will drown for you will sink like a rock. I will not allow you to cause me to lose face in front of my braves. You are lucky I didn't beat you, for that is what they expected me to do. Do you understand?"

Aimée nodded slowly, but she glared at him with burning eyes full of hate.

With a swift graceful push the canoe was in the water. She knew a moment of panic as Sebastian climbed in, for the craft rolled and she had visions of drowning in the muddy brown water of the Wolf River. He, however, quickly stabilized the boat. In a fluid gesture, dipping a single paddle in the water, he had them moving on their way up the river in the opposite direction away from the fort and Mignon.

Aimée refused to look at him, something that was hard to do while facing him. Turning away, she stared first at the heavily forested bank then occasionally at the other canoes that followed behind them. It resembled a regatta, she thought in disgust, but Sebastian would always win, he was their chief. The other braves deferred to him – that was obvious. Well, if he expected her to give him such slavish obedience he was in for a surprise, she thought with conviction. With an aloof air she turned away, watching the river bank slide by.

As the hours dragged on the sun grew high in the sky, beating down without mercy. The mosquitoes were another torment, biting Aimée where it was impossible to scratch with her hands tied. She was determined not to complain, not to give Sebastian the satisfaction. Not a word had been exchanged for hours. Hunger also began to add to her misery as her stomach loudly complained of its lack of subsistence.

Lifting his arm Sebastian pointed to the right and immediately all the canoes followed him to the bank. His every gesture was obeyed, Aimée observed with amazement. For once she was glad his every order was law for perhaps now they would eat and she could see to the infernal insect bites.

"We shall stop for a brief rest – the complaints of your stomach are about to deafen me," he announced, jumping out of the canoe and pulling it up on the grassy bank. Reaching down he lifted her up over his shoulder like a bag of potatoes and carried her to a spot under a large oak where he dropped her unceremoniously on the ground.

"How am I to eat, you oaf, with my hands tied?" Aimée spat.

He took a knife from his belt and sliced through the bonds on her hands and feet. "You are intelligent enough to realize we are far from the fort. If you try to escape we will only find you again. We know these forests – you don't. My braves are watching us for we don't usually stop enroute except at night. I am making an exception, for I realize you are not used to the pace we set, but if you do anything to embarrass me it will be the last time," he ground out, grabbing her arm and pulling her to a standing position.

"Let go of my arm," she spat out, trying to pull from his grasp.

"I said you are to behave, that means keeping your eyes down and acting submissive. A Chickasaw wife does not argue with her husband in front of other men. Come, we will go further down the bank behind those willows. They think that I have stopped because I am so enamored of you that I can't wait for night to have you once more. We shall let them believe it, for it is the only explanation they would understand."

Aimée now understood the laughing jeers the braves were making as they stared at her. They thought they were going to make love. She turned away from their smirking grins, crimson with resentment and humiliation, allowing Sebastian to guide her down the grassy bank on the other side of two huge river willows.

"Here is far enough. Sit, we will eat," he told her, gesturing toward some long grass where wild strawberries grew in profusion. Their scent perfumed the warm, humid air.

"I thought Chickasaw men never ate with the women," Aimée commented stiffly, sitting gingerly on the meadow grass.

"We are alone," he answered, sitting beside her. He took a small clay container from the deer skin bag he had slung over his shoulder. "Eat, this is called pemmican." He offered the opened container to her.

The food had a bland greasy taste, but Aimée was so hungry she ate it eagerly. As she feasted Sebastian walked to the river and filled a jar with water. Upon his return he watched as she ate, taking little himself.

"Aren't you hungry?" she asked, handing him back the jar of water after a long drink.

"A Chickasaw warrior is trained as a boy to go long periods without eating, especially when he is on the hunt or in a war party. A full stomach can dull the mind. A few strawberries, however, cannot hurt." Stretching out his arm he picked a few of the ripe berries from the bushes that surrounded them. "They are delicious, here." Gently he fed them to her one at a time, tracing the fullness of her mouth with his fingertip.

The sun-warmed fruit filled her mouth with a bittersweet juiciness. A rush of sensation filled her being, so intense was her physical awareness of him. Her lips trembled as he placed yet another strawberry in her mouth. Trying to still the wild pounding of her heart she found the strength to shake her head no.

"Enough," she murmured. Turning away she reached for the jug of water. "Please eat some yourself—they are sweet."

"Ah, sweet and ripe. I cannot resist."

The double meaning of his words was not lost on Aimée, causing her to glance uneasily over her shoulder. The Chickasaw braves who had accompanied them were only yards away. She stirred uneasily, remembering what he had said about their reason for thinking they had stopped.

"You have barely eaten a thing. Here, have some of this." She pushed the rest of the pemmican at him.

"I require very little, Green Eyes, but to please you I will finish it."

"And what of the Chickasaw women? Do they also go long periods without food?"

"No, the women do not hunt or fight. They tend the fields. Do not worry, as one of the people you will not go hungry." His deep voice reassured her, teased her, as his black eyes studied her delicate features with a disconcerting intensity.

"Will I be expected to work the fields?" she inquired in a taut voice, boldly meeting his gaze with eyes flashing emerald fire.

"As a slave, most certainly – But as the wife of a chief you will have help," he explained lazily, reaching out to trace a finger up the sensitive inner surface of her calf. When he reached her thigh she moved away slightly.

"I . . . I don't think I can ever live as a Chickasaw. It is too different from what I am used to, Sebastian," she whispered his name, not trusting herself to look at him staring out across the river. It was true, she thought, misery filling her heart. The attraction to him was strong, but the bonds to her sister were also strong. Even if she hadn't had to return for Mignon's sake, how could she live like a savage for the rest of her life?

"I will not ever let you go, Green Eyes." There was a cold finality to his words. "You will adjust. It will take time, but you will learn to live as one of the people. You have no other choice."

"Never," she whispered, tears choking her throat and misting her vision.

"Aye, you will," he admonished, taking her chin in his hand. "You are mine for all time. Remember it."

His mouth came down hard on hers, branding her lips. It was a kiss without tenderness, more an act of possession. She was filled with anger and a hot, overwhelming hunger.

"This is what is between us. It is stronger than anything else," he muttered in a harsh whisper, ebony eyes boring down into her as if to touch her very soul.

After what seemed an eternity, he released her and rose to his feet. His face was once more a stoic visage—only the burning eyes told of his emotion.

"Put this on," he ordered tersely, handing her another small jar he took from his bag. "It is the herb spikenard mixed in bear grease. It will keep the mosquitoes off and help that sun burn. Go on, rub it in," he insisted as she hesitated.

It had a not unpleasant fragrance and it felt cooling, Aimée thought as she applied it to her arms and legs. She noticed Sebastian turned away, fists clenched, as she rubbed in the ointment.

He had to use every ounce of willpower to keep from taking her here and now. She drove him mad with longing. All morning long he had had to stare at her long slender legs with the tiny golden hairs on her thighs that were like the downy fuzz of a delicious peach. She was his silver-and-gold mate, his Moon Maiden, sent by destiny to him. Would she never see that they were meant to be? Would her white mind ever be able to comprehend that, for good or for bad, their lives were destined to be intertwined for all time?

Chapter Nine

The late afternoon sun slanted golden rays of fading light across the tan water of the river as the canoe continued its way eastward. Aimée stared out at the heavily forested banks from her perch in the front of the narrow pirogue. The woods were full of shadows now that the sun was setting. She shuddered, for the land through which they traveled seemed so empty, so foreboding.

The hours had dragged on since their brief stop at noon. She was physically more comfortable, for Sebastian had allowed her feet and hands to remain unbound. The fragrant salve had repelled the mosquitoes and eased her sunburn. Looking down at her arms she realized her skin was beginning to turn a light tan like the waters of the river. What would Leona think of her stepdaughter the color of a quadroon, Aimée mused. How the Creole ladies of New Orleans guarded their magnolia-white complexions from even a hint of sun. Sighing, she knew she was far from New Orleans and its rules of civilization. The man guiding the canoe so skillfully behind her was determined that she never see the city again.

The dying light of the day seemed to underscore her melancholy. A pang shot through her as she thought of Mignon and how frightened she must be now that her older sister, her protector, was gone. She hoped fervently that the young lieutenant who had spent so much time with Mignon would look after her when Rodrigo returned to the fort.

Aimée had been so engrossed in her sad musings she missed the first signs that something had changed in the empty forest. The skittish flight of a flock of mallards into the air from the river caught her attention. She watched in admiration as the setting sun caught the brilliance of the shimmering emerald heads of the males.

"How beautiful," she breathed aloud, turning toward Sebastian. It was then that she noticed the canoe was rapidly heading for the far shore. "Why are we stopping?" she called out.

"Be quiet!" he hissed, giving her a black look from under heavy brows slanted in an angry frown. "Someone is coming—there on thc other shore."

She whirled around to where hc pointed, her flash of anger forgotten. Lifting her hand to shade her eyes, Aimée could see nothing but the shadowy stillness of the trees.

"Get out and follow me," Sebastian ordered tersely, beaching the canoe on a muddy flat.

She obeyed without thinking, jumping lightly onto the long grass of the bank. Her heart was hammering in her chest. She saw over her shoulder that the other braves were following right behind them.

"This way." Sebastian grabbed her arm, pulling her into a dense thicket of tangled bushes. "Lie down and I will cover you with the branches. Don't move or make a sound, no matter what happens. If they are Creeks you could be in great danger if they see you. Stay here till I return . . . if I don't wait till day break and then make your way back down the river to the fort. Be careful and stay as inconspicuous as possible. It should not be necessary, Green Eyes, but the Creeks are a deadly foe. If fate is with us I shall return for you."

Horrified at his words, she huddled in the bushes while he pulled the thorny branches over her. She wanted to pull him down with her, but she knew he, a chief, would never hide from an enemy. Sheer terror swept over her, and she began to shake as fearful images built in her mind of Sebastian slain by the Chickasaw's deadly enemy the Creek. She had heard at the fort of the war that continued between the two tribes. It was a conflict that had first been fueled by the French and British, and now was continued by the Americans and the Spanish. The two nations paid in goods and liquor for each scalp of the rival tribe brought to them. Pitting Chickasaw against Creek was a devilish scheme to keep the Indians from uniting in any strength, thus allowing more Spanish and American settlers to move into their lands.

Huddled on the ground under the prickly branches, Aimée tried to keep some fragile control. She couldn't let herself think of what she would do if Sebastian never returned, for it would mean he was dead. Only his death would prevent him from coming back for her—of that she was certain deep within her being.

Suddenly a harsh cry broke the waiting stillness, a cry that sent chills up her spine. It was a savage, inhuman sound. She pressed her fingers to her ears to block out what she knew she would hear in nightmares the rest of her life. The cry was followed by a piercing scream that instinct told her was the sound of someone dying. She lost all sense of time as she lay under the prickly branches, panting with the terror that swept over her in black waves. A fight to the death was occurring only yards from where she lay. Although she could only hear the sounds of combat, her horrified mind created the images she couldn't see.

Panic welled in her throat when after what seemed an eternity the branches that gave her sanctuary were pulled from her back. She choked back a moan of despair as she turned to face her discoverer.

"Hurry, we must leave. They might have been only a scouting party," the deep reassuring of Sebastian broke through the fog of Aimée's terror.

Accepting his outstretched hand she stumbled to her feet. Unable to control the spasmodic trembling that shook her slender form, her knees buckled and she slumped into his arms. Quickly he picked her up, draping her over his shoulder like a sack of flour. The ground and sky swirled around her as she struggled against his firm grasp.

"Put me down, I can walk," she gasped, beating her fists against the sinewy muscles of his back.

Ignoring her protests, Sebastian strode down the bank to the waiting canoe and unceremoniously dumped her inside. Anger surged through her as she struggled to sit up in the precarious craft. It was then she smelled it, the unmistakable sweet musky scent of blood.

She sat transfixed in horror at the scene in front of her on the muddy banks. Two Chickasaw braves lay dead, sprawled on the muddy bank, their throats cut. There were several other dead warriors beside them she didn't recognize. Creeks, perhaps. Her body stiffened in shock as she watched the cold-eyed brave, who had captured her on the bluff, scalp the roach of black hair from a dead warrior's skull. Nausea surged up in her throat as he held the trophy aloft, giving a savage howl of victory as the blood of his victim dripped to the ground.

Unable to control the wave of sick revulsion that came over her in waves, Aimée leaned over the side of the canoe and vomited into the water as it lapped the shore. When her stomach was empty she leaned back in the bottom of the pirogue. Exhausted, she stared up at the blue sky. If she concentrated on the clean wispy clouds hard enough she could blot out the horrible sounds around her. She could not handle any more, as if her mind refused to recognize any more violence. In her despair she retreated within herself to a quiet, safe place.

Sebastian cursed low under his breath as he stared down at her, seeing the frozen glazed look on her delicate features. He had seen such a reaction before in people when they had been driven emotionally beyond what they could handle. Yelling a few words of instruction to the others he quickly pushed the canoe out into the water. With a swift motion he was seated, paddling the craft eastward on the Wolf and away from the scene of violent death.

Aimée lay quietly staring up at the sky, enjoying the rocking motion of the boat as it sped across the water. It was safe, like a cradle. *Nothing could hurt me on the water.* The thought drifted across her mind like the white clouds above her in the sky. Slowly her eyelids grew heavy in the warmth of the sun. Yes, she thought, sleep would be such a lovely escape.

Sebastian's mouth was a taut, grim line as he

watched Aimée seek the refuge of slumber. She would have to learn to be tough, strong within like a true Chickasaw woman. In time she would learn, he thought grimly, but the lessons would be hard. He would have to bring her out of her dream world tonight when he stopped for the night's rest. It was dangerous if someone was allowed to stay in the dreaming state for too long. There were some who never returned. They would be alone for a few hours before his braves caught up with them after burying their dead. The foolish Spaniard they had captured traveling with the Creeks would slow them down, but he was glad he insisted they bring him along. He was further proof to the Chief's counsel of the treachery of the Spanish.

He cursed the Spanish for the game they played pitting the Creeks against the People. That idiot Wolf's Friend had his tribe, Chickasaw clanspeople, camped at the fort believing the stories of the Spanish, living on their liquor without honor, while behind his back they encouraged the Creeks in their old hatreds against the rest of the Chickasaw. Wolf's Friend was a fool, a dangerous fool who endangered all of the clans of the Chickasaw.

Through a fog of sleep Aimée realized the comforting motion of the canoe had ceased. She struggled to stay in the safe quiet place of slumber, but try though she might she couldn't block out the night sounds of the peeper frogs. The scent of wood smoke stung her nostrils as did the fragrance of cooking fish. The strength of her hunger pangs would not let her dismiss the scent of fresh food. The needs of her body overcame the damage to her mind.

Reluctantly, she opened her eyes to find she was lying on soft pine boughs covered with a doeskin. The leaping orange flames of a campfire rose in front of her, the heat taking away the cool damp of the night air. She realized with a start that she had slept for hours, not even awakening when they made camp. A wave of panic coursed through her as her eyes searched for Sebastian in the dim light of the fire. Struggling to sit up, she pulled the soft blanket of mallard feathers up about her shoulders for she was taken with a chill. Trembling, her teeth chattering although the night was not that cold, she looked about her trying to understand where she was. Where was Sebastian?

"Ah good, you are awake. You have slumbered long, Green Eyes, but now it is time to eat," Sebastian's deep voice spoke with quiet emphasis from across the fire.

She stared at him, ashamed that she felt such relief at his close presence. He was her only security in this new wild land where life and death were a mere heartbeat apart. Vivid images of blood seared across her mind no matter how hard she tried to get them at bay. A startling thought cut through her musings to bring new horror to her soul. How often had Sebastian taken part in such slaughter, reveling in the scalping of the vanquished as did his braves? A shudder ran through her being at the memory of the bloody lock of hair held high by the cold-eyed warrior.

"Here, eat. Do not dwell on what you don't understand," Sebastian ordered, handing her a crudely molded bowl of clay broken open to reveal a fillet of fish done to a golden brown. "It is good – you will feel better with food in your belly."

She wordlessly accepted the bowl, refusing to meet his eyes. She tried to eat the delicious fish slowly, but her hunger was great. Although staring with an aloof air into the fire as she quickly finished the food, pausing only to drink from a cup of water he had also provided, Aimée felt his intense gaze never waver from her face. The silence lengthened between them, making her uncomfortable, but she was loath to speak.

"The others will soon be here. You must prepare yourself," his deep voice finally broke the tension.

"How does one prepare to live with savages?" She flashed him a withering stare of contempt, lifting her chin in a haughty gesture of defiance.

"Carefully, and with intelligence, if one wants to survive."

She flinched at the tone of warning in his voice. "Is that a threat?"

"You may take it anyway you wish." His voice was cold, hard, with no vestige of sympathy. He kept any sign of the relief he felt at her display of anger from his face or words. She would be all right—the dreaming world had been left behind.

The full moon came out from behind a cloud and shone down on the clearing beside the river making it almost as light as day. Satisfied that Aimée was restored to reality, even if that meant he had to put up with her contrary bad temper at being his captive, Sebastian left her and the fire to walk down the bank of the river. Standing very still, he listened to the silence of the night. Then, bending down, he placed his ear against the clay ground of the river bank.

Aimée watched him, intently curious about what he was doing with his ear pressed against the cold ground. Would she ever be able to understand this strange man whose ways were frightening and yet intriguing.

"Pray tell, what was that all about?" She asked, not bothering to keep the tinge of ridicule from her voice.

"Mother Earth has much to tell us if we will only listen," he replied, throwing more wood on the fire. A shower of sparks shot upward into the indigo blue of the night sky to join the thousands of stars that twinkled above them like diamonds.

Aimée experienced a strange bittersweet pang as she stared at his long, lean form outlined against the firelight, his handsome head thrown back, the long ebony satin of his hair loose from the queue flowing across his broad, sinewy shoulders. He was so at ease here in this primitive domain—as if he was one with the giant trees, the dark brilliance of the night. A quality of controlled power and complete assurance seemed to emanate from his being as if he and nature were one. He behaved as if he knew all the secrets of the universe, for he listened to her voice.

A cloud came over the moon and Aimée shook her head at her own fancies. On such a night anything seemed possible, she realized, looking away from where Sebastian stood to stare into the orange-blue flames.

"What did you mean about listening to the earth?" she inquired to break the spell that seemed to surround them.

"It is the way I was taught as a boy to find out if anyone is coming near. The ground is a conductor of sound or vibration. What one cannot hear on the wind one can often hear from the water or the earth."

"And what did you find out?" she persisted.

"My braves will soon be joining us. I must request that from now on, when we are with the People, you address me as Shadow Panther, not Sebastian. Few of the People speak English or French, but they recognize my English name. I must insist on this for otherwise it would be a great loss of face. They would expect me to beat you for such an insult. Do you understand this?" He asked softly, mockingly.

"Should I bow my head in proper subservient manner, oh great Chief Shadow Panther, when I am so bold as to address you, a warrior?" the insolence in her voice was ill-concealed.

"As charming a picture as that brings to mind, I think Shadow Panther is enough. Oh, of course, you must keep your eyes lower for it is lack of respect, showing great rudeness, to meet another's eyes, especially a man's. The Chickasaw would think you a lewd woman."

Hearing his low chuckle Aimée shot him a cold look, staring long and hard into black eyes that glowed at her from across the fire. "I could care less what those ignorant savages think of me," she sputtered, bristling with indignation.

"They would consider it an invitation, Green Eyes. I don't think you want that," he murmured, his words playful, but the meaning was not.

She gave a shudder at his warning, and a vision of the cold-eyed warrior holding his bloody trophy flashed across her mind's eye. The thought of him touching her was repulsive. Feeling trapped, she realized that all that stood between her and the rest of the savage warriors was one man, the man who sat across from her. She hated her dependence on him and his knowledge of it.

"Quiet!" he hissed, rising swiftly to his feet, his finger to his lips.

Mon Dieu, not another attack thought Aimée, her heart in her throat. Throwing the blanket of feathers aside she too rose to her feet, watching as Sebastian strode swiftly without a sound to the water. Panic welled up inside her. She wanted to run, but where would she be safe in this godforsaken wilderness?

The sound of a paddle in the water reached her ears as the moon once more came out and shone on the silver surface of the river. From around a bend she saw the canoes of the other Chickasaw warriors. She couldn't believe she would ever be glad to see them, but better them then an unknown enemy.

As the long slender crafts were beached, she saw with amazement one contained a white man. Moving closer to make sure her eyes were not deceiving her, she recognized him.

Chapter Ten

The exhausted captive struggled to stand as the canoe was pulled up onto the muddy shore. His hands were tied in back, throwing him off balance, and he fell out of the boat face first into the mud. The Chickasaw braves, his captors, howled with derisive laughter, making no move to help him. He struggled, turning his head from the yellow-brown water that lapped his face threatening to drown him.

Seething with a mounting rage Aimée ran down the embankment to kneel beside the struggling man trying to rise from the shallow water. "Here, let me help you, Señor Ximenez," she murmured in Spanish, lifting the man's shoulder as best she could, propping him against her own body. Gently, she tried to wipe the mud from his eyes and mouth.

"*Madre de Dios,* it cannot be! *Señorita* Louvierre, is it really you?" The dirty, bloodied face of the young Spaniard stared up at her with amazement in his dark eyes, full of his pain and humiliation.

"*Si,* 'tis me," she replied quietly, helping him to a sitting position. "You must do as they say, or they will kill you without a moment's hesitation."

"But how did they capture you? The last time I saw you you were moving into the quarters of the Commandant at the fort," the young man stammered.

"I shall explain all later, for now you must keep quiet and do exactly what they want," Aimée cautioned. She felt a strong hand grip her shoulder, pulling her roughly to her feet.

"Leave him! This is none of your concern," Sebastian commanded in a harsh, frigid voice.

"I know him. He was on the boat with Mignon and me. Can't you see how young he is, even if he does wear a Spanish uniform? Keep them from hurting him," she implored, squirming in his grasp as he half-carried her up the grassy bank.

Once they were in the shadow of the great river birches Sebastian stopped. Pulling her to face him he held her in a tight grip by her shoulders. "He is old enough to be an agent of the Spanish Government, old enough to be a Lieutenant in the army, old enough to plot with the Creeks to kill the Chickasaw. You care for him, this boy, this *agent provocateur,* this hired agitator?" His fingers cut into her shoulders as his black eyes fixed on her pale face.

"I care for him as I would any human being who is being tortured and humiliated," she retorted in a low voice taut with anger.

"Enough! You will hold your tongue or your fine friend will suffer indeed." Releasing her shoulders, he pulled her hands together in front of her and, swiftly, before she could protest, lashed her hands together at the wrist with strips of rawhide.

"Why?" She raised eyes that blazed emerald fire, holding out her bound hands.

"I cannot trust you with the Spaniard here. We return

to the fire, the others will sleep near the canoes. It is late, and we must rise with the first light."

Aimée stumbled beside him as he pulled her roughly to where the doeskin lay covering the pine boughs. "You will take Manuel Ximenez with us on the morrow to this village of the Chiefs that you told me about."

"Aye," he muttered tersely, pushing her down on the doeskin. "No more about the Lieutenant. We sleep."

He lay down beside her, drawing the soft blanket of mallard feathers about them to ward off the cool damp of the night. Pulling her against him, his long, lean form lay curved about her, the warmth of his sinewy thighs pressing into the soft backs of her legs. His hand cupped one soft breast, his thumb lightly rubbing the peak till it stood erect and throbbing.

"No!" She gasped, twisting in his arms trying to pull away from his warm, hard body, his tantalizing touch that was driving her mad with longing.

"Don't fight me, Green Eyes, for I will take you no matter your protest. It can be more pleasurable with your consent, but you are mine. Do not forget it," he murmured into her neck, his words a hot breath of desire against her skin.

"I belong to no one but myself," she contradicted, her voice thick and unsteady with the passionate hunger that he was igniting with each stroke of his hand.

A shudder ran through her as his tongue circled her ear slowly, tracing the shell-like contours with a gentle probing. His thumb continued her nipple as his other hand caressed the long length of her thigh. She was filled with both a hot yearning deep within her womanhood and a mortification at the power Sebastian exercised over her body. Unable to fight him, for her hands were still tied in front of her, she knew that there were invisible bonds of passion that held her in his thrall as securely as the rawhide strips about her wrists.

"Untie me," she whispered, making one last attempt to escape from his assault on her senses.

"Nay, my lovely captive, I cannot allow you to escape me," his voice was a harsh rasp of barely controlled desire.

Before she could struggle he had rolled her onto her back. He rose above her, tearing off his breechclout, the well-honed muscles of his chest and shoulders gleaming bronze-gold in the shaft of light from the fire. She glimpsed the tattoo of the moon, the stars, and the stalking panther across his chest before he sprung on her like some magnificent wild beast of the forest proudly claiming his mate. Pulling up the brief skirt his hand sought her honeyed depths preparing her with his knowing touch for the erect length of his manhood.

She was so beautiful as she lay spread under him, her hair a silver river of silk that rippled over the dark of the pine boughs. The sight of her touching the young Spaniard had almost driven him mad. This delicate moon maiden was his and his alone. Tonight he would possess her completely, and the next night, and the next, till she learned that there was no escape from him. Her destiny lay with him and the People. In time she would come to understand this commandment of fate.

His mouth came down on the soft skin of her midriff exposed by the brief bodice. He traced light circles with his tongue on the golden satin of her skin, feeling with satisfaction her shudder of desire. His hands were never still—searching, caressing, probing the most intimate secret places of her delicious body as his warm, knowing mouth followed their path in a passionate exploration of every inch of her beloved flesh.

"Yes . . . oh yes!" She heard the hunger, the wanting, in her own voice and thought dimly she should be embarrassed. The thought disappeared in the swirl of emotions that blocked out everything but the need for complete joining with Sebastian.

Her involuntary plea drove him beyond control and with a moan his swollen shaft sought entrance to her moist waiting depths. His mouth came down on her trembling lips. He plunged into her as she arched up to meet him in a perfect symmetry of movement.

Fire flickered through her veins as his tongue circled her mouth entwining with her own scarlet ribbon, his hips moving in equally passionate thrusting circles of delight. She felt total abandonment, like a wild creature of the night, writhing, arching, wanting all of him deep within her. Moans and sighs of pleasure were torn from her throat as he thrust again and again into her waiting depths. Her legs were now locked about his thighs in a love-knot, encouraging him onward in his quest to bring them both to the pinnacle. When the pleasure became so exquisite it was almost pain the first intense waves of release swept through her body. Her eyelids flew open, and staring up into the starry heavens, she felt wave after wave of throbbing rapture bring her womanhood complete fulfillment. As a shudder shook Sebastian's lean form, a cry of passion was rent from deep within him and he followed her to that moment of perfect joy. All was quiet as he gently eased himself from her and pulled her to his chest. She lay with her cheek pressed against his heart, listening to the slight pant of exertion that he was trying to still. They spoke no words for they didn't want to break the spell of enchantment. What had occurred between them they sensed couldn't be explained with simple words. They lay entwined, listening to the sounds of the woods and watching the stars that twinkled above them in the velvet night sky.

Suddenly a fiery streak shot across the heavens in a high arch to fall to earth on the far horizon. Aimée caught her breath at the spectacle before her. She felt Sebastian tense beside her at the sight.

"A good omen for the future, a falling star. *Ababinili,* the Great Spirit, is happy with us. He gives us his blessing. Rest now, beloved one, for our journey continues on the morrow." Sebastian pulled the mallard feather blanket about them. Holding Aimée in his arms, he slept.

Slumber did not come so easily to Aimée. Lying with her head still on his chest, the fragrance of the pine boughs beneath them mingling with the scent of the low-burning fire, she felt her senses were too alive to allow her to sleep. It was the first time she had spent the night outside without some type of structure to shelter her from the elements. There was an excitement about it, making her feel one with nature. This was Sebastian's world, a strange intriguing world that seemed to call out to some long-buried part of her. It was also a frightening world where there was a fine line between life and death.

Tracing lightly with her finger the raised edge of the cruel and alien-looking tattoo on his chest, Aimée mused on the paradox that was Sebastian, Shadow Panther, Chief of the Chickasaw Nation. He had called her beloved one, said that she was to be proclaimed his wife in ceremonies at Long Town, but in reality she was his captive, his prisoner. How could she ever understand such a man, let alone live with him? What kind of future could she have living with this strange man who was half savage, yet such a tender lover he took her breath away. They came from such different worlds, how could they ever live together as man and wife? Such a life was impossible. How could she ever bear it, but how could she ever bear to be parted from him? Aimée stared up at the stars, wishing they could somehow show her what path she would travel on her life's journey. Her mind was reeling. *Is Sebastian right? Has fate already chosen him as my destiny?*

Chapter Eleven

Staring ahead at Sebastian's gleaming raven hair loose about his deeply tanned shoulders, Aimée tried to forget her aching muscles and her sunburnt skin as she trudged valiantly behind him on the narrow path. They had left the river behind in a deep forest and were now following a narrow path between the soaring trees. She had never been so exhausted as since they began the seemingly endless trek through the wilderness. The sun had risen and set three times since they left the Wolf River behind.

A low-hanging branch struck her cheek as her thoughts wandered and she forgot to watch where she was going. A low moan escaped her lips as the narrow bough lashed her skin, raising a welt.

"A good lesson," Sebastian called over his shoulder. "Pay attention."

He must have eyes in the back of his head, Aimée thought with a flash of anger at his lack of pity for her wound, slight though it was. It was not the first time she had been amazed at the Chickasaw ability to know everything that happened around them. They seemed to have another sense that the white man lacked.

Mon Dieu, how much longer to the Village of the Chiefs, Aimée wondered, wiping the damp from her brow. The pace the Indians set was a killing one, even though Sebastian had told her they were taking it slow because of her. The fate of their other captive, the young Spaniard, did not seem to matter. She gave a light shudder knowing that because she was Sebastian's woman they were showing her a sullen respect, but she had seen the expression of hatred and lust in the brave's eyes when they looked at her behind their chief's back. The fear it had sent through her made her stick close to Sebastian's side. Although they had slept side by side the last few nights he had not touched her, for the others had spread their blankets close by their fire. It had made her uneasy to have the other braves so close, but the clearings had been small since they left the river's bank. She had usually been so exhausted that after eating the evening's meal she had quickly fallen asleep. It was strange, but now that Manuel Ximenez was with them she was embarrassed to be Sebastian's woman, even if it meant her safety. She had a hard time meeting the speculation and outright curiosity in the young Spaniard's eyes.

Narrowly missing another low branch Aimée put her musings aside. Determined to not let her mind wander again, she stared ahead, following the line of canoes the braves carried above the heads as they portaged to the next river. They walked so silently all she could hear was the sound of her own footsteps as she stepped on a fallen stick here and there, and the footsteps of the Spaniard. It was obvious they were the strangers in this domain of the Chickasaw.

As the sun grew low in the orange-violet western sky the monotony of the long trek was broken. As they broke through a thicket of tall river birches and dense canebrake they heard the sound of water gently lapping the shore.

Aimée caught her breath as she stared ahead of her at a swiftly moving, dark river almost a quarter of a mile wide. It was, however, another sight that caused her heart to pound, for there on a slight rise on the far bank stood a house. This was no crude hut, but a fine two-story structure with glass windows gleaming in the light of the setting sun.

"It is a surprise I have been saving," Sebastian murmured. He came to stand beside her, leaving the other braves preparing to launch the canoes.

"We are going there?" Aimée questioned breathlessly.

"Aye, we will spend the night with the Colberts brothers. They are friends of mine."

A crazy hope started to rise in her heart. He had been teasing her making her think he was taking her to this Indian village, when all the time it had been a ploy to get her away from Rodrigo. Perhaps Sebastian only enjoyed masquerading as an Indian. Surely a man who had known the white world of his father couldn't live like a savage in the wilderness. But what would happen now that they were once more back in civilization?

"Come, George has sent over the raft to ferry us across," Sebastian explained, taking her arm and leading her to the bank.

A huge burly man dressed in breeches, tall boots, linen shirt, and leather vest poled the raft into the shore. He jumped to the grassy bank with a graceful leap for so large a man.

"I am come," Sebastian said solemnly, holding out his hand.

"You are; it is good," the man replied, clasping his hand.

Aimée watched the exchange realizing their words were not spontaneous, but some strange ritual greeting. Why did this white man greet Sebastian in such an odd manner?

"Come, my friend, there is food and drink awaiting us at the house." The burly man gave Aimée a brief glance then headed back to the raft.

"We will ride with George across the river. Tonight, Green Eyes, we sleep in a feather bed." Sebastian pulled her up on the raft, then helped his friend push it into the rushing water, jumping on board at the last minute.

Aimée clung to the side of the raft as the two men pushed across the strong current of the river with long poles. The water was much swifter than that of the Wolf. She watched as the braves battled the surging river. The young Spaniard sitting bound in one canoe looked as apprehensive as she felt.

It was with a sigh of relief that she accepted Sebastian's hand to disembark when they reached the far shore. The setting sun cast long shadows across the verdant grass on the rise that led to the inviting house. Following the two men up the path that led to the Colbert brothers' house, Aimée thought of the pleasures of civilization, perhaps even a warm bath.

It was as they reached the top of the rise only a few steps from the front door that she heard first a moan and then the harsh laughter of the braves. She whirled around and saw Manuel Ximenez being prodded like cattle down a path that led along the river. Every time he stumbled the cold-eyed brave yanked him to his feet by his hair.

"Stop them!" she pleaded of Sebastian, grabbing his

arm to get his attention.

"Enough!" There were shards of ice in his voice as he jerked his arm from her grasp, his eyes ebony pools of anger. "It is none of your concern."

"But could he not stay in the house with us?"

"You try my patience, Green Eyes. No more!" He held up his hand to silence her, then his fingers dug into the flesh of her upper arm as he thrust her roughly inside the open door of the house into a large entrance hall.

Seething with mounting rage at both his treatment of her and callous indifference to the young Spaniard's plight, Aimée barely noticed her surroundings. Her mind whirled with all manner of ways she could seek her revenge upon Sebastian. This was the house of a white man. Surely he would not stand for such treatment of Manuel Ximenez.

"Why have you not introduced me to our host?" she asked, permitting herself a withering stare in Sebastian's direction.

"Chickasaw women do not make a spectacle of themselves. They are not forward."

"I am not a Chickasaw woman," she countered icily.

"You will learn, Green Eyes, I promise you that." His words, though spoken quietly had an ominous quality to them.

Aimée had no time for a retort for their host gestured for them to follow him into a large room on his left. She was amazed to discover it was the parlor and very well furnished.

Dying rays of the setting sun fell from long many-paned windows across a turkey rug in shades of deep rose, blue, and cream. The floor boards were a highly polished heart of pine and the walls were painted ivory.

A fireplace with a carved mantel stood against the far wall, and a flintlock gun lovingly polished, hung above it. The furniture was in the English style known as Queen Anne with several upholstered chairs, a settee and several small tables including a gaming table laid out before the fireplace with an elegant chess set containing pieces of ivory and ebony.

For the first time since entering the house Aimée was self conscious of her attire. She had never been so immodestly displayed before a stranger. During their trek through the wilderness she had gradually gotten used to her brief costume, for the others had worn even less then she, but here in a home that reminded her of all she had left behind she was filled with embarrassment.

" 'Tis good to see you again—there has been little traffic across the river the last few weeks. I am ready for a worthy opponent in a game of chess. After dinner, if that is all right with you?" Their host took two long clay pipes from the mantel and filled them with fragrant tobacco from a canister on the table beside him.

"Aye, a game would be fine," Sebastian agreed, taking the pipe and lighting it from the stick his friend held out to him. Aimée watched in surprise as both men solemnly blew puffs of curling blue smoke to the east, the west, the north and the south corners of the room.

Neither men had asked for her permission to smoke as would any gentleman in New Orleans, Aimée thought in disgust. Obviously Chickasaw women were entitled to few courtesies. But surely George Colbert could see in spite of her attire she was a white woman, for Indians did not have blonde hair and green eyes. He had not even invited her to sit down, she mused, her ire peaked by both men continuing to ignore her presence.

"Shadow Panther!" A feminine cry startled everyone

in the room as the door from the foyer was thrown open by a lovely young woman. She ran across the room to throw herself in Sebastian's arms, her raven-black hair cascading down her back in lustrous waves.

Aimée stared in disbelief as he lifted the beauty up in his arms and swung her around, smiling up at her as she clutched his neck, laughing her throaty mock protests. Her dress was a delicate primrose yellow with deep ruffles of ecru lace at her wrists and low bodice. She had a lush, sensuous look about her with almond amber eyes, high cheekbones, full ripe lips, and voluptuous bosom amply displayed in the low heart-shaped neckline of her gown.

"Leila, is this the same grubby little girl who used to trap rabbits with me? What has happened to you since you went to that school in Mobile?" Sebastian joked, letting her down gently to the floor.

"I grew up. Do you think I turned out well?" The seductive Leila gave a graceful turn, sending him flirtatious glances over her shoulder.

"I should say extremely well," he admitted rather ruefully, shaking his head indulgently at her obvious flirting.

It was more than Aimée could take. She had been ignored as if she were some Chickasaw squaw, while this country belle was the center of attention. Well, she would take it no longer.

"Sebastian, aren't you going to introduce me to your friends? Perhaps they can help me return to Fort San Fernado de las Barrancas. I think this charade has gone far enough, or do you want me to tell them that you kidnapped me," she stated in a low controlled voice taut with anger. Seething with rage and humiliation, her eyes blazed green fire as she stared at the three of them, daring him to deny her presence.

Her reaction seemed to amuse him. He regarded her with a slight mocking smile as if she were a temperamental child who didn't understand a private joke. "But of course, Green Eyes, these are my friends George Colbert, also known to the people as *Tootemastubbe,* and his daughter Leila. May I present Mademoiselle Aimée Louvierre, captive, but soon to be my wife."

"Mademoiselle." George Colbert gave a slight bow of his massive head in her direction, while his daughter simply stared, a flicker of dislike in her strange amber eyes.

"Enchanté," Aimée replied in formal tones. Why, she thought, did George Colbert also have an Indian name?

"I am afraid the Colberts cannot help you escape. You see George, like me, is . . . what did you call it? A half-breed. His loyalties are, however, pure Chickasaw."

Her mind whirled with bewilderment as a tumble of confused thoughts and feelings assailed her. She felt she was living a nightmare where nothing was as it appeared.

"Perhaps Mademoiselle Louvierre would like to be shown a room where she could rest from her travels," George Colbert said in polite tones to his daughter.

Aimée stared in disbelief, for her host was now acting as if she were an honored guest. "That would be delightful," she managed through clenched teeth, trying to hold on to her fragile composure. She would show them she could play their game even though she didn't know all the rules.

"Leila," her father said sharply as the young woman

stared, unmoving at Aimée. Her cold amber eyes seemed to be evaluating her rival as dispassionately, and as deadly, as a cat its intended prey.

"Come," she ordered over her shoulder, turning her back and starting for the door.

With one last hostile glare at Sebastian, Aimée followed the lithe, graceful figure of Leila from the room. The young woman spoke not a word as she walked a few paces ahead, never turning to check that her guest was behind her. Aimée was beginning to dislike the Colberts with a vengeance. Their arrogance was insufferable. Suddenly, to her surprise, she wished they had never left the trail. There would be no help for her escape to the fort from this pair, but at least she would sleep in a bed tonight. It was almost worth putting up with Leila's airs.

After climbing a curving staircase they reached a wide hall onto which opened four chamber doors. Leila glided over the polished floor to the room at the front of the house. It was a lovely bed chamber with whitewashed walls, lace curtains hung at the windows, and a huge tester bed with a lace canopy. A pine armoire and four drawer chest stood against the far wall and a brick fireplace with a rocking chair in front of it faced the bed.

"It will do nicely," Aimée murmured in as gracious a tone as she could manage.

"Leave him be, Frenchy," Leila hissed, turning to look at her for the first time. Her little triangular face, high cheekboned and cat-like appearance, was contorted with the intensity of her hatred.

"He won't let me be," Aimée answered flatly.

"You want to leave him?" she asked in disbelief.

"I must return to the Spanish fort on the Mississippi.

Please help me," Aimée implored, seeing her chance to return to Mignon and civilization. If she felt a momentary pang at leaving Sebastian she hardened her heart. What he asked was impossible. She couldn't live like a savage for the rest of her life. She couldn't leave defenseless Mignon in the clutches of Rodrigo. There was no other choice but escape.

"I will help you, Frenchy, and the Spaniard as well. It will look as if you ran off together." Her amber eyes gleamed with malicious triumph. "We must plan well, for Shadow Panther will be filled with anger. He may try to track you for I can see he is foolishly attracted to your vapid paleness."

Aimée curled her fingers into fists at her side, trying not to loose her temper. Leila was baiting her, but this spiteful, feline woman was her only chance to return to her sister.

"I must think on what to do, for now I will send up a slave with a tub and water. You need a bath," Leila said, with a curl of disgust to her full sensual lips. "I will bring you a change of clothes, although you are too skinny to do them justice."

"Merci," Aimée countered icily, her eyes blazing green fire, her lips thin with repressed fury.

"Ah, Frenchy, 'tis hard to be polite to me, but the icc water in your veins allows you to be the lady, always the lady. I am your only hope. You are a fool to give up a man such as Shadow Panther. Only a silly, pale-blooded Frenchy would make such a mistake. Remember me, *Mademoiselle,* when you reach your civilization, remember that now I lie in the arms of Shadow Panther." The sound of her malevolent laughter hung in the air long after she had left the chamber.

Chapter Twelve

"It is rather big on you, Green Eyes. I think I prefer the doeskin to that garment."

"I am sure Leila will be most gratified to hear your sentiments, since this was her idea," Aimée snapped, as she tried to pull the waist of the rough homespun skirt tighter about her waist. The voluminous bodice hung off her shoulders even after she pulled the drawstrings tight about the neck. The clothes were clean but of poor quality, as was the plain, much-washed chemise she wore underneath the badly fitting outer garments.

"These are slaves' clothing. I think I must have a word with mistress Leila," Sebastian muttered, his grin vanishing as he realized the insult she had given his intended wife.

Aimée sighed as he stormed from the room. The bath had been such a luxury with real soap and warm water, but when the African slave woman had brought the crude clothes, and only a rough comb for her hair, she remembered the malice she had seen in Leila's amber cat eyes.

The sun had set, leaving the chamber in shadows. She walked to the fireplace where the slave had started a fire against the spring night's chill. Holding her hands to the fire, she realized how she had gotten used to only the light from the flames of the campfire to chase the dark from the night. There had been no candles on the trail, only the firelight and the moon glow. Tall tapers now burned on the mantle and on the small table beside the bed.

"Here, Green Eyes, this is more to my liking," Sebastian announced, returning in a flourish with the African slave woman behind him carrying an azure-blue silk gown and slippers as well as white silk stockings with blue garters. "This never did suit Leila. The color was all wrong for her."

"I am sure she was glad to hear that," Aimée murmured dryly, but couldn't keep the grin from her face at the thought of the woman's reaction to Sebastian's comment.

"She has the very devil of a temper. She needs a husband, but has refused every offer. George shouldn't have sent her to the school in Mobile. It has made her restless, and she has forgotten what it means to be a Chickasaw woman."

"Is she an Indian? She could pass for Spanish," Aimée commented as she slipped off the muslin outer garments to stand in her chemise. The slave woman then helped her on with the silk stockings and delicate slippers with curved heels. The shoes were a little large, feeling so strange after the heeless moccasins.

"Her mother was half Chickasaw as is her father. Leila does not know which world she belongs in, the way of the People or the way of the white world. She is used to much luxury living here on her father's plantation with his many slaves, and the wealth he has gotten from ferrying white settlers across the river. But the call of the People is strong to Leila. It is in her blood, as it is in her father's. He lives like a white man, as do many of the half-bloods, but in his heart he is Chickasaw."

"As are you," Aimée stated softly.

"Aye, Green Eyes, as am I," he answered quietly, moving toward her, gesturing for the slave woman to leave them.

"I shall bathe in the tub first, then we shall lie together," he whispered, catching her chin in his firm, bronzed hand, tilting it up so she had to stare into his burning ebony eyes. "You shall join me for it would give me much pleasure." His hands slid the chemise from her body till it lay in a puddle on the floor. The stockings and slippers were stripped from her legs till she stood nude in front of him, her ivory skin glowing in the firelight.

He left her side for only a moment to pour more water into the brass tub. Stripping his breechclout from his waist and flinging off his moccasins, he lifted her up and carried her to the waiting bath in front of the fire. The warm water swirled around her as he pulled her down in front of him. Handing her the bar of lavender-scented soap, he motioned for her to soap his chest as he stroked the wet silk of her thighs.

It was soothing and yet erotic—the warmth of the water and the warmth of the fire lulling her senses as his fingers sought her inner lips. She shuddered as he found their hidden softness. Leaning toward him she soaped down his broad shoulders, his sinewy back, down to where his now erect manhood rose to meet her grasp. The soap slipped into the water as she sought the hard velvet feel of his shaft.

The touch of her small soft fingers around him drove him mad with desire, a wild yearning that destroyed his resolve to prolong the delicious bath. With a savage tenderness he lifted her onto his throbbing shaft as his hot mouth searched her waiting lips.

A moan of ecstasy was torn from Aimée's throat when he penetrated her moist depths, his knowing hands kneading her rounded buttocks as she met each thrust with a wanton swirl of her slender hips. Her mouth clung to his as he explored the honeyed sweetness of her cavern, their tongues swirling, dueling, savoring the taste of each other.

The soft moans of her pleasure excited him, driving him to bury himself deeper within her. The need to possess her completely had become an obsession. They would become one flaming entity, a merging so total they were one.

Aimée was all sensation, hot molten fire surging through her veins as his mouth traced long drugging kisses down the slender column of her throat. Beyond shame, she arched up, presenting the taut nipples of her ivory breasts to his avid searching mouth. Her gasp of utter pleasure filled the room as his tongue curled around one rosy peak, sucking it lightly as he thrust in and out of her with long sure strokes.

As he moved to the other lovely globe and its waiting rose bud, he savored for a moment the sight of her slender form arched to his mouth, her graceful hips swaying in the age-old dance of love, her silver hair flowing down her back to touch the water like a waterfall in the moonlight. It was his undoing to see her so beautiful before him, lost in her enjoyment of his passion. With a groan he called out, "Beloved one!" Holding her tiny waist with both strong hands he plunged into her with a frenzied thrust, seeking the rapturous release he knew was seconds away.

At his passionate cry Aimée was filled with a wave of exquisite pleasure that was almost pain. As he drove into her she answered back with a thrust of her own that caused an explosion of wild sensation to shake them both in a shudder of complete fulfillment.

She sank into his arms, laying her head on his chest as they both panted with the exhaustion of their exerations. The wild hunger they had both found in one another had frightened her in its intensity. Nothing had mattered when he had claimed her body with his own. It was as if the world itself had ceased to exist—there was only the touch, the taste, and the feel of each other. This had been her world where time seemed to have stood still. Reality had been his mouth, his hands, the wondrous feel of him inside her body filling her with rapture. Mignon, right and wrong, the life she had known before, none seemed to matter, for it was so right when they were together. It was as if she had been waiting all her life for him. Perhaps, she thought, she had, remembering how she had drawn his strong, handsome visage whenever she had been lonely. In some part of her heart she had known him forever, long before they had met at the ball in New Orleans.

A rapid knock on the door startled both of them, shattering the quiet sanctuary they had both found in other's embrace. "What is it?" Sebastian called out, still holding Aimée to his heart.

"We shall dine on the hour." A terse feminine voice called out through the thick closed door.

"It seems our idyll is over, Green Eyes," Sebastian whispered with regret into Aimée's silky hair.

He had left her, calling for the slave woman to help her dress for dinner. Aimée stared down at the full skirt of her azure gown, and stroked the luxurious silk with her tanned fingers. It seemed an eternity since she had worn such a gown. Her waist was constricted by the boned corset, forcing her breasts to mound fashionably above the low neckline with its deep ruche of blonde lace. Ruffles of the same fine blonde lace edged the long sleeves at her wrists. Silently the maid had indicated she would dress Aimée's hair. She was as talented as a French ladies' maid, pulling the silver blonde tresses high on the crown of her head to fall down her back in silky rolled curls.

"*Merci, er* . . . thank you," Aimée stammered to the enigmatic slave.

The woman bowed in her head slightly in acknowledgment, then left the chamber, having said not a word.

Now that she was alone Aimée tried to accustom herself to the high-heeled slippers. It was wonderful to feel like a civilized lady once more, but why did she also experience the sensation of being restrained—as if her freedom had been curtailed. She chided herself for being foolish. No one could prefer that indecent squaw costume to this beautiful gown, even if it did seemed to hamper her movements a bit and make her breathing shallower. She tossed her curls and smoothed the silk skirt ready to descend to the dining room. Tonight Sebastian would see her once more as the lady of fashion. He would see how ridiculous it was, this plan that she live as his wife among the savages.

As she glided down the staircase she thought of how refined the Colbert house was, even if it was in the middle of the frontier. She remembered something Sebastian had said about many of the half-bloods living like George Colbert. If that were true why couldn't they? A lovely daydream began in her mind of their having a plantation like this one, and bringing Mignon to come live with them. Her mouth curved in a smile of satisfaction for she had found the perfect solution to her problem. She couldn't wait to explain to Sebastian how every thing could work out. Later tonight she would tell him, and together they could plan their future, a future that didn't include living in a hut in the forest among a bunch of half-naked savages.

The dining room was empty, but the long table with a gleaming white damask cloth was set with silver and crystal glasses. Bayberry candles burned in tall silver holders perfuming the air with their rich scent. Leila had set a lavish table intended to impress, mused Aimée with a wry smile. As if her thoughts could conjure, her hostess appeared from the hall dressed in gold-embossed satin, the bodice so low one could almost see the peaks of her full golden breasts.

"I must talk with you," Leila muttered, coming close. The waves of her heavy, musky perfume almost overpowered Aimée. "If you are to escape, it must be tonight when all are asleep."

"I . . . I may have changed my mind," Aimée replied, stains of scarlet appearing on her cheeks at the knowing, disgusted look her hostess flashed in her direction.

"You want him too, Frenchy," Leila spat. "I didn't think fire could ignite that cold body, but I see I was wrong. You shall not have him, that I promise you."

Aimée shrank back from the venomous tone and the pure hatred she saw in the almond-shaped amber eyes. There was a long, brittle silence between them as each took the other's measure.

"What charming dinner companions we shall have, George." Sebastian's deep voice, tinged with amusement, broke through the tension that hung in the room like a heavy mist. He regarded the two of them with perfect understanding of their dislike for one another.

La, thought Aimée, *he knows we were speaking of him, and how he enjoys the idea of our fighting over him. Look at him stand there preening like a peacock.* Then she had to admit he looked magnificent. Gone was the breechclout and in its place tight black satin breeches that clung to his muscular thighs. White silk stockings showed the strength of his calves. The black satin coat was elegant but masculine, displaying his broad shoulders. The waistcoat of silver-embroidered gray silk was the height of fashion and the jabot at his neck was snowy white, setting off his swarthy features. The raven hair was pulled back in a sleek queue tied with a black satin ribbon. He appeared the perfect gentleman, and Aimée was startled by the metamorphosis.

"May I have the honor of escorting you to the table, *mademoiselle?"* He held out his arm to Aimée and she nodded. Placing her trembling hand on his arm she followed him to her chair.

She was so beautiful, this exquisite silver Venus. How could he want her so fiercely that he had to use all his willpower to keep from sweeping her up in his arms and carrying her up to their bed chamber when he had spent the last hour making love to her? She was like a tempting water sprite of the forest who had cast a spell over him till he was bound to her by some magically invisible bonds.

"Merci," she whispered as he seated her. He felt her shudder as he couldn't resist gently touching her bare skin. In the lovely hollow of her throat he could see the throbbing of her pulse.

"Your braves are most restive. I sent food to them at their camp on the river bank, but they were more interested in baiting their captive. A Spaniard by the look of him," George Colbert addressed Sebastian, as they began the lavish meal spread before them by two slave women.

"He was caught with a band of Creeks who attack us. Wolf's Friend, the fool, still believes the Spanish are friends of the Chickasaw. We take this captive to *Chukafalaya* to show Piomingo that he was right. The Spanish speak with two faces," Sebastian explained tersely. Lifting the crystal goblet to his lips he took a long drink of the red wine.

It was hard for Aimée to reconcile in her mind that these people with their civilized manners and elegant home were Indians. All right, she thought, they were mixed-bloods, but in their hearts it was obvious they were pure Chickasaw.

"Will this Spaniard run the gauntlet?" Leila asked, watching Aimée's reaction to her question with a curious waiting quality.

"His fate will be decided by the Chief's Council, as you well know," Sebastian replied with an edge to his voice, avoiding Aimée's gaze.

"Men were killed by these Creeks—fathers, sons. He will suffer long and hard for their deaths before reaching his own fate," Leila continued with satisfaction on her feline features.

"What do you mean suffer for their deaths?" Aimée asked, her voice trembling. She must have misinterpreted Leila's words for people could not sit around a dinner table and casually discuss a man's torture and death. It wasn't possible.

"Every warrior's death must be avenged so his soul can rest. His clan is honor-bound to seek revenge on his killer or his killer's clan. This Spaniard will die slowly for the Chickasaw who died. It is the way of the

People," Leila explained to Aimée. There was a malicious gleam in her eyes for she knew how this would affect the Frenchwoman who sat across from the man she wanted above all others.

"But that is barbaric," Aimée gasped.

"Do the French and Spanish never kill out of revenge?" Leila asked, her voice heavy with sarcasm.

" 'Tis not the same," Aimée protested.

"Why? Because one is white and the other is not?" Leila continued, her amber eyes gleaming with a triumphant hatred. "Perhaps you find it different because this time the man who will pay is someone who matters to you?"

"But of course he matters, but not in the way you mean." Aimée ripped out the words impatiently, without thinking. She had walked into Leila's trap and she struggled to force her emotions under control so she could think rationally.

"If he means nothing to you in a personal way, then why are you willing to risk your own life to save his? Oh, I am sorry! It seems I have given it away, but then it was never in my power to help you. It must be clear to you now that I could never assist you in your plan to escape with this Spaniard." Leila's words were soft, but each cut into Aimée like the slash of a sword. The woman's haughty features were set in a vicious expression of victory as she sought her own revenge on the woman who had taken the man who was her obsession.

There was complete silence in the room as Leila's pronouncement hung in the air. Looking up, Aimée's eyes meet Sebastian's. He had stiffened as if she had struck him. For a moment so brief she thought she imagined it she saw hurt in that dark gaze, but then it was gone. She saw only a cold dignity that created a stony mask of his handsome visage.

"It seems you have asked the wrong person to help you, my dear. 'Tis strange to find you would be such a fool." His voice cut the silence and Aimée's heart.

There was an icy contempt in those obsidian eyes that had looked at her with so much warmth and desire only hours before. With a sinking feeling in the pit of her stomach she realized that he believed her false. He thought she had been pretending a passion for him while all the while she had been planning an escape with the young Spaniard. In a way it had been like that, she thought with a sigh, but the passion had been real, not feigned. He would never understand, and it was useless to try and explain. She would never give Leila the satisfaction of seeing how much she had succeeded in her act of revenge.

Taking her napkin from her lap she placed it back on the table then rose to her feet. "I feel unwell, and if you will all excuse me I shall retire," Aimée stated, suddenly anxious to escape from the disturbing undercurrents in the room.

"You will stay here until I am ready to leave," Sebastian lashed out, rising to his feet. His arm reached across the table to grab her wrist in a firm, unyielding grip. "We have not been served our dessert," he continued, his voice now soft, mocking her, but his eyes flashed a warning that she must obey.

Crimson with humiliation and resentment, Aimée countered icily, "As I seem to have no choice, release my arm and I shall endeavor to comply, *M'sieur.*"

Their eyes locked for a few breathless moments that seemed like an eternity to Aimée. Then he suddenly released his fingers and sat back in his chair. She sank into her own, realizing for the first time that she was trembling.

The rest of the meal passed in a blur as Aimée sat staring at her wine glass, refusing to touch the dessert plate placed in front of her. Conversation ebbed and flowed around her as the others carried on as though nothing had happened. The room seemed to close around her. She was stunned with the realization that for all his tenderness during lovemaking Sebastian had her his captive, his to do with as he pleased. The quality of her life for good or ill depended on this one man.

She felt that she was suffocating, that there was not enough air in the room. This chamber that appeared so normal, so civilized, was really a trap. Pressing her hand to her throat she knew if she did not leave this table and its overpowering scents of food and bayberry she would be sick. Lifting her eyes for the first time in what seemed hours she glanced at Sebastian's sleek head turned in George's direction. He was her jailer, she was his prisoner.

Chapter Thirteen

The moon cast long beams of light across the floor of the bed chamber as Sebastian lay, unable to sleep beside the slumbering Aimée. Occasionally she would moan as she tossed and turned, troubled even in her exhaustion. He clenched his fists tight against the linen sheet to keep from taking her in his arms and comforting her like a fretful child. He must fight the weakness she caused inside his heart.

The evening had been torture for them both – he had insisted she sit in the parlor with him as he engaged George in a game of chess. That witch Leila had flirted with him throughout the game, leaning over him, pressing her breasts against his shoulder. Aimée had said nothing, staring into the fire lost in her own thoughts. It was as if she had removed herself mentally from their presence since she couldn't leave physically. When he told her coldly to go to bed she had obeyed without comment, leaving the room as if still in her far away trance.

After an hour more of their chess game Sebastian had conceded victory to George. His mind was not on the strategy of winning but on the silver-haired woman who lay upstairs in his bed. She had feigned sleep when he entered the chamber. For a moment he had been tempted to take her even if she fought him, his anger and desire had been so strong, but he resisted. He must not allow her to know how she obsessed him, how the mere thought of her ivory body drove everything else from his mind.

Now he lay awake beside her as the slit of pearl-gray on the eastern horizon told of the coming of first light. He rose from the bed to slip on breechclout and moccasins. The room seemed to be trapping him, closing around him till he couldn't breathe. Once outside, he could think again if he was away from the temptation of her silken body, her silver-gold tresses that spilled across his pillow.

The slight touch of a hand on her shoulder brought Aimée from the land of slumber where she had found the oblivion of complete exhaustion. Her eyelids flickered open and she met the gaze of the African slave woman bending over her.

"Eat," the woman spoke to her for the first time in English. Seeing Aimée was awake she turned and pointed toward a tray placed on the small table in front of the fireplace. "Leave soon," she continued, gesturing this time toward the Indian costume and soft moccasins Aimée had worn when she arrived.

Struggling to wake up, Aimée realized she was being told to eat, and then dress once more in the brief skirt and bodice. Looking down at the linen chemise she had kept on as a night rail she wondered what Sebastian would do if she appeared in it and the silk gown she had worn for dinner. Glancing about the chamber she realized the gown and slippers had vanished. Pushing her tangled hair from her face, she considered wearing only the chemise and moccasins. It would certainly cover more of her than the Chickasaw skirt and bodice. Somehow she knew that the strong looking slave woman would not stand for such an act of rebellion. She stood, arms folded, watching Aimée like a hawk. The slave woman seemed to imply by her expression that she had her orders, and would put up with nothing but complete compliance.

After washing at the basin provided for her, Aimée reluctantly donned the freshly cleaned skirt and bodice. With relief she fastened the pin with her sister's picture in it at the low neckline. She pressed it against her heart for a moment, thinking it was all she had left from her former life. It was all she had to remind her of who she was and where she had come from in this strange new world.

"I do," the slave interrupted her melancholy musings, gesturing she would braid Aimée's hair in two long braids.

With a sigh of defeat, Aimée allowed the woman her way. It was obvious her transformation back into Chickasaw squaw was to be complete.

The morning sun was rising, and Aimée left the house with a pang of regret. She had seen no one but the slave woman who escorted her out to the veranda. Leila, if she was awake, was no where in sight as Aimée joined the two men waiting for her beside a sleek black stallion.

She recognized the steed as one of the famous Chickasaw Running Woods horses, so called because of their fleetness and stamina. They had been the talk of the fort, every soldier wishing he could possess such an animal. The horses were a cross between the early Spanish ponies and the breeds from the American Colonies.

The Chickasaw had worked for years developing this special breed famous all along the Mississippi Valley for its long stride and striking appearance.

"We leave," Sebastian said to George Colbert as Aimée appeared. He stared at her, his bronze visage impassive, his dress once more pure Chickasaw. The elegant gentleman of the previous evening was gone, and in his place stood a fierce, unyielding warrior.

Aimée returned his stare with an icy glare of her own. She would not let herself be intimidated by this perverse game he seemed to delight in playing. In the days she had spent with the Chickasaw she had come to understand their respect for a stoic demeanor where all emotion was under complete control. She would give them a lesson in dignity.

"Come, we leave," Sebastian spoke tersely. "You will ride in front of me."

Walking past George Colbert deliberately, but without haste, Aimée ignored him even though it was rude to not thank him for his hospitality. This, however, was not the civilized world, she reminded herself. He had not responded to her appeal for help, treating her as Shadow Panther's woman, his captive. George Colbert might live and dress as a white man, but underneath he was pure Chickasaw. Sebastian watched her with surprised respect, careful that she should see none of what he felt. He had expected her to plead once more for her freedom, but she did not. Every curve of her body spoke defiance, but she did not beg. Head up, shoulders back, she carried herself like a queen, boldly meeting his icy gaze with a look of disdain. She might be his captive, but there was nothing of defeat in her demeanor. *What a woman,* he thought with admiration, *a chief's woman.* She was his, everything he wanted, and their destiny been foretold years before in his vision quest. Lifting her up, he wondered how long it would take before she too realized it was fate that they be together. He feared she would fight long and hard before accepting her place beside him with the People. Silently he prayed to *Sawgee Putchehassee,* the Giver and Taker of Breath, that she learn before her magnificent spirit was broken in the harsh days to come. He must be careful. It was such a delicate balance to instruct her in the ways of the People, to break down her resistance to their ways without breaking her, destroying the very essence of her that was his beloved Aimée, his obsession.

They left the Colbert plantation and ferry alone on horseback. Aimée wondered about the other braves, and especially the fate of Manuel Ximenez, but she dared not ask knowing how Sebastian felt about her interest in the Spaniard. She must think of the man so close behind her as Shadow Panther. He was not her beloved Sebastian, but a savage who could kill ruthlessly and without remorse. A Chickasaw chief who was taking her against her will to live in a squalid hut in the middle of a god-forsaken wilderness.

They rode for hours, not speaking, through a wild, verdant paradise. Majestic trees of great variety soared overhead covering the hills and valleys they traversed. The ground was concealed under a thick, dense carpet of emerald grass two feet high, intermixed with wild flowers of every shade of color. The wild ripe strawberries were profusely scattered amid the grass and their scent in the warm sun was a fragrant perfume.

When the sun was high they forded a shallow stream. Aimée caught a glimpse of a graceful deer and her exquisite fawn drinking from the clear, sparkling water before the shy creatures caught their scent on the warm breeze and vanished into the dense primeval forest.

"How lovely," she breathed aloud, forgetting her resolve not to speak.

"Aye. It is time to stop," he replied quietly, slipping from the horse to tie the reins to a low-hanging bough.

A quiver surged through her veins as his strong hands grasped her waist and her own fingers touched his sinewy bronzed arms as he helped her dismount. She thought she detected a flicker of response in his intense black eyes as he stared down at her. Standing so close, she could feel the heat of his body. She found his nearness overwhelming. His gaze seemed to hold her immobile, unable to look away, as he seemed to search into her soul. What was he looking for? What response did he seem to be waiting for in the still, stalking posture of some great predatory beast of the forest?

Suddenly, his hands grasped her head at the temples, pulling her in one fierce motion to his hot, hard mouth. His kiss was punishing, angry, and deeply passionate. She was shattered by the depth of the hunger his demanding lips invoked. Wanting him with a desire that left her weak, she felt her tongue seek his and coil around him like the wild honeysuckle vine to the stalwart oak. Sinking against his almost nude form she seemed to melt into him. His savage kiss was like the soldering heat that joins metals into an unbreakable bond.

Sweeping her up into his arms he carried her a few brief steps to the mossy bank, her head buried in the corded muscles of his neck. She felt the soft velvet moss on her back as he lay her down, flinging his breechclout beside him. She saw for a brief moment his erect manhood throbbing his hunger before he lifted her skirt to her waist and thrust inside her waiting depths. His moan of possession and rapture hung in the heated afternoon air as he took her again and again. His hands lifted her rounded bottom up so he could thrust deeper and deeper as his mouth covered hers with a devouring intensity.

It was as if he could not get enough of her, and Aimée responded to his raw sensuous need with her own uncontrolled passion. Her own moans of erotic pleasure joined his as she moved with him, challenging him with her thrusting hips, digging her fingernails into the muscles of his back. Aroused to the peak of her desire, she was drawn to a height of passion she had never known before as her body began to vibrate with a liquid fire.

As her breath came in long shuddering moans she experienced tremor after tremor inside her throbbing loins as together they soared higher and higher. Reaching her peak of ecstasy, she no longer recognized this wild female creature who clung to her mate with such fierce abandonment. He freed her in a burst of exquisite sensation that gave her a rapturous fulfillment.

All was quiet as they lay side by side, their breathing still harsh, like the pant of exhaustion. The overhead sun streamed down upon them, bathing them in its bright, hot light.

"You are mine, Green Eyes," his voice was a husky whisper beside her.

"It would seem that was obvious," she answered, embarrassed at her wanton response to what had almost been an attack. His lovemaking had been wild, urgent, and without his usual tenderness. To her shame she had reveled in it.

"Never try to leave me again. Once we reach Long Town we shall be married before the People. As the wife of a chief you will have a certain status, a protection from what can often be a harsh life for a white captive. There is much you must learn about our ways. I shall place you under the tutelage of one of the wisest women of the tribe, a healer. She is consulted even by the elder chiefs. It is an honor accorded only a few women to be called a Beloved Woman of the Chickasaw, but that is what French Nancy is called."

"French Nancy?" Aimée questioned, lifting one delicate brow as she turned toward where he lay beside her.

"Aye, she, is as you guessed, a white woman taken as a small child by one of the fiercest warriors. Her parents were killed as the Chickasaw hate the French for their years of treachery. When this warrior chief, my uncle, saw the beautiful little girl with hair of flame and eyes like the sky he took her back with him to Long Town. He watched and waited as she grew to be a lovely young woman schooled in the ways of the Chickasaw. Although eleven years older than she, he had never married, waiting for the time when she would be of age to become his wife."

"Did she marry him?"Aimée asked in a whisper.

"They married in the month of the mulberry moon. Although they were saddened to have no children to bless their union, they were very happy. I think their love only grew with time, for when my uncle died French Nancy was by his side, and one could feel the strong bond between them. She made him promise to wait for her in the land of shadows, for only when they were together again would the empty ache in her heart cease."

"She never wanted to return to her own people?"

"The Chickasaw are her people, Green Eyes. She is more one of us than if she had been born a Chickasaw. Is it so hard to believe that a woman could love a man so much his life became her life?" he inquired, a tinge of disdain in his voice at her question.

"No, but she was a small child when taken captive. It was much easier for her to adjust to living like a . . . well, in such a primitive way."

"Easier to live like a savage, you meant," he spat out in exasperation. "Green Eyes, you are going to be a hard case. The lessons you must be taught are many."

"Perhaps I am not worth the trouble," Aimée retorted tartly. "You, or this French Nancy, will never turn me into a Chickasaw, never! You might as well not try for it is useless."

"Oh, I will try all right, and I will succeed if it takes the rest of my life," his voice cracking with a sardonic weariness. "Don't ask me why, but you are worth the trouble. Yes, you are definitely worth it."

She felt his hand travel up her thigh in a sensual caress as his eyes raked her with a fiercely possessive look. They had just made love, but the intense physical awareness of each other was still as strong, sending a tingling of delight through her.

"Come, we bathe," he announced suddenly, rising to his feet and pulling her along with him.

Like two children they discarded their clothing and waded into the swift-flowing, chest-high water of the stream. The cool water washed the sweat of travel and heat of the day from their bodies. Floating on her back, letting the crystal clear creek soothe the sunburn of her skin, Aimée let her thoughts drift like the small fish that swirled about her.

Could she, like French Nancy, learn to call this wilderness home? Would a hut in the forest with this man called Shadow Panther be enough for the rest of her life? He fascinated her, of that there was no doubt, but what he asked of her she didn't know if she was capable of giving. She couldn't forget Mignon, turn her back on her sister and leave her to Rodrigo. It was as if her heart was tearing in two, one half wanting to stay with this man who lifted her to heights of ecstasy, and the other reminding her of her duty to her beloved sister.

A muffled cry shook her from her musings. Turning over in the water she surfaced to glance toward shore. Sebastian was striding toward a group of men silhouetted against the sun. They were only black shapes, but even that much told her they were the braves who held Manuel. She kept low in the water so they could not see she was nude and watched as they spoke to their chief.

He had casually slipped on his breechclout and moccasins and now stood talking with the warriors. They, too, had horses, and the steeds stood beside them grazing on the long grass. Moving downstream Aimée tried to squint into the sun to see if she could spot Manuel. After finishing their conversation the braves began to move further down the bank, obviously at Sebastian's request so she might leave the water and dress in privacy.

It was as the last Indian left that she saw their prisoner. Manuel had a length of rawhide tied about his neck in a noose and was being led by a seated rider. Exhausted and off balance with his hands tied behind him, he stumbled and the braves jeered his misery.

A white-hot anger blazed through her at his plight. It was torture, pure and simple, she thought with despair. These were the ways of the Chickasaw she was to learn and make her own. She could never condone such cruelty, let alone accept it as a fact of life.

Once the men were out of sight Aimée hurried from the stream to dress. Her wet braids dripped water onto her bodice, but she barely noticed, so great was her anger at what was being done to the young Spaniard.

"We eat, then we must be off now that we have met up with the others," Sebastian told her, handing out a flat corn cake and some smoked venison.

"How can you allow them to treat him that way," Aimée demanded, ignoring his outstretched hand.

"All men captives are treated such. If he survives the journey he may be allowed to live if he can survive other trials of courage. If any of us were captured by other tribes we would expect the same treatment. You can do nothing about this. Eat. There will be no other food till after last light."

"Non!" Aimée hissed in French, knocking the food to the ground. "I am tired of being told to do this and do that."

"You are a foolish woman, Green Eyes, and by nightfall a very hungry one," he sighed in exasperation. "Then you will watch me eat."

"I hate you," she muttered, glaring at him as he enjoyed his food.

"It changes nothing." He shrugged finishing his meal. "You are mine. It does not matter if you like it, but I think there are times you do like it, Green Eyes." He pulled her to him roughly pinning her arms behind her back as his mouth came down on hers, forcing her lips open with his thrusting tongue.

She tried to fight him but he held her tight, immobile, pressing the long length of his body to hers. His hot tongue moved inside her with strong, impelling strokes, fueling a raw, primitive desire deep within her. She wanted to fight him, but her body, alive with a deepening hunger, yearned for her conqueror. Her own aching needs were betraying her resolve.

"Hate me, my little wild cat? Aye, but you will never be free of me as long as we have this between us." He gave a soft moan as he pulled himself from his breech-clout and took her there, standing up.

As he lifted her skirt and thrust his manhood inside her waiting depths, Aimée gave a wild cry of surrender. Shudder after shudder tore through her as he braced himself to thrust and thrust again. Her arms now clung to his shoulders as he lifted her rounded bottom so he could fill her completely with his steady thrust of possession. Abandoning herself to her spiraling climax she arched her hips to meet him, and he took her past naked desire to complete fulfillment.

She thought with sudden clarity as he spilled himself inside her that he was right, she could never be free of him. But how could she live with him? How could she become a Chickasaw?

Chapter Fourteen

Moist, hot air surrounded Aimée like a wet blanket smothering the life energy from her bones. She was thankful that at least she was on horseback. The pitiful image of Manuel Ximenez being dragged by the noose while his captor rode a sleek Chickasaw Running Woods horse was burned into her brain. It seemed as if they had been riding for days through the dense forest, she thought, wiping the perspiration from her face with an equally damp hand. How the young Spaniard had lasted so long in the stifling heat she couldn't understand, for he had walked the entire way. Every time he had stumbled she felt her heart catch in her throat, but always he had staggered back up and continued on behind the brave's horse.

"Oh, why do you allow it?" she implored Sebastian, turning to face him on the stallion.

"We shall not speak of this. You can do nothing. It will only cause him more trouble if they hear you beg for him." He had stared ahead over her concerned face, his features stony, remote.

She sighed, remembering how all hope had died in her heart at reaching some part of him that could respond to a white man's plight. He was a Chickasaw Chief in every inch of his bearing. This was the side of him she couldn't reach or understand. It seemed as they journeyed further into the heart of the Chickasaw domain he became more Indian, and more of a stranger to her. Seeing him now with his ebony hair flowing down his bare back it was hard to remember the elegant gentleman of the ballroom in New Orleans, or even her dinner companion at the Colberts. Her old life was becoming a memory like a half forgotten dream, for as the long days drew on Aimée realized she would never leave this land of the Chickasaw. "The time is soon approaching when we reach our destination. I must ask you to listen very carefully." The heretofore silent man who held her fate in his hand, spoke quietly into her ear so that the others could not hear.

"When?" she asked, keeping her voice also barely above a whisper. She stared straight ahead not turning to look at him. She sensed that secrecy was in her own best interest.

"By last light we will see the smoke of their fires. You must keep your eyes low, look no one in the eye. They would take this as an insult from a captive. Keep your head high, but withdraw into yourself, appear and be remote, aloof. Show no sign of fear no matter what happens. Remember, I am with you and as my woman, under my protection, no one will hurt you. Under no circumstances, and I cannot stress this hard enough, do not try to go to the Spaniard's aid. There is nothing you can do to help him, but your interference could get him killed. Stay close behind me when we dismount in the village. I shall take you to French Nancy's lodge as soon as I can, but we have been gone many days and there will a celebration at our return. Do you understand,

Green Eyes?" There was a husky softness to his voice as he asked the question.

Nodding her head, Aimée didn't trust herself to speak. The warmth of his breath was like a caress on her ear and the back of her neck. Sparks of unwanted excitement shot through her with an intensity that unnerved her. He had not made love to her since the day the others arrived. He slept beside her on the ground at night only inches away, but never touched her. She saw the others stare at them with curiosity and it made her skin crawl. The hardest gaze of all to meet was Manuel's, for he looked at her now with contempt. She was an Indian's woman, and he despised her for it.

It was as Sebastian had said, as the sun sank lower in the sky Aimée noticed a growing excitement among the braves. They were nearing home. She listened in amazement as they trilled a series of bird calls into the seemingly empty woods, but by concentrating she could hear an answering call. They were signaling to unseen sentries that they were returning to Long Town.

Sebastian felt Aimée tense and realized she was listening to the calls of the braves. He was constantly amazed at her courage and strength. She would need all of that aristocratic poise when they reached the village. He was surprised to find how much he had come to admire her grace under the pressure she had endured. Never had she broken down or begged, as if such gestures were beneath her dignity. A bittersweet pang tore through him as he realized he wanted so much more from this silvered-haired beauty than just her lovely body. He wanted to share her thoughts, to know her mind, to feel she also understood him with every fiber of her heart and soul. He wanted her to desire to live with him, to share his secret hopes and dreams, to make a life together wherever fate took them. Staring at her glistening hair, the tender part where it was pulled into braids that he wanted to kiss, he wondered if she would ever surrender more than her body to him. Would she ever give him her heart, or was he a fool to think she could ever come to love the Indian side of him?

Aimée experienced a curious sensation that they were not alone, that they were being watched. She felt a tingling up and down her spine as they continued down the single faint trail toward the Town of the Chiefs.

The deepening shadows of evening had fallen when they saw the glowing orange light ahead of them. It was the glow of many fires lighting the night sky like a beacon. There was the fragrance of wood smoke and simmering food drifting toward them on the humid air to add its beckoning lure of an oasis in the empty wilderness.

Breaking through the dense undergrowth they reached a large stockade made of fifteen-foot logs set in the earth with an embankment thrown up at the base. The enclosure ran for as far as the eye could see into the dark of the immense forest. A huge gate of enormous logs stood open. A messenger had been sent ahead. They were expected.

Fear of the unknown knotted and writhed in Aimée's stomach as they rode through the open gate into the heart of the Chickasaw town.

From groups of conical and rectangular houses, neatly arranged in geometric blocks along wide paths, poured men, women, and children as the cry was sounded that the warriors had returned. Aimée shrank from their curious stares. Leaning against the man called Shadow Panther she sought reassurance from the touch of his strong, warm presence. There was speculation in the many dark eyes that seemed to devour her as they rode past. Everywhere, however, she sensed the respect accorded the man who held her lightly as he stared straight ahead, not acknowledging by so much as a glance the curiosity of his people or their jubilant cries of welcome.

The cheers soon turned to jeers as the young Spaniard entered the compound led by the long thong about his neck. Aimée flinched from the sound of the crowd, and was glad she could not see his humiliating entrance.

They were accorded the respect of a returning emperor, a Caesar, as they rode down the wide dirt path to the center town plaza. There a huge fire bonfire blazed red-gold and blue flames into the night sky from the center of the ceremonial ground. Structures built like the rest, only much larger, ringed the plaza.

As the braves entered the ceremonial ground behind them the cheers of the crowd quieted till there was only a low hum as the people pressed in on all sides. Suddenly a sharp wail of grief pierced the night causing Aimée to flinch as chills ran up her spine. The cry of sorrow was now echoed by several other high-pitched women's voices.

"What is it?" Aimée whispered, barely moving her lips so the others would not hear.

"They have discovered we lost two men to the night land of the shadows. The women of their clan are beginning the ceremony of mourning. From now on, Green Eyes, you must remain quiet," he ordered in a terse voice, pulling the stallion to a halt in front of a large round house. The walls were made of clay mixed with grass, the roof thatched with a tall pole like a spire that displayed the carved figure of an eagle on the top.

Shadow Panther dismounted in one quick movement, signaling for Aimée to follow. He did not help her, turning his back as she slid down in an awkward maneuver. Standing behind him, Aimée remembered his words on how to behave. Lifting her head, she held herself in a stiff pose, shoulders back, chin up, but eyes lowered. Icy fear twisted around her heart, but she fought for control. She must not lose her dignity, for she could feel hundreds of pairs of eyes watching her, waiting for the least sign of fear.

From a low, narrow door in the round house came a commanding figure. Rising to his full height he stood as tall as Shadow Panther, but on his head a crest of swan feathers made him appear much taller. From the light of the bonfire Aimée could see he was old, his visage a bronze leathery mask of wrinkles.

Shadow Panther approached the impressive old man, taking from his back a square wooden ark he had told Aimée was called a medicine bundle. Filled with holy objects and vessels made by old women, it was considered sacred. It accompanied them on all journeys, especially war parties and hunts. The War Leader's responsibility was to see that it came to no harm, and for his diligence it would guard them from the harm. He placed it on pieces of wood at the foot of the war pole opposite the door of the Great Warrior's house.

Her mouth dry and her pulse beating erratically, Aimée watched as the cold-eyed brave strode forward, two scalps tied to his belt. As the crowd watched in tension-filled silence he took them from his belt and held them high in the air. Again the piercing wail of mourning rent the uneasy stillness.

At a brief nod of the brave's head the young Spaniard

was thrust forward. The noose was gone from his neck, but his hands were still lashed behind him. Exhausted, he stood with head bent hardly seeming to be aware of what was occurring in the plaza.

Tears filled Aimée's eyes as she heard the hiss of the crowd as they viewed the captive. Here was a man who could have been the one who killed their warriors. She was certain they would show him no mercy, but to her surprise he was led across the plaza to vanish inside a large rectangular house constructed of wattle and daub walls with a gabled roof.

Quickly, lowering her eyes before anyone could see, she stared at the ground and waited. She sensed the expectation of the Chickasaw as they scrutinized her standing in the firelight. Who was she? The unanswered question hung in the air like a fog.

Shadow Panther strode to the center of the Plaza with the confident grace of a great predatory beast. His deep mellow tones rang across the square as he addressed the People gathered in hushed expectation. They listened as he told them of his vision quest so long ago, and how it had foretold the future of his meeting the woman with silver-gold hair. Standing quietly, they nodded as he spoke for his reputation as an orator was great. The Chickasaw took dreams and visions with great seriousness. They considered them warnings, prophecies, and revelations. In the dreaming state one could find the true path revealed, the road one should take in life.

Aimée listened to the rich deep sound of his voice in the language she could not understand. He held his audience spell-bound, she realized, and her frustration grew that she knew not what he said with such eloquence.

Shadow Panther continued his story, weaving the facts of his dream with the actual facts of their meeting in New Orleans. He explained that this French woman was an artist and that she had drawn his face many times before she ever met him. There was a great sigh from the people at this, another sign that they were indeed destined. She had been sent to them by fate to learn the gifts of healing from their own Beloved Woman French Nancy, he continued. *Sawgee Putchehassee,* Giver and Taker of Breath, knew Beloved Woman was growing old, and it was time she passed on her gifts as they had been given to her. Since she had been granted no child of her own loins she was sent this moon maiden to carry on her work. When this woman, now to be known as Moon Flower, learned the ways and was deemed ready by French Nancy, she would become his wife.

A low murmur rose at this pronouncement, but then he reminded them that this was how their own Beloved Woman had come to them. She had lived with the healers and grew in their knowledge, while the man who loved her waited and watched till she was ready for marriage. They agreed this was so, but they withheld their complete acceptance as a slight figure made her way from the crowd to where Aimée stood.

The sense of expectation was so great Aimée felt it like a physical presence. A graceful, lined hand touched her cheek, then tilted her chin up so she stared into penetrating sapphire-blue eyes.

A small-boned woman of her exact height with an intelligent still lovely visage, although quite old, stood in front of her. Dressed in a loose garment of ivory doeskin that reached mid-calf with high, heavily ornamented moccasins, she appeared a Chickasaw till one noticed the piercing blue eyes and long braids of auburn dusted with silver white. Her skin was deeply bronzed from her life outdoors, but the delicate bone structure and narrow nose belonged to a French aristocrat.

"Do you love him, *ma chère?*" The frail voice whispered an elegant French.

"Oui, God help me, but I do," Aimée replied, her gaze locked with those all-seeing magnetic blue eyes.

"You are frightened of this bond between you. 'Tis good you are wary—it shows intelligence. Your life will be completely different with the People then before. 'Twill be as if you are reborn, but then I think your old life was not so happy. *Oui,* there was much pain—I can see it in your eyes. It shines out from your soul, *petite chère,* but so does your courage."

Turning to face the crowd French Nancy took Aimée's hand in hers and said in Chickasaw, "I welcome Moon Flower to my lodge. The goodness of her soul shines through her eyes. She will learn the healing ways of the People so she may carry on my work."

"Agigaue! Agigaue! Beloved Woman! Beloved Woman!" The cheers of the crowd echoed across the square as the two women, one young, one old, walked with dignity from the plaza.

Aimée clung to French Nancy's hand as they exited down a narrow path beside the large round house with the eagle spire. Her gaze had met Shadow Panther's for a brief instant before turning and following the older woman. She had seen admiration and desire burning in those ebony depths. It was the only emotion he could not control on his stony visage. Standing in the glow of the flickering fire light he was every inch the proud, arrogant sovereign of the Chickasaw Nation.

The two women walked only a few yards when French Nancy pulled Aimée inside a low narrow door, only four feet high, into a circular structure with plastered walls of clay mixed with grass, but no windows. A fire burned low in the middle of a large room some forty feet in diameter. Couches made of cane raised up on posts three feet high were arranged along the wall. The frames were covered with split-cane mats and soft doeskin. Fur blankets lay across them. From the walls, and four large pine posts in the roof, hung bunches of drying herbs. Their scent gave a pleasant aroma to the large chamber. Small clay lamps of scented oil with floating wicks hung in a netting from hooks on the walls and from the ceiling beams, lighting the lodge with a mellow glow. Large clay pots in colorful designs, as well as baskets large and small, were stored beneath the couches. The hard-packed dirt floor was covered in woven mats.

"It is so large," Aimée commented in awe as she stared about the vast structure. It was much bigger than the hut she had shared at the village on the Wolf River.

"A Chief's house should be large. 'Tis expected. Also as a healer I am accorded certain priviileges," the older woman explained quietly.

"This is the house of Shadow Panther," Aimée stated softly.

"*Non,* the houses and property belong to the women. I allow Shadow Panther to share my lodge as a member of my clan. He has no woman to care for him and my husband was his mother's brother. The mother's brother rears the boys of their sister in the Chickasaw world. The actual father has little to do with the teaching of his son. It was different with Shadow Panther as his father was white, but when he was here with his mother's people it was my husband who led him in the ways of the people," French Nancy explained gently, understanding the surprise on Aimée's lovely face.

"The children and house belong to the mother?"

"Oui, I must say I find it much more agreeable than the French way of descent through the male line." There was a slight smile on the older woman's still aristocratic features.

"I quite agree." Aimée gave a soft laugh of understanding. "Who arranges the marriage among the Chickasaw?"

"The woman is free to choose her husband, although a Chickasaw mother, like any other, may try to influence her choice. In the end the woman has the final say in the matter. She cannot be forced into a union with someone she does not want. She is also free to divorce her husband if later he displeases her, but she keeps the houses and children."

"Houses?"

"This is the winter house. There is also a summer house behind this one for the warmer weather, a menstruation hut for the time of a woman's monthlies, and a storage building," the older woman elaborated as Aimée stared at her in amazement.

"It is all so different than I expected," Aimée murmured, unable to quite take it all in.

"You are weary, *ma petite.* Rest here by the fire while I fetch you some food. There is much for you to learn, but I can see your heart is good if a trifle confused. Fate has sent you to me. How I shall enjoy instructing you in the ways of the People." The older woman pushed her gently down on a luxurious black fur rug next to the fire.

The warmth of the flames felt good, for the May

night was cool, and Aimée found she was shivering. A great weariness washed over her as she stared into the hypnotic fire. She had entered a new world, a world where everything was strange and different from anything she had ever known, but to her surprise she was not afraid. French Nancy had such an aura of gentleness about her that it was impossible to feel fear in her presence. The older woman was the most unusual person she had ever met.

"You will have time to rest, *ma petite fleur,* for Shadow Panther will spend the next three days in the medicine lodge fasting to purify himself along with his braves. It is done whenever blood is shed, for this is very polluting to the soul. On the morrow when you are rested we will begin your instruction." French Nancy threw a piece of meat into the fire before handing the bowl to Aimke.

"Merci, but why did you do that?" she questioned, lifting the spoon made of deer horn to her lips.

"Before a Chickasaw eats he offers some of his meal to the one above in appreciation and hope that his belly will always be full. If it is meat one asks also the pardon of the spirit of the animal that was killed to feed one's hunger."

"I believe I have had my first lesson," Aimée said softly.

"You have an understanding heart and a sympathetic soul, Aimée Louvierre. Shadow Panther has, indeed, found the woman of his vision quest, his destiny." The older woman stroked her cheek lightly, then with a sigh rose to see to her own meal.

Aimée stared into the blue and orange flames, pondering French Nancy's words. Was it to be her destiny to live with these strange people she had known only to be savages? For savages they seem to have a deeply felt sense of honor, community and reverence for nature. These were Sebastian's people, no she corrected herself, Shadow Panther's people, for here in this forest domain he was all Indian. But could she ever belong here as one of the Chickasaw nation?

A vision of her sister Mignon's sad face flashed across her tortured mind. She was not free to cast her past aside and become a child of nature as one of the People. Her ties to her sister would not allow it, for her responsibility to Mignon would haunt her day and night. Her heart was torn between her duty and her overwhelming passion. She could not give up her life as she had known it for Shadow Panther, but how could she leave him and live without the only man she had ever loved?

Part Three

Come forth into the light of things,/Let nature be your teacher.

William Wordsworth

Friendship is a single soul dwelling in two bodies.

Aristotle

Chapter Fifteen

The June sky was a pale pearl gray as the dark of night gave birth to the new day. Drops of sparkling dew hung from the lacy spider webs draped across low branches of the stately oaks, as Aimée followed the graceful form of French Nancy along the forest path, and her moccasins made no noise as she tread solemnly along the narrow trail. In the ten days she had spent with the older woman she had learned how to walk as a Chickasaw, as well as many other ways of the People.

The air was still cool without the full rays of the sun to burn away the dampness. Aimée shuddered as she thought of the purpose of their walk. They were going to greet the morning as they did each sunrise at the swift cold waters of the crystal clear stream. Today she must take more time with her bath as she had just finished her monthly cycle and must purify herself for the coming month. The water would be freezing for a long ritual, but she knew French Nancy would give her no quarter. The ways had to be followed. Had she not just spent a week in the seclusion of the menstrual hut? She sighed. Although it had not been as bad as she thought, for the small structure was comfortable and her every need had been attended to by the older woman. She had even been given an herbal tea for cramping . To her surprise the herb had been most effective. It was the way of the tribe for the women to be excused from all duties and seclude themselves during their monthlies and childbirth. Afterward they performed a special purifying ceremony.

A circling red-tailed hawk coasted past them to settle on the top of one of the enormous cedars. The clean scent of the pines lent its freshness to the morning as the two women reached the moss-covered banks of the stream. They were alone, for they had walked far up the creek away from the other women for this special ceremony.

She had seen very few people since the night she had been introduced to the tribe and taken to the lodge. She felt a pang of longing as she thought of Shadow Panther, for her last glimpse of him had been when he watched them leave the town plaza. He had spent several days on the purification ritual upon his return. When she had thought finally he would come to French Nancy's lodge she had started her moon time, as it was called by the women of the tribe. She had been whisked away to the small hut in the back of the property, and had not been allowed to see him.

It was thought a woman during her time could curse a warrior and make his war medicine weak if she came in intimate contact with him. It was not a custom Aimée liked, although she had at first enjoyed the peace and quiet. The solitude gave her time to think and rest from the arduous journey she had taken from the fort, and she had been relieved to find she was not with child. Although she knew she loved Shadow Panther, their future life together had so many unresolved questions.

She knew a child would bind her to him so that she would have no choice in leaving or staying.

"Here, *petite fleur,* we stop here," French Nancy told her as they halted beside a huge willow. They faced east and the rising sun as the older woman began a prayer chant welcoming Grandmother Sun.

Aimée stood watching with great respect as the woman sang her song in the lilting Chickasaw language. She had become very fond of French Nancy in the days she had spent with her. The woman had a great spirituality about her person, and a loving reverence for all of nature and her creatures.

"Come, ask the Creator of all the earth, the sun, the moon, the wind, and fire to purify you and bless you with a healthy long life," French Nancy called to her, taking her hand to lead her into the crystal waters of the stream after she had gestured for Aimée to drop the bear robe she had wrapped around her nude body.

"Bless me, Great Spirit, and find me a worthy, kind soul," Aimée whispered as the older woman had taught her, then with a gasp submerged herself in the cold water. Holding her breath for a few moments she felt the sharp sting of the stream like hundreds of needles stabbing her skin. When numb she raised up and accepted the soap weed from French Nancy and quickly lathered. Another quick dip in the icy water and she waded out.

As if hearing their prayers the sun rose, casting golden rays down on the stream, turning the water to a million prisms of light. Aimée welcomed the solar warmth and stood for a moment letting it dry the wet from her ivory skin. Standing there, she suddenly felt someone or something watching them. Looking about she saw the older woman was also aware that they were not alone.

"You are learning to be aware," she whispered to Aimée, quickly gathering her robe about her and picking up her hide bag.

"Forgive my intrusion, but you are needed," a deep familiar voice echoed from the trees as the lean sinewy form of Shadow Panther emerged from a dense thicket.

Aimée felt a dizzying current run through her as his eyes met hers with the intensity of a caress. She was shocked at the swift reaction of her body to his presence. Her skin ached for his touch as a flame of desire ran through her, kindled by his ebony eyes that bore into her in silent expectation of their being together once more.

"They are making the Spaniard ready for his time of trial. You as Beloved Woman are needed to witness his performance," Shadow Panther told French Nancy, his eyes never leaving Aimée's delicate features.

"And Moon Flower?" the older woman asked.

"She too must bear witness," he replied tersely, a flicker of regret in his dark eyes.

" 'Tis the gauntlet," Aimée whispered, for French Nancy had explained once the Spaniard had rested and been interrogated by Chief Piomingo he must under go the running of the gauntlet. If he survived and proved himself a brave man he would be adopted by one of the families who had lost a man at the skirmish where he was taken prisoner. It was the Chickasaw way to provide for new blood in the tribe, and for the widows and children of slain braves to have a man to hunt for them.

The walk back to the lodge was swift, with little conversation although Aimée was aware of Shadow Panther's eyes on her as she walked in front of him on the trail. She felt shy in his presence. The time they had been apart now made her all the more aware of his Indian heritage. He seemed strange and foreign to her with his flowing black hair held by a beaded band with red swan feathers about his forehead. His muscular bronzed torso with the intricate tattoos of the stalking panther, moon, and celestial stars added to his alien appearance. He moved along the trail with a deliberate graceful swiftness that gave the impression of a strong, controlled vitality. It was the walk of an Indian chief—proud, self-contained, independent like the solitary beast he had tattooed on his chest.

Could she ever really understand this enigmatic man, Aimée pondered as they entered the small opening in the stockade that led into the compound. There was a sense of excitement in the air as they strode past the other blocks of houses that made up the households of the Chickasaw. Each of the households consisted of a matron, her daughters, and her unmarried sons. The husbands of the matron and her daughters lived there, but the households with which their allegiance lay were those of their sisters and other matrilineal relatives. Aimée realized how glad she was that Shadow Panther had no sister. It came as a shock how deeply she didn't want to share him with anyone.

"We must dress, my son," French Nancy told him as the three entered the low door of the lodge. "There is food in the cook pot if you are hungry."

Aimée paused before the couch that had become her bed since her first night in the house, clutching the robe close about her nude body. Below the raised platform were several baskets where she kept the few belongings French Nancy had given her. Even though Shadow Panther had seen her unclothed many times, including a few minutes ago at the stream, she suddenly felt shy in front of him. Peering over her shoulder she saw he was helping himself to the hot hominy in the cooking pot, his back to her. Dropping the robe she quickly bent down and opened one of the baskets, pulling out a doeskin skirt and new bodice of yellow calico with tiny blue flowers across it. She had made it from some material French Nancy had given her.

"What a shame to cover such beauty, Green Eyes. Let me enjoy your loveliness a few moments longer before you don your garments."

Aimée whirled around clutching her clothes in front of her at the sound of his deep-timbered voice. The underlying sensuality of his words captivated her, causing her heart to flutter wildly in her breast.

His gaze slowly and seductively slid downward from where a rush of pink stained her high cheekbones to the creamy expanse of her slender neck, ever downward to where her full breasts strained against the garments she held like a shield in front of her. He heard the quickening of her breathing as his eyes, black as onyx, traveled like a soft caress down across her hips to where her slender ivory thighs trembled beneath his scrutiny.

Aimée realized dimly that French Nancy had disappeared behind a deer skin that hung as a barrier across a part of the lodge. She stood entranced by his compelling eyes that seem to have captured her and held her immobile by their intensity. Those ebony orbs, so deep set and magnetic, seemed to blink far less rapidly then any others she had ever seen. Her body felt heavy, warm, pulsating with a growing need to be touched, kissed, caressed. How her mouth thirsted for his moist lips, his teasing tongue. As the hot ache grew in her throat she implored him with eyes of emerald fire.

"I have hungered for you, Green Eyes," his voice was

thick, unsteady, reminding her of sensual pleasures he had taught her in those nights of abandon.

"I too," she whispered, as at the base of her throat her pulse beat quicken against her translucent skin like a trapped bird.

"Later, when there is time, I shall remove your clothing piece by piece till I can touch every silken part of you," he continued, each word a caress that fired her blood. "Would you like that, Cat Eyes? Tell me if you would like to feel my hands on you, the taste of my mouth, the feel of me inside you."

" 'Tis not fair to say such things," she gasped, their eyes locked as their breathing came in unison.

"Have your nights not been haunted by the thought of me next to you, touching you, making love to you?" he persisted, his husky words seducing her from across the room.

"Oui, yes!" She was amazed that he could know how she had tossed and turned, restless without him beside her. The yearning for his touch was like a wound that never healed.

"You are surprised. Do you not know yet that we are one, that we walk in each other's soul?" He smiled, but there was a tinge of sadness in his dark watchful eyes.

"It is a lovely thought," she murmured, a tender smile flashing across her delicate face.

A deliberate rustling from behind the deerskin curtain startled them both. They turned to see French Nancy appear in a white doeskin shift heavily encrusted with red dyed quills and beads. It reached below her knees. Her lined face was painted in red and yellow as was the part in her hair. Swan feathers dyed crimson were entwined in her gray-auburn braids and silver earrings flashed from her ears.

"Dress, there is little time," she ordered Aimée, not showing any surprise at her being unclothed. There was, however, a twinkle in her blue eyes as she busied herself with cleaning up the remnants of Shadow Panther's meal.

Experiencing a stab of disappointment that they were interrupted, Aimée chided herself for such a wanton thought. Quickly she donned her garments and new moccasins of white doeskin, also a gift from French Nancy. Standing patiently she allowed the woman to paint a streak of cinnabar down the part in her hair and place silver loops in her pierced ears. She knew she must not let the older woman lose face in front of the tribe. French Nancy had shown her kindness and extended the hand of friendship – the least she could do was go along with what was expected of her as the Beloved Woman's protegé, but a flicker of apprehension began in the pit of her stomach as she thought of facing all those curious Chickasaw eyes.

"I am proud, Green Eyes. You honor both of us, and our lodge," Shadow Panther said as if sensing her unease. He rose and came toward her with a tender smile of encouragement.

"I will try and not disgrace you and French Nancy, but I must warn you I dread having to witness such an inhumane display," Aimée replied, her soft voice edged with distaste.

"The armies of the white man also have the gauntlet. Not only the Chickasaw have such a custom." Shadow Panther frowned in exasperation.

"But that does not make it right, or any easier for Manuel Ximenez," Aimée spoke with light bitterness.

"We leave." He stared down at her intensely for a brief moment before turning and with lithe strides left the lodge without looking back.

The sun was harsh, almost blinding, after the artificial darkness of the hut. The two women followed behind Shadow Panther. A shiver ran down Aimée's spine even in the humid heat of the morning as she heard the sound of drums. The booming, measured sound echoed off the domed houses as they walked down the hard-packed dirt path toward the plaza.

They were joined by scores of Chickasaw, as male and female, young and old, poured out of their lodges lured by the monotonous throbbing of the drums. Excitement crackled in the air like lightning as they ran laughing, shrieking from every direction into the large plaza. Everyone was carrying some manner of switch or stick. Some would lash them through the air to the accompaniment of howls from their companions. Dogs caught up in the mood of anticipation and exuberance added to the pandemonium by leaping and adding their howls to the melée.

Aimée shuddered, wishing she could run from the scene. It was obvious the crowd was looking forward to the young Spaniard's ordeal. French Nancy had explained the Indians thought of the gauntlet as a test of nerve and courage. Young Chickasaw boys were trained to run the gauntlet in order that they might acquire skill and learn to endure pain. They were not asking any more of Manuel Ximenez then they did of themselves, but it seemed to Aimée another example of the strangeness of the Chickasaw ways. It served to remind her of how different these people were from anything she had ever known. How different Shadow Panther's life was from her own. The Indian side of him was an enigma that both fascinated and repelled her.

The gathered crowd parted and let them pass

through as French Nancy, her carriage as proud as a queen, led Aimée to the center of the plaza where a double line of the tallest, strongest warriors stood, each waiting with a stripped cane switch, a spear, or a club in their hand. At the far end of the gauntlet lines was a striped pole with a crown of eagle feathers upon its top. Nearby was a large domed lodge where refuge might be taken if the captive successfully ran the line of flailing missiles.

A gasp was torn from Aimée's throat as she saw the young Spaniard, totally nude, brought with courteous treatment from the lodge of Chief Piomingo to stand at the gauntlet line. The sun caught the auburn lights in his dark chestnut hair and made his skin glow ivory on his thin boyish body. He appeared so vulnerable next to the sinewy bodies of the warriors. She looked around wildly for Shadow Panther. There must be something he could do to stop this horror.

"Control, Moon Flower," French Nancy hissed, clutching her wrist with fingers of steel. "The young man has been told what to do. It is now up to him to show his courage."

"Barbaric," Aimée breathed, as the drums fell silent. Her body stiffened in shock as she saw Shadow Panther move from the crowd to stand in front of the pole with the fluttering eagle feathers. Lifting his arm he signaled that the ordeal begin.

The young Spaniard entered the line with panic-stricken eyes as he spirited down the line with the fleetness of a deer. The air was filled with the sound of the swish of the striking canes. Although his back was soon crisscrossed with red stripes he avoided any of the blows of the clubs. Reaching the post his laugh of triumph mingled with the cheers of the crowd. He had been brave and quick, qualities admired in a warrior.

"The Spaniard has proven himself worthy of adoption into the People," French Nancy murmured with approval as he was escorted into the lodge of refuge.

"Worthy!" Aimée spat, eyes of emerald fire flashing her outrage.

"He will now be an honored member of the tribe, *petite fleur.* Do not waste your anger on that which you cannot change. The ordeal of the gauntlet symbolized his new birth into the Chickasaw Nation. He is now being washed in water that has been charged with transformation magic in the lodge of refuge. He will be dressed in the garments of a warrior," French Nancy explained softly in Aimée's ear.

The crowd milled about the Plaza as they waited for the Spaniard to reappear. Shadow Panther stood aloof from the others with Chief Piomingo, but Aimée felt his gaze return to her again and again.

A cry went up again as Manuel Ximenez appeared at the entrance of the lodge. He was dressed in breechclout and moccasins, his hair loose about his shoulders, a beaded headband about his forehead. Streaks of red and yellow paint were across his cheekbones. His chest and facial hair had been removed so he was as sleek as the warriors.

The crowd grew silent as two ancient crones led him on a ceremonial walk a number of times about the fire burning in the middle of the Plaza. Slowly, with great dignity, they led him to where an older heavy-set woman stood with two younger women, one delicate-boned and fair of face, the other attractive but heavier.

"They are giving him to his adopted family to replace the husband of the one daughter Soft Wind who was killed by the Creeks. The mother Thunder-Sky Woman is a widow, and Dark Dove is not married, so he will take the place of Soft Wind's husband who was the only man of the household," French Nancy told Aimée as they watched while the women led him away to their lodge to the cheers of the gathered throng.

As the one called Dark Dove passed by Shadow Panther, the young woman gave him such a burning glance it startled Aimée. She realized that a man as compelling as Shadow Panther would be attractive to many women, but there was more in that exchange of eyes then mere admiration on the part of Dark Dove.

"Who is that woman and why does she look at Shadow Panther with such knowing hunger?" Aimée whispered, unable to stop the surge of jealousy that rushed through her till she thought she would be ill.

"Beware of that one, *ma petite*. She is trouble. Several winters ago when Shadow Panther returned from the college called William and Mary he took up with her. He was confused, lonely and hurt by the rejection he found in his father's world. He and Dark Dove lived together for a few moons in what the People call a *Toopsa Tawa,* a make haste marriage because there is not the usual ceremony or duration of the other more enduring marriage. Young warriors and maidens with their blood running hot often strike up one of these matches, usually only for a few moons till each tires of the other. Shadow Panther soon grew tired of Dark Dove for she is a self-centered vicious young woman. He realized she could never be the wife of a chief. When they parted Dark Dove saw her dreams of power and glory as the wife of a war chief vanish. She was desolate and this soon turned to anger. All other offers of marriage she has turned down and now grows old for a Chickasaw maiden. She still wants to be the wife of a chief and will stop at nothing to realize her goal of getting him back," the older woman commented in disgust. Dark Dove was called by her mother to follow them to their lodge. Reluctantly, she obeyed, casting smoldering looks at Shadow Panther over her shoulder.

Aimée listened to French Nancy, tormented by conflicting emotions. The knowledge he had lived with this woman twisted and turned inside her. Was that what he wanted from her—*Toopsa Tawa,* a companionate marriage? He had taken her from her sister, led her through a god-forsaken wilderness to live with savages whose ways were strange and foreign, only to perhaps leave her alone to fend for herself when he tired of her. Her face paled with anger as she shook with impotent rage and fear. Had his honeyed words of their intertwined destiny been only lies to lure her to his bed furs? In time would he leave her as he had the seductive Dark Dove?

Chapter Sixteen

The moon was an ivory crescent in the navy-black velvet of the sky as the two women walked back from the communal corn fields. It had been a long day. After the adoption ceremony of the young Spaniard, French Nancy had insisted they tend the fields allotted to them. Aimée rubbed the small of her back where her muscles ached from the strain of bending over and building up small hills of earth with a digging instrument called a mattock.

"You are tired, Moon Flower," the older woman commented, seeing her gesture. "Soon you will get used to it. Your muscles are weak but with time they will become strong. It is good for your body to work. You will see how the energy will flow with renewed vigor as your muscles strengthen."

"I hope you are right, but for now I feel I have a long way to go," Aimée answered dryly. Every nerve and muscle cried out for rest as the women approached the lodge.

They had been joined in their labors by other women and girls of the village. There had been a cheerful atmosphere among the workers as they planted the fields the men had cleared, even though the men had stayed behind in the village. Planting and caring for the crop was women's work, French Nancy had informed her when she complained that there were many able-bodied men to do such back-breaking work.

"Women are more connected to our Mother the Earth. We, too, give birth to new life and nurture it. We understand its secrets," the older woman had explained, as she showed Aimée to build up the small hills then drop seven corn kernels into each hill. Seven was a sacred number, she had confided before she began her reverent prayer to the elements asking for soft winds, warm rains, and the blessing of Grandmother Sun upon each hill.

Aimée had to admit she had enjoyed the feel of the warm earth on her hands, the scent of the wet fecund soil as she watered each small mound, but she still thought the men should have helped. When it was explained to her that the fields belonged to the women who worked them, not the men, she felt somewhat better. The Chickasaw women labored hard in Long Town, but they had a freedom and power in the community that white women didn't even dream about.

Aimée had mulled the rights of the Chickasaw women over in her mind all the long planting day. The sight of Dark Dove and her mother had set her to thinking. They had come to plant their fields, leaving Soft Wind to become acquainted with her new husband. She had often felt the penetrating gaze of Dark Dove upon her as she worked. There had been enmity in those black eyes. The young woman would not easily accept her as Shadow Panther's bride, the wife of a chief.

Aimée sighed as she bent low to enter the low portal

of the lodge. Weary in both body and mind she wanted only to wash, eat, and then sleep. She entered the large chamber and stiffened as she saw the familiar masculine figure reclining in front of the center fire with an indolent grace.

"I have been waiting long for your return," he murmured. There was an invitation in the smoldering gaze he turned on her.

Although tired and hungry, she raised her chin and assumed all the dignity she could muster. "I assume you have spent the day lolling about the village while we have been working like slaves in the field," she spat out, for there had also been black slaves captured from white settlements working with their new Indian masters in the corn fields. "No Frenchman, no *gentleman,* would have allowed women to do hard physical labor while they amused themselves by lying about in the sun."

"We have been planning the next hunt and discussing the intrusion of the Spanish into our lands, Green Eyes. It is the way of the People—the men have their tasks, the women theirs."

"I am sick of hearing about the ways of the People," Aimée cried, flashing into a sudden fury.

"You are tired. There is warm water here in this bowl and hot food in the pot over the fire." He spoke with an indulgent tone as if to a fretful child.

She walked with stiff dignity to the fire and took the bowl. It was heavy with the hot stones that warmed the water. It was how the Indians heated all liquids. Taking the soap weed from a nearby basket, she washed the dirt from her arms and hands. She would not look in Shadow Panther's direction, but she was conscious of his presence, his dark intense gaze.

"The night is warm," French Nancy commented as she came from behind the deerskin partition, her washing completed. "I shall sleep in the summer house tonight." There was a twinkle in her knowing blue eyes as she scooped out some of the bubbling stew with a horn spoon from the pot over the fire.

"You are a wise and thoughtful woman," Shadow Panther murmured, giving her a gentle smile of gratitude.

"Be patient, my son, with Moon Flower. She is finding her journey a rocky one, but she has great courage and a loving spirit. We must allow her to find her own answers even if it causes us pain. She cannot easily forget all she has been taught in her life by her own people," the old woman reminded him in a low voice, before moving with her bowl to the low portal that led to the summer house.

"Where is French Nancy going?" Aimée questioned with more than a hint of panic in her voice, standing by the fire with her bowl and spoon in her hand.

"She gives us time alone on our first night together since coming to Long Town." The fire in his piercing onyx eyes, seemed to penetrate and read the very thoughts of her heart, leaving no question in her mind how he planned to spend the night.

Ashamed at the trembling of her hand as she ladled the stew, she fought for control. Carefully she walked to the other side of the fire and sat on a mat across from him. She ate staring into the flames as if she were alone. It took every ounce of strength at her command to appear so calm. She was learning how the Indian valued control of one's emotions, and it was a lesson she was determined to master. Her dignity was all she had left to her. It seemed every other facet of her identity was being slowly changed as her resistance was worn down inch by inch. She felt like a grain of sand constantly buffeted by the strength of the mighty ocean called the Way of the People.

"You are learning control, like a Chickasaw," he commented softly with a trace of regret.

"Is that not what this is all about," Aimée grimaced in disgust, "to turn me into the perfect squaw."

"I wish only to show you your destiny."

"And you are privileged to know my destiny?" Aimée inquired, each word etched with scorn. Her withering stare lashed across the leaping orange-blue flames of the fire.

"In my vision you were revealed to me, Green Eyes. French Nancy has explained to you that the Chickasaw believe they are given brief flashes of enlightenment in dreams, that we are shown the hidden corners of our soul. Dreams connect this world with another world which may be more real than this one; they connect the past with the present, and the present with the future."

Aimée felt the tiny hairs on the back of her neck rise at his words. She shifted uneasily, not sure how to answer for he had struck a cord deep with in her, a cord she did not want to acknowledge.

"You understand what I am saying even if you will not admit it, but I see it in your eyes. Who was the man you drew time after time? Was he a stranger, a fantasy to while away the lonely hours, or was he your future?"

" 'Tis hard for me to believe in . . . in such things."

"For now, believe in me, in us, in the bond that is between us" he suggested, the rasp of barely checked passion echoing across the fire burning with a smoldering warmth.

It was too warm a night for a fire, Aimée thought as

The Publishers of Zebra Books
Make This Special Offer
to Zebra Romance Readers...

AFTER YOU HAVE READ THIS BOOK WE'D LIKE TO SEND YOU

4 MORE FOR *FREE*
AN $18.00 VALUE

NO OBLIGATION!

ONLY ZEBRA HISTORICAL ROMANCES
"BURN WITH THE FIRE OF HISTORY"
(SEE INSIDE FOR MONEY SAVING DETAILS.)

MORE PASSION AND ADVENTURE AWAIT... YOUR TRIP TO A BIG ADVENTUROUS WORLD BEGINS WHEN YOU ACCEPT YOUR FIRST 4 NOVELS ABSOLUTELY *FREE*

(AN $18.00 VALUE)

Accept your Free gift and start to experience more of the passion and adventure you like in a historical romance novel. Each Zebra novel is filled with proud men, spirited women and temptuous love that you'll remember long after you turn the last pag

Zebra Historical Romances are the finest novels of their kind. They are written by authors who really know how to weave tales of romance and adventure in the historical settings you love. You'll feel like you've actually gone back in time with the thrilling stories that each Zebra novel offers.

GET YOUR FREE GIFT WITH THE START OF YOUR HOME SUBSCRIPTION

Our readers tell us that these books sell out very fast in book stores and often they miss the newest titles. So Zebra has made arrangements for you to receive the four newest novels published each month.

You'll be guaranteed that you'll never miss a title, and home delivery is so convenient. And to show you just how easy it is to get Zebra Historical Romances, we'll send you your first 4 books absolutely FREE! Our gift to you just for trying our home subscription service.

BIG SAVINGS AND FREE HOME DELIVERY

Each month, you'll receive the four newest titles as soon as they are published. You'll probably receive them even before the bookstores do. What's more, you may preview these exciting novels free for 10 days. If you like them as much as we think you will, just pay the low preferred subscriber's price of just $3.75 each. *You'll save $3.00 each month off the publisher's price.* AND, your savings are even greater because there are never any shipping, handling or other hidden charges—FREE Home Delivery. Of course you can return any shipment within 10 days for full credit, no questions asked. There is no minimum number of books you must buy.

4 FREE BOOKS

TO GET YOUR 4 FREE BOOKS WORTH $18.00 — MAIL IN THE FREE BOOK CERTIFICATE TODAY

Fill in the Free Book Certificate below, and we'll send your FREE BOOKS to you as soon as we receive it.

If the certificate is missing below, write to: Zebra Home Subscription Service, Inc., P.O. Box 5214, 120 Brighton Road, Clifton, New Jersey 07015-5214.

FREE BOOK CERTIFICATE

4 FREE BOOKS

ZEBRA HOME SUBSCRIPTION SERVICE, INC.

YES! Please start my subscription to Zebra Historical Romances and send me my first 4 books absolutely FREE. I understand that each month I may preview four new Zebra Historical Romances free for 10 days. If I'm not satisfied with them, I may return the four books within 10 days and owe nothing. Otherwise, I will pay the low preferred subscriber's price of just $3.75 each; a total of $15.00, *a savings off the publisher's price of $3.00*. I may return any shipment and I may cancel this subscription at any time. There is no obligation to buy any shipment and there are no shipping, handling or other hidden charges. Regardless of what I decide, the four free books are mine to keep.

NAME

ADDRESS APT

CITY STATE ZIP

TELEPHONE ( )

SIGNATURE (if under 18, parent or guardian must sign)

Terms, offer and prices subject to change without notice. Subscription subject to acceptance by Zebra Books. Zebra Books reserves the right to reject any order or cancel any subscription.

089002

GET
FOUR
FREE
BOOKS
(AN $18.00 VALUE)

AFFIX
STAMP
HERE

ZEBRA HOME SUBSCRIPTION
SERVICE, INC.
P.O. BOX 5214
120 BRIGHTON ROAD
CLIFTON, NEW JERSEY 07015-5214

her cheeks flushed crimson, but it was from his intense gaze, not the flickering logs. She couldn't help it, she felt herself flowing toward him, toward the magnetic pull of his masculine need. He wanted her and refused to let her go. Suddenly she knew she was glad he persisted in his belief of their intertwined destinies. It was such a wonderful feeling to be wanted that much. She had known so little love in her young life, rarely any affection, that now to hear such words was overwhelming. Tears blinded her eyes and choked her throat so she was unable to speak.

"Nay, my sweet lost love, we are here together. The wind, the moon, the stars, have decreed it. We no longer walk alone but travel life's pathway together in each other's souls." Kneeling down, he gathered her into his arms and gently rocked her back and forth. She buried her face against the corded muscles of his throat.

It was so safe in the circle of his sinewy embrace. She felt she had found a sanctuary from all the pain and uncertainty of life. Wrapping her arms around the satin warmth of his skin she relaxed, sinking into the all-encompassing security of his touch.

"Tonight we are one," he whispered, his breath hot against her ear, his hand caressing the hollows of her graceful back. His tongue traced the outline of her shell-like ear in a tantalizing circle.

Aroused by his touch as his hands moved lower underneath her brief skirt to stroke each soft mound of her saucy bottom, she caressed the length of his nude back with trembling fingers. His mouth pressed down in the hollow of her throat as her body arched against him, telling of her desire.

He fought the roaring in his head and the wild urge to

throw her down on the mat and claim her again and again. There would be time for all the delicious variations of lovemaking in this splendid night, but she needed cherishing, gentling, till she felt secure enough to tease and play at love.

Slowly, with a gentle reverence, as if she was made of porcelain, he removed her bodice. Lifting each small globe in his hands he circled the nipples with his thumbs till they were taut with desire. His tongue tantalized the throbbing buds which had swollen to their fullest. Her senses reeling. She panted lightly between parted lips as she watched him suck first one taut peak, then the other.

The whole hut seemed to swirl around her, the smoky scent of the hickory and the clean wood-musk fragrance that was Shadow Panther, mingling together in one exciting aroma. It was hot and dark in the lodge, but it only added to the intimacy of their lovemaking. The golden glow of the embers turned their nude bodies to bronze, as they touched and caressed the satin of each other's skin. Their hands feathered over each other's bodies, reveling in the gasps and moans of pleasure that they evoked.

Tenderly, with a barely leashed passion, he stretched her out beside him on the mat, his mouth now following the path of his hands over her voluptuous curves. The teasing touch of his lips triggered primitive yearnings that she didn't know she was capable of experiencing. Her hands intertwined in his long black hair, as she writhed under his ravaging mouth, ragged whimpers of wanton hunger escaping from her lips.

He parted her legs to kiss the soft inner thigh and she saw as if in a dream their shadows thrown against the side of the lodge by the firelight. The giving and receiving of their rapture made them partners in a dance of light and shadow.

A moan of ecstasy was torn from her throat as she arched up to meet his insistent touch that probed the inner petals of her woman's rose. Her response was shameless, instant, and total. He rose over her, and his sinewy bronze beauty took her breath away. His blazing eyes commanded hers to lock with his as he entered her. Her small fingers wrapped around the cords of his forearms. He took the weight off her slender body, thrusting into her with a slow measured rhythm that sent fire bolts of desire arching through her.

"Are we one, Green Eyes?" he demanded in a harsh rasp as he fought for control, bringing her once more to the brink of climax with steady thrusts of possession. Her hot tightness almost brought the end of his restraint.

"Oui, yes, we are one!" she gasped. Passionately she arched to meet him and abandoned herself to the spiraling climax of complete rapture.

"Beloved!" He uttered a fevered moan from deep within as the throes of fulfillment shook him.

They lay in silence, the hunger they had for each other satisfied for a brief time. Their limbs entwined, their hands clasped, they listened to each other's breathing as if to the sweetest music.

Shadow Panther raised her hand to his lips and kissed her small fingertips reverently. He felt the still-rapid throb of her pulse in the delicate wrist. Turning her hand over he placed his lips on the fragile vein where her hand met the soft ivory arm.

"Little one, I shall cherish you always," he promised, smiling down at her, his expressive dark eyes touching her everywhere, but especially her heart.

Her small ivory visage glowed like a magnolia blossom in the firelight, the features cast in a wistful mood, the moss-green eyes awash with tears of joy and deep emotion. "And I you," she replied in a tremulous whisper.

Tenderly Shadow Panther kissed away the tears at the corners of her eyes, lingering on her eyelids, then the tip of her nose, before caressing her lips with such aching gentleness Aimée thought her heart would break.

"What a life we shall have together, my beloved one," he murmured, pulling her down so she lay with her head on his chest. "Someday you too, like French Nancy, will be Chickasaw in your heart. She sees you as the daughter she never had, you understand. There is much she can teach you. Listen well."

"Can she teach me how to forget my sister and my obligations to her?" Aimée asked in a low troubled voice. "Can she erase my past and all I know of civilized life?"

"Civilized?" He snorted, his hand holding her tight to him as if she would try and run away. "You call the cold and brutal way the white man treats each other civilized. The filth in his streets, and his aversion to bathing—the harm and waste they do to our Mother the Earth and her creatures. They hunt for pleasure, not needing the meat, leaving it to rot after the thrill of the kill. They hold themselves superior to the birds that can fly, the deer that can outrun any man, the fish that swims with such grace. Never do they ask forgiveness of the spirit of that which they kill. Instead, they rejoice in the slaughter. This is the civilization that you hold in such high esteem?"

"I . . . I have never thought of it that way," she answered, her voice troubled.

"Think, Green Eyes. Listen, learn, and then decide for yourself what is civilized. I realize it is all so strange, but you are different from the other whites I have known. There is a kindness and largeness of soul within you. I could see it in your eyes that first night in New Orleans, and the sadness as well. You are right, however, in worrying about your sister. I have thought on this and have decided there is something I can do."

"You will take me back to the fort?" There was excitement in her voice as she raised her head to stare into the deep-set black eyes that seemed to look right through her.

"You are mine. I shall never let you go. Forget the fort, forget Rodrigo Hernandez. You are no longer Aimée Louvierre, but Moon Flower. You are Chickasaw," he said flatly, his voice as cold as his eyes.

"I *am* Aimée Louvierre! Do you hear me? Aimée Louvierre! You cannot take that from me. You cannot change me because you want it to be so," she spat out the words, glaring at him with a burning, reproachful stare.

"You are Moon Flower, my chosen bride," he repeated, rising to his feet, tying on his breechclout. As he turned to leave she saw his face. It was a frozen mask, all emotion pulled within. He had withdrawn into himself, a private place she could not reach. All Chickasaw were taught from childhood to hide their emotions, to wear this stoic mask so no one knew their thoughts. It was a point of pride among them, French Nancy had explained, to learn this control over their feelings and their bodies.

Aimée watched with tears of rage and despair filling her eyes as Shadow Panther walked to the narrow portal of the lodge. She clenched her teeth to keep from asking him not to leave.

"Rest, little one, you are tired," he said huskily, turning for a moment to stare through the gloom of the chamber. He studied her pale face for a brief heart-stopping moment, then disappeared into the night.

A flash of frustration and wild grief ripped through her as tears slowly found their way down her cheeks. It was like battling a fog—he heard only what he wanted to hear. He could be such a sensitive, tender lover one moment, then this cold stubborn stranger the next. Why couldn't he understand that she couldn't lose her identity, her name, forget all she had known her whole life to become what he wanted. She wasn't, would never be a Chickasaw, she vowed, whispering into the dark heated air of the lodge. But she found no release from her vow, for a voice within reminded her that the man she loved would always be an Indian, no matter his father's blood. He wanted her to become a part of his world, for he could never be a part of hers. Did she love him enough to try, or would the very essence of her be destroyed in the process?

Chapter Seventeen

"Awake, *petite fleur,* 'tis time to gather the herbs." French Nancy's insistent voice continued in Aimée's ear like a bothersome insect. "Awake, there is illness in the lodges of the People."

Struggling to sit up and rub the sleep from her eyes, Aimée saw that the old woman was dressed, carrying a large basket over either arm. She had become accustomed to waking at dawn since living with French Nancy, but it seemed that this was earlier than usual. There was no light coming through the portal, and she could see the stars overhead when she stared up through the small smoke hole over the banked coals.

"Why are we rising so early?" she questioned, quickly donning her garments.

"Eat and drink, then we shall go to the stream to welcome Grandmother Sun. After bathing we must gather the herbs I will need today. 'Tis important we gather them right before use if we are to derive their full power. Today you will learn much about healing, but you must listen and remember."

"You said there was sickness in the village," Aimée repeated, breaking her fast quickly as she sensed the older woman's anxiety to be about her work.

"Have you had the disease the French call *la rougeole,* the measles?

"Oui, when I was a child."

"Bien, good," French Nancy said with satisfaction, "so did I. You will be of help to me. I believe that is the sickness that is starting in the lodges. Foolish men brought back blankets and pots from a white trading post where there was much illness among the settler's children. *La rougeole* is a disease of children among the whites, but to an Indian village it is disaster. Everyone, young and old, will come down with the illness. Many will die, Moon Flower, so we must prepare to fight."

Aimée flinched at the somber prophesy and the shadow of alarm she saw in those ancient blue eyes. In the three weeks she had been with French Nancy she had never seen her show fear of anything.

"Shadow Panther?" Her question hung in the air and she regretted asking it, but couldn't help herself. He had left the village the morning after their quarrel to go off hunting alone. She had not seen him since. It had been almost a week and still no word. Now there was a dangerous epidemic in Long Town and he would soon be returning. She hated that she cared so much, but she couldn't stand the thought that he might be returning to an agonizing death.

"He also has had the disease as a child when he stayed with his father in Charles Town," French Nancy told her briskly, but there was a look of understanding in her azure eyes.

The two women left the lodge as the dark of night was turning into the pale gray of a new day. No one stirred as they traveled down the deserted streets and out the front gate to the clear waters of the bathing stream. Only the uneasy bark of a dog and the fretful wail of a child broke the stillness of the dawn. *Is it the cry of sickness,* Aimée thought, her face clouding with alarm as she remembered French Nancy's words of foreboding.

A cloud of steam rising off the water lent an eerie atmosphere to the bathing spot as they approached through the fragrant stand of giant cedars. The damp fog swirled around the women as they placed their baskets on the mossy bank. Aimée shivered as she slipped out of her garments and joined French Nancy in her morning prayers. They slid into the cold waters of the spring-fed stream. The night had been warm and humid, and the June day promised to be hot, but Aimée couldn't keep from shivering as she rose from the water.

She had been amazed when she realized the Chickasaw bathed every day, summer or winter. It was considered a great wrong if one did not do this each and every morning. Violators were punished by a light scratching on the arm with the dried teeth of a long dead rattlesnake. It did not hurt much, French Nancy had explained, but it did cause much humiliation to the one who had violated the strict law of the morning cleansing. Aimée had thought with chagrin of the many wealthy citizens of New Orleans who could have learned something from the Chickasaw custom of daily bathing.

The sun was high enough to break up the wispy banners of ground fog when French Nancy led Aimée deeper into the forest, her eyes intent on the ground beneath her moccasins. Nothing seemed to escape the sharp gaze of the old woman.

"Here is the bark of the willow, good to reduce fever," she told Aimée as she approached the dwarf gray willow tree. "Always take the bark from the east side of the tree." Taking a knife from her basket, she stripped long strips of bark from the trunk.

Aimée watched in amazement as they continued on their way, stopping whenever the healing woman found a wild herb she sought. She explained its name and use to her young apprentice and made her repeat it after her till she was sure Aimée understood. She taught her the incantations that must be spoken as well. Every time she found a plant she desired she circled it four times counter-clockwise, chanting, then facing east she dug up what she wanted.

"You always leave some. Why not take more so you will not have to come back so often?" Aimée questioned as she helped gather wild sorrel, wilana, and wormseed.

"Healers prefer to gather fresh plants because their life force is strong. Mother Earth will always have a supply ready when I need them again."

Their baskets were full when they started back toward Long Town. The pungent scent of the cut herbs was strong in the heat of the morning. Women nodded respectfully to French Nancy as they passed the fields where some were tending their crops and others were frightening away the birds who were trying to eat the seed. Aimée sighed, wondering if that was next on their agenda. Her back was growing stronger from all the vigorous exercise, but she hated how unkempt her hands had become with callous palms and broken nails.

Although some of the women and children had been in the fields it seemed quieter then usual as Aimée and French Nancy entered the village. An eerie pall hung over the clustered huts like an early morning fog. Men passed them with taut expressions, walking with a determined stride toward the plaza and the council house of the chiefs.

"Stay close by my side and do not leave the lodge unless I accompany you," French Nancy cautioned as they entered the low portal. "The Chickasaw believe disease can be caused by witches amongst them and by vengeful animal spirits. You are new to Long Town, and white. They may feel you have brought the sickness to the People to cause mischief and pain."

Aimée felt a whisper of terror run through her at the old woman's warning. She knew that if the Indians thought she had brought the disease that would kill many of them her own life would be in danger.

As the two women were tying the bundles of herbs into bunches and hanging them from the beams in the hut, there was a call from a husky feminine voice as a slight form entered the lodge. Aimée met the hostile gaze of Dark Dove as she listened to the soft sound of the Chickasaw language. French Nancy had been instructing her, but she knew only a few words. She couldn't understand Dark Dove's rapid speech, but she sensed the urgency in her questioning of the healing woman.

"There is sickness in Thunder Sky Woman's lodge. The young son of Soft Wind is ill with fever. Gather the willow bark, the wormseed, the queen of the meadow, white snake root, and the coltsfoot snake root," French Nancy ordered Aimée as she placed thoroughwort and Lobelia in her basket.

There was a sharp command in Chickasaw from Dark Dove, full of animosity, as she stared at Aimée with eyes full of hate. Her arms crossed in front of her chest, she stood in front of the entrance of the lodge as if to bar the white woman's exit.

"She goes with me for she is *Aliktce,* one of the Chosen—a healer," French Nancy commanded stiffly in Chickasaw.

Aimée recognized the word *Aliktce* for it was Chickasaw for healer, but it didn't seem to pacify Dark Dove. The woman stood silent, unrelenting, as the tension in the lodge grew in intensity. The three women stood locked in a silent battle of wills.

Suddenly, with a shrug, Dark Dove turned and disappeared through the low tunnel that led to the portal. French Nancy picked up her baskets and leather bag, then gestured for Aimée to follow her.

The pathways through the village were strangely deserted for the middle of the day as they made their way to the lodge of Thunder Sky Woman. Dark Dove hurried ahead, never checking to see if they were following. A moan of pain or illness echoed now and then from a hut as they passed. Aimée shivered. French Nancy had been right in her prophecy.

The fetid scent of sickness was thick in the air of the lodge as they entered. The cloying warmth and smell was overwhelming, causing a wave of nausea to wash over Aimée. Willing herself not to faint or throw up, she helped French Nancy soak the willow bark in a pot of water to make an infusion.

"Done all right for yourself, I see," the sneering male voice spoke in an accented French. "Made you some kind of medicine man as well as a squaw."

Aimée looked up from where she knelt by the center fire to stare into the contemptuous eyes of Manuel Ximenez. He was dressed in a breechclout and moccasins, his hair long with a beaded headband about his forehead.

"And you are now a Chickasaw brave," she answered calmly, not showing how stung she was by his obvious disdain.

" 'Tis advantageous to let them think so, the fools," he sneered.

"They have treated you well, have they not," she asked, wondering what French Nancy made of their conversation. It was obvious the Spaniard was unaware the older woman spoke French.

"Indeed, my little squaw is most passionate, even with her sister and mother in the same hut. Don't believe in privacy, these savages," he jeered. "I like their idea of having more then one wife, though. I might make the sister mine also. Enjoy the thought of a little variety. How's your Indian chief feel about that custom, or hasn't he told you?" The sound of his obscene laughter filled the lodge.

Aimée felt sick. When she met him aboard ship, she had thought the Spaniard a nice young man, but his attitude had changed toward her since their arrival at Long Town. In his eyes she was little better than a whore now that she had an Indian as a lover. With a sinking heart, she knew that would be the attitude of all white men to her when and if she ever returned from the Chickasaw. Once a woman had lived with the Indians, even if taken against her will, to the whites it was as if she was tainted. They would pity her, but treat her as if she was not quite human.

"I know about the custom of some Chickasaw to have several wives, sometimes sisters, but it is not universal to all," she replied quietly.

"Well, I plan on having them both before I leave," he told her with a lewd grin.

"You are planning on leaving?" she asked, one delicate brow lifted in disbelief.

"Figure they will soon be so busy with all these savages dying like flies they won't have time to notice I'm gone. The brat over there is in a bad way."

His callous cruelty made Aimée want to slap him. She was aware of French Nancy's slight stiffening of manner, and knew she felt the same. The Chickasaw had treated him well since his adoption into the tribe, but he felt only scorn toward the woman who treated him like an honored husband and her innocent sick child. She realized with both despair and anger that to Manuel Ximenez, these two people who had shared their food and lodging with him were little more than animals.

When the child began to whimper in his fever delirium Manuel left the lodge in disgust to sit outside. Aimée was glad to see him go. He was a reminder of the world she had left behind, a world that would never allow her to return to the same life she had known. She would always be the woman who had been a white squaw, an object of piteous contempt. Caught between her past and present, she belonged nowhere.

"Come. We attend the child," French Nancy said softly, rising to her feet. In her blue eyes there was complete understanding of what Aimée had just realized, and there was also compassion for her loneliness.

Soft Wind's son tossed and turned on his mat in the throes of high fever. His moans caught at Aimée's heart, as did the terrified look on his mother's distraught face. She bathed his slight form with cooling water and held his head as French Nancy forced the infusion of willow bark between his lips. As the older woman poured the liquid into the child's mouth she chanted an incantation to banish the invading animal spirit who had intruded itself into his body and caused illness. French Nancy had explained the People believed when the world had been formed, the animals had invented disease in order to cope with mankind's intrusion, but help to man had been furnished by the plants of Mother Earth in supplying the medicine to cure them.

"I have heard the hooting of the night owl this last moon, and the cry of the raven," Dark Dove announced as the two women tried to help the suffering child. "When Small Bear was first stricken I raked all the smoldering coals in the sacred fire together in a cone-shaped heap and sprinkled sacred tobacco on the heap of coals. A spark flared up, but not far. You know French Nancy as an *Aliktce* that this proves there is a witch nearby."

"Perhaps," the older woman mused with a slight shrug. "The blankets and pots that were brought from the trading post could have belonged to powerful witches. This could have been the sign you were reading." The woman kept her eyes from turning in Aimée's direction. She knew that Dark Dove was filled with jealousy and would use any excuse to vilify the woman who she saw as stealing Shadow Panther from her. There was an unease in her heart and a growing anxiety for Aimée.

"I shall go to the *Archi-Magus,* the head priest, and ask him to consult his crystals," Dark Dove persisted. Her onyx eyes stared with unwavering hatred as she watched Aimée bathe the sick child.

"There is no more I can do at the moment," French Nancy announced, rising to her feet. "You must continue to bathe the child with cool water and give him this mixture after every attack of diarrhea. After seeing to my other patients I shall return," she promised the concerned mother and grandmother. She ignored Dark Dove, knowing she was set on a path from which she would not be easily discouraged.

Although Aimée understood very little of what had been said, she sensed French Nancy's anxiety and Dark Dove's enmity. She gathered up the baskets and followed her teacher out of the stifling hut, glad for the breath of clean air. Manuel had disappeared for which she was thankful.

"You shall return to the lodge, *ma petite,* where you must stay within the walls whilst I shall see to the sick. There is danger for you to be seen about. There is talk of witches in the air as often happens when there is illness. Hide yourself, I beseech you, till I return." French Nancy's voice was grave and sent a chill through Aimée.

She nodded her understanding, she left the old woman in the plaza and strode swiftly toward the lodge. Her thoughts were in a turmoil. If French Nancy sent her home instead of continuing on with her lessons in healing, the danger must be great. Aimée felt a cold knot of fear grow in her stomach. Caught between two cultures, she belonged to neither. She had experienced rejection from both the white and Indian world today. Never had she felt so alone.

The path between the blocks of houses was empty, unusual at this time of day. Not one child or dog darted out to play. The eerie atmosphere began to wear on her nerves which were already on edge. She began to imagine she could feel someone watching her, and she continually glanced over her shoulder as she hurried to the lodge.

It was as she reached the winter house that she heard the crack of a stick breaking under a moccasin behind her. Whirling about, she glimpsed the flash of dark brown hair and a bare chest, a white man's chest, before she was grabbed and dragged behind the winter house to the long rectangular hut that was the summer lodge. A man's hand was clamped across her mouth so she could not call out, and strong fingers clasped her against a hard male body.

The summer house was dark and cool, smelling of the woven grass mats that hung on the walls as he pushed her inside and onto the floor. Twisting and turning she fought to free herself from his grasp.

"Be still Frenchy, or I will break your neck," the man hissed as he threw her to the floor.

Manuel, she thought, it's Manuel. She stopped struggling, thinking he wanted only to speak with her alone where no others could hear. Perhaps she had been wrong about him. Did he want her to try and escape with him? It was the wrong time, couldn't he see that?

"That's better. You are tired of these savages too, my beauty. I could see it in your eyes. Now I will take my hand away from your mouth, and we can have a little time together before I leave."

His voice was a raspy whisper in the gloom as he removed his hand, but kept her pinned to the floor. She couldn't see him, but could feel his hot breath on her face.

"I couldn't leave without having you just one time, touching that silver hair. You knew what you were doing to me, teasing me with that little skirt and that bodice that shows those nipples right through the calico. Tired of those dark ones and that dark skin. You are not so high and mighty now, *Mademoiselle,* as on the ship. Imagine you would be glad for a white man after that dark savage. Almost begging for it, weren't you today," he crooned as he stroked her blonde braids.

"You . . . you don't know what you are saying," Aimée protested, shrinking back from the touch of his hand. It was a nightmare from which there was no awakening.

"Take your hair down. I don't want it like that. Take it down!" he demanded, tightening his hold on her waist, his fingers digging into her skin.

Fighting for time, she obeyed, as fear, stark and vivid, rendered her almost senseless. Slowly, she unbraided her long tresses till they fell about her shoulders, the harsh rasp of his breathing echoing the frantic beating of her frightened heart.

"*Si,* 'tis the way I imagined—it would feel like silk," he sighed, slipping it over his fingers winding it about them till her head was pulled back. "Now take off that teasing little skirt and bodice."

As she opened her mouth to protest she suddenly felt they were no longer alone. As her eyes darted about the gloom of the hut she heard a gasp and then a gurgle. She fell back against the mat as Manuel released her hair. He collapsed beside her face down on the floor, to lie still and lifeless.

Chapter Eighteen

"He is dead," the hoarse whisper of Sebastian, the man the Chickasaw called Shadow Panther, broke the silence.

"It is you, thank *le bon Dieu,* 'tis you!" Aimée gasped, scrambling to her feet.

"Go to the winter lodge. Wait for me there," he ordered in a flat, expressionless tone.

She paused beside him, feeling the warmth of his body in the dark. Her hand reached out to touch him, to seek reassurance in contact with him. She stopped, her hand hovering inches from his arm, for she sensed his withdrawal, his cool aloofness.

"Leave me," he repeated tersely.

Without reply, she left the hut, tears blinding her eyes as she struggled to find the portal. A man lay dead, killed by the hand of the man she loved. Manuel had shown himself to be a man without honor, but his death left her filled with a sense of shock and horror. It was only as she sought the sanctuary of the winter lodge that she realized that Sebastian, Shadow Panther, didn't know what had happened between them. Did he think she had sought Manuel's company?

Her question was soon to be answered. As she huddled on her bed of doeskins trying to blot out the memory of those last horrid moments when the young Spaniard had tried to rape her, Shadow Panther entered the lodge. She saw his silhouette in the smoldering light of the center fire. He stood motionless in the shadows watching her, not speaking a word.

"He was going to escape," she stated, rising to a sitting position on the bed platform.

"And you were going with him," Shadow Panther replied with a taut resignation.

"Non, no," Aimée whispered, shaking her head in emphasis.

"Do not lie to me, Green Eyes."

"I do not lie," she answered with indignation.

"Why did you go with him to the summer lodge if not to plan your escape? Was your body the price he asked?"

She felt, rather than saw, the intensity of his gaze as he stood in the gloom of the hut only a few yards away from her. His question and mocking tone roused her ire as only he could do.

"Do you think me capable of such treachery?" She answered in a low voice taut with anger.

"I fear I know you less than I thought," Shadow Panther's voice was quiet, controlled, yet held an undertone of contempt.

"Then you know me not at all if you would even consider I would use myself in such a way." Disappointment and regret etched each word.

"Explain, then, why you were with him in such a manner."

"Would any explanation restore the trust between us now that I find you have such a low opinion of me?" She sighed bitterly.

"Tell me, Green Eyes," he growled, finally showing emotion as he strode to where she sat and jerked her to her feet. His fingers dug into her forearms as he pulled her up against him.

"He followed me from Thunder Sky Woman's hut and dragged me into the summer lodge where he tried to rape me," she told him in a choked voice filled with bitterness. "He did not succeed. Now let me go. I have had enough of man's brutal treatment of woman for one day."

Slowly, he lessened his grip on her, but instead of releasing her he bowed his head to tenderly kiss each forearm where his fingers had cruelly dug into her skin. He could feel the quickening of her pulse as his tongue lightly circled her skin, tasting the slightly salty flavor of her.

She hated the unwelcome surge of excitement he could elicit so easily by his tender touch. She knew it was foolish, but she wanted to hold on to her anger, not give in so quickly. He had hurt her by his accusation, and she wanted to make him pay for that hurt.

"I lose my reason when it comes to you, Green Eyes. I am like a man without a center, lost and wild. When I saw his hands on your beautiful hair I became like a crazed animal. It is not an excuse, just a fact. You are right to feel anger that I should question your honor. To a Chickasaw his honor is everything, and his word his bond. The Spaniard is dead, he is forgotten."

Aimée gave a light shudder at his words. It was not so easy for her to dismiss death as it was for the fatalistic Chickasaw. She realized once more how differently she and this man looked at life. But strangely the differences between them didn't change the strength of the bond that held them together. The invisible link that held them enthralled might be stretched, but never broken.

"How I have missed the taste and feel of you," he murmured, his hands slipping up her arms, bringing her closer. His warm lips were kissing her temples lightly where tendrils of silver-blonde curled in the humid heat of the lodge.

"No," she protested, "not now. I can't . . . not after . . ."

"Aye, now. You should know the joy of man and woman, the beauty of joining. Let me erase the ugliness and replace it with what is so right between us," he crooned into her hair, rocking her in his arms like a beloved child.

Hating her easy surrender, but unable to resist, she relaxed, sinking into his cushioning embrace. Her arms locked about his sinewy chest, her fingers tingling at the feel of his warm bare skin. Molded against his narrow hips and muscular, hard thighs she felt the rigid arousal of his shaft press into her belly.

The world and its horrors vanished in that magical way it always did when she was locked in his embrace. There was only this magnificent man, and his all-encompassing passion lifting her to a plane where mere mortals didn't dwell. Her sense of the physical reality about her ceased to exist, yet every sense was exquisitely tuned to his touch, his scent, his very essence. She seemed to flow into him, and he into her, till they were one entity.

He pealed her brief clothing from her body as if unwrapping a longed-for precious gift. His fingers and eyes caressed each inch of her as it was revealed. Lifting her, he laid her on the bed of soft doeskin with a sigh of pleasure.

"Ah, let me look at you, Moon Flower of ivory and gold." His eyes traveled down the length of her, as his hands teased the rosy peaks of her breasts till they grew to pebble hardness. Taking her long tresses he held them to his lips for a moment, then draped them over her breasts allowing the nipples to peak through so he could tease them with his tongue. His lips continued on down to trace a sensuous path to ecstasy as he tasted the satin of her soft ivory belly.

Aimée moaned as the spiral of rapture grew within her, whirling hotter, and faster, as his hands stroked her hips, the silk of her thighs. She was all pulsating sensation. This is what she was made for, her body cried out with primitive knowledge. This was life's joy and fulfillment.

As he kissed and caressed her silken form he paused to whisper his love for each part of her body. "So beautiful are these, your soft white doves, your breasts. How perfect is the symmetry of your form, the tiny waist, the perfect hips. I taste the nectar of your thighs sweet as the wild lily flower," he breathed against her heated skin.

Tears filled her eyes and slid down her cheeks like tiny diamonds at his poetic words. It was the Chickasaw side of him that he revealed as he made exquisite love to her. The People had the most beautiful words for every part of nature. Then there was no more time for thinking as he spread open the petals of her intimate flower, and she knew only the incredible power of his surging body. They came together with the reverence of tender love, and the fiery passion of overwhelming hunger. Soaring on wings of ecstasy the earth fell away and they reached that perfect place of rapturous fulfillment, utterly consumed, knowing complete contentment.

Exhausted, she lay with her head on his chest. He had been right, for in the act of loving Shadow Panther she had felt cleansed from the horror of Manuel. How could she ever leave this strong, wise man who had come into her life, but could she stay and live as a Chickasaw?

The image of her sister flashed across her mind, causing her to stir uneasily in Shadow Panther's embrace. She realized the high mournful sound of a flute was coming from outside the walls of the lodge, and it had triggered the memory of Mignon.

"What is wrong?" Shadow Panther asked softly sensing her agitation.

"The flute, do you hear it?"

"Aye, 'tis called a flageolet. Someone is playing a healing song. There is much sickness in the village."

"French Nancy and I were treating Soft Wind's son for the measles. He was very ill. That . . . that is where Manuel saw me." She sighed as the terrible images flashed across her mind once more.

"I know. I had to tell Thunder Sky Woman of her son-in-law's death. She did not like the Spaniard and was glad to hear of his passing to the shadow land, but her daughter was distraught. She had become fond of her husband even though he treated her badly. You must stay away from their lodge for awhile, Green Eyes. There is one there who would do you harm."

"Dark Dove," she whispered against his chest.

"Aye," he agreed, pulling her closer to him as if he could protect her from the enmity of his former lover.

There seemed to be malevolent forces swirling about them in the Chickasaw village. Aimée felt the lovely sense of security and warmth from their lovemaking slowly seep away. When they were together it was wonderful, feeling so right, but always the world intruded, shattering their idyll forcing them to face how different were their ways of living.

The flute continued its mournful song, adding to the

disquiet inside Aimée. She listened as the music seemed to haunt her till she sat up, pulling away from Shadow Panther.

"You are thinking of your sister," he said quietly, stroking the planes of her back as she sat staring out into the gloom of the lodge.

"Oui, yes. I am afraid she is calling to me. You know how fragile she is. It is hard to think of her alone at the fort without me to protect her."

He was struck through by the nobility of her spirit. This was a good woman he loved. He experienced an ache deep within his being like a wound at the thought that he was to blame for her heartache. Somehow this wrong he had done her had to be righted.

The flute music stopped as suddenly as it had started. They heard in its stead the sound of a light scratching on the outside wall of the lodge near the portal. Dropping his hand from her back, Shadow Panther rose to his feet, pulling on his breechclout. Aimée followed suit, hastily donning her skirt and bodice for she could not appear unclothed in front of others. The light scratching meant they had a visitor who wished to come inside.

A young woman entered the lodge at Shadow Panther's low call. Aimée recognized her as a mother of two children, a boy and girl. Their fields were near French Nancy's, and she had often spoken her few words of Chickasaw to the children. She was startled at the woman's appearance. Dark circles ringed the woman's worried brown eyes, and deep lines seemed etched on either side of her trembling mouth.

"She wants French Nancy. The priests have sung and danced over her children and mother, but to no avail. They are worse, delirious in their fever. Do you know where she is?" Shadow Panther asked after speaking with the tired woman in Chickasaw.

"She has gone to see to others. I know what herbs she uses. Tell the woman I will come," Aimée replied, taking down bunches of herbs from the rafters and placing them in the large gathering baskets with a couple of small jars.

A gleam of tender admiration shone in his black eyes for a brief moment as he stared in surprise at her, before carefully concealing his emotions behind a cool mask of authority. Turning back to the worried mother he explained Aimée would come since French Nancy was attending another. The young woman gave them a grateful smile, her weary eyes showing a small light of hope in their velvet, dark depths.

Night had fallen as they followed the Chickasaw mother to her lodge. Aimée was grateful for Shadow Panther's escort to the hut of Morning Light. He had told her the woman's name, and that her mother's uncle was a high priest of the tribe, what the whites called a medicine man. She then understood why he was accompanying her, the uncle would probably not welcome another healer, especially a white woman.

The family had moved into their summer lodge for the warm weather and because of the fevers of the children and grandmother. Even in the roomy summer hut with its high ceiling, the air was fetid as they entered.

Morning Light ran to where her young daughter of about four years lay covered with the tell-tale red spots of measles. The child was delirious with fever and cried insistently. Two fierce-looking men dressed in the skins of the red fox, and wearing buzzard feathers in their hair as a sign that they were unaffected by exposure to death and impurity, danced around the child, chanting. Their eyes flashed their anger as

Aimée approached the little girl.

"I must have a pot of warm water. Please tell her," she told Shadow Panther, avoiding the bitter glances of the priests.

While he explained her needs to the young mother, Aimée took out of her basket a small jar. She opened the lid and rubbed the child with a balm of bear grease into which had been mixed several herbs that would cool her skin. She made an infusion of willow bark in the water, and spooned a little between the child's lips. Remembering French Nancy's admonition to always sing an incantation, Aimée sang in French a song about the new moon, a baby moon, a papoose canoe that sailed around and around making the little girl well once more.

All around her in the crowded, evil-smelling lodge she could feel the hatred of the priests and distrust of other members of the household, but when she looked up she could see Shadow Panther tall and proud, standing near her as if to guard her from all harm. A curious peace came over her just knowing he was there. She sensed the others' awe of this man who stood watching, yet detached from the scene as a warrior should be in such a situation.

Unafraid, she went about her tasks next with the little boy, showing Morning Light what she must do to make each child comfortable. Her heart sank, however, as she moved to the next room where the grandmother lay barely breathing, the rattle of congestion of the lungs obvious with each labored breath the woman took. She would die, Aimée was sure. The disease was deadly to the old—even young adults often died. There was little she could do but try and make the woman more comfortable in her last hours on earth.

"Why do the priests not come in to the chamber where

the grandmother lies?" Aimée questioned Shadow Panther, as they were left alone with the old woman except for Morning Light.

"They realize she will die and they do not want to be blamed for her death. 'Tis no shame for a healer to say his magic is not strong enough and leave a patient. Leave the medicine for Morning Light. Do not tend the old woman yourself, for you too could be blamed for her death," he explained, casting uneasy glances at the priests. They seemed to be regarding Aimée with a malevolent anticipation in their hard black eyes.

"It would be inhuman to not make her more comfortable," Aimée protested, preparing to help the old woman drink a little of the infusion of willow bark.

"Nay!" he ordered, suddenly grabbing the cup from her hand and giving it to Morning Light with a terse command in Chickasaw. "We leave. You have done what you can."

Startled by his reaction, she allowed him to drag her by the arm out of the lodge. Taking a deep breath of the fresh night air, she couldn't help but be relieved to be out of the fetid-smelling hut.

"Come, there is danger about," he said in cryptic tones, hurrying her away before she could speak.

There was a different atmosphere about the village—Aimée could feel it as they strode between the houses. The aura of fear and death seemed to permeate the very air. She shivered as one of the camp dogs howled at the crescent moon that hung pristine and remote above them in the dark night sky.

French Nancy was waiting for them as they returned to her lodge. She rose from where she knelt stirring a cooking pot. Her azure eyes stared up at them full of worry and concern. For the first time since she had come to stay with her Aimée saw fatigue and a kind of despair on that still-lovely face. She looked really old, and to her surprise the thought smote Aimée's heart. She realized with a sudden flash of insight how much she had come to care for the older woman. Nancy had, indeed, become a mother to her.

"There is great fear among the People tonight." French Nancy spoke softly to Shadow Panther. "They sense death has come to visit Long Town. He is a guest they hope does not tarry. In such an atmosphere Moon Flower is in great danger."

"I have thought long upon this, and have decided we should leave the People for a time till 'tis safe for our return," he answered, to Aimée's surprise and French Nancy's grim agreement.

"You must leave tonight," she admonished, reaching for a bundle of skins that Aimée recognized from their trip to the village.

Stunned, Aimée watched as they prepared for their hasty departure. Could the danger be so great that they must steal away in the night?

Suddenly, the skin in front of the portal was rudely flung aside. Two warriors dressed as priests entered without asking permission, accompanied by a familiar figure. With a smile of triumph and hatred gleaming in her black eyes, Dark Dove extended her arm to point at Aimée and declared in Chickasaw, "There is your witch. There is the one who robs the dying of their life. Rid the People of her and all will be in balance once more."

Chapter Nineteen

Panic like she had never known before welled in Aimée's throat when the two frightening priest-warriors moved to take hold of her arms, one on either side. The triumphant smile on Dark Dove's haughty visage burned into her brain. She had not understood everything the young woman had said, but she had recognized the Chickasaw word for witch.

"Stop! This is my woman," the cool authoritative voice of Shadow Panther broke the tense quiet. The priests stepped away from her as he motioned for them to let go of her arms.

Aimée thought she would faint, her legs threatening to give way underneath her, but she fought for control. She had been among the People long enough to know how much they respected courage. Lifting her chin, she held her head high, boldly staring into Dark Dove's hate-filled eyes.

The young Chickasaw woman seemed to become less sure of herself after Shadow Panther's command. Nervously, she licked her lips, her eyes now darting around the hut, no longer locked with Aimée's jade-green gaze.

One of the priests spoke a few terse words to Shadow

Panther in Chickasaw. He nodded in the affirmative. Turning to Aimée he spoke reassuringly, "They must take you before the council of elders. This is tribal law when one is accused of being a witch. Do not worry—all will be well. You are my woman. No harm will come to you."

Her stomach sank as Shadow Panther walked out of the hut. The two priests again resumed their hold on her, pulling her toward the portal. Stumbling, she allowed herself to be led away.

"Courage, *petite fleur,*" French Nancy called to her as they disappeared into the waiting night.

The walk to the council house in the plaza seemed to take an eternity. They followed Shadow Panther, with Dark Dove bringing up the rear. Cries and moans of sickness echoed from the lodges they passed. Aimée shivered at the sound, realizing the epidemic was growing, an epidemic a jealous young woman was trying to blame on her presence in Long Town.

Entering the large ceremonial rotunda of the vast council house, Aimée was startled to see it filled with so many people. Everyone who was not down with the sickness was crowded on the raised platforms that lined the huge lodge. The hot, humid air was hazy with smoke from the long pipe the elders were passing among themselves where they sat in front of the sacred fire.

Rivulets of perspiration rolled down her bodice as she stood, trying not to cough in the choking air. Avid black eyes devoured the sight of her from all directions. A low hum of whispers like the sound of cicadas rang in her ears. They had all gathered for a show, and she was the star attraction.

Out of the corner of her eye she saw French Nancy

enter the council house and felt strangely comforted by her presence. There were two in the room now who would fight for her cause, and they were worthy champions.

A silence full of anticipation fell over the council house as Shadow Panther came and stood in front of the elders of the tribe. Taking the pipe they held out to him he took a puff from the long stem, blowing the blue-gray smoke into the four corners of the universe.

His lean, bronzed form stood as stalwart as a mighty oak, the firelight gleaming off the sinewy muscles of his back and thighs. A curious peace came over Aimée as she watched him performing the ritual of smoking the pipe. It was as if his mere presence protected her from all harm. She had experienced this strange phenomenon before during their flight from the raging fire in New Orleans. He seemed sent by fate to be her defender, her champion, her refuge.

"I come before you to tell the People of a great wrong that has been committed," Shadow Panther began softly, but with a voice that was strong of purpose and command. "My woman, who in my eyes and the eyes of *Ababinili,* the Great Spirit, is my wife, has been accused of doing harm to Long Town. This woman who has worked to help save the lives of your children has been called a *Hattakyushpakummi*—a witch."

There was a low murmur from those gathered on the benches as he paused. Aimée felt all eyes turn from Shadow Panther to her with a question in those numerous dark orbs. There was anticipation in the air as they waited for him to proceed. He was a splendid orator, Aimée thought, even though she couldn't understand but a few words. He had the audience hanging on his every word, and the Chickasaw were a people who honored a good speaker with the name Long Talker. She only hoped he was winning her case, for her life could depend on his skill.

"I say there *was* a raven-mocker, a stealer of breath among us." He paused once more as the audience gasped at this admission. "But I say to you that the night-walker, the witch, was the Spaniard who came among us to do harm. Did he not already kill Chickasaw warriors? But he was greedy, wanting more souls to steal. I saw this man who walked among us drink a concoction made from duck-root, not once, but seven times. Seven times, my friends. We all know is proof this of one who wishes to transform himself into a raven-mocker, a *hattakyushpakummi.*"

There were knowing nods as the audience whispered among themselves at this revelation. Aimée sensed the tide was turning in her favor as she watched the people enthralled by Shadow Panther's words. How she wished she could understand what he was saying.

"After consultation with our Beloved Woman, French Nancy, who as a *Aliktce,* a healer, recognized this raven-mocker among us, I sent him to the western quarter of the shadowland where evil ones are sent upon taking their last breath. His bad magic is still among us and will take several moons to disappear, for 'twas strong. He made those in Thunder-Sky Woman's lodge believe it was those who came to help them that were the night-stalkers who steal the breath of the sick. Dark Dove still is under his power, but with our help will see the error of her ways." Shadow Panther turned in the direction of where the young Indian woman sat glowering at his words.

She had been bested and could not continue any longer with her accusation without looking as if she too were still under the witch's power. How she hated the gold and silver white woman. Someday she would pay for tonight's humiliation. Dark Dove rose to her feet and admitted she might have been wrong, confused by the strength of the Spaniard's magic.

A sigh of relief rose from the gathered crowd. The sickness had been explained. While many might still die, now that the witch, the cause of the epidemic had been killed, in time the tribe would recover.

"On the morrow I will formally join with Moon Flower, making her my woman-wife. Together we will pledge to renew the spirit of good for the People. She is learning the ways of healing from French Nancy and will work the rest of her days to minister to the needs of the Chickasaw." Shadow Panther turned and walked to where Aimée stood, slightly bewildered at what was occurring, only knowing that somehow he had made everything all right once more. She was safe.

"Hold your head up high, Green Eyes. I have just announced we are to be married on the morrow." He held up her hand in his and announced in a clear, strong voice, "I leave to prepare and purify myself for the ceremony, as does my woman." Dropping her hand he turned and strode out of the lodge indicating she should follow behind like a true Chickasaw wife.

Weak with relief, Aimée walked stoically behind, seeing French Nancy join her as they left the smoke-filled lodge. The three did not speak as they strode swiftly away from the plaza. Each step that carried her toward the familiar lodge block of French Nancy made Aimée breathe easier.

"I leave you here, Green Eyes," Shadow Panther turned and said softly as they reached the portal of the winter house. "Till the morrow," he murmured, clasping her hand in his strong warm grasp, those intense ebony eyes devouring the sight of her for one brief moment. Then he was gone, vanished into the night.

"Come, *petite fleur* these old bones are weary." The old woman guided her toward the low entrance. "We must move to the summer house before too long. The nights are getting warm," she commented as they entered the hut stuffy and warm in the humid night air.

"Not tonight!" Aimée gasped, overcome with panic at the thought of staying in the structure so soon after seeing Manuel slump to his death beside her.

"Non, no, not tonight," French Nancy reassured her.

The events of the last days had left Aimée exhausted. She slumped onto the raised platform that had become her bed. As if through a fog, she heard the old woman moving about the hut, but a troubled sleep soon claimed her. Tossing and turning she tried to flee from the images that her overtired brain conjured up.

Mignon's tortured visage and hands outstretched beseeching her to return haunted her sleep, as did the last terrible moments of Manuel Ximenez. In the unreal world of Morpheus she could make no one understand that she was unable to return and help her sister. Both Mignon and Manuel chided her that she was not a prisoner—that she wanted to stay with the Chickasaw, that indeed she was one of the People. Suddenly Shadow Panther appeared in her dream, and when she reached out to embrace him she was pulled away by the hands of her sister and the Spaniard. Crying out to him to wait, she was pulled farther and farther away from him by these two, who only laughed at her protests. The scene changed and she was searching through a dark wood for someone, or something. Wearily, she trudged a narrow path that seemed to never end. Tears of frustration streamed down her cheeks as she moaned in her tormented sleep. Loneliness overwhelmed her, leaving such an emptiness in her heart she thought she would die. Then there was a light at the end of the dark wood, and she knew she would find what she sought if she could only reach it. Running through the wisps of fog that clung to the swampy woods, gnarled branches tore at her clothes as she passed, but nothing would deter her from that glowing light. She was almost there, almost to the end of her quest.

"Wake, *petite fleur,* wake," the crooning voice of French Nancy brought Aimée reluctantly from her dream. " 'Tis the morning of your wedding day, and there is much to do."

The sun was rising as the two women bathed in the creek and greeted the day with the usual ceremonies. Aimée felt tired, as if she had not slept at all. The memory of her dream still affected her mood, as nightmares can often do. She walked slowly back to the lodge. The hot sun, beating down, erased the mists of the night and finally helped to erase the haunting horror of her slumber.

Once back at the lodge, French Nancy instructed her to lie down on an outstretched doeskin so she might remove her maiden hair. Blushing, Aimée complied as the old woman showed her how to pluck all the hair from her body except from her scalp. This was how a married Chickasaw woman groomed herself, she explained. Then she was given a lotion that smelled like the fragrant scented magnolia blossoms to rub all over her body, including her most intimate parts.

"I give you my gown, Moon Flower, as there is not time to make your own," the old woman said softly, taking a lovely doeskin tinted a warm ivory by time from a chest under her sleep platform. The loose dress reached her knees where fell a deep fringe to the middle of her calf. Across the bodice were sewn blue quills and fresh-water pearls. There were more pearls on thin wires of gold for her ears.

"It is lovely," Aimée breathed in admiration as she donned the treasured garments. Sitting on the platform bed, French Nancy stood behind her and brushed out the long silver-blonde hair that reached almost to her waist.

"Shadow Panther has left this headband for you to wear. He has been working on it in anticipation of this day," the old woman told her with a slight smile. She placed the band, decorated with pearls and green quills to make a design of magnolia blossoms, about her head.

"I have nothing for him," Aimée said with a sigh, touching the band with trembling fingers.

"Ah, *ma chère,* but you do," the old woman chuckled. She placed a warrior's necklace of four broad silver crescents that was worn suspended upon the breast in her hand. But on this warrior's necklace there was a fifth silver ornament hanging in the middle. Aimée recognized her brooch. "I took out your sister's miniature and placed it in this pouch of doeskin. In its place, across from your portrait, I put a small lock of your hair that I took while you slept. He will be greatly pleased to carry your likeness next to his heart, and you can look upon your sister when ever you please. I hope you do not mind that I took such a liberty."

Rising to her feet, Aimée embraced the old woman, kissing her weathered cheek. "I am honored to have found such a friend as you."

"And I a daughter to gladden my heart," French

Nancy told her with tears in her azure eyes.

A scratch on the wall near the portal told them it was time for the ceremony. Several young women awaited them outside the lodge to escort them to the plaza. The kept their eyes lowered but the air was filled with their excited giggles. The joining of their war chief was a welcome respite from the horror of the sickness that was making deep inroads into the camp. But for this afternoon and evening, they could forget their fear and enjoy the happy event.

The preparation for the ceremony had taken most of the day. Long golden streams of light from the setting sun turned her hair to a silver-gold shimmer as Aimée made her way with her feminine escort to where Shadow Panther stood waiting. In her hand she carried French Nancy's necklace to give to him as her only dowry, and in the other a basket of cakes she had made to show her domestic care and gratitude for his protection as her husband.

The sound of the drums reached her ears as they drew close to the plaza, then they were joined by a high trill like the song of a bird from the Chickasaw reed flute. Suddenly the young woman beside her began to shake gourd rattles with beans inside.

Aimée's heart sang with the music as they reached the plaza and she saw her beloved. He stood with his back to the fiery rays of the setting sun so it seemed he was surrounded by light. His tall, lithe form seemed to tower above her as she came to stand across from him. He was dressed in heavily fringed white buckskin breeches that fit like a second skin and she could see the muscular outline of his sinewy thighs. The ceremonial breechclout was ornately decorated with quills and beads in the pattern of the celestial heavens and phases of the moon, as were his moccasins. About his forehead was a band that matched hers in design except for the addition of a stalking panther among the magnolia blossoms. His long raven hair shone in the light. Arrogant, proud and handsome as a god, Aimée knew she was drawn to this man as if she were fulfilling her destiny. As she drew close and met his dark blazing eyes, eyes that reached out to bind her to him with invisible bonds, she remembered her dream. This was what had awaited her at the end of her search, here was the person waiting for her in the light at the end of so much darkness.

The drums and flute reached a crescendo and then stopped. The gathered throng waited silently but one could feel their anticipation in the hot, late afternoon air. Here was a great talker, and they waited impatiently to hear his words of marriage to the gold and silver woman he had brought to them.

"I take this beloved woman, twin half of my soul, given to me in a vision as my destiny as my wife. She is heart of my heart, as much a part of me as my eyes, my mouth, my hands. Together today we merge into one being, one heart, one soul, as it was told in the beginning. We will walk the seasons of time on our journey from the planting time, through the flowering, to harvest, and on into the winter of our life together. We will look back and say it was good, but know always that we travel together the spiral path, never ending, only changing and growing, always finding each other once more, the mate of my soul." He spoke slowly, his deep voice carrying across the plaza first in Chickasaw and then translated into French for Aimée.

She listened to the beautiful words, so moved that her heart seemed to rise into her throat and her eyes blurred with tears. Standing before him, she tried to tell him with her gaze of her love and gratitude for a ceremony that fulfilled all her dreams. The crowd stood puzzled as he took her hand and slipped a circle of gold about her finger. She smiled and whispered thank you at this touch of her world that he had remembered. It was roughly made, but more precious to her than a wedding band made by the most famous jeweler in Paris.

"This, my husband, is my dowry," she said in Chickasaw as French Nancy had taught her, handing him the necklace of silver circlets.

"I am honored, but your beauty is your dowry," he answered in French then spoke again in Chickasaw so the crowd might understand. There was a sigh from the crowd as he placed it about his chest, his hand stroking the brooch allowing Aimée to know he understood the significance of the necklace.

From behind him, a brave led a magnificent rare white horse. The dainty mare was all grace and beauty. Magnolia blossoms had been intertwined in her mane. Shadow Panther explained the horse was hers, his gift her bride price since it could not be paid to her clan.

"She is so lovely—thank you, my husband," she murmured, stroking the animal's soft nose.

Then handing the reins back to the brave she followed her husband to where stood the village priests and French Nancy. Taking an ear of corn and dividing it in two, Shadow Panther gave one half to Aimée while she handed him the basket of cakes of corn bread. The chief of the priests chanted words and prayers for a fruitful long life over them as they stood hand and hand. The drums began again as did the flute and rattles, but this time the song was joyous, not somber as before.

Taking her hand in his, Shadow Panther led her gently to where the white mare stood waiting next to an ebony stallion. Helping her mount, he swung up onto the back of the stallion. They rode from the plaza as the People chanted songs of blessing. Riding out the front gate of the stockade they left the village behind.

The indigo-blue twilight was touching the sky as they followed a babbling brook into the verdant forest deep with the shadows of approaching night. They followed a trail along the bank through a maze of river birches and slender green cane stalks. The clean astringent scent of the giant cedars was all around them, mingling with the rich fragrance of the damp fertile earth.

Breaking through a dense patch of wild grape vines and tangled blueberry bushes, they came upon a secluded glade bordered on two sides by limestone outcroppings. The stream fell over the rocks, cascading in a small waterfall to form a willow-green pond. On the mossy banks of the pond stood a small summer house made of black locust posts set in the earth, a pitched thatched roof of grasses, and walls of cypress whitewashed inside and out with clay.

"But I have never seen this before," Aimée exclaimed, as they entered through the low door hung with a mat that moved away at the push of a hand.

"Often I have need of a quiet place to think, so I made this house some time ago," he replied, happy to see how much she was taken with this place that meant so much to him.

The interior was clean and spartan with a center fire outlined in gray stones. A hard-packed, freshly brushed floor and several baskets hung from the rafters. Against one whitewashed wall stood a platform bed. The coverings were of soft ivory doeskin and across its surface were strewn stalks of tiny white fragrant wild lily blossoms. The perfume of the lilies added to the scent of the numerous magnolia blooms that were floating in shallow clay dishes of water about the chamber, making the bower a virtual garden.

"It is so beautiful," Aimée breathed, tears in her eyes at the care her husband had taken to make the chamber lovely on their wedding night.

"As are you, my beloved woman-wife. How proud I was of you as you stood in the plaza. This is the woman who will walk beside me on my life's journey. Together we will have children of our love, and when we are old we will remember today and know it has been forever written on our souls."

She stared up into those black piercing eyes that seem to penetrate and read the very thoughts of her heart. She felt the flow of her soul into his with a certainty that was total and all-consuming. Holding out her arms she came into the sanctuary of his embrace.

It was as his arms encircled her, their gazes locked, lost in the emotion they saw reflected in each other's eyes, their very breath in unison, that they heard the sound. It was a deep roar that struck a primitive fear in every human's heart. It was the fierce cry of the panther, cruel predator of the forest. And by the sound coming from outside he was very close.

Chapter Twenty

"What is it?" Aimée's voice quaked in fear as she clung to Shadow Panther's reassuring form.

" 'Tis the cry of the forest panther," he answered in awe. "Do not fear, he has come to give us his approval."

"I . . . I don't understand," Aimée, stammered, looking at him with disbelief.

"The panther is my personal totem, my dream animal, Green Eyes," he explained, listening with every sense alert to the movements of the restless great cat outside. "A Chickasaw's totem will always appear at the most important times of a warrior's life. 'Tis been said they have often come to warn of danger, or to give their blessing. Come, he will not harm us." He took her hand firmly in his strong grasp and pulled her to the low door of the lodge.

Aimée allowed herself to be led to the door although icy fear twisted about her heart and her limbs so trembled with panic she could hardly stand. She had faith in her husband, but the cry of the wild predatory cat outside struck a primitive cord deep within her brain that demanded caution.

"Do not make any quick movements when we go outside. Do not speak, stand quietly beside me. You may be amazed at what you see," he cautioned her as they moved to the door.

Pushing the skin barrier away from the portal, Shadow Panther walked outside pulling his reluctant bride with him. The glade was lit in the dim silver-gray light of twilight, but the image of the sleek form of the great cat was easily seen. He stood only yards away from them on the ledge of outcropping of limestone. At their appearance he lifted his mighty head and roared, a fierce sound that echoed in the glade chilling the blood.

Shadow Panther stood as still as a statue staring into the gaze of the predatory beast. Aimée cowered beside him barely breathing. Then he began to chant, singing in a low, husky voice ancient words of Chickasaw, his gaze never leaving the golden eyes of the cat.

Aimée watched in amazement as the wild cat seemed to listen to the song, standing so still he appeared carved from stone. It seemed an eternity that her husband stood chanting his song to the great beast. Suddenly the song ended, and as they stood motionless, their gaze locked with that of the animal, he turned and walked into the dark shadows of the forest from which he came. The full ivory moon appeared over the tops of the cedar trees as he disappeared.

"What did you say?" Aimée asked, breaking the unearthly spell that hung over the glade.

"I thanked him and the celestial spirits above for showing you as my destiny in my vision quest so long ago. I told him tonight we dedicate ourselves to one another, as we have done before in our previous lives together that I was privileged to see in my visions as a young man. Finally, I asked a blessing that we may find true happiness on our life's journey."

"I see," Aimée whispered, not really understanding at all. There was much about the Chickasaw religion and philosophy of life that she found hard to understand and accept. She knew that what a young warrior saw on his vision quest guided him throughout the rest of his life. Somehow her husband felt he had been told that one day they would be together, and he believed it with all his heart and soul. There was much about their meeting and love for one another that was indeed strange, as if out of their hands. Their destinies did seem intertwined. She did not know if she believe as did he, but she would not question what he so fervently accepted as their predestined fate.

"Come inside, for tonight we will eat together," Shadow Panther said softly, pushing aside the hanging skin over the p ortal so she might enter before him. She smiled her appreciation of this politeness that was of her world, not his.

Taking hot stones and a few smoldering coals from a basket he had brought from the sacred fire in the plaza, he placed them in the center fire circle inside the lodge. Slowly, he began the laborious chore of starting a fire by placing dry pieces of moss over the coals and blowing to ignite a spark.

As the fire burned, small and direct as all Chickasaw fires burned, not blazing away and wasting heat and fuel as did the white settlers' fires, Aimée prepared the rabbit on a spit that fit over the cooking fire. She was always amazed at how precisely and thoughtfully everything was done in a Chickasaw household. There was a real effort made not to waste anything in nature. The gathering and preparing of food was to be done in the most efficient way possible.

Preparing the corn cakes and placing them in a clay pot resting on the ash bed, Aimée remembered to sing the songs of blessing over the food as French Nancy had taught her. She mused on what the old woman had told her. She had stressed that it was important to dwell on only good thoughts while preparing food so it would turn out well. Bad thoughts on the part of the cook could spoil the flavors of the freshest food.

Shadow Panther allowed himself a faint smile as he watched his beloved woman-wife prepare their meal from where he reclined against the skin and wood back rest. He felt such love and contentment here in her presence he thought his heart would burst, but as a warrior he kept all thoughts to himself and his visage was carefully neutral. Somehow he wished to tell her of his joy. Rising to his feet as she prepared the food, he strode to the bed platform and reached underneath into a chest made of cypress. In his hand he held a silver flute, a fine instrument he had bought in a shop in Williamsburg. It had been made in Europe. He had not played it in months. Lifting it to his lips he played a quick trill.

Aimée, startled, dropped the basket of berries as she whirled around. "But that is a white man's flute," she gasped at the mellow sound, much richer than that of the Chickasaw reed flute.

"Aye, I learned long ago from a priest of the tribe. This I picked up on my travels," he explained, reluctant even now to speak of his sojourn in Williamsburg. "I thought you might miss your sister's music. A bride should have a minuet on her wedding day." Lifting the instrument to his lips he played a sprightly minuet that brought back to Aimée memories of balls in New Orleans.

The forest receded, and she was once more dressed in

satin and lace dancing to the tunes she had heard many times. She could almost smell the burning candles in the wall sconces and hear the laughing of the other guests. Suddenly, the harsh cry of some creature of the night broke through her reverie, shattering the illusion, bringing her back to the reality of the hut deep in the woods. She gave a light shudder, bringing her husband's song to an abrupt halt.

"Is my playing that bad, Green Eyes?" he inquired quietly, his dark eyes studying her intently as if he already knew the reason for her change in mood. He had been a fool. The playing only made her remember her sister and her responsibility to the fragile Mignon.

"Non, no, 'tis beautiful," she reassured him, reaching her hand out to touch his bronzed forearm.

"Then what brings such melancholy to your soul?" His long tapered fingers closed over her hand, his gaze searching her delicate visage for the secret of her pain.

"Just a pang of bittersweet memories and worry about Mignon," she confessed with a rueful smile. "The contrast of the music with where and how I am living . . ." She stopped, seeing some dark and unreadable emotion come into his ebony eyes. Although he had not moved, she felt that he had withdrawn from her into some private place she could not follow.

"This life with the People is so terrible for you?" His bronze features were a cold remote mask.

"Not terrible . . ." She hesitated, groping for the right words, ". . . just very different. French Nancy has become very dear to me, and I . . . I am your wife. I consider our ceremony as binding as if in the cathedral in New Orleans." She raised her eyes, a soft misty green in the firelight, to reach out to him and penetrate the wall he had built between them.

"Aye, to me also," he answered huskily, tracing the curve of her lip with his finger.

The sensation brought a flush of warmth to her inner depths. She hungered for the taste of his lips on her trembling mouth. A moan of delight was torn from her throat as he bent his head and kissed the pulsing hollow at the base of her slender neck. His arms encircled her, pulling her to him as she gave a sigh of anticipation.

The scent of magnolia blossoms, and the wild lily of the woods, was in his nostrils as he tasted the milky softness of her skin. Her declaration had given wings to his heart, piercing the wall he would erect between his inner-self and the world.

Aimée relaxed, sinking into the wonder and security of his cushioning embrace. The touch of his hand as he stroked the length of her spine was almost unbearable in its tenderness. His tongue now traced her lips, following the path of his finger, leaving her mouth burning with the blaze of her urgent desire. Tentatively she touched his tongue with her own as if beckoning him to explore the inner recesses of her moist cavern.

A groan of delight surged through him at her invitation. Slowly, with a sensuous joy, he entered the dark velvet sweetness she offered to him with such abandon.

Clinging to his lean, sinewy form, she tasted him with a new hunger that was all consuming. It was as if her soft femininity was responding, merging into his strong masculine depths. They were twin flames merged into one blazing flambeau of desire.

Lifting her up into his arms he carried her the short distance to the bed platform. His lips in her hair, her head nestled in the hollow of his neck.

She moaned as he placed her gently on her feet next to the bed, not wanting to leave the delight of his embrace. It was only a brief second before his hands were once more touching her as he removed her wedding garment.

There was reverence and awe on his usually stoic visage as he beheld the beauty of her nude body. His eyes as dark as the night sky caressed her, following the lead of his knowing fingertips. Kneeling before her in a pose the proud warrior had never taken with her, he seemed to pay her homage as if she were some goddess of the forest. Leaning forward he pressed his lips to the smooth ivory mound of her belly, murmuring against the satin of her skin, "Flower of the Moon, most beloved woman of my soul, twin half of my being. Tonight we become one once more on our journey through all eternity."

"Oh yes, *mon coeur,* my heart, my dearest husband, tonight we are one," she gasped, as he rose to lay her back upon the lily-strewn doeskins.

Quickly, shedding his garments, he joined her, gathering her to the warmth of his lean, sinewy form. Their mouths met with an aching tenderness as she wound her arms about his neck the black satin of his long hair brushing her fingertips. His lips seared a path down her neck, her shoulders, to capture one erect throbbing nipple. Sucking lightly, his sensitive fingers stroked the other full breast till she was arching up for each kiss, each stroke, that brought her closer to the peak of desire.

Her hands were caught, wrapped in the long ebony strands of his hair, as she moved in an age old dance under his knowing touch. *This is life, its very essence,* she thought through clouds of desire. The scent of the wild lily was stronger now from where their bodies had crushed the delicate blooms, releasing the sensual fragrance.

His hands and mouth both teased and adored her breasts, the slender hips, and then down to the sensitive inner satin of her golden thighs. How he wanted to plunge into her like the fierce jungle cat, again and again, till he knew exhaustion. Fighting for control he tried to hold back to prolong this ecstasy. Pulling away from her, he laid back beside her, only his hand continuing his teasing stroking path through her innermost feminine petals.

"We shall play awhile, Green Eyes, on this glorious night," his voice husky with his barely controlled passion.

She looked at him from under eyelids heavy with desire, her eyes burning green coals, her mouth full and slightly bruised from the intensity of his kisses. "Play?" she breathed, her fingertips now tracing his nipples and then down to the proud, erect shaft of him.

"Aye, a warrior is taught control in all matters of life," he whispered, groaning as her hand found his shaft, enclosing the velvet sword with her tiny hand and gently mimicking the motions of lovemaking. "Ah, you are an apt pupil at this game of love," he gasped.

"And how is the winner decided?" she asked, rubbing her long slender leg down his muscular thigh.

"Both are winners in the game of love-play, there are no losers," he moaned aloud with the sheer erotic pleasure she was evoking with her touch. His heart was filled to overflowing with this sign that she too wanted to give him joy with their union. A man could not ask for more than to find a woman, who in the fullness of their love, would give as well as receive passion.

"Ah, but I so enjoy winning," she gave a low throaty laugh. Suddenly she rose up, and taking his manhood in her hand, straddled his slender hips, lowering herself onto his erect masculinity with a cry of triumph and rapture.

"I surrender, Green Eyes," he gasped, with surprise and pleasure so all-consuming he thought he would never forget a moment of this extraordinary night. Fate had indeed blessed him with such a woman for his mate. This was joy beyond his deepest hope and longing. What nights of love-play they would have together, and days too, he thought, for he knew there would be times he couldn't wait for the darkness to taste her passion. There would be long afternoons of delight to savor with this splendid woman. He trembled at the mere thought of the rapturous adventures they would have in the coming years. But would he ever get enough of her? Looking up at her he doubted he would ever tire of such complete perfection.

Her head thrown back in ecstasy till her silver-gold tresses trailed down his thighs, the rose peaks of her breasts erect and throbbing, she was a glorious sight. Holding his hands at her tiny waist, he began to move inside her tight, hot, moist sheath. She followed him, her hips moving in slow circles, till they moved in perfect harmony, the sound of their moans of rapture an exquisite symphony of love.

Filled with the wonderful sensation of him inside her, she experienced a wanton joy she had never known. It was as if she was taking him, making him her own. She was riding him harder and harder now, and like some splendid stallion that she had always wanted to ride, he followed her every nuance. Arching, her hips moving in faster and faster circles of abandonment, tremor after tremor began to quake within her. Wild cries were torn from her throat as her fingernails dug into the muscles of his arms.

Never had she felt as she did at this moment. There was a feeling of complete freedom in her mind and body. All false constraints of the society in which she had been reared were gone. He had freed the real essence of her feminine being, given her pride in the splendor of her sensuality. She was all living, passionate woman, ablaze with the sense of what it was to experience the ultimate fulfillment. Together they merged into one racing, burning entity, a flame that reached ever upward till both were consumed with the ecstasy of becoming one. As their pinnacle was reached, their cries of rapture and capitulation were joined by the fierce, deep, echoing roar of the panther from the clearing outside the hut. The sound rent the quiet of the wilderness night, as he roared his message to the full silver circle of the moon. His spirit was with them.

Chapter Twenty-one

A shaft of hazy light from the smoke hole in the ceiling of the hut fell across Aimée's face as she lay slumbering on the bed platform. Stirring from the deep sleep, she reached out her hand for her husband's reassuring chest. Her fingers touched only doeskin. Her eyelids quickly opening, she stared at the empty place beside her. Feeling the strength of the ray of light coming into the lodge, she realized it was late in the morning. Shadow Panther had probably risen much earlier.

"I fear the world calls to us, Green Eyes," the deep mellow tones of her husband came from the direction of the portal. "A brave has brought word from the village that French Nancy needs your help with the sick, and I must attend a council of the chiefs. The epidemic is worsening as we speak."

With regret, but knowing he spoke the truth, she rose from the bed to wrap a robe of mallard feathers about her nude body. Placing soapweed in a basket, along with a wood comb for her hair, Aimée touched her husband's shoulder as he knelt in front of the smoldering embers of the fire.

"I shall greet the morning and bathe before we leave,"

she said softly as his hand rested over hers for a brief moment.

"There is a little food left from last night. I will leave it here for you as I prepare for our return." He gestured toward a covered clay pot as he extinguished the fire. Only his touch on her hand told of his love; his voice was cool and preoccupied. He was once more the self-contained Chickasaw warrior.

I am learning his ways, Aimée thought as she exited the lodge. The morning was glorious, but hot. The humid, warm air had almost a weight to it as she flung her feathered robe on the bank and walked into the cool spring-fed water. Repeating the morning prayer she had been taught, she quickly lathered the soapweed and cleansed herself. Submerging her body in the cool clear water, she wished she had more time to enjoy the quiet glade, but Shadow Panther was right—they were needed back at the village.

Floating on her back for a few precious minutes before returning to the lodge, she mused on how she was starting to behave as a Chickasaw. The morning prayer had come almost automatic, as if she had been doing it all her life. Her responsibility toward the People in their hour of need had also been an automatic response as if they were, indeed, her people. How had it happened, this subtle change in her thinking? Realizing there was no answer, and time was fleeing, she left the tranquility of the pond to dry herself on the bank with a piece of calico she used for that purpose.

It was as she reached down for her feathered robe that she heard the tiny chirps and saw four pair of tiny black eyes peering up from the middle of the garment. Four small mallard ducklings had made her robe their nest.

"Come off, *mes petites,*" she crooned, trying to move them off the robe. "Your mother is close by," she whispered, looking around for the missing hen. It was then she saw the female laying on the ground not far away, her neck broken by some predator. The ducklings were now orphans.

"Bring a basket, quickly," she called out to Shadow Panther who stood watching her from the entrance of the lodge.

"What have you found?" he asked, appearing beside her a few seconds later.

"The mother has been killed. I am going to take them back with us and raise them myself." Taking the basket from his hand she pulled up tufts of moss from the bank and made a nest in the bottom of the deep basket then picked up each tiny fluff ball and placed them inside.

" 'Tis quite a task you have taken upon yourself, Green Eyes. They might still die with the best of care. They are wild creatures, birds of passage, and when grown will leave you."

"But I cannot leave them to starve. I must try. Just because we love something it does not mean we own it. We have to let it go sometimes, when 'tis time for it to do so, even though it is hard." She looked up at him with a sad smile that smote his heart. Was she talking about herself?

"Dress. We must leave." His voice was terse. He turned and walked down the bank leaving her to stand and stare after him in bewilderment.

When, what she had now come to call his Chickasaw face, came over his proud features she always felt he was locking her out. There was always this wall that would come between them when she knew she had touched on something that was like an old wound. How could they be so close the night before and now be like strangers? She gave a Gallic shrug of her delicate shoulders, and then picked up the basket to walk back to the lodge and dress for their return to Long Town.

The village was filled with an atmosphere of fear that was palpable in the oppressive humid air as they entered through the main gate. Even the camp dogs moved in restless circles snapping and barking at anything that crossed their path. They had sensed the fear of their masters.

"French Nancy awaits you. I go to the council," Shadow Panther told her in remote tones as he left her at the plaza without a backward glance. But then, that is as it should be between a Chickasaw brave and his wife, Aimée thought with a sigh.

The old healer woman was stirring a decoction over the fire in the summer house as Aimée entered her house block. The house block that would now be her and Shadow Panther's home. Among the Chickasaw, upon marrying the man moved into the wife's house with her relatives. French Nancy as her adoptive mother would share her house block with the young couple.

"There are now many old ones sick," the old woman said after greeting her. "They will die, but we must make them comfortable as they prepare to enter the shadowland." Her thin lips had curved into a weary smile as she looked at the tiny ducklings. " 'Tis good to see the beginnings of life once more instead of so many endings. There is an enclosure near the corn shed in which I once kept chickens my man had stolen from the whites. 'Twill be good for the little ones."

Aimée had no time to ponder her wedding night the

next week, for she followed French Nancy from lodge to lodge tending the sick and dying from morning into the late hours of the night. They tried to make the dying more comfortable, but the unmistakable signs of congestion of the lungs told the two women that these patients would only find complete relief from their suffering when they breathed their last. Often these patients had been tended by the priest shaman, but when he saw his chanting and dances were doing no good he would withdraw from the lodge. There was no loss of face in this among the Chickasaw, the family would simply try another healer until they found one who could effect a cure, or the patient died. If they died it was considered that the spirits were too strong for any healer, and it was the person's time to leave the earth.

As they stood beside the bed platform in Thunder-Sky-Woman's lodge late one night, Aimée knew this would soon be the case with the grandmother. Her grandson was much better and although his mother was now ill, as was Dark Dove, the grandmother was by far the sickest. The baby was being nursed by a great-aunt, the two younger women too ill to tend to his needs. As weak as Dark Dove was with fever she refused to take any medicine from Aimée. Her black eyes had flashed disdain as she hit the spoon out of Aimée's hand.

"Come, I will do that." French Nancy had pushed her aside, taking the spoon from the floor. *"Netak intahah* – your mother's day are completed. Do you wish to follow her to the shadowland?"

A flicker of fear showed in the young woman's expressive eyes. She then quieted, taking the willow bark infusion from the bone spoon without protest. Aimée saw the tears of grief slide down Dark Dove's cheeks before she turned her head to the wall. She had heard the Chickasaw expression for death too many times these last few days to not understand what French Nancy had told the young woman.

Soft Wind wept softly for her mother on the other bed platform. When Aimée helped Dark Dove's sister to drink the willow bark liquid the young woman tried to smile her thanks. She was as different from her sister as night and day. Of course, Aimée reminded herself, Soft Wind had not loved Shadow Panther.

Gathering up the medicine bag the women prepared to leave so the family members of Thunder Sky Woman who were not ill could attend to her burial. Aimée thought longingly of her husband. She had been exhausted every night, having spent the days nursing the sick. He, too, had been weary for the men of the tribe had been trying to deal with the epidemic as well as raids from the Creeks. The rival tribe, knowing of the sickness in Long Town, had seen the opportunity to attack hunting parties and even raid the fields, as they were sparsely guarded now that so many were ill.

There had been little time to even speak, let alone make love, as they both fell into an exhausted slumber each night, only to rise at first light. The sensual beauty of their night in the wedding bower seemed almost a dream in the midst of the horror around them.

Following the sure-footed old woman healer down the path to their own lodge, Aimée stumbled with weariness on a root exposed by the daily treading of the villagers. Hitting the hard clay ground, she lay for a moment, her energy so drained from her that she felt she could not get up.

Suddenly strong masculine arms were lifting her up from the earth, cradling her like a child against his chest. She buried her face against his throat as she wrapped her arms around his neck. In the midst of the horror of the epidemic she had found sanctuary in his solid embrace.

"Rest, little one, we will soon be home," he murmured against her hair.

She remembered only his stripping the clothes from her body with the tenderness of a mother, and then the feel of his lips briefly against her forehead before she fell into a deep slumber. When next she stirred she felt him beside her, his quiet breathing telling her that he was deeply asleep.

Trying to return to the realm of Morpheus she found herself strangely uneasy. Her memories of her terror at the Spaniard's hand in this same summer house still made her uncomfortable, but the weather had become so hot the other lodge would have been unbearable. A woman's high-pitched cry of grief rent the night and caused a shudder to run through Aimée. Another one of the People had died of complications from measles.

"Has a dream frightened you, Green Eyes?" Her husband's deep voice startled Aimée, erasing the awful contemplations of death that were troubling her mind so she could not sleep.

"I did not mean to wake you, but the woman's cry—it brought back memories of the horror I have seen today." She turned on her side to face her husband. He was so controlled he had awakened without moving a muscle, but then he had been trained as a boy to be a Chickasaw warrior.

"You have made me proud, beloved wife. No one with the exception of French Nancy has worked harder to help heal the People. Your actions have brought honor to your husband and caused the village to regard you with respect. There is much talk in the council that you are indeed one of the Chosen Ones, one of the true healers. For most it takes a great age to learn such kindness and compassion for the sick, but sometimes the great spirit bestows a gift—as if the chosen one is born knowing what is the right way. They believe that since the disease was brought to the People by a white man that 'tis only right that two white women should know the cure. Since French Nancy is growing old they believe you have been sent to take her place."

"Do you believe this, that fate has sent me to help the People?" Aimée asked quietly with skepticism.

"Who is to say about the ways of fate. I think we are all put on this earth to accomplish some task, learn some lesson. I believe you were destined for me. 'Tis enough." He turned toward her so they were facing one another.

Tracing down her neck, his finger sought the fullness of her ivory breast. Slowly he circled the rose-hued tip as his ebony eyes stared into hers, black pools of mystery in the dim firelight.

Her breath caught in her throat as a hunger rose and flared in her like a savage, demanding animal. As if it had a will of its own her foot, slowly with long sensual strokes, rubbed the calf muscle of his sinewy leg. Her green eyes were held by the spell of his gaze as they continued their teasing touch, breathing in unison, heavy, harsher, faster then before.

This is what he loved about her, her total passionate response. The response of a woman who felt life deeply in all its aspects. She met a man on her terms, her feminine terms that were full of the joy of giving and receiving.

Her mouth quivered as he leaned toward her and

traced her lower lip with his tongue as his hand slid down over her thigh and back up to the curve of her buttocks. A moan was torn from her throat as he pressed her belly tight against him, and she felt the urgent press of his erection into the soft curling hair of her woman's mound.

She felt the heat of his body radiating toward her as her fingers moved across the ropy muscles of his back. Ragged whimpers of sheer need escaped her lips as his tongue sought entrance and swirled inside. She twisted and arched against his sinuous body as if she could not get close enough to him. Languidly, his tongue entwined with hers as she sucked and tasted him with a passion that knew no bounds.

The steadily tightening coil of hot desire in his loins made him want to unleash his hunger and satisfy it with quick, brutal force, but this was Aimée, his beloved woman; for her he would use control. With leashed passion he pressed her down on her back as his hand stroked through her triangle of soft silver and gold curls to part her tender inner lips.

Fire bolts of flaming desire arced through her as his fingers moved inside her, caressing, teasing, preparing her for him. Her body quickly understood his rhythm opening to him like a flower thirsting for rain.

Her hands were not still for they traced a teasing path down his back to caress the backs of his strong lithe thighs. His gasp of raw hunger told her of his delight as his mouth moved from hers to lightly suck each throbbing nipple that rose to meet him with eager anticipation.

Arching, twisting, she sought release from him as her fingernails dug into the hard muscle of his buttocks. He would give her no quarter, continuing his sensual exploration of her inner depths, bringing her to the brink time after time only retreating for a few brief moments so that they could prolong their delightful, exciting love game of arousal.

"Now, *mon coeur,* my heart!" she demanded, as her ecstasy grew beyond any boundary she had ever crossed. On this night, he had brought forth a new, passionate, wanton woman that had been deep inside her. Her body alive in every nerve with a desire that was almost primitive demanded a conqueror. The magic of his mouth and touch had vanquished any lingering inhibitions till she was all molten sensation.

"I want you . . . I need you in . . ." she paused unable to say the words.

"Aye, Green Eyes, where do you want me?" He teased her with his words, his hands, his mouth, till she was a pure flame of gasping passion that must be fulfilled.

"I want you inside of me, filling me." The words were pulled from the very depths of her being as he led her to the pinnacle of rapture.

Rising above her, he tenderly parted her thighs and lifting her saucy bottom, thrust his throbbing manhood inside her moist velvety depths. Her body opened to him; wrapping her legs tightly around his lithe hips she pulled him into her deeper, and deeper still.

His thrusts were at first slow and measured, but as he felt her trembling need for him, he was lost. With a wild groan of possession, he took her with hard-driving thrusts that she met with all the passion in her soul.

She was filled with the hard throbbing shaft of him that made her vibrate with liquid fire. Abandoning herself to the whirling, building sensations, she rose with the spiraling climax of ecstasy to the shuddering pinnacle of total fulfillment. With a raw moan of exploding sensation he joined her, completely sated, utterly satisfied. Together they lay exhausted, merged body and soul.

Drifting on the cloud of afterglow they lay not speaking for words were not necessary. They had experienced total communion in each other's arms.

It was only later as Shadow Panther rose from the bed did Aimée realize she had slept once more. Even his slight movement, however, had awakened her to his absence. Brushing the sleep from her eyes she saw the pale gray light of dawn peeking through the smoke hole. Her husband sat by the smoldering embers of the fire staring at her with a shadow of pain in his dark eyes.

"What is the matter?" She rose up from the bed, wrapping a doeskin about her like a sarong. So attuned were they to each other she felt his pain like it was her own.

Gesturing for her to sit beside him on the mat, he dipped into the thick clay pot that held the corn drink. With a gourd dipper he filled a cup and handed it to her before he spoke.

"As you can see, it is first light and soon I must leave you for a time. I do not know for how long," he paused, staring at her with an unreadable emotion in his ebony eyes. "I go with a war party. If destiny decides I shall not return French Nancy will take you to a trader a days journey from here, if you wish to leave the People. You must tell no one of this. I have already received a promise from the old woman to help you, although she says 'twill not be necessary—that I will return."

"But why must you go?" Aimée pleaded in an agonized voice.

"I am a warrior," he answered simply, as if no other answer was needed.

It was his Chickasaw side again, Aimée thought in despair, always this wall, this side of him she could not understand. A dull ache of foreboding seemed to come over her like a fog.

"I hate the warrior part of you," she muttered in a low, tormented voice.

"Then you hate me, Green Eyes, for that, too, is part of who I am." There was anguish in his voice, and for a moment he looked like she had struck him across the face. Rising to his feet, he stood in front of her, his visage once more the stony mask of cold dignity that was the demeanor of a Chickasaw warrior.

"Non! No, do not go!" she cried, reaching out her hand as if to stop him.

"I go, beloved wife, because I must." Then he was gone, and she was alone with only her fearful heart and her memories.

Chapter Twenty-two

The excited chirps of the four bright-eyed, hungry ducklings greeted Aimée as she poured a mixture of corn and water into shallow clay dishes. It was always a good way to start her day—feeding the little orphan ducks. Their antics and continued good health lightened her mood. She had already seen to the lovely white mare given to her on her wedding day. The graceful animal had been named *Ivoire,* Ivory. Stroking the sleek neck of the beautiful horse she had watched the comical ducks with pleasure. On this sultry, hot morning there was the hint of a storm in the air. She needed to try and forget her worry and depression.

Shadow Panther had been gone for over two weeks and the days were beginning to drag. The epidemic was for the most part over. Although many had died, there had been no new cases and those recovering were doing well. She and French Nancy had returned to tending their ripening fields of corn and beans, as they were needed less and less for healing the sick. Often she would take long rides out into the wild forest surrounding the village even though French Nancy objected to her going alone. There had been several raids by the

Creeks on Chickasaw hunting parties. It was dangerous, but she had to work off the tension that grew with each day of Shadow Panther's absence.

At night, worn out from her physical exertions, Aimée could still not find solace from her worries about her husband in sleep. She would toss and turn in the close humid air of the summer house, images of Shadow Panther flitting through her mind. It was more than body hunger for her husband that made her restless, although there was that too—without his presence she felt so alone. French Nancy lay on the other side of the mat partition that made two chambers out of the summer house, but she was so much a Chickasaw after her long years with the People that there was much Aimée could not speak of with her, for it had been a long time since she had lived with the French.

"They are doing well, soon they will be ready for the stream," French Nancy commented, coming to stand beside Aimée in the enclosure.

"But I shall hate to let them go," Aimée sighed, as she watched them try to swim in the small flat dishes of water.

"You need a *bébè* to care for, *ma petite,*" the old woman said, patting her flat stomach.

Aimée stared down at the woman's wrinkled, age-spotted hand against her belly. She had been relieved when they had first arrived in the village, and she had experienced her monthly flow. Would it come again, or was she perhaps already carrying Shadow Panther's child? Conflicting emotions surged through her at the thought. Her love for him was something she could not help, it was beyond reason or logic. But to carry his child she would be tied to this village for the rest of her life. Did she want to raise a child as an Indian with no knowledge of any other kind of life? She wasn't sure of the answer to that question. As close as she had come to the People caring for them during the epidemic, she wasn't sure she wanted to spend the rest of her life among them. They were in many ways a good, kind people, especially with children. No child was ever struck. They were gently led in the correct direction if their behavior was considered naughty. The worse punishment was verbal correction, or a light scratching of an older child's arm by a dried pair of snake fangs that didn't hurt, only caused embarrassment.

"You fear a child would tie you to the village," the old woman said softly.

"I . . . I do not know, but to raise a child here . . ." she stopped, reluctant to go on.

"Is this New Orleans a better place? I hear there is dirt and illness there also. Until the white man came there was little disease among the People. Every child is loved by the Chickasaw. I have heard this is not always so with the whites."

"Sadly, 'tis true," Aimée agreed. "I just do not know if I am ready for such a commitment."

"Ah, nature will decide this matter, as she usually does. We shall see what comes." French Nancy gave a slight smile then said briskly, "But at this moment nature has commanded us to help at a birthing. You shall learn the way of all women, be they white or Indian. Come, we go to the Woman's hut of Running Fawn. Her daughter's time has arrived. Bright Star is small through the hips and 'tis her first child. We will be gone a long time."

Aimée had gone pale at the old woman's command. Childbirth among the Creoles was a private affair only for married women who had borne children, and perhaps an African slave midwife. If there was trouble a doctor was called in, but the topic had not been discussed in front of young unmarried girls. She really knew very little about what happened when a woman gave birth. She only knew many times the woman died as well as the baby.

"You must not worry about Shadow Panther, he will return safely, I assure you. Before he left I made sure both red and yellow crystals, the strongest male power colors, were put into the medicine pouch that he carries about his neck. The priests also gazed into their own crystals and foretold a great victory. I tell you this so you may concentrate all your energy into the birthing and not be distracted by bad thoughts," French Nancy told her as they walked through the village. " 'Tis most important that the birthing mother feel only positive healing energy coming from us. It will reassure her, and she will be able to help us bring the little one into this earthly world."

Aimée nodded her understanding of what the old woman was telling her. Any conflict or concern she was experiencing about Shadow Panther could be perceived by their patient as apprehension about the coming birth. She must practice the Indian stoic face, not showing her feelings. Her anxiety must be controlled behind a cool mask of competancy. French Nancy was a wise woman; she had learned well the ways of the Chickasaw healer. If she was to be a healer, as well as a *sage femme,* a midwife, she would do well to follow the old woman's example.

The lodge block of Running Fawn was empty of all males. The birth of a child was a woman's work. Aimée wondered with a start if the father of the soon-to-be-born child was with Shadow Panther and the war party.

She felt a shudder run through at the thought that she could be in throes of labor and her husband could be miles away in mortal danger. No, she thought, she could not imagine having a child in such a situation. But she must put all such thoughts away, and show only the mask of a cool, controlled healer.

The woman's lodge was hot and smoky, and Aimée's heart went out to the young woman, fragile as a young fawn, who stood with legs apart over a shallow hole lined with soft furs. She grasped the birthing pole with all the strength in her frail arms. She uttered not a moan as she contracted her muscles trying to help the child toward the light of birth.

"She is strong in heart," French Nancy said with approval as she threw sacred cedar chips on the fire to purify the lodge. "Prepare an infusion of slippery elm bark and wild cherry for Bright Star to drink," she ordered Aimée. "It will help with the pain and encourage the little one to jump down."

The other women in the lodge watched with approval as the old woman lubricated the mother-to-be's loins with a bear grease mixture of spotted touch-me-not to help ease the child's entrance. Songs of encouragement were sung to the laboring mother by her female relatives as she panted in pain. Aimée helped her drink a little of the infusion, then wiped the sweat from her brow.

"Courage," Aimée whispered to the young woman in French. Even though Bright Star did not understand the language she seemed to comprehend the meaning, and gave a grimace that passed for a smile.

Hours of sweat and pain dragged by for the young woman, but the support of the other women and the two healers was unflagging. When it came to be that there was no time between contractions, French Nancy slipped a piece of rawhide between Bright Star's lips that she might bite down on it in the intensity of her pain.

"The head is appearing," the old woman announced, and the other women sang faster songs of joy and encouragement.

They were all with Bright Star in spirit, both white and Indian. She took courage from them for the last exhausting push, and the child was born. The tiny girl slipped from its mother's body into French Nancy's hands. Aimée had clutched the young mother's hands where they grasped the birthing pole as if to add her strength to Bright Star's in the final moments of birth.

French Nancy tied the umbilical cord close to the baby's body then cut it with her knife. Washing the infant in warm water scented with herbs she packed puffball fungus over the knot and navel, wrapping a clean cloth like a bandage around the baby to keep it in place. Handing the child to Aimée to wrap in a soft rabbit fur, she warmed her hand over the fire then rubbed Bright Star's abdomen as she sang the song to bring down the afterbirth. When it came, she wrapped it in a pouch prepared for that purpose and handed it to Bright Star's mother to bury in the sacred ground to insure fertility for the tribe, and more children for Bright Star.

Aimée held the baby to its mother as she lay exhausted on her bed. Tears filled her eyes as she saw the wonder in the young mother's dark gaze as she looked upon her child for the first time. Looking up at Aimée she whispered something in Chickasaw.

"She says she names the child Silver Cloud after the beautiful woman, with the cloud of silver hair, who helped bring her into the light of this world," French

Nancy explained, when she saw Aimée's puzzlement.

"Thank you," she whispered in Chickasaw, so touched she could barely speak. Bright Star smiled, then closed her eyes and slept.

"The husband will be told when he returns with the war party," French Nancy said, wrapping the newborn child in a doeskin as she was female. If the baby had been male it would have been wrapped in a cougar skin. From the moment of birth the Chickasaw sexes were treated differently. They believed that the "communicative principle" of the skins would convey qualities they desired in the child. The doe would cause the female to be shy, timorous; the cougar skin would cause the male child to have strength, cunning, and a prodigious spring to his running ability. After placing the infant in a light rectangular frame of wood called a cradle board, the old woman inserted a wad of soft moss to absorb the child's excrement. The women of the family crowded around to admire the baby.

"We go now. The others of her family will see to Bright Star." The old healing woman motioned for Aimée to follow her out of the woman's lodge.

The pearl gray of twilight had fallen since they had entered the hut, and long shadows streaked across the hard-beaten paths of the village. The scent of roasting meat hung in the sultry air of late summer in the month the Chickasaw called Big Ripening. It was the month Aimée called August. As she strode beside French Nancy she thought of how familiar the sounds of early evening in Long Town were to her. The barking of the camp dogs as they begged for scraps, the low conversation of the old men as they sat out in front of their lodges trying to catch a breath of cool air, the cries of the children as they played in the last dying light of day.

It all had such a familiar, comfortable ring to it. She realized with a start she had been with the People almost three months. Suddenly a pang of melancholy struck her so hard she felt it like a physical pain. What had happened to her sister in these three months that she had been gone from the fort, these months she had been becoming a Chickasaw?

"You worry about Shadow Panther?" French Nancy asked observing the pain in the young woman's jade eyes. "I tell you he will return safe to you, perhaps by tomorrow's sun."

"I am sure you are right," Aimée gave a slight, tired smile. The old woman seemed to have some sixth sense that told of happenings others could only guess at the result. "But 'tis not my husband I think of tonight, 'tis my sister."

"You are a good woman, Moon Flower. You take your responsibilities with great seriousness of purpose, but there is nothing you can do about your sister so far away. She has her destiny, you have yours. You have the ability to be an excellent *sage femme*. This is not given to everyone. It is, indeed, a gift to be a healer. You must wait and see what your destiny is to be in this life. Fate cannot be changed or hurried. All will be known in its own time."

Aimée sighed as they reached the center plaza, wishing she had the old woman's calm acceptance of fate. Then her attention was diverted from her own problems as she noticed a heightened activity coming from the council house. Priests were coming from their lodges to enter the large domed structure. The drums began to beat slowly with a deep resonant voice.

"What is it?" Aimée asked French Nancy.

"The war party is returning, scouts have been sent

ahead. They were victorious, capturing many slaves." The woman's voice was cool and matter-of-fact, but Aimée sensed there was something bothering her, something she did not want her to know.

"Many slaves?"

"Oui, yes, Moon Flower, many slaves to be given away to the People as trophies of victory. Come, you do not want to see this, you are tired." There was an unaccustomed note of anxiety in the old healer woman's voice.

"They will give all the prisoners away as slaves?" Aimée inquired, pushing French Nancy to reveal what she was trying so unsuccessfully to hide.

"Not all, the men . . . the men will be tortured to death," she said quietly, taking Aimée's arm, trying to pull her away from the plaza. The air was filled with the wild war cries of the returning braves entering the village gates.

"I see," Aimée replied through clenched teeth, her stomach rising in disgust and anger.

"You do not see, *ma petite*. You will watch with your white eyes and feel revulsion. But 'tis the way of all tribes. There is honor in retribution, righting a wrong. The Creeks they bring here today would do exactly the same if they were the victors. The women will be taken as slaves to help the women of the People, or if lucky taken as wives. The children will be adopted by those families who lost sons and daughters to the sickness. They will be loved and treated as if they were their own. Understand this, but do not watch what is to come. You have not been with the People long enough to accept all their ways. Later, perhaps, you can learn to live with this part of their beliefs."

"Never! Never will I be able to understand such barbaric behavior," Aimée spat. Turning to leave the plaza as the old woman wished, she was stopped by the appearance of a warrior proudly astride a black steed. His lean muscular body, with its broad shoulders and slim hips was familiar although painted a ghastly red and black, as was his stern visage. He wore only breechclout and moccasins, but a strange square box was strapped across his broad, sinewy back. Looking neither to the right or left he rode in front of Aimée, never acknowledging her presence, his dark unreadable gaze fastened straight ahead of him. She shuddered. This horrible, unrelenting figure was Shadow Panther, war chief, her husband.

"Wait for him in your lodge," French Nancy hissed, pulling the young woman with all her might from the scene. She had seen the horror on those delicate features and feared for her in what was to come.

The plaza was filling with joyous Chickasaw, as they watched the war chief followed by twenty braves dragging prisoners behind them, long ropes of rawhide about their necks. The women surged forward to spit and pelt the men with rocks. Creek women were not treated quite so badly, although they were jostled as the Chickasaw tried to ascertain their worthiness as a slave. The children were left alone, although many clung to their mothers, crying.

"I have seen enough," Aimée muttered, her face white, her eyes huge green pools of anguish. She had seen too much, all the contempt she had been taught of the Indian came flooding to the surface. The People she had come to care about as she nursed them had vanished, to be replaced by this cruel, vindictive crowd crying out for blood.

" 'Tis for the best, *ma petite.*" The old woman led her

away, through the crowd pushing into the plaza eager for the coming ceremony.

Aimée ran to the sanctuary of the lodge block of French Nancy, the savage cries of the crowd echoing in her ears. She wanted to blot it all out, to forget the avid blood lust she had seen on familiar faces she had come to care about. No matter how hard she tried she could not forget the image of Shadow Panther riding at the head of that barbaric display.

"He will not come to you for three days, that is how long the ceremonies of purification will last. You should stay here and avoid the plaza, for you will not like what you see there," French Nancy said quietly, entering the summer house to find Aimée huddled on her bed skins.

"That is where they will conduct the torture and slave auction," she said flatly.

"It is where the Creek warriors will endure their test of courage. Do not the whites also have slaves?" The old woman stared with compassion in her blue eyes at the young woman she had come to care for like a daughter.

"Oui, but they do not torture," Aimée insisted in stubborn tones.

"Then you have obviously never seen what happens when the whites take prisoners after a battle," French Nancy said dryly, bending down to uncover the smoldering coals of the center fire. Placing dry moss and the ends of sticks on the coals she began to gently blow the fire alive.

"What are you telling me?" Aimée asked, rising from the bed to come and sit beside her on the mat.

"That all people, be they white or red, have their dark side, their savage side, you might say. They do these things because they believe they have the right. Only a very few are given the insight to question. 'Tis not easy to be a questioner in any society, *ma petite.*"

"You are very wise, I think," Aimée whispered, touching the old woman's hand in a gesture of affection.

"I have lived a very long time and have seen much. But always I, too, have been a questioner; it has not been easy. I have learned when to keep my doubts to myself, here in my heart, and when to speak."

"And your husband, was he a questioner also?"

"He was a man, a good man. He had his doubts at times, but like Shadow Panther he had responsibilities that had to come first. This is what it means to be a man, I think. In some ways, *ma petite fleur,* they are less free than we to act on their feelings, their doubts."

"Less free then women?" Aimée gave a snort of disbelief.

"Man lives a very rigid role in both white and Indian society. Always man must be brave, responsible, never show fear. Is this freedom? I think not," French Nancy said with a sigh as she shaped corn cakes to bake in the heated coals.

The old woman's words stayed with Aimée the next long days as she stayed secluded in the summer house. There were times she cringed at the sounds she heard coming from the plaza. Then, on the third day, all was still. Gradually the village began to come back to normal, and the laughter of children playing could be heard once more in Long Town. Shadow Panther, however, had still not come to the summer house.

"We go this morning to the fields—they have been without us long enough," French Nancy told Aimée as they greeted the sun by bathing in the stream.

"It has been four days since the war party returned," Aimée commented softly, as she donned her garments.

"He will come," French Nancy assured her, "but the corn is our concern for the moment."

The fields were filled with woman and children tending to the corn, higher now then some of their heads. She smiled as a little girl and boy played in the corn rows where their mother could not see them. It was as she bent down to pull a tenacious weed that she saw the strange woman dragging herself with an awkward gait from one stalk of corn to the other.

"What is the matter with her?" Aimée asked her companion.

"She is a slave, a Creek. They have cut the tendons in her ankles so she will not attempt to escape again," French Nancy muttered in a low voice.

A wave of revulsion came over Aimée at the explanation. This is what they did to slaves who tried to escape It was inhuman.

"I feel a bit faint. I am going to go over there under that tree and rest," she told the old woman, gesturing toward a large cypress.

The hot, hazy air seemed to shimmer in the light of mid day as Aimée sat with her back against the shaggy bark. Her nostrils quivered at the fresh, clean fragrance of cedar that surrounded her. The dizziness had stopped, but there was a sour taste in her mouth as she observed several new woman with fear in their eyes working the fields. They were more Creek slaves, but they did not limp. These had not tried to escape—they had learned their lesson watching what had happened to the other slave. There were children she had not seen before playing with their new Chickasaw sisters and brothers. Children were so adaptable, and, in truth, they had probably been better treated than the women. They had been adopted into the tribe.

Closing her eyes against the glare of the sun now straight above her, she tried to stop her thoughts of what had taken place in the village. It was impossible. She realized she would always feel an outsider among these people, for she was not a child to put the past behind so easily.

The still, humid heat surrounded her, lulling her into an uneasy slumber. She tried to fight it but it was like a hot, heavy blanket pressing her down, down, into the blank refuge of sleep.

It could have been only seconds, or a bit longer, that she slumbered, but something was pulling her back, back from where she didn't have to think about the strangeness of where she was and the horror that had taken place. Her eyelids, heavy with sleep, flickered open almost against her will. She stared up into the white blinding haze of the sun. Blinking, she could make out the outline of a figure, tall and lean, silhouetted against the light.

" 'Tis me, Green Eyes. I have come back to you."

Chapter Twenty-three

"You are back from the torture and killing," Aimée said in a dull, troubled voice, holding her hand to shield her eyes from the glare of the sun.

"I find your soul troubled by what has occurred," he stated quietly. " The killing, unfortunately, could not be avoided. The torture by the women of the People is their way of seeking revenge for their losses in battle. It was expected by Creek warriors. Their women would have done the same to us."

"The women were the ones who carried out the torture," Aimée breathed in shocked tones of disbelief.

"Did not French Nancy explain this also?" He knelt down beside her on bended knee, his dark gaze searching her delicate features, as if to read her thoughts.

She tried not to look into those ebony, depthless eyes for they had the power to hold her to him, weakening her resolve, till her body ached for his touch.

"Non, she did not." Aimée stared down at her lap where her fingers were tightly interlaced as if to keep from reaching out for his embrace.

He wanted her with a hunger that tore at him, for he had been unable to rout her from his mind during the time he had led his men into battle with the Creeks. It had almost made him hate her for lighting such a fire in his blood, but she was his destiny. It was useless to argue with fate, he had reminded himself on those long, lonely nights when he fought his hunger for her, and his worry that she was safe.

"It has been the way of the People since the beginning. The women, who do not go to war, are allowed in the torture ceremony of their enemy to release the fear and hatred they carry in their hearts. The women whose men were killed by these prisoners will seek their revenge. If they do not, they believe that the restless ghosts of those slain in battle will haunt the dwellings of the living until they are avenged. Ghosts can do much harm to the living."

"Do you believe such nonsense?"

"There are many mysteries in life. I cannot say what is true and what is not. I can only tell you why the People do as they do, for as in most things in nature there is a reason."

"I find it savage; never will I understand such a thing," Aimée said, an edge of desperation in her voice.

"Why must this come between us?" he asked tersely.

"You are Chickasaw, or have totally embraced that side of your heritage." She continued to refuse to look at him, although she could feel his intense gaze touching her everywhere.

"The Macleod heritage would be more appealing to you, the Macleod fortune, perhaps," he replied with a biting sarcasm, rising to his feet.

"Non, 'tis not that . . ." she began, looking up at the tall, towering length of him. His image was hazy, lost in the burning white-hot rays of the sun.

"You disappoint me, Green Eyes. I thought you . . . well, it does not matter, for in spite of everything I find I am weak. I want you. For many nights I have thought of touching you, tasting your mouth, feeling you under me. I will wait no longer." His dark liquid voice with its inflection of barely restrained sensuality sent sparks of unwanted excitement shooting through her.

Anger warred with desire within Aimée, as he reached down and clasping her arm with his long tapered fingers pulled her roughly to her feet. Ashamed of the heated reaction she had to his touch she tried to resist him by pulling away, but it did no good. Her resistance only seemed to inflame him. She could feel the angry warmth of his hunger, the barely leashed intensity of his passion unnerved her, as it sent tremors of pure desire down her spine to her aching loins.

"Come, or I swear I will take you now in full view of the women in the fields," he ordered in a harsh voice raw with sensual hunger.

"Beast!" she spat, twisting in his grasp.

"Aye, and I will have my mate, Cat Eyes." He lifted her up against him pinning her to his chest.

She could feel his uneven breath against her cheek as he held her to him, her face buried in the strong tendons of his neck. Crimson with resentment, humiliation, and some wild primitive hunger, she heard the women laugh as he carried her to his stallion. Placing her roughly in front of him on the steed, he held her to him with an arm of steel as the animal surged forward at his command.

He felt his manhood rise and press against her rounded bottom in front of him. His hand sought one full breast, as with his thumb it stroked the nipple till it was erect and throbbing. She was furious at his treatment, but he could tell she was also aroused, and it drove him wild with desire. All the trappings of civilization fell away from him. He was pure Chickasaw and she was his woman, his wife. The blood pounded in his veins as he thought of taking her time after time like the stallion his mare, the forest panther his fierce mate.

The steed made its way into the deep forest on a path only Shadow Panther could see. He was unmerciful in his seduction of Aimée, caressing each breast till the peaks were hard, aching with ecstasy. Bending his head he circled her ear with his tongue, her answering low moan sweet music urging him on.

"Please. . ." she moaned, as the fire he ignited pulsed through her veins. How could it be to feel such anger and such wanton desire at the same time? Her body ached for him, the press of his erection against her bottom was slowly driving her wild. She wanted to arch and move, feel the long velvet length of him inside her bringing her to the pinnacle of rapture.

"Soon, this beast, your savage beast will take you, my wild cat, and how you will love it," his words were a husky caress into her ear as his tongue darted, licked the shell-like curves.

"I hate you," she groaned, her hand finding the hard muscle of his thigh in long sensuous strokes that told of her need, her wanton hunger for what only he could give her.

"Aye," he whispered, licking down the side of her neck, his hot breath coming in quickened gasps. "And what else," he coaxed, teasing her right nipple with his thumb and forefinger.

"I must have you in me . . . I love you," she sighed, surrendering to the awakened abandonment he had so knowingly aroused.

"You drive me beyond reason," he muttered, lifting up her brief skirt to caress the delicious bare mounds of her bottom. "No, 'tis too much," he gasped, spreading his hand under her to caress the soft intimate lips that fit into his palm.

She was swept away on heated waves of a new vivid sensation as his finger plunged into her waiting moist depths. Her pearl nails dug into the hard muscle of his thigh as he slowly, achingly, brought her to the climax of passion as they rode through the dark, fragrant shadows of the cedar forest.

The final explosion of sensation left her weak, trembling, utterly consumed. Long, shuttering breaths shook her slender frame as he held her slumped against his chest.

" 'Tis only the first, Cat Eyes, only the first," he murmured as she trembled in his arms, exhausted by the intensity of her satisfaction.

"You must be mad," she managed to gasp as the intent behind his words penetrated the cloud of contentment that surrounded her.

"Ah, my sweet Green Eyes, as the poet Dryden said, There is a pleasure sure/In being mad which none but madmen know."

A husky, throaty laugh welled up from deep within her as she realized how mad, indeed, was her life. She was being ravaged by an Indian on horseback who quoted the English poet John Dryden.

"Very sensual, that laugh, and very satisfied," he murmured, kissing light butterfly kisses at the nape of her neck where the part of her golden braids started.

"You make me wanton," she whispered, as to her disbelief little shivers of desire were once again building within her at his unrelenting, seductive touch.

"Ah, but you are wanton, sweeting, my silver and gold wanton, my joyful playmate in the game of love."

His destination was soon clear to Aimée as the sound of a rushing stream was carried to her on the still, humid air. Within minutes they rode into the clearing where stood the summer house of their wedding night. How many restless hours she had tossed and turned remembering the brief night they spent in the secluded glade.

There was an almost unearthly silence about the lagoon. Not a breath of wind stirred the lacy leaves of the cedar trees. The cool, olive water of the pool under the waterfall beckoned to Aimée, hot from the heat of the day. She welcomed the peace and privacy the glade offered. It was hard for her to adjust to the constant presence of others that was so much a part of Chickasaw life.

"Ah, sweet wife, now for what you French call the *lune de miel,* the honeymoon. We will have time to understand each other, to grow strong together in each other's soul." Shadow Panther slid from the stallion's back and reached up to help her down.

" 'Tis a lovely thought," Aimée murmured, giving him a shy smile. He was so natural about lovemaking, but she felt embarrassed about what had just taken place.

"We shall make it true," he said softly, the light of desire growing like a steady flame in his dark intense gaze. Holding out his hand, he grasped her trembling fingers. "Come, let us refresh ourselves in the cool water."

Hand and hand they walked to where the mossy bank sloped into the pond. The branches of a river willow shaded them as it stood sentinel over the clear, quiet water. The only sound to break the primeval stillness was the dance of the sparkling stream as it fell over the limestone outcroppings across the lagoon.

Stepping out of his moccasins, he stripped off his breechclout in one swift gesture, then turned to Aimée. She, feeling the flush of rose touch her cheeks, turned her eyes to the pond as she fumbled with her bodice.

"Allow me." His voice was a husky rasp as his fingers gently unlaced the calico bodice. "You are so beautiful, Green Eyes. There is no shame between us. Look at me."

Turning her head she stared into black eyes that smoldered with his hunger, then slowly allowed her gaze to drop, following the long, lean line of his magnificent form. Her breath quickened as she saw his manhood erect with his need, his hunger.

" 'Tis for you," he told her, his voice thick and unsteady. Taking her hand he placed her fingers about his shaft as he slipped her brief skirt from her hips. "I, too, like to feel the touch of my beloved."

She felt the blood surge from her fingertips, where the touch of him set her pulse racing, to the center of her aching womanhood. Slowly, she caressed him, delighting in the sound of his quickened breath that came in a hard rasp with each stroke of her hand.

"Enough!" he gasped, pulling away from her with a groan. "Not yet, Green Eyes." Taking her hand he led her quickly into the cool waiting pond.

As the water swirled around them, he led her out till it reached his waist and the tips of her breasts. Sweeping her into his arms, he took her mouth with a savage passion that caused her to mold her feminine softness to his lean, hard contours. Her lips opened to him as his tongue demanded entry and their tongues intertwined in a wild dance of desire. Licking, tasting, circling, they were insatiable.

Her hands caressed the honey-colored skin of his sinewy back, her tiny nails digging into him as he aroused the smoldering coals of her passion into a leaping flame. She felt the steady beat of his heart pounding against her breasts, delighting in the feel of his raw warmth pressing the aching peaks that throbbed for his touch.

His hands cupped her saucy bottom, lifting her up off her feet till she wrapped her legs around his thighs. Stroking her wet, satin skin he parted her delicate, throbbing petals.

She arched at the teasing caress of his hand. The wild, wanton feelings were once more overcoming any inhibitions as her hips moved against him in sensuous invitation.

He could not control his white-hot hunger any longer. He had to feel her tight, moist hotness around him. With a fevered groan he thrust his erect aching shaft inside her welcoming body.

"*Oui,* oh yes!" she gasped, wanting him deeper and deeper still. Wrapping her legs tighter around his hips she pulled him into her, meeting each slow, measured thrust with a sensuous rhythm. The water swirled around them aiding in their rapture till all of nature seemed to nurture their passion.

Suddenly, both seemed to break all restraint as they moved faster and faster, seeking that total union, that total fulfillment. They abandoned themselves to the spiraling pinnacle in an exquisite harmony of movement, sensation, and joining of spirit. In a dizzying, uncontrollable explosion of rapture they found the peak they sought, and together achieved a fiery release in a melting of two into one. The cry of union was torn from the depths of their beings, sounding like one voice, one exclamation of total joy.

The velvet dark nightfall found them outside in the glade in front of the summer house once more, still basking in the glow of their earlier joining. They had finished eating the evening meal, and in the sultry heat sought the coolness of the eventide. A light breeze was blowing, and they lay on boughs of cedar covered with doeskin, staring up at the stars, their fingers intertwined.

"The stars are so close you feel like you could reach out and touch them," Aimée murmured with a sigh of contentment. If only she could always feel this right with the world when she and her husband were together. They were only man and woman celebrating the joy they found in each other. The clash of culture and tradition for a brief time did not exist.

" 'Tis called the spirit's road by the People," Shadow Panther explained. "The stars are celestial souls that shine in the Sky World to guide earthly wayfarers on their journey. They watch over man, as well as protect and inspire him."

"The People have such a poetic way of looking at nature. I find their words quite lovely," Aimée replied, as her eyes scanned the starry indigo heavens. The warmth of the night surrounded her like a velvet comforter filled with black downy feathers.

"There is something, then, you like about the Chickasaw," he teased, squeezing her hand lightly as it lay captured in his strong fingers.

"I find I have grown quite fond of one Chickasaw," she replied.

"And whom do you refer?"

"Why, French Nancy, of course," her voice was all teasing innocence, but he heard the deep rich chuckle that followed her statement.

"Ah, my sweet afternoon delight, you will pay for that, aye, indeed, you will." With one swift graceful movement he was on top of her, holding her hands above her head with one strong hand, as he began to tickle her with the other.

The sound of her laughter rose on the heated air like

smoke till it mingled with the crystal credence of the waterfall in one joyous song. It was only moments till the lilting sound turned to a *chanson* of love. Tickling strokes became caresses, and laughter sighs of desire.

Later, as she lay exhausted across his chest, still tingling from the rapture of her fulfillment, she knew that for the first time in her life she was happy. In spite of all the difficulties in adjusting to her life in the Chickasaw village, she had experienced moments of a rare contentment unlike anything she had ever known. Perhaps, in time, she could become one of the People and leave the life she had known behind. She hoped so, for she feared she would never be happy away from this magnificent man who brought her such rapture.

The measured rise and fall of Shadow Panther's chest told her that he slumbered. With heavy eyelids she snuggled against his stalwart form and sought the renewal found in contented sleep.

Yet it was not to be that she would find a peaceful rest. She tossed and turned in a myriad of dreams, till the last hideous visions caused her to cry out in despair.

"Mignon!" Her sister's name was torn from her throat as she saw the figure, as if in a mist, running by a vast river. The tormented visage of the young woman she could see clearly as she stumbled in her haste to outrun the pursuer who was almost beside her. Aimée had to stop him, she had to help her sister.

"Wake, all is well. 'Tis only a dream," the deep, reassuring masculine voice called to her, pulling her from the hallucination of terror that had been her slumber. Strong, male arms rocked her like a fretful child.

"It was terrible," she sobbed. "Mignon was in danger, and I could do nothing to help her." A shudder tore through her slender form as she remembered the nightmarish illusion her tired mind had conjured.

"Have you had this dream often?" Shadow Panther asked quietly.

"Not like tonight. There was such an urgency about it. I am frightened. French Nancy says often the truth comes to you in dreams."

"Aye, 'tis thought so," he agreed, his voice troubled. It was not the first time he had regretted not returning for the fragile Mignon. He should have seen to the capture of Aimée himself, making sure her sister was taken as well. His beloved wife would never be completely at ease without her sister safe beside her.

Aimée sighed, fatigue still with her even though she could see the gray of first light above the trees. A dull headache throbbed at her temples. Her troubled sleep had given her little rest.

"Rest a while longer, sweeting. I shall lay beside and hold you safe from all the demons of the night," he whispered into her hair, as she snuggled into his arms, her head on his chest.

Soon her light, regular breathing told him that she slumbered. He hoped this time her dream would not return to haunt her. Although he could protect her from physical danger, he knew the real danger to their love lay within her own mind, her deeply felt sense of duty. How could he protect her from her tie of fealty to Mignon? There was only one way, and it was a dangerous path. He had no other option, it must be taken.

Chapter Twenty-four

"I wish we could stay here forever," Aimée sighed, watching with regret as Shadow Panther smothered the coals of the fire in the summer house. She knew fire was sacred to the People as the earthly representation of the sun, and as such was never to be polluted with water. Thus they never extinguished fires with water. Always they must be suffocated with the dirt of Mother Earth.

Today she was glad for anything that delayed their departure from the glade where for five sleeps, as the Chickasaw reckoned days, they had known such happiness. No one had come to interrupt their idyll. But now they would be returning to Long Town and the constant presence of the People. She would once more see her husband as a chief, bound to follow the tribal ways that were so foreign to her. With a sense of unease she walked outside to gaze one last time at their private glade where all had seemed so easy.

"Do not fear, Green Eyes, we will still be together, perhaps not as much as here, but in our hearts we are always one," Shadow Panther said quietly, coming to stand behind her as she stared out across the clear, olive water of the lagoon.

His firm hands clasped her shoulders as he bent his head to lightly kiss the part in her hair. Turning her head she glanced up at him, giving him a sad smile. How she hated the thought of returning to the village.

"We must leave," he whispered against her hair, then taking her hand led her to where the black stallion stood waiting.

The brilliant glowing circle of the sun beat down as they rode through the dense forest. Even here in the shade of the giant cedars, the sycamore, and cottonwood, it was hot, a stifling humid heat that made the air seem close and suffocating like a heavy wet blanket. There had been little rain and the leaves had a dry dusty look about them. Everywhere there was silence as if the forest creatures in their wisdom slumbered through the heat of the day, not stirring till the cool of evening.

The scent of wood smoke hanging in the still air was their first hint that they were near Long Town. Even in the heat of summer the cooking fires were maintained. As they neared the fields Aimée saw women and children were working between the tall green stalks of corn. Large pots filled with water from the stream were being used to give the thirsty plants a drink in the heat.

It was as they rode along the edge of a field of waving corn that Aimée saw a sight that struck her through. A young Creek woman, large with child, labored to carry an enormous clay pot full to the brim with water. As she struggled the water would spill onto the ground, with each spill she was struck with a narrow cane whip by a woman Aimée knew all too well—Dark Dove. The pregnant woman was obviously her slave.

"You must stop her!" Aimée cried out over her shoulder to Shadow Panther.

"There is nothing I can do. She is Dark Dove's slave, her property," he replied in terse tones.

"She is with child. Even on the plantations a slave

would not be expected to do such hard labor." As the crack of the whip rent the sultry air one more time Aimée stiffened, a sudden anger lighting her eyes with an emerald fire. Watching as the exhausted woman slid to the ground in a faint, she knew she couldn't stay silent any longer.

Before Shadow Panther could stop her, she slid from the back of his stallion and was stalking across the dry burned grass of the meadow toward Dark Dove and her prostrate slave. Reaching the two women, she pulled the whip from the startled hand of Dark Dove and broke it across her knee, flinging the pieces on the ground.

She knelt down beside the unconscious woman and saw the rhythmic contractions of her swollen abdomen—she was in labor. Gently, she tried to examine her to see how far along she was, but before she could complete her task a feminine hand grabbed her shoulder pushing her roughly to the ground. Rising back up, she stared into the malevolent black eyes of Dark Dove glaring at her with pure hatred.

"Leave her alone," she hissed in Chickasaw. "She is going to have a child," Aimée spat back, understanding her and somehow finding the Chickasaw words to reply.

"My slave," Dark Dove muttered, her hand reaching out to slap Aimée. It never reached her, for the woman's arm was clasped by a strong masculine hand that stopped her gesture in mid air.

A curious expression came over Dark Dove's furious visage as she stared up into the stony mask of Shadow Panther. A cunning came into those beautiful almond-shaped eyes as she leaned against him, rubbing her breasts in a suggestive gesture across his chest.

"You want her?" she asked, staring up at him with bold eyes. "You can have her, she is worthless, but Soft Wind wants the child. She fancies another baby," Dark Dove's voice was a low sensual purr as she rubbed her long slender thigh against his.

"Leave us and the woman. We will take her to the lodge of French Nancy for the birth." He dropped her arm as if the touch of her was distasteful.

Dark Dove seemed not to have heard him for she continued to press against his chest, her head thrown back to stare up at him with a bold sexual invitation in her eyes, her tongue tracing her lower lip in unmistakable invitation.

"Leave us," he commanded, his voice as cold as his eyes, "or your nose will surely wear the slit of the whore."

She shrank back at his words, for to be branded an adulteress in Chickasaw society was a serious matter. The man in the affair would experience some censure, but the woman's nose was slit and deformed so all might know her crime. Other men would not marry her, only keep her as a concubine.

Aimée flinched at his words for she had seen a few women to whom this had been done. They were disfigured for life and were outcasts from the rest of the tribe, earning their living as prostitutes. As much as she disliked Dark Dove she understood her fear, and shuddered to think of that lovely face so disfigured. It was with relief that she saw the young woman flounce off after giving Shadow Panther one last burning look.

"We must get her to French Nancy—her time is upon her. It will not be long," she told her husband as the woman regained consciousness, moaning with the pain of her labor.

Taking two long sticks he found near the fields, Shadow Panther made a rough travois from a deer skin that lay across his horse under the saddle. Placing the slave woman on the travois, Shadow Panther led the steed into camp with Aimée walking beside the woman.

They attracted much attention as they made their way to French Nancy's lodge. The sight of a slave woman riding on a travois behind a warrior's horse was strange indeed to the People. When they saw she was in labor they understood; children were precious to the Chickasaw, even slave children, for they would soon be adopted. Aimée realized little of what was going on around her, for her complete attention was on the moaning, suffering woman.

She was thankful the old healing woman was at the summer lodge seeing to the mixture of medicines from the herbs she had picked that morning. French Nancy took charge of the situation, sending Shadow Panther away to the council house, for the birth of a child was for women's eyes only. It was very bad medicine for a warrior to be anywhere near the birthing hut. He could be cursed from such an offense against the law of separation, that most important Chickasaw rule that maintained certain things must be kept apart in order to maintain the spiritual purity of the individual, and the People as a whole.

Aimée watched him leave the summer house with a sinking heart. There had been no word or physical touch of goodbye, as was proper for a warrior in front of others, but it reminded her so much of the difference between them. It made him seem so very much a Chickasaw chief.

Stirring the infusion of slippery elm over the fire as French Nancy had bidden her do, Aimée pondered what he had told her of the Chickasaw concept of balance in their world. They felt the cosmos was conceived of consisting of parts which were in opposition to each other. The forces of the north were opposed to the forces of the south, fire to water, bird from four-footed animals, and man to woman. When the People failed to keep such opposing forces apart during certain times dire consequences could be expected to result. She sighed, wiping the perspiration from her lip. How could she ever live among a People that had such beliefs? It was impossible. There were so many taboos, taboos she thought ridiculous. Why, she thought not for the first time, had she fallen in love with man who was so totally wrong, so different from everything she had ever known or believed?

"I need you," the voice of French Nancy interrupted her musings. "The birth will be difficult. The child is making his appearance on the earthly plane feet first. This is most dangerous, and the mother is worn out."

The next hours were exhausting as the old healer woman tried every method she knew to move the position of the baby by manipulating the womb, but nothing worked. The mother was wan and still, having exhausted all her strength.

"I shall take the child," she told Aimée, motioning for her jar of bear grease mixed with herbs. After applying the mixture to her hand and the birth canal, she began the laborious task of removing the child from his almost comatose mother.

With her breath caught in her throat, Aimée watched the large perfect male child leave his mother's body. Within seconds French Nancy had him crying lustily.

"He is big, but perfectly formed," the old woman commented, handing him to Aimée as she prepared to deliver the afterbirth. "Take great care after such a delivery," she instructed, "to keep the pressure firm on the belly. There can be much bleeding after such a birth. Bleeding that can kill."

While washing the child in tepid water, Aimée watched the motion of the old woman's deft hands. She felt a sense of privilege to be taught the secrets of such a talented *sage femme,* midwife, as French Nancy. If anyone could save the young mother's life it was this wise old healer.

"Will she live?" Aimée asked, wrapping the baby in a cougar skin as befitted a male child.

"It depends," the old woman mused, giving a shrug, that after all her years with the Chickasaw could only be described as Gallic. "She is young, perhaps. See, her eyes open, give her the child."

The sad dark eyes of the mother stared up at Aimée with gratitude as the baby was placed in the crook of her arm. A tear traced down her wan cheek as she touched her child for the first time.

Aimée was filled with a quiet pride that in some small way she had contributed to this happy scene. French Nancy too seemed satisfied as the mother lifted her infant to her breast.

"Bien, good, nursing will help the womb to contract," the old healer told Aimée, "it will help lessen the bleeding."

Realizing how weary they were now that the excitement of the birthing was over, the two women returned to the summer house and their evening meal. It was as they were finishing the last of their food that they heard the high-pitched wail pierce the quiet of the night. Both women dropped their bowls and ran from the lodge, for the sound was coming from the birthing hut.

"What do you think you are doing?" Aimée demanded in French, as she ran into the hut to find a figure bent over the weeping slave woman.

At her words the figure rose to her feet clutching the newborn child to her chest. In the dim light of the hut Aimée saw to her horror it was Dark Dove.

"Soft Wind wants the babe. She wants another son.

She is still nursing her daughter, but 'tis time she is weaned. There will be enough for the boy," Dark Dove hissed. The wails of the child's mother almost drowning her out.

"You can't have him!" Aimée exclaimed, grabbing for the infant, but Dark Dove darted out of her grasp.

"Enough!" French Nancy ordered. "The woman is hemorrhaging. I need your help," she called to Aimée as she bent over the hysterical mother. "Leave the child, Dark Dove."

The fleeing young woman hesitated for a moment at the authority in the old healer's voice, but as the light caught the silver in Aimée's hair she stiffened. Her black eyes flashing hate and need for revenge, she gave a light laugh of triumph before disappearing into the night with the baby clasped tightly in her arms.

"Stay!" French Nancy admonished Aimée as she rose to chase after her. "Help me. You must hold her down while I press on her belly or she will surely die." The old woman was working frantically to stop the flow of blood that was gushing from the tormented mother.

Aimée watched, horrified as she soon realized she was not needed to restrain the slave woman. She lay pale and still. Her blood seemed to permeate the floor of the hut, the sight and smell causing waves of nausea to wash over Aimée. In spite of French Nancy's most heroic efforts the woman had bled to death.

"She killed her," Aimée muttered through teeth clenched in anger and revulsion.

"Perhaps, or she might have died anyway. With such a delivery, and as weak as she was, it could have happened even if the child had not been taken from her. 'Tis fate. At least the baby will be nourished by Soft Wind. He would have been hers according to Chickasaw law regardless if the slave had lived or died. Soft Wind will raise him as her own. A mother cannot have enough sons."

"So she simply takes another woman's child," Aimée said bitterly. "I will never understand these people, never." There was despair and a great weariness in her jade eyes as she stumbled to her feet. She had to get out of this place of horror and death.

Leaving the birthing hut behind, Aimée stood for a moment in the humid night air breathing deeply, savoring the fragrance of life, the scent of the magnolia blossom, the wild lily, the cedar forest that surrounded the village. But even here she felt confined, she had to be free. The earthy smell of horse came to her nostrils along with the perfume of nature, and she knew what she must do.

Ivoire, the beautiful milk-white mare that had been her wedding gift, seemed to sense her need as she saddled the sleek animal. There was no plan of escape, simply a need to feel free, to once more be allowed to come and go as she pleased. Mounting the horse she urged her forward down the village path toward the main gate.

It was late for there was little sound coming from the lodges that she passed. Would she ever get used to never knowing the time, never seeing a clock. Hours had no meaning for the Chickasaw. They reckoned time only by days and months, sleeps and moons.

She could see the tall open gates looming up ahead of her and she urged Ivoire on. To ride with the wind in her hair, to feel free and in control of her own life once more was all she sought. It was not to be, for as she reached the gates where the path opened into the forest a figure out of the dark appeared grabbing hold of the reins of the mare.

She stared down into the cruel visage of the warrior who had first kidnapped her on the bluff. He held firmly to the mare as she shied from him.

"Let me go!" she ordered in Chickasaw.

Impassively he stared up at her with hard, cold eyes that were unrelenting. She shuddered at the contempt she saw on that stony visage. There would be no freedom for her, not on this night or any other night. She was being watched by men whose only allegiance was to Shadow Panther. To resist any more might bring injury to Ivoire, and was obviously futile.

Sitting stiffly in the saddle, she allowed the warrior to lead her back toward the lodge. She felt empty, drained of all emotion, even anger, as they made their way through the sleeping village. All she wanted now was her bed platform and to forget in slumber what had happened on this awful night.

But she soon realized she would not be allowed to simply return to French Nancy's house block. The cold-eyed warrior was leading her in the direction of the center plaza and the summer council house. She was to be shamed in front of all the assembled braves.

The summer council house was in reality four sheds, or arbors, arranged around a square with a sacred fire of four logs in the middle. The orange-blue flames flickered into the dark night as Aimée was led into the square. She could see only shapes and shadows silhouetted against the flames, but she felt the tension in the air as a palpable presence. Dark hostile eyes were following her entrance. She caught herself glancing uneasily over her shoulder feeling as if surrounded by a pack of hungry wolves eyeing their prey waiting for the first sign of weakness.

The warrior led her to the main building on the west side of the square. He stopped the horse in front of the structure. Aimée shuddered as she saw the front posts were carved birds of prey with blood dripping from their mouths. Eagle feathers topped the posts hanging motionless in the hot, still night.

"This woman has tried to escape," the warrior announced in a harsh voice. There was a low murmur like a swarm of mosquitoes at his words.

Aimée held herself erect trying not to show any fear. What he was accusing her of called for strict punishment, but she would not let them see her tremble. The Chickasaw admired courage more than any other trait. She would not lose face in front of these men, in front of Shadow Panther. She knew somewhere in that shadowy, hostile throng was her husband, the war chief. What side would he show tonight, the lover or the vengeful Chickasaw chief? Would he defend her, or leave her fate to these jackals?

Chapter Twenty-five

"This woman is the wife of a war chief," the deep familiar commanding voice spoke from the dark shadows. "She is not a prisoner. She is free to go where she pleases as an *aliktce,* a healer."

Relief and joy flooded Aimée as she translated the Chickasaw words of her husband. He had come to her defense. She fought to maintain her stoic expression as her heart sang with happiness. Peering through the darkness, she tried to see Shadow Panther's beloved visage, but all she saw was the frown of vexation on the brow of the cold-eyed warrior. He had been thwarted and was furious.

"There are no sick outside the stockade," the angry brave thundered.

"Perhaps she sought medicinal herbs or communion with the healing spirits," Shadow Panther replied calmly. "This chief's wife was treating a woman in childbirth. We, as men, do not know of such things, as it should be. Let her speak and confirm what I say." The tall, lean masculine form appeared out of the gloom to come and stand next to Ivoire.

Aimée stared down into the black compelling eyes of her husband. There was a private message of warning in that intense gaze. It was as if he were speaking to her, telling her that he knew what he said was not the truth, but that she must for her own good confirm his speculation.

Panic welled up within her as she sought for an answer that would satisfy these hostile judges. Then as she stared down at Shadow Panther a slender invisible bond seemed to run from his being to her own heart. A wonderful feeling of calm came over her as his strength seem to flow into her, reassuring her, guiding her in this terrible hour of need.

A sense of strength filled her as she lifted her head announcing in a clear strong voice, "I sought the guiding spirit of *Hushininakaya,* the moon, to take the soul of a slave woman who died this night. I ask that she travel the spirit's road to the sky world to live with the Great Composite Force, and not stay here to bewitch the People. She was wronged by one of the People, but I ask her forgiveness and lead her from the village to where her soul may rise in peace to the sky. That is why I leave the gates of Long Town when the moon is high."

There was a low rumble of conversation as the men discussed such a courageous act. To guide a troubled spirit away from the People so it might find peace was truly worthy. This woman was as valiant as a warrior, but then she was the wife of Chief Shadow Panther.

"We salute you, and wish you well in your journey. You may go," the deep, solemn tones of Chief Piomingo echoed from the porch of the hut with the bird of prey posts.

Startled, Aimée realized they were accepting her explanation, but that now she must indeed leave the village, for they were expecting her to carry out the ceremony she had described. She knew how frightened the Chickasaw were of discontented spirits. There were elaborate rites to burial. It was believed if these were not carried out exactly the dead person's soul would stay about the village as a ghost haunting the living, and causing mischief as well as illness.

As if sensing her turmoil at what to do next, Shadow Panther whispered as he handed her the reins, "Go to our marriage bower by the stream. I shall join you as soon as I can. Do not stop anywhere. Go!" he hissed.

Signaling to Ivoire, Aimée rode the sleek mare out of the plaza and down the dirt path to the village gates. This time no one stopped her. A sense of inadequacy swept over her, as she left the village behind riding out into the blackness. Unfamiliar sounds of the creatures of the night began to haunt her as she sought to follow the path to their summer house deep in the woods. Everything looked so different in the night even though the full moon shone down a silvery light.

Leaving the corn fields behind, she followed the faint path she would never have noticed before she lived with the Chickasaw and learned their subtle ways of marking nature. The thought of losing her way and wandering lost through these dark woods gnawed at her confidence. She tried to keep a fragile control and not let the black panic that welled in her throat overwhelm her.

The towering cedars turned into frightening giant shapes as she rode deeper and deeper into the forest. Was she on the right path? Suddenly, as if she could hear him, she remembered what her husband had told her about using all her senses to tell her direction.

She looked about trying to remember if anything looked familiar in the veil of night. Ahead of her a beam of moonlight caught the huge white blooms of a magnolia tree. A sense of glee shot through her as she recognized the magnificent tree. They had traveled past it for she had remarked to her husband on its beauty. With a smile on her lips she remembered how Shadow Panther had told her it would always have special meaning for her as she was named for its alabaster blooms, Moon Flower. As she rode past she heard the sound of water falling across rocks and knew she was close to the stream and their marriage bower.

The moon cast down an unearthly glow as she rode into the clearing next to the babbling brook. Their marriage bower stood deserted and dark. Tying Ivoire to a low hanging branch, Aimée rubbed her down with the stalks of long dry grasses.

Reluctant to go inside the darkened lodge, she decided to sit in the moonlight beside the stream. She had no way to start a fire to lighten the dark night. The air was hot and humid inside the structure, while outside there was a slight coolness next to the rushing stream.

Staring up at the starry night she remembered the death of the young slave woman. It had been a hideous savage deed on the part of Dark Dove to steal the baby. She gave a deep sigh, knowing that no matter how long she lived among the Chickasaw there would be things she could never accept.

A hoot of an owl high above her in a cedar tree caused her to give a slight shudder. She felt so alone, so vulnerable. Her wish to ride free through the night had long since deserted her. Now she wished only that Shadow Panther join her, comfort her from the terrors of the night and those she conjured up in the deep recesses of her troubled mind.

The crack of a stick broken by the step of a human foot caused her heart to be filled with relief. Shadow Panther had arrived. Rising to her feet she turned to greet him, but her joy turned to ashes. A figure stood near Ivoire, but it was not her husband. In a shaft of moonlight she saw it was a warrior, a warrior painted in the red and black of the war party. He was a Creek, sworn enemy of the Chickasaw.

Fear, stark and vivid, glittered in her emerald eyes as she met his fierce, cold black orbs. She watched as if hypnotized as he took a knife from his belt. The blade gleamed in the moon glow as he held it in his powerful hand. They stood, eyes locked, as unmoving as statues in a frightening tableau of predator and cornered prey.

It was the terrible cry of the forest panther that finally caused the Creek brave to glance away for one brief second. The great cat's roar echoed in the clearing, telling of its nearness. Some primitive sense of survival spurred Aimée to take advantage of that brief lapse in his attention. She turned and ran into the dark pool of the stream. Diving under the water, she swam till she thought her lungs would burst, swam toward a hidden cave under the limestone outcropping where the stream tumbled down to form the lagoon. Shadow Panther had showed it to her on one lazy afternoon as they played and swam in the cool water. Now it was her only chance to evade the Creek intent on her murder.

Blood pounding, her body crying out for air, she surfaced behind the small waterfall and crept into the dark mossy cave. Trembling, she huddled as far back as possible, her every sense alert. The warrior had followed her into the water, but in the dark had temporarily lost her. She could only pray he would not find her.

Suddenly, above her, she heard the heart-stopping roar of the panther. He was above her on the ledge that overlooked the cascading stream. His fierce bellow seemed to be all around her. She cringed against the cave wall, her body ridged, her fists clenched, a scream of pure terror clawing at her throat.

The sharp piercing death cry of a human joined the great cat and then all was still. Aimée didn't know how long she stayed huddled in the cave, her mind and body numb, listening for any sound of the Creek brave, but there was only the sound of the falling water. As she stared out at where the moonlight shone on the rippling stream as it fell down in a mist of crystal droplets, she saw a figure floating in an unnatural pose, a dark oily cloud surrounding him.

Her hysterical screams echoed in the forest night, as she realized it was the dead body of the Creek, and the dark cloud was his life's blood seeping from his wounds. The sheer horror of it overwhelmed her.

"Green Eyes, is it you?" The call echoed in the cavern piercing her hysteria till her voice became only a frightened sobbing.

"Here! I am here!" she sobbed, unable to move, only to cower in the sanctuary of the cave.

Within seconds he was beside her, holding her to his chest as if he would never let her go. When he had reached the clearing and found Ivoire carefully tied, but no sign of Aimée, he had been filled with anxiety. The roar of the panther as it struck its final blow to the Creek brave had drawn him to the waterfall and the sound of Aimée's terrified screams. The great cat had disappeared into the forest as he reached the cave.

Unable to stop sobbing, Aimée allowed him to lead her from the cavern. As they passed the body of the brave she felt her gore rise and was sick into the swirling waters of the stream. Humiliation and fatigue threatened to tear her apart as Shadow Panther carried her into the lodge.

"We must leave here, Green Eyes, for there may be other Creeks with this one. The village should be alerted that they have come so close. It is retaliation for the Chickasaw raid," he explained. He dried the wet from her hair and body, then wrapped her in a cloak of mallard feathers, for she continued to tremble even in the sultry night air.

"The panther killed him," she muttered, through clenched teeth.

"Aye, he was protecting you, my beloved Moon Flower. You are my wife, the panther is my totem animal."

"You really believe in such things?" There was scorn and a great weariness in her voice as she huddled in the downy robe.

"Have you lost none of your white skepticism since living with the People?" he asked gently, realizing how exhausted she was with trying to make sense out of her new life.

"None," she replied flatly.

"Ah, then you have refused to acknowledge the voice within you who hungers for the truths in life, the power and wisdom that can come from understanding what you really seek in your journey."

"What journey? My journey to becoming a Chickasaw?" she said contemptuously. "I tell you that will never happen. There is too much horror, too much savagery in your way of the People."

"We leave, you are tired." He spoke gently, taking her arm. "Can you ride?"

"I think so." She mounted Ivoire with Shadow Panther's help. "The body . . . the Creek." Motioning toward the water she averted her eyes.

"His comrades will come for him. We must be off before they arrive."

The village was slumbering as they rode inside the gates. Aimée had shuddered to see a shrouded figure laying on a raised platform some distance from the stockade on a small rise in the woods. The shaman priests had wasted no time removing the slave's body from Long Town. As a slave she would not be entitled to any of the burial rites of the Chickasaw. Soon wild animals and the elements would erase her earthly remains. Shadow Panther had sent Aimée to Nancy's house block while he rode to alert the chiefs to a possible raid. The old healer woman was deep in sleep when Aimée crept into the summer house. The scent of smoke was heavy in the still, humid air, telling Aimée that the woman's hut had been burned to the ground. On the morrow another would be erected a few yards away from the ruins of the old. The spirit of the dead would be at rest.

Worn out and trembling with fatigue, Aimée tried to seek the oblivion of sleep, but her over-stimulated nerves would not allow that release. When the first pale light of dawn shone down through the fire hole, Shadow Panther slipped into the lodge and beside her on the bed platform.

"You are not at slumber," he whispered, seeing her pale tired visage with the huge dark circles beneath her eyes. "Stretch out beside me I shall release the tension."

Rolling over so she lay on her stomach she felt his long tapered fingers stroke down her spine. In her ear he chanted a low, quieting song as if she were a fretful child. His touch was soothing as he rubbed sore muscles, nerves that had been tense with fear. He rubbed down the backs of her thighs to the aching muscles of her legs, his fingers always firm but gentle.

When he turned her over with a firm but tender touch she felt excitement rise where there had been only fatigue. Looking up into those ebony eyes that were now lit with a smoldering fire, a dizzying current of desire surge through her veins. Her arms lifted up to embrace his broad shoulders gleaming bronze in the flickering light of the center fire.

His arms encircled her as he slowly pressed her to his long length. His lips were warm as they lightly kissed her temples then down to eyelids, the tip of her nose and finally pressed against her moist waiting mouth. His kiss sang through her veins as he devoured the softness of her lips.

They spoke not a word, allowing their touch, their warm bodies, their mouths that tasted and caressed, to communicate their longing and total joy in one another. They were gentle, teasing with one another, taking time to explore, to arouse, to give each other a sensual pleasure.

When he entered her she was ready, crying out for release from the exquisite delight of her arousal that caused her to vibrate with a liquid fire. Together they moved in perfect rhythm finding a tempo that bound their bodies as one. She melted against him till all the world was filled with his essence. Soaring higher and higher, they found the pinnacle of ecstasy and, exploding in a shower of fiery sensations, found perfect contentment.

Aimée sighed as the anxiety of the night slipped away. She experienced a sense of peace flowing between them as she lay held in his tender embrace, her head on his chest, listening to the music of his beating heart. When she entered the quiet of sleep she did not know, but it was when the sun was high that she opened eyes still heavy with slumber.

What had awakened her? She looked about the lodge then saw her husband sitting quietly across from her on the mats strewn across the hard dirt floor. He was cleaning the long rifle he always carried in a buckskin pouch slung from his saddle. His handsome visage was the mask of a stranger, painted half red, half black. She knew what that meant, and it made her blood run cold. He was going out with a war party.

"No!" she cried, struggling to a sitting position not caring she was nude.

"I must, Green Eyes. The Spanish wish to meet with us. They have sent a messenger. We will hear them out. Foolish Wolf's Friend asked for a council."

"You go to the fort?"

"Aye, we meet outside the gates."

"Take me with you," she pleaded, hand outstretched as if in supplication.

"That I cannot do, Green Eyes. You are safer here." He bent over his rifle not looking at her.

"Here with savages," she muttered scornfully.

"Would you prefer the company of Rodrigo Hernandez?" He asked in icy tones, his eyes flashing fire.

"Oui, to that of a wild pack of barbarians who would steal a mother's child from her arms," she spat out, the memory of the previous day flooding her frightened mind. Terror made her thoughtless and cruel. She knew only that she didn't want to be left behind alone with the Chickasaw. An icy contempt flashed in his eyes as he rose to his feet. His handsome features were arranged in a cold remote mask as he stared down at her. "You will stay with French Nancy. I travel alone. I see that you still have ties to the white world in your heart. 'Tis no matter. You stay here. You are the wife of a chief. Remember it."

"I want to see my sister!" She cried out, as she watched him leave the lodge without a backward look. She pressed her hand over her face in despair as tears blinded her eyes and choked her throat. He had left her, and their last words had been said in anger. What if he never returned, and they were the last words they ever spoke to one another? She yielded to the compulsive sobs that shook her slender form.

Part Four

Destiny grants us our wishes, but in its own way, in order to give us something beyond our wishes.

Gothe

There's a divinity that shapes our ends,/
Rough-hew them how we will.

Shakespeare

Chapter Twenty-six

A smoky blue haze that was part wood-smoke, part fog, not yet burned away by the rising sun, hung in the lowland near the stream. It veiled the two women giving them privacy as thcy greeted the morning in their daily ritual of bathing. The feminine voices rose in the still air calling their good morning to Grandmother Sun, and the song seemed to beckon the golden light as it broke over the tops of the giant cedars. Aimée shivered as she quickly dressed after bathing in the icy water. The early morning air was heavy with the harbinger of autumn. Lifting her head she breathed deeply of the wood-smoke fragrance that struck a cord of remembrance. It was true, she thought, each season has its own particular scent and color. Here in the domain of the Chickasaw she was even more aware of each nuance as Mother Nature changed her attire.

She dressed quickly and looked skyward once more as the dark vee silhouetted against the azure sky came closer to land with perfect grace on the sparkling water of the stream. It was her ducklings, now grown almost to maturity, trying their wings. The instinct that called them was strong, stronger then their tie to her.

"They are wild creatures, *ma petite.* You must allow them to fly free. They will return to you in time," French Nancy said wisely from where she gathered the last of the season's herbs.

"Will Shadow Panther also return in time?" Aimée asked in wry tones, bending to fondle the fat little puppy she had adopted a few days before. The creature had one leg shorter than the other and its owner had been about to put it to death. She had intervened—to everyone's shocked amusement, for a dog that could not work would not be tolerated. The little black and white pup was now her constant companion, helping to assuage some of her loneliness.

"He will return unharmed as I have said before," the old healer-woman muttered, "you must have patience. The life of a chief's wife is one of enduring long absences. You have the little one for company, and perhaps soon a babe as well." Her blue eyes twinkled at Aimée's shocked expression.

"How do you know?" Her hand touched her still flat belly.

"You have not gone to the woman's hut in two moons. Did you not realize what this could mean?" French Nancy asked as she gathered bunches of sweet fern and wild mint.

"I tried to put it from my mind," Aimée murmured, with a frown creasing her delicate features. Could she be carrying Shadow Panther's child? The thought was both thrilling and frightening. She didn't want to give birth out here in the wilderness. The memory of the slave woman was still with her, even though it had been almost two months since that tragic night. Almost two months had past since Shadow Panther had left for the council meeting with the Spanish at the fort on the bluff overlooking the Mississippi—the fort where her sister lived in the house of Rodrigo Hernandez.

"You are frightened," the wise old woman stated, as she tied the gathered herbs in bundles and placed them in her basket. " 'Tis always so with the first one, but I will take care of you. There is nothing to fear.

Come, we return to the village."

Nothing to fear, Aimée thought as she felt a whisper of terror run through her. Perhaps she was only late with her monthly—it had happened before when she was worried. Sighing, she prayed this was one of those times. Tying the long leather thong about the puppy's neck to use as a leash, she gathered up her basket. Leading the dog she had named Bijou, because of its bright black eyes that shown like jewels, she followed the spry old woman back toward the village.

As they neared Long Town the corn fields of the women were filled with tall stalks, an emerald wave of leaves blowing in the light breeze. It was late September, the month Aimée knew the Chickasaw called the moon of the Maize, or Great Corn. The sunflowers that edged the fields were turning their black faces up to face the rising sun as they passed. Purple martins darted in and out of the gourd houses the People had placed on poles throughout the fields, catching insects.

"The harvest begins," French Nancy said with satisfaction, as they approached where women and children were going down between the rows collecting ears of corn in large pack baskets carried on their backs.

Aimée gave a weary sigh, now realizing the purpose of large oddly-shaped baskets they had carried with them to the stream. Today was the beginning of the harvest. It would be a day of backbreaking work.

" 'Twill be hard work, *ma petite,* but then comes the Green Corn Ceremony. Shadow Panther will return for this, the most important ceremony of the year." The old woman's blue eyes twinkled as she saw how her words caused Aimée to straighten her slumped shoulders. The thought of her handsome beloved banished the weariness from her slender form.

"What is the Green Corn Ceremony?" Aimée asked, as she slung the pack basket across her shoulders.

"Ah, 'tis many things, a rite of thanksgiving, a quest for purity, a time of forgiveness for past transgressions. For all, it is a time when people try to straighten out their affairs and make resolutions to make their lives better then the year before. The lodges are cleaned and the fires relit from the sacred fire in the plaza."

"You are sure that Shadow Panther will return in time for this ceremony?" Aimée kept her face averted from the knowing old woman so she could not see the concern in her jade eyes.

"He will come, for the village on the Wolf as been invited to the ceremony. Here he has made his camp while holding council with the Spanish. The Wolf village has been sent their bundle telling of the time of the Green Corn."

"The bundle?"

"When the day was decided by the chiefs, pieces of split cane were tied into bundles representing the number of days remaining until the ceremony would begin. The bundles of sticks then are given to messengers who travel to all the Chickasaw towns. The *Miko,* or chief, of each village will throw away one stick each sunrise till all are gone, then the clans will know it is the day to assemble in Long Town."

So, thought Aimée, her husband would be staying very near the fort at the village where she had been first taken after capture. He would be so near Mignon, she realized with a pang, wondering how close the council would be held to the fort. Might he see her sister, even speak with her to tell her that Aimée was all right?

Lost in her musings, Aimée picked the golden ears of corn without really being aware of what she was doing. It was with a start that she heard a gentle voice call her name.

Looking up, she felt Bijou pull on the rawhide leash as the little dog leapt toward the women approaching her from the opposite field. It was Soft Wind carrying the dead slave's baby and beside her, Dark Dove.

"The little one is fussy. I believe he is teething. Does French Nancy have something I could rub on his gums?" The gentle visage of Soft Wind smiled at her, but Dark Dove simply gave her a sulky stare.

Aimée could now understand Chickasaw quite well and even converse slowly in the language. Swallowing both the anger she felt at seeing the baby in the cradleboard on Soft Wind's back and the memories the child evoked, she gestured toward where French Nancy was working.

"Why do you work these fields when Shadow Panther has fields as far as the eye can see at Eagle's Roost?" The silky voice of Dark Dove questioned her after her sister had walked over to confer with the old healer.

"What do you mean?" Aimée stared into the triumphant black eyes of the waiting woman. A woman bent on some twisted game she realized dimly.

"He has not told you of this, and you being his wife. This is very surprising," Dark Dove feigned shock, but it was all too obvious she was enjoying baiting Aimée.

"No, but I am sure you are about to tell me," Aimée replied in dry tones.

"I will show you," Dark Dove answered, casting a look over her shoulder at the other women working not far away. "You must say nothing to the others. This afternoon when all rest I will come for you. I will show you Shadow Panther's secret."

She was gone before Aimée could make a startled reply, swiftly vanishing into the tall dense stalks of corn. Aimée pondered Dark Dove's cryptic statement. She couldn't remember anyone mentioning the name Eagle's Roost. Her curiosity was aroused, but she was uneasy about accompanying Dark Dove anywhere. The woman hated her, it was obvious. What mischief was she up to now? Would she come that afternoon when the village took time to rest from their labors, or was this just another attempt to taunt her? Placing another ear of corn in the basket, now grown heavy with the morning's work, she decided only time would tell.

The transparent golden rays of late afternoon sun slanted down in front of the winter lodge, falling across Aimée's shoulder onto the soft ivory doeskin stretched out in front of her. During this time every day she tried once more to draw, for she had missed her sketching. Taking several feathers dropped by the mallards she had cut the tips into finely pointed quills. French Nancy had taught her how to make pigments from the various clays and berries. Impressed with her skill, the old woman had given her several doeskins stretched taut between sticks for canvas.

"Sit still just a few moments longer, Gray Rabbit," Aimée pleaded of the bright-eyed little girl who giggled and teased Bijou with a ball as she sat for her portrait. The children had been amazed at first that the silver-haired white woman could paint their likeness with such accuracy. They crowded around to watch until finally their interest was drawn to something else. Aimée had been trying for weeks to paint portraits of a representative group of the village. Children, old people, young mothers, warriors if they would allow her to stare at them, but this charming little girl was rapidly becoming tired of posing.

"Where you learn this?" The peevish voice of Dark Dove startled her, so intent had she been on capturing the countenance of Gray Rabbit.

"It has always been with me since I was very young," she

replied, continuing with her drawing. It was true, it seemed she had been sketching since she could first hold a pen or piece of charcoal in her hand.

"This I would never allow, to have my face on a skin. A witch could do such a thing to capture my soul," Dark Dove pronounced in haughty tones, holding the reins of a Chickasaw pony in one hand as she stared down at the portrait of the little girl.

"I think your soul is safe from me," Aimée murmured dryly.

"What you mean by that?"

"It is not important. Are you here to show me this Eagle's Roost?"

"We must be careful not to be seen. No one is allowed to speak of this to you on Shadow Panther's orders," Dark Dove explained in a hushed voice so the child couldn't hear.

"I see. May I ask why you have decided to disobey his orders?" Aimée asked, as she put away her pens and the pots containing the pigments.

"No one tells Dark Dove what to do. You want to see his secret or not?"

"You may go home, Gray Rabbit. I shall paint you again tomorrow." Waiting till the little girl had gone Aimée said," I will go with you against my better judgment. First I must tie up Bijou, and then fetch Ivoire."

The village slumbered in the warmth of late afternoon as the two young women rode out the front gates. There were few about to see them, but Aimée knew that the braves that guarded the stockade were aware of their leaving. Perhaps they thought they were only out for a ride now that the tasks of the day were finished.

Dark Dove took a path through the woods that Aimée had not seen. It was faint, but now that she was learning the Chickasaw way of tracking could tell it was well traveled. The twisting trail lead in the opposite direction from the communal fields and the lagoon where she and Shadow Panther had spent their wedding night. Dark Dove set a breakneck pace, but Aimée urged Ivoire on, keeping up with the devious Indian maiden. They rode through flat bottomland that was swampy in places till they reached a swiftly flowing river. Here the path seemed to widen and she could see the wagon tracks in the rutted soil.

Where in the world was Dark Dove taking her, Aimée mused. The wagon tracks had surprised her for she had seen no wagons among the Chickasaw. What were they doing out here so far from any settlers? Her questions were soon answered for as they rounded a bend in the river she saw to her amazement a dock of wooden planks jutting out into the water. The sound of men working turned her amazed gaze away from the river and there on a slight rise she saw it. A house of two stories, a white man's manor house, painted white with beaded siding and green shutters at the long glass windows. A lane of cypress trees led from the river to the front double door shaded by a portico supported by two slender columns. Beyond she could see outbuildings, stables, a barn, and slave cabins. Further in the distance she saw cleared land and arpent after arpent of fields fertile and lush ready for harvest.

"What is this place?" she called to Dark Dove, who had reined in her horse and was watching her with an expectant expression.

"Eagle's Roost. Shadow Panther's, or should I say Sebastian Macleod's plantation." There was triumph and a wicked glee in her voice as she watched the expression of shock, and then disbelief, come over Aimée's stunned visage.

"It cannot be," she breathed, staring at this vision. It was so unlike from the village of Long Town and the endless forest that surrounded it.

"Come, I show you," Dark Dove called, starting down the lane of Cypress trees.

Following beside her Aimée noticed African slaves working the fields. She knew that the Colberts who ran the ferry had slaves. French Nancy had told her of other half-bloods who owned slaves and plantations, like the white settlers who were streaming into the Chickasaw domain from the former colonies, now states, of Georgia and the Carolina's. Could all this belong to her husband? She knew his father was wealthy, but she thought he had left all that behind to live with his mother's people. Why had he never told her of Eagle's Roost?

Reaching the house they dismounted, tying their mounts to an iron hitching post that might have come from New Orleans. A tall, aloof woman had come to the double doors seeing them ride up the alley. She was dressed in the muslin dress of a slave with a tignon of gingham about her head. Gold earrings dangled in her ears, but she was neither African nor Chickasaw but a blend of the two. She did not look pleased to see them.

"What you doing here?" Her words were harsh and directed at Dark Dove, but she could not help staring at the woman in Chickasaw dress with the hair of silver-gold and eyes of jade.

"Proud Eagle Woman, I bring you Shadow Panther's wife, Mistress Macleod," Dark Dove announced, malicious glee in her black eyes. "This is the woman who takes care of the white man's lodge when Shadow Panther is with the People."

Aimée could only nod as the housekeeper stared coldly at her. What the woman thought she could only guess. She gave a brief nod, but said not a word.

"We come in," Dark Dove stated in commanding tones, brushing past her.

They entered a wide entrance hall that ran the width of the house. A large parlor lay on the left while a dining room and library shared the right side of the mansion. A broad staircase rose at the back of the hall to the second floor.

Aimée observed the beautiful woods used in the wainscoting of the walls of each chamber. The house was furnished with fine English furniture and turkey carpets on the polished floors. She remembered her husband had lived in the American towns of Charlestown and Williamsburg. Eagle's Roost showed the influence of their architecture and furnishings. But what drew her eye was a large portrait over the mantel in the parlor. It was of an older man dressed in the formal dress of a gentleman, but the handsome visage so like her beloved told her this must be his father. There was no mistake—this luxurious house belonged to Shadow Panther. *No,* she corrected herself, this was the abode of the white half of her husband. This was the manor house of Sebastian Macleod.

As she stared about the lovely chamber, so unexpected in the wilderness, her shock turned to fury. He had taken her to the Chickasaw village, let her live in primitive conditions while all the time, not even an hour's ride away, there had been this comfortable house. She now understood his frequent absences when he would be gone for several days. Instead of hunting, he was here at Eagle's Roost seeing to his plantation.

"You see enough. Time we leave," Dark Dove interrupted her thoughts, a smile of pure revenge on her sensuous mouth. She sensed Aimée's anger and hurt at her husband's secret.

On the ride back to Long Town Aimée's mind raced with the implications of what she had seen. Her hand touched her belly. She realized if she was carrying Shadow Panther's child it would not have to be born in a hut, but in a strong wood house that would shelter it well from the coming winter. She experienced a gamut of emotions—anger, relief, frustration, and a deep sense of hurt that he had not confided the knowledge of Eagle's Roost to her. What could have been his reason, she wondered again and again.

The mauve shadows of the early autumn twilight were falling across the village, mingling in the air with the lavender-gray wood-smoke from a myriad campfires. The sweet melancholy of the harvest season seemed to permeate the atmosphere as they rode through the tall open gates of the stockade. A few dry golden leaves scattered under Ivoire's hoofs as the dainty mare made her sure way home.

Dark Dove had disappeared the minute they reached the village. Aimée had hardly noticed her departure, for her mind was occupied with the startling sight she had just seen. She could not wait to question French Nancy, and then realized with a pang that the old woman had kept this information from her all the time they had spent together.

After seeing to the mare, Aimée scattered corn for the ducks that still flew into the lodge garden to roost for the night. She could not put off facing French Nancy any longer. Her feeling that the old woman had some how let her down, betrayed their friendship by withholding the secret of Eagle's Roost, had to be dealt with for her own peace of mind.

The fragrance of roasting meat sent her nostrils aquiver as she entered the winter house. Bijou hopped to meet her from her place by the fire with a frantic wagging of her tail. They had moved back into the sturdier structure when the nights cooled. Her stomach ached with hunger, but she could not wait to demand an explanation from the old healer woman she had become to look upon in one sense as a mother.

"You are late, *ma petite fleur,*" French Nancy observed, as she stirred the pot hanging on a hook over the fire.

"There is something I must speak about to you," Aimée replied in a voice that cracked with emotion.

Piercing blue eyes looked up at her from the mat where the old woman sat. She had noticed the tremor in Aimée's voice, and her fine-tuned awareness of the hidden feelings of people alerted her to the mood of the trembling young woman she had come to look upon as a daughter.

Holding up a wrinkled hand to stop her she said," We talk, but first there is someone here you have waited for these long days."

Peering into the dark shadows of the lodge, Aimée saw a movement from behind the hide partition. Joy flooded her heart as she saw a beloved masculine form appear and come toward her. Shadow Panther had returned.

"Mon Dieu!" A soft gasp escaped her as she stared unbelieving at the other figure that joined him. Standing transfixed, her jade eyes widened with astonishment as she gazed at a face she thought to never see again.

Chapter Twenty-seven

"Mignon!"

The cry was torn from the depths of Aimée's heart. Holding out her arms, as tears of happiness flooded her eyes, she ran the few feet that separated them to clasp her sister into her embrace.

The two young women wept with joy as they held on to one another as if they would never let go. Bijou ran in circles around them lending her yelps to the confusion. The winter lodge was filled with a sense of rejoicing that made the old woman smile, and the proud warrior watch with an intent gaze.

"I . . . I thought to never . . . never see you again," Mignon sobbed into Aimée's arms. "Sebastian . . . Sebastian saved me from . . . Rodrigo. He wanted me to . . . to marry him." Mignon lifted her head and gave the silent warrior a radiant smile.

"Merci, thank you," Aimée said fervently, her heart in her eyes that pierced the distance between her husband and herself. Never had she loved him as much as she did at this moment. His quiet strength, his ability to read the innermost secrets of her heart, his gentle care of the fragile Mignon – it all overwhelmed her.

"I must go to the purifying lodge, beloved woman-wife, as is custom after a warrior's return, but I shall return to you," his controlled voice almost broke as he stared hungrily at his beautiful wife. He wanted her with a passion that warred with his sense of duty and honor. His ebony eyes smoldering with the fire of desire devoured the shimmering sight of her for one brief moment, then he left while he still could find the strength of will.

"No, oh not yet," the moan was pulled from the depths of her being as she pressed her fingers to her trembling lips. She knew the ritual of a returning warrior. She would not see him again for three days.

"Sebastian . . . will come back," Mignon repeated, hugging her sister's shoulders in an attempt at comfort.

"The little one is right. Come, we eat, and then you must tell me of your journey," French Nancy told them calmly, gesturing to the mats beside her and the bowls that rested there.

Only after hearing of Mignon's daring capture by Shadow Panther did Aimée realize she had not thought once about Eagle's Roost since she had returned. Her sister had taken to French Nancy in the same way that she had to Sebastian. Aimée did not want to do anything to upset the tired girl. She knew the old woman also felt it was best they talk later, for she had sent her a warning glance as Mignon had haltingly told her story. There would be time to find out why the two people who professed to care about her had in fact kept many things from her. She was beginning to wonder what else they had neglected to tell her.

Yet somehow, in the next two days, she and French Nancy were never alone. Mignon had become the old woman's shadow, eager to learn everything she could about the life of the Chickasaw. Aimée realized that instead of being frightened of the strange new life she was leading, Mignon felt safe for the first time in her life. French Nancy was the mother she never had, and since she could not speak Chickasaw no one required her to talk at great length. It was startling, but with French Nancy, as with Shadow Panther, Mignon could converse with barely a stutter.

The two sisters were kept busy morning to night as they helped French Nancy prepare for the coming Green Corn Ceremony. Everyone was busy in the village as Long Town was filling with clans of visiting Chickasaw from every part of the domain. The warriors repaired the public buildings, and the women cleaned their houses, renewed their hearths, and tried to find room for all the visitors.

"Today at sundown the men will observe a strict fast until the second sunrise," French Nancy explained to the two young women as they greeted the morning at the stream. "They will meet in the plaza, but all women, children, and dogs are to be excluded from the square. Women and children are to speak in a gentle tone and to preserve harmony. Four sentinels will stand at the four entrances to the plaza to keep out impure animals and people. Keep Bijou on a leash or tied in the lodge. She would be shot if she happened to enter the vicinity of the square."

Aimée picked the little dog up and held it to her breast. Once more she was faced with the way of the People, and she found it angered her. Shadow Panther had been gone for almost two months, but instead of coming to her he spent his first days in the sweat lodge. Now he was now going to fast and keep away from her because it was the way of the People. No man could touch a woman till the last night of the ceremony.

"Are we allowed any part in the celebration?" Aimée inquired in a peevish tone.

"On the morning of the fourth day we will carry

cooked food to the plaza, having relit our fires from the sacred fire. After serving the warriors, in strict accordance with rank, the men will dance for us. By evening they will ask the women to dance. Anyone who does not will be given a fine, but that seldom happens. The ceremony ends and all are purified for the coming year. All crimes except murder are forgiven. People who are angry at each other are forgiven and become reconciled. 'Tis good to have a time when all are cleansed and make resolutions to live a better life."

"Are lies forgiven as well?" Aimée asked, as they reached the lodge and Mignon left them to see to the chores French Nancy had assigned.

"Lies, *ma petite?* Why do I feel you are troubled about something?"

"I have seen Eagle's Roost. Why was I not told about the plantation?"

"Dark Dove showed you," French Nancy stated, sighing at her nod. "Shadow Panther did not think you were ready. You still had much to learn about the ways of the People."

"And why must I learn these ways when he has a fine house and plantation? Why must I learn to live as a Chickasaw?" There was anger and confusion in her voice.

"Because Shadow Panther is a Chickasaw chief. Whatever else your husband is, he is in his own heart a Chickasaw. He desires that you understand this side of him, that you accept with all your heart who he truly is in the deepest part of his being."

"And if I cannot?" Aimée inquired bitterly.

"Then you are, indeed, a foolish woman." There was rebuke in French Nancy's voice, and disappointment in her blue eyes, as she entered the lodge with her basket full of nuts she had gathered at the stream.

The old woman's words stayed with Aimée in the next days as the Green Corn Ceremony took over the attention of everyone in Long Town. Mignon was entranced by everything Chickasaw, even the soft doeskin skirt and bodice she had been given by Aimée. It had not taken her long to learn to play the reed flute of the People, and she would delight the children with her song as she had done at the fort.

"They consider her one of the Chosen Ones," French Nancy confided to Aimée , as the women prepared the food to take to the plaza on this morning of the fourth day of the ceremony. "She talks with her flute, her voice is music. Only a Chosen One would have such a gift, they have decided."

"She does seem to have found a home here," Aimée admitted. "She is accepted for herself, even if she is different then the others. This was not the way in New Orleans."

"Your sister does not fight her destiny. The way of the People is comforting to her for her wants are not large. A simple way of life allows her a certain security that she was lacking."

"You are a wise woman," Aimée said quietly as they lifted up the food baskets to take to the plaza.

"As are you, *ma chère* when you listen to your heart. Come, the men await us, and I have a small part to play in the ceremony as an old honored woman of the tribe."

There was an excitement among the gathered women at the entrance of the plaza. The evening before they had been given splinters of flaming pitch pine from the sacred fire to relight the fires that had been extinguished in each lodge. The Chickasaw women then had outdone themselves cooking large quantities of the new corn and vegetables for this feast on the fourth day of the festival, and after days away from their men they were eager to take part in the dancing and celebration that would signal the end of the ceremony.

Mignon, usually shy to the point of being reclusive, was eager to see the dancing and happily accompanied the two women dressed in her finest Chickasaw dress. Today she would be presented to the People and given her Indian name of Singing Bird. About her forehead she wore a headband beaded with the outline of a bird as blue as her eyes.

The tension among the women was building to a fevered pitch when one of the high priest's assistants motioned for them to enter the plaza. Led by French Nancy carrying a basket adorned with white feathers for purity, the women moved forward, the tortoise shell rattles on their legs joining the sound of the pottery drums coming from the center of the square. Mignon proudly lifted a Chickasaw flute to her lips and the high quick sound floated on the autumn air to mingle with the others in the sacred song French Nancy had taught her.

Aimée felt the fine hairs on the back of her neck rise so stirred was she by the solemn pagentry. Following the old healer woman she walked to the men seated on mats in front of the council house. Each man was served food in strict order according to his rank. As they moved down the line of the chiefs Aimée's eyes met the blazing black orbs she knew so well.

His features were as if cast in stone, but as she raised her head he captured her eyes with his and they alone betrayed his ardor. They held her for a brief moment when time stood still and all the others around them vanished into dust. They sent her a private message of passionate yearning and desire. Twin flames smoldered in those black coals, kindling a fire that raced through her being. She felt the strong bond that seemed to draw them together till they merged into one steady flame of spirit. It always took her breath away when it occurred, shaking her to her very core.

"Come!" French Nancy hissed, bringing her back to reality, back from that special place where only the two of them could go.

The women seated themselves with the children across from the men. All feasted on as many as fifty or sixty different dishes. There were all kinds of dried meat, fish, oil, corn in a dozen different dishes, beans, pumpkins, squash, wild fruit and honey. The People ate their fill, celebrating the abundance of the harvest. Later the high priest gave a speech admonishing all in eloquent language to stay pure, to keep the rules of separation and behave properly so they might all enjoy good health, and the rainmaking spirits would bring plenty of rain, that they would be victorious over their enemies; but if they failed to abide by the rules of the People they could have drought, death or captivity from their enemies, witches would walk among them and cause disease. His speech ended and the warriors, their heads covered with white swan feathers and carrying eagle fans in their hands, danced in three concentric circles around the sacred fire as the early autumn twilight fell in long gray-mauve shadows across the square.

Aimée watched the lithe figure of her husband, his form glowing bronze in the light of the center fire as he moved around it with the other warriors. Across the square she saw Dark Dove, her eyes glued on the dancers, and she saw the longing in those feminine almond-shaped eyes. A slight shudder shook her as she knew that the young woman would never give up trying to gain Shadow Panther's affections. He had become her obsession.

"Look, he wants you to join him," Mignon hissed without the usual stutter, pointing to where her husband stood. He stood silhouetted against the orange-blue flames in the gloom of early twilight extending his hand. The gaze that glowed with a savage inner fire was so compelling, his magnetism so potent, that she moved forward as if in a dream.

Was it the drums that beat with such an erotic rhythm or her heart? She heard the crowd begin to chant a low, husky chant that spoke of the joining of a man and woman. She began to move and sway with the rhythm of the drums and the low song. Facing Shadow Panther, but not touching, they moved in perfect time with one another. She could not believe this was her body that was dancing with such uninhibited ardor, slender hips rolling, teasing this man who devoured her with hot, dark eyes. She was woman—sensuous, ripe, hungry for her man with unashamed passion. Remembering the other woman who also wanted and watched her husband with unabashed yearning, Aimée moved closer to him till her breasts and hips almost touched him, flinging back the long silver-gold hair that she knew he loved so much. She arched backward, offering up her lush body in a graceful movement that caused a moan to spring from his throat.

He could not wait to have her a moment longer. As she arched low in front of him he swept her up into his arms. The crowd gave a collective sigh as he strode from the plaza, her arms about his neck, her face pressed into the hollow of his throat. The cries of the women joining the men in their dance echoed in his ears as he left the square for the winter house and Aimée's bed furs.

The lodge was dark and warm from the newly lit center fire, fragrant with the cedar shavings French Nancy had scattered about the floor and the ceremonial herbs that burned in the low flames. As he placed her on her feet beside the bed platform they drew back together, pressing against each other as if to relearn the beloved contours of the other's body. Soft breasts against hard sinewy chest, erect manhood pressed into the soft ivory belly, thighs intertwined as the flowering vine around the towering cedar. Hands stroking the beloved planes of back and spine. Only the sound of their quickened breaths and deep sighs of yearning and desire broke the silence of the night.

"How I have wanted to hold you, touch you, taste your sweetness," he breathed against her temple, brushing a kiss into the silky tendrils that curled out from under her head band. His hands stroked her back under the shining fall of hair that she had worn down about her waist to tempt him. From time to time he would wind the tresses about his fingers.

"I am without a center when you are gone, my husband," she whispered, her hands caressing the planes of his back, reveling in the feel of his heated skin.

"I, too, feel incomplete without you. And when first I see you again, I feel such joy, for in your eyes I see a reflection of my soul."

Looking up at him she gave a smile of recognition. Tenderly his mouth claimed hers in a kiss that was a seal of deep abiding commitment. Her lips parted to receive him fully like a morning glory the first rays of the sun. Together their tongues danced in a silent melody of love.

A mutual shudder ran along the length of their two bodies as they both knew they must be closer still. Trembling hands pulled breechclout, skirt and bodice from their heated bodies. A deep sigh rose from both throats to mingle in the dark lodge as they sought the pleasure of each other's satin skin and nude form. There were no barriers between them. They could touch, stroke, caress the beloved texture they had hungered for in the long nights they were apart.

Pressing her down on the ebony fur of the bearskin that covered the bed platform, he spread her silver-gold hair out from under her to rest like a radiant fan from the pale flower of her visage. Slowly, almost with reverence, he circled each throbbing rose nipple. Taking one dainty rose bud in his moist mouth he sucked it lightly till she moaned with pleasure, her hips arching up. Long tapered fingers sought her moist waiting womanhood, moving inside her, stoking the fire that smoldered in the center of her being.

Her nails dug into his back as he rose above her, mounting her as she begged him for release. She raised her hips up in wide circles of passionate abandonment as he plunged inside her velvet sheath, cupping the soft ivory mounds of her bottom so he might penetrate her deeper still. They both desired a joining so total, so complete that they were for a brief splendid time, indeed, one entity. Twin flames that joined and burned as one all-consuming radiant light.

Later as they lay in each other's embrace they knew a perfect contentment. The world did not exist for them when they were together. It was as if they were on another plane where nothing else mattered but that they were in the solace of each other's company. They felt in these quiet times that there were no boundaries, no barriers, only a complete acceptance of this strange bond that nothing could destroy.

"There are many differences between us, Green Eyes, but when we are like this they are only small specks of dust. They are only illusions. What is real is this belonging we feel to one another. Apart we feel incomplete, only together do we feel in perfect balance. This is all that matters," he spoke softly holding her to his chest, his lips against her hair.

Staring out into the darken lodge where the only light came from the center fire, Aimée sighed, touched to her core by his words. She understood his meaning about the strange bond that drew them together, before they had even met. His face had haunted her a thousand times in dreams before she had ever set eyes on him. He claimed to have seen her in his vision quest, the most important event in a young boy's life. They seemed destined to become lovers, but what strange twists did fate have in store for them. Her husband had many sides to his character, sides he had kept hidden from her. Unwilling to break the spell of their lovemaking she would put off revealing her knowledge of Eagle's Roost, but the time of reckoning must come. Would their bond of love withstand that test, or would it break apart under the revelation of the two sides of the mercurial, compelling man who held her to his heart.

Chapter Twenty-eight

The early morning sun shone on the frost that lay like a lace cloth on the ground, making it appear to be sprinkled with diamonds. Aimée, shivering in the cold air, pulled the light but warm mantle of mallard feathers close about her chest. How she wished she were back in the warm sanctuary of the winter lodge still nestled under the bed furs in the circle of Shadow Panther's embrace. It was not to be, for as she was a chief's wife she must be an example to the other women. The winter was approaching, and there was food to be gathered for storage. Every moment of the waning daylight must be used in the forage.

The forest was a patchwork quilt of color, the brilliant red of the sumac, the yellow-gold and amber of the sassafras, tulip poplar, and sweetgum on this early morning. A few leaves drifted on the veils of blue smoke that wafted through the trees. The Chickasaw women and children were carefully burning away the debris on the forest floor. When all was consumed and the flames died out, they gathered the nuts that lay exposed to view. Aimée tried to warm herself on the meager heat from the burning leaves as she waited to fill her basket.

"It is going well. There should be no hungry bellies in the starving time of late winter," French Nancy commented with satisfaction, as she directed the boys who set the small fires.

"You have seen starvation?" Aimée questioned in surprise. This was something she had never considered. The Chickasaw were able farmers and excellent hunters. She couldn't imagine any of them going hungry, there seemed such abundance in the village.

"When the rains do not come, or come too much, and there is little corn and beans the winter can be harsh. 'Tis when the children cry in the lodges from hunger, and the warriors must hunt far afield to feed their families."

Aimée unconsciously touched her still-flat stomach thinking of the baby she carried in her womb. She had not told her husband yet that she was with child, but soon he would notice for her breasts were already growing fuller. He had been back with her in the lodge for several days, and still she had not broached the subject of Eagle's Roost. She had in some strange way hoped that he would confess its existence to her now that the cold weather had come, the time of the Eagle, the Chickasaw called it. Surely, he didn't expect her to spend the winter in a lodge, snug though it might be, when he owned a wooden house, a mansion that would better keep out the frigid winds.

"Come, we gather the nuts. The fire has died," French Nancy told her, interrupting her musings. Mignon was already quickly filling her basket.

Staring down at her hands, the nails broken from hard work, the palms callused as well, Aimée felt a growing anger. If her husband would not tell her of the plantation then she would inform him this very night that she knew of its existence. She would not have their child born in a hut when its heritage was a fine house and land. She had reckoned the child would be born in late March. It could still be cold then; under no circumstances would she endanger her baby's life.

The sun was high overhead before the women stopped their gathering to return to the village with overflowing baskets. Aimée was exhausted with a low pain in the small of her back. How she would welcome a long rest in the sun in front of the winter lodge.

"Ah, it is a good year, indeed, plenty of corn in Long Town's storehouses. Many skins to treat, much meat to smoke," French Nancy said in triumph as they passed the huge communal storehouses filled to the roofs with ears of corn protected from insects by wrapping each one with grass and then plastering it all over with wet clay mixed with grass.

Aimée and Mignon both rolled their eyes in remembrance of the backbreaking work preparing those ears for storage. Every woman and child had worked from dawn to dusk the last few days since the Green Corn Ceremony. Aimée sighed as she realized there would be continuing hard work preparing the numerous skins the hunters brought back from the hunt. A Chickasaw woman's life was certainly not one of leisure.

Bijou greeted them with delight as they untied her from her stake as they entered the lodge block. They had been afraid she could have gotten burned in the clearing fires.

"Rest a moment, *ma petite*" the old healing woman told Aimée as they entered the lodge, now pungent with the scent of the drying berries, pumpkins, and squash that were piled high in baskets around walls of the winter house. Huge bunches of herbs hung from pegs in the walls and from the rafters.

Aimée sank down gratefully on a bear rug by the smoldering fire. She accepted with thanks a gourd cup of the delightful drink French Nancy made from the ripe pods of the honey locust. She helped herself to the stew that simmered in a pot over the fire. It was delicious, made of rabbit, various roots, and flavored with wild onion, and the roots of the sassafras to thicken and flavor it. In fact it reminded her somewhat of the gumbo that was a staple of the diet in every New Orleans home. They too used sassafras as an ingredient, only they ground it very fine and called it filé powder.

"You look . . . t. . . tired. Are you feeling well?" Mignon inquired as she too helped herself to the stew. The Chickasaw usually ate only a morning and evening meal, but a pot of food was kept cooking over the lodge fire for those who felt hungry any time of day.

"I am fine," Aimée reassured her sister, sending French Nancy a warning glance. She did not want to tell her sister of the baby till she told Shadow Panther. "After we finish I shall show you how to sew a feather mantle. I have gathered baskets of feathers. 'Tis a warm garment for winter."

"I have long admired yours," Mignon replied, content that there was nothing wrong with her older sister.

When the frigid wind and ice come we shall be snug in Eagle's Roost, Aimée thought with satisfaction, careful to let none of her emotions show on her calm visage. It was a lesson she had learned well from the Chickasaw—to show always a stoic face. It had served her well in the last few days with her husband.

"We still have a few hours of light to work," French Nancy told them, gesturing for them to follow her outside where she was treating several deer hides.

With a weary sigh, Aimée rose to her feet and followed her sister and the spry old woman out to the ground behind the lodge. Here, next to the small garden plot they tended stood wooden vessels of water to which pulverized deer brains had been added. The noxious odor made Aimée sick to her stomach. It was in these vessels that French Nancy soaked the deer skins after removing all the flesh and scraping off the hair with a piece of flint.

As the old woman pulled the skins from the murky water pieces of the deer brain clung to the surface. Aimée felt her stomach turn over and the world suddenly spin around her. Seeing the ground come up to meet her, she welcomed the black oblivion that mercifully closed over her.

"Ma petite, Moon Flower, lie still for a moment and 'twill pass," the soft reassuring voice of French Nancy came to her through the fog and led her back to consciousness. Her face was being bathed with cool fresh water, and she was covered with a blanket of mallard feathers like her match coat.

"I am sorry, but I do not think I can work the skins today," Aimée whispered softly.

"Rest in the lodge. I shall make you a tisane of citronella and red raspberry for the nausea. Do not worry—I shall teach Singing Bird how to make the feather mantle." French Nancy helped her inside to her bed furs. While Mignon hovered worriedly over her sister the old woman made her an herbal tea to help the sickness.

When the two women were assured she was all right, they left her to slumber and to resume their endless tasks. Feeling relaxed and less nauseous after drinking the herbal remedy, Aimée dozed off into a light sleep, her hand resting protectively over her flat abdomen.

It was dark in the lodge when next her eyelids flickered open to stare into luminous black eyes that looked down at her with concern and love. A bronzed hand gently lifted a tendril of silver from her cheek as his lips curved into a slight smile.

"You give me concern, beloved wife. When I returned from the council house Mignon, Singing Bird, tells me you have fainted. Are you ill?"

"Where are they?" she answered him, looking about the darkened lodge, hearing no sound of the other women.

"French Nancy has been called to a lodge to set a broken arm of a child. She has taken your sister with her."

"It was only fatigue and the sight and smell of the curing hides. I fear I have a way to go before I become the perfect Chickasaw wife," she said in wry tones with a slight shrug.

"You are my wife, Green Eyes, 'tis all that matters. The ways of the People will come in time. Together we travel the road of marriage, and often it is a rocky road." He smiled down at her with teasing affection. "Share my meal with me." He gestured for her to join him on the mats beside the fire.

Wrapping the skin of a black bear about her shoulders like a blanket against the night chill, she sat beside him helping herself to more of the stew. She found she was always hungry now, even with the nausea. They ate in companionable silence at ease in each other's presence. It was enough. They didn't need to speak, for to touch and gaze on the other was enough. As they finished their meal Aimée remembered her vow to mention the plantation to her husband. It was a good time, they would not be disturbed.

"Since we are alone I wish to speak with you about . . . about a matter that has been bothering me." She stared up at him, her jade eyes large and serious in her pale face. "I do not know where to begin. It is painful to me that I had to find out about this from another. Perhaps it is the reason I have waited to speak of it, for I had hoped you would finally tell me about . . . Eagle's Roost."

There was a long silence that lengthened until it hung between them like a palpable presence. The familiar mask had descended over his proud features as he withdrew into himself. Aimée knew that cold stony visage all too well. It was the face of the stoic warrior that gave nothing away.

"How do you know of this?" His voice was cool and distant.

"Dark Dove took me there. I saw all of it." Her tone was flat, showing little emotion. Whatever she had expected his reaction to be, it had not been this remote reply. A core of fury grew deep within her as she thought of the anguish she had undergone since knowing of his deception. She wanted something from him to acknowledge her hurt, her sense of betrayal.

"Aye, she would do such a thing," he answered wryly, a flicker of distaste crossing his features for a brief moment.

"Why?" The word was thrown out at him like a challenge. Clenching her fists, her pulse beating like the war drum, she steeled herself for his answer.

"There was much you had to learn and understand before you were ready for Eagle's Roost." There was a wary, waiting quality about his tall, lean form as his depthless ebony gaze studied her with a curious intensity.

"And were you the one who would decide when I had learned all my lessons?" Each word was etched in scorn. "I detest games between people. If this is another twist to your game, then I shall refuse to play."

"It was no game, Green Eyes—only a way of showing you how our life together must be. There can be no Eagle's Roost if you do not learn first to live in Long Town."

"How much longer shall my lessons continue?" There was a light bitterness to her words, as her eyes blazed an emerald fury.

"Life, my beloved wife, continues to teach us until we take our last breath."

"How tired I am of your Chickasaw way of talking around and around a subject. Your words are like smoke drifting around me, but I cannot find any substance to hang onto," Aimée sputtered in exasperation. "Do you insist I freeze here in a hut all winter while only a few miles away there is a house with all the comforts of civilization? 'Tis madness, or do you wish to punish me because I was not born a Chickasaw? Can you not accept me as I am?"

"I cannot leave the People. There is much unrest among the clans, some wanting to follow that fool Wolf's Friend, the others in the camp of Piomingo. The Spanish fill the warriors of Wolf's Friend with whiskey till they are like helpless children. I want more for my People then being kept like a pet dog, led around by a leash to do his master's bidding. The Americans claim to be the true friend of the Chickasaw. While I do not trust them, at least they are a known enemy. I have studied their laws and understand their ways. I agree with the old chief Piomingo that the best interest of the People lies in smoking the pipe of peace with the Americans for now. The Spanish fear this alliance for it will drive them from the lands they covet. They have bought the loyalty of Wolf's Friend and his clans with whiskey and cheap trinkets. I cannot leave Long Town until I know that none here will ever follow this path."

"And where you stay so must I?" Aimée lifted a delicate brow in question. She was torn, knowing she was acting stubbornly, for her husband's desire to guide his People was a noble one. But there was a greater concern that gnawed at her heart, it was the growing love and fear for the child she carried. She wanted a safe haven for her baby; it was a maternal instinct as strong as that of a mother bird intent on finding the perfect nesting spot for her young.

"You are my woman, my wife. Your place is at my side, or providing an example to the others if I am gone. You have been adopted into the People, you are Chickasaw. Come, you are tired. We will settle this beneath the bed furs." He stood up, reaching down for her hand, his eyes glowing with desire.

"Non, this cannot be swept away in a moment of passion," she protested, rising to her feet but keeping her hands in tight fist at her sides.

"Green Eyes, 'twill be much longer than a moment, I promise you," his voice was a husky, seductive growl. There was a twinkle of humor in those ebony eyes that slowly slid downward to rake her trembling form with a gaze that was as sensual as a caress.

Fighting the quiver of excitement she felt, she lifted her chin trying to keep her features cold, allowing no reaction to show on her visage. This time he would not end her protestations in a knowing embrace that was like a drug that dulled her mind till she was only sensation. Try as she might, she felt herself weakening. *No, not this time* she thought, strengthening her resolve.

"You say you love me, that it is our destiny to be together, yet you do not care if I am happy living in this place. These are the actions of a mean, pig-headed man who cares only that he has his own way in everything. Enough, I have had enough of your honeyed words that mean only to bend me to your will." Pulling the bear robe closer about her shoulders she turned and left the lodge before he could stop her. He would not win this time.

Shadow Panther stared after her in complete disbelief. Then a grin tugged at his firm mouth. What a woman she was, strong-willed, proud, bowing to no man—a fitting mate, indeed, for a chief. A woman such as this, with the bearing and will of a queen, would some day become part of the legends that were told by the People around the fire on long winter nights. She would not give in to him so she left before she was tempted any further. He admired her for that, and how he loved the challenge of it. But tonight she deserved to lick her wounds. When she returned after becoming chilled, he would pretend to be asleep so she might salvage her pride. He gave a shrug of regret, for he had wanted to lie with her before leaving on the morrow.

Staring into the flames of the center fire, as he smoked a pipe of tobacco, he tried to quiet his desire. He regretted he had not told her of his mission to the American settlement at Nashbrough before she left the lodge in anger. Perhaps it was for the best they were apart a few days; he had to decide if she was right. Was he wrong in not accepting her as she was? Did he want her a submissive squaw? *No,* he thought with a rueful grin. It was her fiery spirit as well as her beauty that drew him to her, that kept her always on the edges of his mind. The ride to Nashbrough to talk with the American agent Robertson would be long. There were be much time to ponder his wife's words. Now that she knew about Eagle's Roost, he realized nothing between them would be quite the same. The road they traveled together on life's journey was about to take a new and dangerous turn.

Chapter Twenty-nine

The haunting cry of an owl carried on the gusts of cold autumn wind that blew through the summer lodge chilled Aimée's body as well as soul. The mournful sound was said to be bad luck, she remembered, and quickly she made the sign of the cross. How she wished she were back in the snug warm winter lodge, but there was no way she would crawl back to her husband. When she had made her defiant exit in the heat of anger she had not thought of where she would go. Walking out into the cold, dark night, lit by only a moon that played hide and seek with a mass of indigo clouds, a moment of panic had set in as she faced the slumbering village. Then in a brief shaft of moonglow she had seen the vacant summer house. It would have to be her refuge for the remainder of the night. Pride would not allow her to return to the warmth of the winter lodge before first light.

It had taken her a while fumbling in the dark, lit only for a few seconds here and there by a shaft of moonlight, to find the apparatus for fire starting. For what had seemed an eternity she had sat trying to start the center fire by means of the rod drill as French Nancy had taught her. Every lodge had the apparatus as well as a bit of dry shredded cedar bark stored away, but it had taken her a long time to remember where it had been stored. She had no intention of returning to the winter house and allowing Shadow Panther to think he had won. Tonight she would sleep in the vacant summer house at the end of the lodge block behind the remains of the garden, no matter the temperature. If only she could get the fire started she wouldn't freeze.

Her frozen fingers fumbled twirling the rod, but she continued till the spark finally caught and a small fire soon was burning. Wrapped in the bear robe she lay down beside the smoldering flames, trying to sleep a few hours before dawn. It was an uneasy slumber at best for she would wake at the slightest noise, a crack of a limb in the wind, the cry of a night creature in the woods, or the rustle of dry leaves.

The third time her eyelids flew open it was because of the sound of low voices, men's voices speaking in Chickasaw. The fine hairs on the back of her neck rose as she glanced about the darkened hut wondering where the sound was coming from. With her heart pounding, she realized with relief it was coming from outside the walls where a seldom-used path led from the plaza to the front gate. Someone was meeting out there, thinking it a good deserted place to talk as the summer houses in the lodge blocks were vacant at this time of year. Their low voices and the late hour told her they were meeting in secret. Pressing her ear to the wall she strained to hear what they were saying.

The words 'Shadow Panther' captured her attention, and she strained to hear what the men were saying. Fear like the stab of a knife cut through her as she heard them tell of a Spanish regiment coming to Long Town with a band of Creek Warriors to kill her husband. They laughed as they revealed how they would make it look like the work of the Americans from the nearest settlement. At the same time a group of Chickasaw that sided with Wolf's Friend and the Spanish would raid the settlement, killing several of the Americans. The treaty between the two would be broken, making it easier for them to lead all the Chickasaw to the side of the Spanish.

Stunned by what she was hearing, Aimée peered out carefully through a crack in the wall of the hut. At first she could see nothing, then as the moon came from behind a cloud she saw the warriors clearly. They were all men her husband thought his friends, but she realized they were Spanish spies. Her blood turned to ice as she saw the cruel visage of the brave who had first captured her on the bluff.

She stood as though fastened to the wall listening to the men go over their plan till finally they left as the pearl-gray light of dawn streaked the horizon. Breathing in shallow, quick gasps, Aimée hurried from the summer house only taking time to smother the fire and extinguish all sparks. Shadow Panther must know that there were traitors among the warriors—Men who even now plotted his death.

The white frost blanketed the village giving everything a pristine cover as she made her way across the grounds of the lodge block. Everyone appeared to be aslumber in the gray-white of early morning, but Aimée knew differently. Somewhere in the quiet town the braves made ready their provisions to leave on what appeared a simple hunting trip, but what was really a rendez-vous with the Spanish.

All was quiet in the winter lodge when Aimée entered. To her surprise the sleeping platform where she and her husband slept was empty. Where had he gone?

"You look for your husband?" the hushed voice of French Nancy broke the stillness.

"Where is he?" Aimée demanded, peering into the shadows searching for the old woman.

"He has gone before the light begins in the east. Your

angry heart has caused you to miss him." There was reproach in her voice, as she came from behind the partition to stoke the banked coals of the center fire to flame.

"I must speak with him. Where has he gone?"

"To the American settlement at Nashbrough to speak with the white agent Robertson. He is one of the few white men Chief Piomingo trusts. There is nothing you can do till he returns."

"You do not understand. I have overheard warriors that Shadow Panther thinks are his friends plotting to have him killed so they might join with the Spanish. He must know this," she pleaded with French Nancy.

"There is naught that you can do till he returns in several suns. Keep you ears and eyes open on our rounds among the sick, so that we may inform him if there are others in this plot when he arrives back in Long Town."

Aimée sank down beside the fire, sighing in frustration. Bijou woke from her place nestled in the furs by the fire, and stretched, then burrowed down on her lap. She knew French Nancy was right, but she feared for her husband and wished only to run after him. He, however, had long been on the trail. She would have a hard time catching up with him.

As the two women broke their fast Mignon joined them, having awakened at the sound of their voices. Helping herself to the refreshing corn drink and flat corn cakes smeared with honey she watched her sister thoughtfully.

"Did you and Shadow Panther argue?" she inquired in innocent tones.

" 'Tis of no concern, *ma petite*. Have you been learning the healing skills of French Nancy?" She smiled wearily at her sister who seemed to have bloomed under her stay with the Chickasaw. She was accepted here, even honored for her fair looks, blue eyes, and skill with the flute. As a healer she would be assured an honored place with the tribe.

"It is fascinating learning all the herbs and the healing songs that go with them. But before I forget I must give you something. Shadow Panther made me promise before he left. He said it was very important, and that you would understand." Mignon handed her a small doeskin bag with a draw-string closure.

Puzzled, Aimée turned the bag over in her hand. It was plain, not even decorated with quills or beads. It was as she held it in her fingers that she felt an object inside. Pulling the drawstrings apart she shook out a long metal key. It was the kind that opened a large door.

"Fancy that! A key," Mignon exclaimed. "There is not a door with a lock on it in the whole village."

A tender smile curved Aimée's mouth as tears filled her eyes. She understood the significance of the key. It would open the door to Eagle's Roost. The mistress of the house always kept the key in her possession, usually on a chatelaine at her waist. He was telling her the plantation was also her home.

"This key I think opens someone's heart," French Nancy said softly, giving Aimée a perceptive smile.

The next few days Aimée did in fact carry the key on a rawhide thong about her neck over her heart. Frequently while doing the myriad tasks that made up a Chickasaw woman's day she would touch it like a talisman and think of Shadow Panther. Always she was listening for any indication of others that felt like the traitorous braves and wished to follow Wolf's Friend. Every evening when the long violet shadows of twilight fell across the village she faced the setting sun and prayed that her husband would be returned to her safely.

It was the morning of the fourth day since he had been gone that the three women were called to the lodge of the great chief Piomingo to treat his wife who had a fever and cough. Aimée was curious to see the great man close up, for always before she had seen him at a distance at some ceremony. It occurred to her that perhaps she might tell him of what she had heard that night in the summer house.

"Do you have any proof of what you heard?" French Nancy asked quietly, when she told her of her plan. "You must realize that the warriors you have accused are of great importance, chiefs. They will deny what you say, and as a woman your voice will not count as much. They then will know they have an enemy in their midst. Your life will not last long. Wait and tell Shadow Panther what you know. He will believe you and can act on your knowledge."

"You are wise, but I fear so for my husband's life. What if they are waiting for him on the trail as he travels back to Long Town?"

"He is a great chief and fleet as the wind in the forest. It would be hard to kill one such as he for he moves as carefully as the panther for which he is named, and his medicine is strong," French Nancy reassured her, as they packed thc healing herbs in the baskets.

Mignon followed behind the two women carrying her flute. Often she played the healing songs while they administered the herbal concoctions. The music always seemed to soothe the patients.

The winter lodge of Chief Piomingo was filled with his female relatives, all giving their advice on the best cure for his wife. Their chatter sounded like the chirping of birds as they entered the large, smoky structure, the air hot and close from so many people crowded together.

"All must leave," French Nancy demanded, not giving an inch as a general uproar occurred at her command. Reluctantly, one by one, the relatives left the lodge. The patient gave a gentle smile of thanks as the chamber became quiet.

"You are, indeed, a miraculous woman to clear out that group of clacking hens." The deep voice that they had heard address the town on several occasions congratulated French Nancy from the shadows by the patient's bed platform.

"Their hearts meant well, but they were fouling the air of your woman-wife," French Nancy replied, kneeling down beside the fire to make a tea of willow bark to lower the fever.

"You are the wife of Shadow Panther," the old chief stated as he came forward to stare down at Aimée. "Your husband is my wise council. I look forward to his return, as I am sure you do, from the Chickasaw trace. Let us hope that he brings good news with him from the American settlement that the agent Robertson will help us in our fight with the Creeks and the Spanish."

Aimée nodded her head in agreement, making sure she kept her eyes lowered so as not to give offense. French Nancy could talk to him as an equal, but then she was an honored, beloved woman of the tribe whose advice was sought by even the council of chiefs. Aimée was a young woman, a new wife, and the rules governing her behavior in Chickasaw society were strict. She did not want to bring shame on French Nancy who had been so good to her.

As soon as the dignified old chief had left the hut, however, she turned to the old healing woman and said, "You did not tell me he had taken the Chickasaw trace—'tis clearly marked, they say. I could have followed him, if you would have showed me its beginning."

"And risked the dangers alone? *Non!* I do not want for you to do such a foolish thing. Come, we talk no more of the impossible. Help me make a poultice for her chest."

While she helped nurse the very ill patient, and Mignon played her soothing music, Aimée's thoughts were racing. If she could at least ride out and meet her husband he would be aware of what awaited him when he returned to the village. The Spanish and Creeks might even be waiting in the dense forest of the Chickasaw domain at this moment for his arrival, and the completion of their plan.

The early autumn twilight had fallen when finally French Nancy felt they might leave their patient to her rest. She allowed only the woman's daughter back into the lodge to care for her.

Purple-gray wood smoke from two hundred lodge fires hung in the late afternoon air as they crossed the plaza, kicking piles of dried tan, amber, and rust leaves till they crumbled into dust. It was as they reached the center near the ever-burning sacred fire that they heard the high keening cry of the returning warrior. For a heart-stopping moment Aimée thought that it was Shadow Panther, but the thunder of horses' hooves told her it was more than one man.

Pressing back against the council houses that lined the square to avoid being trampled, the women watched as a party of braves rode into the plaza. Two fresh scalps dangled from the lances they held in their hands. One wore the coat of a Spanish officer as a war trophy. They led several Spanish horses captured in battle. A gasp escaped Mignon as the women saw a man being dragged behind one horseman, a rope about his neck. Even though his clothes were tattered and blood-stained it was easy to see he was a white man. He had not been allowed to ride his horse, having been forced to walk to show he was a captive.

"Stop! Oh please . . . stop . . . them!" The high stuttering wail tore from Mignon's throat as she ran passed a stunned Aimée.

"Singing Bird, halt!" French Nancy cried after her, as the braves circled the plaza, their cries calling people from their lodges.

"Luis! Luis!" Mignon's cry echoed across the square as she ran between the horses, barely escaping their thrashing hoofs.

"Who is that man?" The old woman asked Aimée.

"Mon Dieu, I believe he is a Spanish lieutenant who was very kind to my sister at the fort. I had no idea she cared so much for him," Aimée muttered in surprise, as they watched the agile young woman reach the prisoner's side and hold up the exhausted man with her own body.

Dark eyes watched and murmured in avid curiosity, as they watched the woman they called Singing Bird cling to the prisoner who seemed only half alive. Old and young women gave the white man measured glances, trying to see what excited Singing Bird so much she was making an unseemly spectacle of herself. He was well-made and strong looking they agreed, but perhaps she had known him before, they mused as they watched.

Aimée and French Nancy made their way through the throng to reach Mignon's side. Men and women watched avidly as the young woman held the wounded man in her arms as if she would kill anyone who would try and take him from her.

"This man is important to you?" French Nancy hissed as they finally reached her side.

"Oui he . . . came all this . . . way to find . . . me,"

Mignon sobbed.

"Then you must keep your head about you. When the chief comes out of the council lodge you must announced that you wish as a Chickasaw woman alone to have this man for your husband. It is your right, but you must ask now, for he is in no condition to endure torture. Stand tall and proud. Ask with strength; do not grovel or beg. Demand this man as your husband."

Mignon stared at French Nancy, her sapphire eyes glittering with fear. She stood like she was carved from stone, then turned to stare at the man she held against her. She nodded.

Aimée's heart broke for her sister. She understood what it was to love a man so much that nothing else mattered. Love that strong could transform and that was what she was seeing before her very eyes. Mignon suddenly had a new maturity in her lovely features, the slightly fey quality had vanished in her concern for the handsome man she loved.

A hush fell over the crowd as Chief Piomingo strode from the council house to come before the returning braves. If he was surprised at the sight of Mignon clutching the exhausted prisoner he gave no sign. His weathered, creased visage was dignified, aloof, as he received the Spanish scalps from the victorious braves. Turning in the direction of the prisoner he asked in Chickasaw if he had fought with courage. When he heard from the warriors that he had, he turned his piercing gaze on Mignon.

"Do you know this man?" he asked of the trembling young woman.

French Nancy translated his words to her for in her anxiety she had forgotten what little Chickasaw she knew. "Speak with strong words in French, I shall interpret for you," the old woman told her. "You must ask now for the prisoner if you want to save his life."

Reaching down deep within her being, Mignon found the courage she needed. Lifting her head proudly to stare into the remote black eyes of the chief she said," I know him. He is a good man, a man who came to see if I needed his help. As a Chickasaw woman alone, I claim him as a husband to hunt for me and protect my lodge."

After a long time when his eyes never left Mignon's face, strong now with purpose, he slowly nodded 'yes,' then turned and walked backed to the council house. The silent crowd soon buzzed as they considered this latest twist. The young gifted one who usually spoke with her flute had stood her ground like a wildcat demanding her mate. Dark female eyes once more pursued the tall, exhausted prisoner, discussing his merits as a husband. Aimée was glad Mignon couldn't understand for some of the comments were quite bawdy.

"Come, we take him to the lodge. He will need much healing," French Nancy told the two young women as they helped Luis de Vargas from the plaza.

"It will take a miracle to get that one so he is worth anything in the bed furs," an aged crone yelled to the glee of the other woman.

"Pay them no mind," French Nancy cautioned to Aimée. Mignon was so preoccupied with the young lieutenant she didn't even listen to the jeers and lewd jokes.

Later, after bathing the wounded man and dressing his cuts and bruises as well as giving him nourishment, they listened to his story of how he came to be in the domain of the Chickasaw.

"Rodrigo Hernandez is heading this way with a regiment of soldiers and Creek warriors. He is determined to kill the Chief Shadow Panther, who he feels has made of fool of him. He has spies here in the village who only pretend to support Piomingo. They will join with the Spanish after discrediting Shadow Panther," he told the women haltingly as he lay on a bed platform. His expressive dark eyes never left Mignon's adoring gaze.

"But how did you get captured and Rodrigo escape?" Aimée questioned.

"We were sent ahead as a scouting party. I convinced him that it was necessary. I wanted only to find you, *querida*. He means to find both you and your sister, for his thoughts are filled only with revenge. When you were taken by Shadow Panther and his men, he was furious seeing any chance at his marriage settlement gone. He claims he will marry one of you for he has waited long for your dowry. I am afraid then he will kill you both, making it appear the work of the Indians. You must come away with me, Mignon. They are only a brief ride away. We will find sanctuary in the American territory. He can't touch you there," Luis told her firmly with eyes glazed with exhaustion.

"Do not worry, Lieutenant de Vargas. You are safe here under my husband's protection. Later, if you wish to travel to one of the American settlements you may have to discuss that with Shadow Panther. In the eyes of the Chickasaw you are Mignon's husband. She has declared it so if front of everyone. Rest, regain your strength. When my husband returns there will be time to speak of your future," Aimée told him with a weary smile.

Rising to her feet, she left the two young lovers alone and joined French Nancy at the fire. "You see what I must do."

"I see you have your mind made up. It will be dangerous, *ma petite*, but you are determined so I shall give you my help. At first light I shall point out the trace to you—it is well marked to one who knows what to look for.

Shadow Panther is perhaps a day's ride away, for I feel strongly that he is on his way back to the village. He has been gone long enough to have conducted his business with the American agent. I had hoped he would have returned by now so this would not be necessary, but you are right. If it is a few more days till he returns he could be walking into a trap. Here, take this with you. In the morning point it toward the horizon and then follow straight north on the trail." She held out a small case; opening the lid she showed Aimée the Spanish lieutenant's compass. "It was in his clothes. He will not need it here."

"*Merci,* beloved mother, thank you for understanding that I have no other choice," Aimée whispered, placing a kiss on the woman's withered cheek.

"May the spirits guide you, daughter of my heart, on your journey. My prayers travel with you and your beloved till you both return to me." Tears filled her eyes as she pressed the compass into Aimée's hand, then haltingly made the sign of the cross in a gesture that came as a half-remembered memory from her distant French childhood.

It was that gesture which smote Aimée's heart. She realized how much French Nancy loved her and how frightened the old woman was that she might never see her again.

She felt no fear for herself, only a terrible anxiety that she would be too late. Nothing mattered but that somehow she find her beloved husband and warn him of the trap that lay waiting for him.

Chapter Thirty

The black mystery of night had turned a misty pearl-gray with the dawn. The sun had yet to burn away the fog of the autumn eventide. Aimée, astride Ivoire, urged the alabaster mare northward through the still-dark forest, following the Chickasaw Trace to the Tennessee territory. She had left the village of Long Town far behind.

Shivering in the cold early dawn, Aimée didn't know if it was the bitter morning air or nerves that set her teeth achatter. A flock of malevolent ebony crows took flight suddenly from the dry branches of a pin oak, their raucous craws only adding to her unease. The forest seemed shrouded in shadows as the wisps of hoary gray fog clung to branches, some pointing like skeletal fingers toward the sky, their leaves lying in deep brown piles on the hard ground.

How long, she wondered, would she have to ride before meeting her husband? He had been in her thoughts constantly since leaving the village. She saw his lean form, the outline of his ebony stallion in every shadow, every gnarled tree, barely visible in the fog. If wishes would make it so he would be beside her. She fervently hoped French Nancy had been right in her premonition that Shadow Panther was on his way home, that around some bend in the trail she would see his beloved visage. Never had she felt so alone. The trip to Nashbrough was long, and for a woman alone fraught with danger. The eerie atmosphere of the morning did nothing to reassure her.

Morning turned into afternoon and still she rode, stopping only to water and rest Ivoire. She took food from the buckskin bags she carried behind her saddle, and ate while the mare drank from a stream. Glancing up at the sun, now moving lower in the west, Aimée knew she would have to think of stopping for the night.

Sighing, she looked about the bank of the stream at the bottom of a steep ravine. She had hoped that by this time she would have met her husband, for she didn't relish spending the night on the trail alone. This seemed as good a place as any to stop. There were trees close to the water with slender low branches she could use to make a small sleep bower covered with the deer hides she carried in her saddlebags. But for some reason she felt uneasy, as if there was some unseen danger only waiting for her to relax her guard.

Shrugging away her apprehension, Aimée began to cut down the slender limbs, cutting their ends into points that she would pound into the earth. When the hut was finished she scooped out a fire spot in the earth, lining it with stones from the creek bed. Carefully, she lifted a smoldering punk. French Nancy had rolled it that morning into a tight cylinder and placed it within a hollow corncob. She placed dried moss and leaves under the kindling and added the smoldering punk, carefully blowing till it caught flame. Soon she was rewarded with a cheerful fire that gave a welcoming glow as the last of the afternoon light vanished in the west with the setting sun.

Wrapping herself in a bearskin, she sat in front of the sleep hut cooking flat corn cakes on the heated stones of the fire. The sounds of the night creatures of the forest echoed in the ravine, sending shivers up Aimée's spine. She moved Shadow Panther's long gun closer to her side.

Images of the nights she and her husband had spent in their private lagoon flitted through her thoughts as she stared into the orange and blue flames of the campfire. A yearning for his strong arms and passionate kiss tore through her like a knife. Her loneliness washed over her in waves as she shivered in the cold, damp air of the late autumn night, wishing that somehow he would appear. *Can you hear my heart longing for you* she wondered, staring into the fire. There was such a strong bond between them she wondered if it could transcend time and space. Could she send out her longing, her need for him into the dark night, and would he hear her?

How long she sat lost in dreams she didn't know, but it was the sharp crack of a breaking stick that jolted her back to the reality of her situation. Lifting the loaded gun she cocked the trigger and stood up. Turning in the direction of the sound that had come from the dense woods, she lifted the weapon to her shoulder and looked down the sight.

"Come out!" she cried in the strongest voice she could muster.

Only silence answered her command. It was too quiet, she decided, for even the night creatures seemed to be waiting, frozen in anticipation of the danger that quickened her pulse and made the fine hairs on the back of her slender neck rise.

Suddenly, it seemed everything happened at once. Her gun was knocked from her hand as it went off, sending the bullet into the ground. Strong arms lifted her up against a hard masculine chest. A musky male scent was in her nostrils, the bare skin of his chest telling her he was an Indian. Struggling, she knew despair as his strength overpowered her, and her hands were quickly lashed behind her back. Roughly she was thrown to the hard, cold ground, her face buried in the dry dead leaves till she thought she would suffocate.

"Enough!" a strangely familiar voice called out in Spanish as her feet were also tied together with rawhide sinews.

Struggling to sit up, she rolled over so at least she could breath. Staring up at the night sky she caught only a quick glimpse of the stars before a figure loomed over her. In the light of the fire she saw the visage of her captor. A scream clawed at the back of her throat, but with a numbing sense of doom she knew there was no one in this forsaken forest ravine to come to her aid. There was only Rodrigo Hernandez and two Creek warriors.

"So, my fine French lady, you have become nothing more than a white Chickasaw squaw. Oh, yes, I have heard of Moon Flower, the silver-blonde Indian princess, the chief's wife who is some kind of witch doctor, healer. The stories about you have gone up and down the river. Didn't even have the decency to kill yourself after that savage had his way with you. Well, my little Chickasaw *puta,* you have disgraced me. Hear that loco sister of yours is in Long Town as well. Seems I have a score to settle with Shadow Panther. He took my women and my money." Rodrigo spat on the ground, his porcine eyes narrowed with hate.

"We were not yours, and our money was certainly never yours." Aimée spoke the words contemptuously, without thinking. Her anger and disgust had overridden her fear for the moment.

"You damn well are mine, you cat-eyed bitch," he snarled, slapping her hard across the face. "I will collect the money your stepmother promised me, but first you need to be taught a lesson. See those two fine specimens of Creek braves leaving us to stand guard outside camp? Why, they have just been itching to sample the silver Chickasaw. Thought you would ride out and join your savage husband, did you? Well, we will have a real surprise for him. His little squaw will be all softened up, shall we say. You will be used goods, my dear, and that will be the last sight he sees on this earth."

A glazed look of despair began to spread over Aimée's face as she realized the full horror of her situation. With the best of intentions she had led her husband into a trap. They would simply wait for him to appear, setting her out as bait. In his fear for her he would not be as cautious. The panther who was as quick and as elusive as a shadow would be coaxed into a trap. From deep within her she prayed that somehow he would realize what was happening. If he was on the trail, as French Nancy thought, she must concentrate with all her will to send him some kind of warning. She knew it was insane, but she had to try. She could not be responsible for his death.

"Shall I call them, my dear? 'Tis time for you to suffer a little for my humiliation." His sadistic laughter echoed on the cold night air.

It was as he rose to his feet from where he crouched beside her that she saw an amazing sight. He took one small step forward, then reached out to clutch the arrow that had somehow pierced his throat. A strange gurgle was the only sound before he collapsed face-down in the dead leaves.

"Do not speak aloud, Green Eyes," a wonderful deep voice whispered in her ear, as strong hands quickly untied her hands and feet.

"Shadow Panther! Oh my beloved," Aimée whispered, through her silent sobs of thanksgiving.

"I have killed the two Creek guards as well, but there are others not far away. We must leave before they discover what has happened. Can you walk?"

"Oui, yes, I think so." Rubbing her ankles to restore the circulation, she watched as he picked up Rodrigo's limp body and carried it to the sleep hut, dumping it inside.

"I have disposed of the others upstream, and if the rest come looking they will think you are in there together." His eyes glittered with anger as he spread a fur over the dead man so he appeared to be sleeping.

Wrapping the bear rug securely about her shoulders, Aimée followed him as he untied Ivoire, placing his hand on her neck in a gesture that he had taught her meant to make no sound. Quietly they stole away from the ravine. After walking what seemed like a long time, they reached a huge cypress where Shadow Panther's stallion waited patiently.

It was only then that he turned and pulled her to him, holding her in the circle of his arms as if he would never let her go. She buried her face against his throat, letting the tears of relief flow down her cheeks as she haltingly told him of what she had heard that night in the summer house and why she had come alone on the trace after him.

"You are safe, little one. My love will shelter and protect you for as long as I have breath in my body, and then into eternity. You are part of my soul, beloved one. Never doubt that our love is everlasting, no matter what trials await us. Come now, we ride for Long Town to warn them of the enemy that lies within their village, and the enemy that comes to conquer them."

The full ivory moon, the harvest moon, shone down on the faint trail that Shadow Panther had chosen instead of the more well-traveled Chickasaw trace. Only an Indian could even see that it was a path, Aimée thought as she rode beside her husband. The full moon worried him, for while it made it easier for them to see, it also made it easier for them to be seen. She touched the knife that rested in a pouch tied about her thigh like those the other Chickasaw women wore. Shadow Panther had given it to her as he helped her mount Ivoire and insisted she wear it. She had always refused before, thinking it barbaric, but she would never be so foolish as to go about unarmed again.

"How long had you been waiting in the trees?" she asked when they were far enough away to talk in low voices.

"Not long. I would have stopped earlier for the night, but I had the strangest feeling—as if I could hear you calling to me. At first it was that you were simply waiting down the trail for me, but then it changed. You were in trouble, but I had to be very careful. It was as if I heard your voice. It made no sense for I knew there was no reason for you to be on the trace alone, but the feeling was so strong I could not deny it. So I started to look for any sign of there being anyone else around and by pressing my ear to Mother Earth I heard the sound of horses. Then I saw the smoke from your fire and carefully approached your camp. I went mad when I saw you tied up and that sadistic Spaniard slap you, but I had to kill the others first so there would be no one to stop us. Forgive me for having you go through his torment, but I had to wait for just the right moment." There was pain in his ebony eyes that glowed like coals in the moon glow.

Glancing at him she gave him a smile so full of love it smote his heart. "There is nothing to forgive. I called to you, or rather my heart called to you, and you answered."

"Ah, Green Eyes, so you did try and contact me. My beloved one, our destiny is indeed intertwined." He reached across and clasped her hand for a moment. There was no need for spoken words, their touch, the invisible bond that held them one to another was enough. They rode on through the starry night content that they had found what they had been searching for all their lives.

It was morning, with the sun well up in the sky before they reached Long Town. There was such an air of normalcy about the village that Aimée and Shadow Panther shuddered for them. The gates were wide open and people walked in and out of the walled town to hunt in the woods for nuts and late autumn berries.

"We must make haste to the council house, beloved woman-wife, for there is much to be done to prepare the village for attack." He urged his stallion forward through the open gates of the stockade.

Aimée felt every nerve tense as she realized she would have to speak to Chief Piomingo and the others, denouncing those who claimed allegiance to him and her husband but who were instead Spanish spies.

The men were still meeting in the *Tcokofa* or winter council house, as they did every morning, when Shadow Panther and Aimée rode into the plaza. If the Chickasaw warriors were surprised to see a woman enter the large round council house behind her husband they gave no sign. At his direction Aimée took a place near the entrance on one of the benches that ringed the chamber. She watched as her tall, stalwart husband advanced with long, lithe strides to the middle of the structure where burned the sacred fire.

After smoking the long pipe with the other chiefs and

braves Shadow Panther asked for permission to speak. They listened intently, but without expression as he told of the enemies that lived within their village—The men who wore the faces of friends, but who were really spies for the Spanish.

Aimée's heart caught her throat as she noticed out of the corner of her eye a slight movement on the part of one of the warriors. It was her old nemesis, the cold-eyed brave who had captured her on the bank of the Wolf River. He was moving slowly, keeping close to the wall and low like a cornered animal, toward the entrance. No one else saw him for their backs were to the door, and they were concentrating on Shadow Panther's words.

She had to stop him, for he was one of the spies for the Spanish, but how? If she called out it would take the others precious time to reach him, and he was almost at the door.

Her fingers grazed her skirt and she felt the outline of the knife. Quickly she pulled it out, and with a lunge caught the warrior in the back as he tried to slip out of the council house.

"Shadow Panther!" she cried. She felt the brave slump to the ground trying to twist away from her.

The chamber erupted in pandemonium as the warriors came rushing to her aid. It was in the general melée that the two other spies tried to escape, but the others were alerted and stopped them. Aimée shrank from the hatred she saw in the dying brave's eyes as his life's blood slowly seeped out into the ground.

"Come, my brave little wildcat, I take you back to the lodge. The chiefs know that you speak the truth for these three gave themselves away." Shadow Panther's arms holding her up were all that kept her from collapsing as he led her away from the plaza. Their horses were being tended by several young boys who hung around the council house hoping someday to become warriors.

The tranquil village seemed to have become a beehive of activity as the warning of attack was passed from lodge to lodge and the mighty doors of the stockade were pulled closed. Women ran to gather up children as Aimée and Shadow Panther made their way to the lodge block of French Nancy.

"I am frightened," Aimée whispered, clinging to her tall husband in a way that was distinctly not Chickasaw, but no one seemed to notice, so intent were they on seeing to securing the town.

"We are well prepared, Green Eyes. Our enemies will find a surprise awaiting them," he said in cryptic tones as they stooped to enter the low portal of the winter house.

"Aimée, you have returned, and with Shadow Panther as you promised!" Mignon cried in happiness without a hint of a stutter, rising from where she prepared medicines for French Nancy.

The old healing woman gave a slight smile as she lifted her head from her tasks, but even in the dim light Aimée could see tears in her eyes. A masculine figure reclined on a fur rug by the fire, his back resting against the woven cane backboard. Luis de Vargas said nothing, but the two could sense the tension in his long frame and the question in his sable-brown eyes.

"You are the husband of my wife's sister. She has told us of how kind you were to her at the fort. We are grateful and accept you as a Chickasaw. My wife has told me of the information you gave regarding the coming attack. I have told the Chief so we may prepare for attack. Word has also been sent to the American settlement. It was an act of courage to do what you did in coming here. I think you see now that your wife Mignon, known as

Singing Bird, is happy here in Long Town, but if you both wish to travel to the American settlement to live I shall help you when you are well. Until you are recovered, and decide what you want, you are welcome here in our village." Shadow Panther spoke gravely, but bent down and held out his hand to the wounded man.

"Thank you," Luis de Vargas replied simply, shaking his hand with what little strength he had.

The tension cleared from the lodge at his words like smoke blown away by a breeze. French Nancy gestured for them all to sit as she brought cups of corn drink from the pottery jug in the corner. As she began to serve the men first from the rabbit stew bubbling in the iron pot over the fire, Shadow Panther motioned that the women too were to be served with him and Luis.

The men talked of the coming attack while Mignon and Aimée tried to eat, but the food tasted like so much sawdust in their mouths. They listened to the discussion of guns and number of warriors, as well as probable battle plans. Slowly, they stopped, placing their bowls on the mats beside them.

"Why are you not eating?" Shadow Panther asked, noticing the bowls still half-full, resting beside the fire.

"War is only the delight of men," French Nancy said softly. "As the carriers of life we women find it abhorrent."

"This has been said before to me, many years ago by my mother," he said quietly. "To men war is exciting, almost a game; to women 'tis loss and grief."

"She was a very wise woman," Aimée said softly, reaching out to touch his hand.

"I shall return to you, beloved wife, but now we must part. I have stayed long. Do not fear, my medicine is strong, and I feel in my bones that we still have many miles to go together on this life's journey." He rose to his feet and Aimée did likewise.

There was a silence in the lodge as he stared down into the pale flower of his wife's lovely face. Her features were frozen like the face of a porcelain figurine. Only one crystal tear that slid down her cheek told of her pain. He lifted his hand and tenderly caught it with one bronze finger tip, his ebony eyes reaching down, down deep inside her to her very soul. Then he was gone to a battle from which he might never return. He had left like a true Chickasaw warrior without a kiss or last embrace. She turned from the empty portal and stared into the sad, pitying eyes of the others.

Chapter Thirty-one

The cold drizzling morning rain fell in a monotonous patter on the roofs of the lodges, turning the streets of Long Town into thoroughfares of mud. Aimée huddled next to the fire, Bijou nestled in her lap. She had slept very little the night before. Her thoughts were constantly of Shadow Panther and as the hours passed her fear grew.

" 'Tis so quiet about the village," Mignon observed. She came to sit by her sister and helped herself to the corn porridge that cooked in the black pot. Luis slept behind the partition, a heavy sleep induced by the pain-relieving tisane French Nancy had given him the night before.

"There is the scent of fear in the air," the old healing woman murmured as she stirred the bubbling porridge. "Always it is like this when the People prepare for an attack. The Spanish and Creek come with revenge in their hearts. All know the fighting will be brutal."

"No one goes to the stream this morning. That is why it is so quiet," Aimee said softly. "They will all wash in their lodges and greet Grandmother Sun silently outside their lodges with a prayer that their men be spared."

"What must we do as women?" Mignon asked of French Nancy to her sister's pleased surprise. It was an adult, responsible question, and showed how much the formerly shy young woman had grown since coming to stay with the Chickasaw.

"We do as women have done since the beginning of time when their men go off to fight. We wait and pray that we will be spared a grievous loss." The old woman rose to her feet and moved toward where many herbs were tied in bunches hanging from pegs in the wall. "I shall also prepare medicine for the wounded."

The words tore at Aimée's heart. There would be wounded and worse before the battle was over. Pushing Bijou onto a fur rug she rose to her feet. "I cannot stay here waiting. I must go outside, at least I will not feel so confined. This waiting is driving me mad."

"Be careful. Stay on the streets that are in the middle of the village. Do not go near the walls. Bring us back news of what is happening," French Nancy replied with understanding in her tired blue eyes. "Singing Bird will stay and help me." The old woman put a restraining hand on Mignon for she could see the young woman was ready to accompany her sister. Aimée needed to be alone, she knew. Thanking the Great Spirit that she was no longer young and in love at such a time, she turned back to her work.

Pulling an oiled deerskin about her head and body Aimée walked out into the rain. The leaden skies seemed to press down on Long Town as she trudged through the muddy streets toward the plaza. The cold drizzle was enough to sap the strongest spirit, she mused, as she passed lodge after lodge with the portal skin pulled tight against the damp. Even the camp dogs were inside next to a warm fire. She heard the whimper of a child here and there as she made her way to the center of the village. They sensed their mothers' fear for their men and for their own lives if the Chickasaw were not victorious.

The plaza was empty except for four sentries dressed in the fierce red and black paint of war. Across their chest was slung a bow and around their waist was lashed a war club. In their hands they held a gun.

"Go back." A fierce-looking brave ordered her in Chickasaw as she tried to enter the square. He gestured with his gun toward the direction from which she had come.

"Have any warriors left yet?" She could not stop herself from asking. Desperate for information, she pleaded, but he only stared at her stonily. She had to know if Shadow Panther was still in the council house.

"No women. Go back." The brave repeated, pushing her now with the butt of his gun.

Sighing, she nodded her understanding, and turning around made her way back toward the lodge. War was the business of men and she would not be tolerated. Familiar masculine faces slipped across her mind like that of the wise old Chief Piomingo. She said a silent prayer that the People would be spared great losses in the coming battle. Strangely in the last months as she had come to treat their illnesses and come to know their families they had in some way become a part of her. She knew them, each and every one, and she feared for them, understanding the pain and hardship each Chickasaw woman and child would experience if their warrior lost his life in the coming battle. Suddenly, she wanted the security of French Nancy's lodge and the peace she felt emanating from the old woman. Slipping and sliding in the mud she realized how good the warmth of the cozy winter house would feel. She was trembling from the cold and damp as well as fear.

It was as she reached the lodge that she heard the sound that sent chills up and down her spine. It was the fierce war cry of the Chickasaw. Immediately the air reverberated with the sound of gunfire. Crouching low, she ducked inside.

French Nancy was calmly pounding herbs into leaves to be boiled into a medicinal infusion. Mignon was trying to restrain Luis as he stumbled to the fire.

"It has begun. We can do nothing," the old woman's voice was controlled, but her hand shook with a slight tremor as the sounds of the battle outside the walls escalated.

"My gun, I must have my gun," Luis pleaded, his face white and drawn. He swayed before collapsing on the bear furs beside the fire.

"You are too weak, *mon coeur,*" Mignon cautioned, dropping down beside him and cushioning his dark head on her lap.

"I understand how you feel, Luis. 'Tis maddening to wait here like an animal in a trap, to not be able to know what is happening," Aimée said, clenching her fists in frustration.

His expressive dark brown eyes flashed her a thank you as he lay panting, his fever once more rising. Beads of perspiration stood out on his pale forehead under the shock of sable hair.

"Here, you can make yourself useful. The lieutenant needs tea of willow bark to bring down that fever. Bring a fur from the bed platform. He will take a chill after the fever drops." French Nancy gave Aimée orders, wisely knowing that if she was busy it would help pass the agonizing wait.

The long day was somehow passed as the sounds of battle overrode the steady patter of the rain. The gates were never stormed although everyone sat in the close dark lodge with the terror that it could happen at any moment. As the early autumn twilight fell across the village, the guns stopped. There was a moment of agony while all waited to hear if the Creeks had entered the stockade. Their hearts in their throats, the women clasped each other in joy as the Chickasaw cry of triumph echoed through the anxious streets.

"You are needed," the deep voice of a warrior drew their attention to where he stood just inside the portal. He had come in so quietly they had not heard him in their noisy rejoicing. His fearsome appearance, his stern visage painted half red, half black cast a somber pall over their rejoicing.

"Come, Moon Flower, take this basket. I will need your help. Singing Bird must stay here with her husband."

The two women followed the tall warrior through the winding streets till they came to the gate. Women and children swarmed about the entrance, spilling out through the now-open gates to the grounds outside. A ghostly white fog swirled up from the nearby river adding to the confusion of the scene.

Here and there an anguished cry of sorrow rent the air, but they were not as many as feared. Aimée walked behind French Nancy, her pulse pounding as she searched through the fog and crowd for some sight of Shadow Panther. His tall, lithe form was nowhere to be seen. Dead Creeks lay on the damp ground while here and there a Spanish officer lay fallen victim to a Chickasaw gun. It was a ghostly sight in the fog, and the People fled from the dead for they believed their ghosts now haunted the ground. A few warriors quickly began to drag the dead from near the village to the forest where animals would finish the job of decomposition.

The few Chickasaw wounded were being lifted up on litters to be carried by their comrades into the village. French Nancy supervised the bearers, calling out here and there not to jostle the men.

"He is not here," Aimée hissed, as the old woman gestured for her to follow the wounded inside.

"I have asked for you, *ma petite.* A brave told me he saw Shadow Panther chase after a Spaniard into the forest by the stream. It was the last time he was seen. Come, he will return, 'tis over," French Nancy tried to reassure her. "The Creeks were surprised by the Chickasaw hidden in the trees and fled in disorder along with some of the Spanish officers. The American guns given to the Chickasaw were many, and that, with the plan of surprise, enabled our victory. The Chiefs' being told in advance of their planned attack by Luis, and by you and Shadow Panther, allowed us to triumph. The Great Spirit sent us you three as messengers to show us the way. The People are grateful, Moon Flower. They see your destiny as one with the tribe. Your husband will return, his medicine is strong."

As she began to follow the old woman back inside the stockade the strangest feeling came over Aimée. Something, or someone was calling to her through the fog. Suddenly in the murky shadows of the forest she saw what she thought was the figure of a panther. He stood staring at her, willing her to follow him, then turned and vanished along the trail that led to the bower beside the stream. She knew what she had to do. She knew what he was telling her.

Leaving French Nancy's side without explanation she ran toward where all the horses had been penned during the raid. She could see nothing in the fog, for it was denser here. Standing at the gate she whistled her special sign for Ivoire. The mare trotted to her side out of the gray fog that clung to the bottom-land. Moving backward a few steps Aimée ran and leapt up on the animal's back. She had no reins, but with the motion of her thighs and knees she told the lovely creature of her intent. They were off into the darkened wood, the rider and horse moving as one.

There was only the leaden sound of the cold November rain in the silent forest. Thick piles of leaves muffled the sound of Ivoire's hoofs as they rode on and on driven by what Aimée knew in some deep recess of her being. Shadow Panther was injured. He needed her and the panther, his totem animal, had come to fetch her, to lead her to him.

The black of night had almost blotted out any light when the rain stopped. The indigo clouds slowly parted, and a shaft of moonglow shone down on the lagoon beside the stream as she entered the clearing. The whinnying of a stallion told her she was right. Shadow Panther's black horse stood tied to a low branch of a magnolia. From the limestone outcropping over the stream came the cry of the panther. Turning, she saw the magnificent animal, his ebony coat glistening like satin for a moment in the shaft of moon light. It was as if he were telling her she had found what he had wanted her to see. Slipping from Ivoire's back, she secured her to a branch then ran to the bower where she had spent her wedding night. Flinging aside the mat that covered the door, she stepped in.

"Shadow Panther, my husband, are you here?" she called out. The hut was dark; only a thin stream of moonlight came through the door.

"Green Eyes, I am here on the bed platform. A

Spanish bullet is lodged in my leg." His voice directed her to him, but the dark of the hut did not allow her to see him. "How did you know to come here?"

"The panther came for me. He led me here." Another roar filled the cold night from the direction of the waterfall.

"Aye, he is powerful medicine. The Panther takes care of his own."

"I would not have believe it if I had not experienced it myself. He led me to you. I shall never doubt our People's ways again," she said with wonder, trying to feel in the dark for the fire starter bow.

"You said *our* People, beloved," he whispered huskily, trying not to groan with the pain of his wound.

"I did," she answered in surprise. "I think, my husband, I have become Chickasaw, and I hope this Chickasaw wife can start a fire, for your wound needs tending." She couldn't see his tender smile in the dark, but she felt it, so attuned were they to each other. "I am glad you are pleased, for you have won."

"My victory is beyond comprehension, for how can I explain what it is to gain the other half of one's soul."

She turned toward him just as the spark lit the dry moss in the fire hole. Quickly, she bent down to blow the smoke to flame. Soon she had a small steady fire going that equaled the fire in her heart. Lighting one of the small clay lamps that contained bear oil, she hurried to her husband's side.

"Mon Dieu," she breathed, staring at the festering wound in her husband's thigh.

"You must dig out the bullet. I can not ride back to the village for I am weak and have lost much blood. I thought if I rested here I could return, but the fever has begun."

"But I have never done such a thing before. Let me fetch French Nancy," Aimée insisted, panic-stricken at the thought of what he asked her to do.

"Nay, she will be occupied with the wounded. Take my knife and heat it in the flames. When it has cooled you must pry out the bullet. You must do it, Green Eyes—or I shall die." He grasped her wrist in his hand, still strong, although his skin felt hot with the fever that even now was rising. His black eyes glittered with the rising infection in the light from the fire.

"Let me fetch water from the stream and see if there are any herbs still alive on the bank. What I need usually grows next to water," she explained. He nodded, releasing her hand.

"Be careful, take my gun. There may be still a few Creeks hiding, waiting for first light," he murmured, lying back against the bed skins, exhausted by the effort of the last few minutes.

Grabbing a basket and clay pot from where they were stored under the bed platform, she left the lodge to hurry out into the cold, dark night. The clouds had vanished leaving a bright moon that showed a silver path to the water's edge. Filling the pot with water, she bent down, searching the bank for the tiny plants. Her heart leapt with joy has she found what she sought. Rising to her feet, she saw the slender willow tree with its fever-reducing bark gleaming in the moon glow. Quickly, she stripped long slender curls of bark from the tree and hurried back to her ill husband.

While the pot of water heated on the coals she allowed the knife to cool. In another pot she made an infusion of willow bark to drink as a tea against the fever. Hanging from a rafter the firelight caught the outline of a large spider web. She smiled softly to herself, remembering how French Nancy had told her a spider web placed over a gaping wound would pull the two edges together. Taking a deep breath to steady her nerves and her hands, she knew she had everything she needed to begin.

"I am ready, husband," she said softly, approaching where her husband lay burning with fever.

"Take my head band from my head and place it between my teeth that I might have something to bite down upon," he ordered coolly.

Silently, with tears in her eyes, she obeyed him. When it was between his strong white teeth, she dashed the tears from her eyes that she might have no obstruction to her vision. Taking the knife in her hand she began to probe the gaping wound. Black oozing blood began to run down the sinewy bronze thigh that she had stroked with such passion and love. Forcing an iron control over her emotions she tried not to think, only work as quickly as possible. The blood, bright red now, threatened to obscure her field of vision and she felt she was probing blind, hurting this beloved man with no result.

"Please guide my hand," she whispered, in a frantic prayer to the dark night as Shadow Panther passed out from the pain. Then she felt metal, not bone. Moving the bear-oil lamp so it shone on the vicious wound she reached with two delicate fingers and pulled the Spanish bullet from his thigh. Blood seemed to be everywhere as she washed the wound, then packed it with herbs as she remembered French Nancy telling her to do. It seemed almost as if she could hear the gentle voice of the old healer woman. She took the delicate silver spider web from the rafter with great care and placed it over the packed wound, then pulled the bed furs over her husband's inert form to ward against the chill of the night.

There was nothing she could do but wait beside the fire for Shadow Panther to regain consciousness. The summer house was not built for November's cold. There was only the one bear rug now about her husband, so she made do with a soft doeskin that was all that was needed in the summer. Tonight, with the wind whistling through the airy summer lodge, it was not enough.

As the first pale light of dawn came through the smoke hole, Aimée woke from her fitful sleep to the moan of Shadow Panther's voice. Flinging the doeskin aside she hurried to his bed.

"I am thirsty," he whispered from fever-parched lips.

"Mon coeur, wait, I have a tisane for you," she told him with happiness in her voice and love shining from her jade eyes. He was awake, and although feverish, he was able to speak.

She lifted his head and helped him drink the willow bark tea. All through the morning she made him drink the willow infusion every few hours. By the time the sun was high, he was able to eat a bit of the corn cakes she had made from some meal she had found in a storage basket. There was a pot of honey as well to give him energy.

"You have saved my life, Green Eyes," he said softly as she carefully checked the dressing on his wound to see if there were any red streaks running from it.

"As you have mine, many times," she replied, meeting his intense gaze. She saw nothing but the depth of his love, remembering the first time she had met those eyes across a New Orleans ballroom. It seemed in another lifetime, when that man and that woman saw each other for the first time but knew that they were not strangers. They had only been waiting – waiting to meet and complete their life's journey together. She knew this was the time to tell him.

"What is it?" he asked, seeing something new and uncertain, but proud in her lovely visage.

"Together we have . . . have created a new life," she said with quiet pride.

"Beloved woman-wife, heart of my heart, soul of my soul, you have filled my being with joy. I had noticed the changes, but when you said nothing I thought you were not pleased. I felt so torn. I was filled with such elation that you were carrying the child of our love, but I saw no such elation in your eyes."

"In my heart I have been happy, but at such a time a woman is filled with worries, ancient worries that all mothers have experienced."

"Having a child while living with the People frightens you," he said gently, taking her hand and holding it to his cheek.

"Yes, but if I am with you, husband of my heart, I will fear nothing." Her voice quivered with emotion as she stared down at this man who was the very center of her life.

It was only the sound of horses' hooves entering the clearing that pulled Aimée from his side. Grabbing his gun she crept to the door. Lifting a corner of the mat covering, she peered out into the setting sun. She saw a figure approaching the lodge.

"Moon Flower, Shadow Panther, 'tis French Nancy," the old woman called out.

"Come, come in," Aimée answered, flinging back the mat cover.

With the old woman's help, and the ample food

stores she brought with her, Shadow Panther soon regained his health. She allowed them their privacy, coming every other day with provisions and news of the village, and of Mignon and Luis.

By the first of December, the month the Chickasaw called the Moon of Big Winter, Shadow Panther was able to leave the summer lodge, their wedding bower. With the cold winds blowing through the cracks in the walls they both knew it was time to leave.

"I shall miss having you to myself. Now I must share you with the others," Aimée said with regret as they mounted their horses to leave.

The trees were becoming bare of leaves, their dry branches rattling in the wind. A frost covered the ground like a dusting of sugar. Morning hoarfrost covered the bushes and undergrowth as they made their way down the forest path. A white-tailed deer bounded across their path, startling their horses.

Aimée's chin sunk down in the black bear fur of the heavy rug she held about her body, seeking shelter from the cold wind. The forest was a frozen tableau this early frigid morning. As beautiful as it was, she looked forward to a warm fire, even if it meant sharing the close quarters of the winter lodge with the others.

A brilliant scarlet cardinal soaring from the bare black branches of a tulip poplar drew her attention away from her contemplation of the cold. "How lovely," she murmured, lifting her chin from the fur, her breath a white wisp of fog on the still brittle air.

"It will not be too much farther till we are home," Shadow Panther told her with an understanding smile. He realized how cold she was, and once more realized his decision was the right one.

"This is not the way I remember," Aimée said, turning toward her husband. They had left the well-worn trail to take a path through a stand of tall dark pines. The wind moaning through the trees sounded like the roar of the sea.

"We are going home, Green Eyes, home to Eagle's Roost. You will not be cold inside its sturdy walls."

She stared at him in shocked surprise. They had made no mention of the plantation during the long cold days in the summer house. What had changed his mind?

"I cannot say I will not enjoy the pleasures of the hearth once more, but you are my husband, and the Chickasaw are my people." Her jade eyes gave him such a serious, loving look it smote his heart.

"And you are my wife, beloved one. Forgive my doubting you, the goodness of your heart, the largeness of your soul. You have stood beside me, fought beside me, learned my people's ways with a grace that few would have shown in the same circumstances. Now you carry my child inside your lovely body. I want to give you some token of my love, to thank you in some small way for all that you are, and all you bring to me. A Chickasaw woman owns her house, her land, to do with as she sees fit. I give you, beloved woman-wife, your house, your land. I give you Eagle's Roost."

Breaking through a dense grove of pines they stood on a ridge looking down at the beautiful white manor house sparkling in the winter sunshine. Gray-blue wood smoke drifted up into the air from the four brick chimneys at each end of the house.

"Merci, thank you, husband of my heart, twin of my soul. I have waited all my life for you. How blessed I am by fate to have been allowed to find you." Her voice trembled as tears misted the emerald jewels that were

her eyes. Holding out her hand to Shadow Panther she gave him a smile that said all that was in her heart.

He lifting her hand to his lips as a few white flakes swirled around them. He spoke softly. “I shall be at your side through your journey in this life, beloved woman of my soul, and beyond into all eternity.”

Epilogue

"Whither thou goest, I will go; and where thou lodgest, I will lodge, thy people shall be my people, and thy God my God."

Ruth 1:16

Eagle's Roost
June, 1796

The humid heat of early summer pressed down on the plantation. Huge alabaster blooms on the magnolia trees perfumed the still, warm air, mingling with the scent of the honeysuckle vine that wound around the columns of the portico. Aimée stood on the shaded porch and surveyed her newly planted fields which already showed rich promise of the fall harvest. She would not be back till the leaves turned to red and gold.

"You are sure you want to do this, Green Eyes?" The deep rich voice of her husband made her turn and give him a smile full of love.

" 'Tis time they knew the rest of their heritage. They are also Chickasaw." She gently rocked the green-eyed, ebony-haired, little male child lying in his Indian cradle board. He was wrapped in the skin of a cougar.

"I fear that their heritage may not be there for them when they are grown. Now that the Spanish are gone and the Creeks peaceful, the Americans pour into the domain of the People. They will not be satisfied till they have it all, as they have done on the other side of the mountains. Our son and daughter may not spend many more summers at Long Town," Shadow Panther replied soberly, a deep sadness in his dark expressive eyes. He tenderly touched a tawny wisp of the downy hair that covered his baby daughter's head. She opened her unusual amber eyes and seemed to stare at her father with perfect comprehension. He held her closer to his chest.

"I hope you are wrong, for I want them to learn the ways of the People. Their love and respect for nature and all her living creatures, their sense of honor, their love for children. I want them to have the freedom of a happy childhood, beloved husband."

"As do I, but change is coming, Green Eyes. We will have to face it soon, for there is nothing that can stop this. I feel it deep within my soul." The ebony eyes captured hers and caressed her with a melancholy tenderness.

"They will have their golden summers with the Chickasaw as long as fate allows, but we will always teach them the old ways. Come, it starts today," Aimée said softly, as Ivoire and the black stallion were brought from the stables by a servant.

"You do not hate the thought of leaving your house, and all its comforts behind, to live as a savage for the summer months?" he teased, but there was a wary, waiting quality about his proud features.

"They are your people, the twins' people, they are my people," she said simply, as if there should be no more question about what she had decided. They would spend each summer with French Nancy in Long

Town, so that the twins might know the unconditional love and joy of a Chickasaw childhood. Proud Eagle Woman would watch over the plantation as she had done for many moons.

"Have I told you how much I love you, beloved woman-wife, or how even now those green eyes set my blood afire?"

"Many times, my husband, but I never tire of hearing it. Perhaps tonight you can say it again, when we are alone in our bower by the stream and the twins are with French Nancy."

"You are a wicked woman, Green Eyes, to entice me so, but what joy you bring my soul. No matter what lies ahead, I shall travel life's journey with a light heart with you at my side."

As they rode down the avenue of cedars, the babies in their cradle boards in front of them, Bijou running beside the horses, they left the plantation behind and rode into the domain of the Chickasaw for their golden Indian summer. From the dense, verdant forest the panther roared his welcome.

Author's Note

The site of the Spanish fort *San Fernando de las Barrancas,* on the Chickasaw Bluffs over looking the Mississippi River is now a park located in Memphis, Tennessee. Nothing remains of the fort. The Chickasaw village of Long Town has also vanished. It was located near the modern city of Tupelo, Mississippi.

Several of the characters in the novel were actual figures in history. George Colbert and his brothers were a mixed-blood family that ran a ferry over the Tennessee river, and were also active in tribal affairs. French Nancy was a French woman who lived with the Chickasaw, having been captured by her future husband as a little girl. She lived to a great age and was honored and revered by the Indians with whom she made her home till she died. Chief Piomingo was a great chief, friendly to the Americans. He signed several treaties with them that later proved a great harm to his People's welfare.

Shadow Panther's fears for the Chickasaw turned out to be valid. By the end of 1795 the Spanish-supported Creeks sued for peace with the Chickasaw because Spain, after signing the Pinckney Treaty with the United States, withdrew from the region and demolished their fort on the Chickasaw Bluffs. The Americans raised their own fort on the same site and began their domination of the region. By 1819 the city of Memphis, Tennessee was laid out on the Chickasaw

Bluffs, and the sacred hunting grounds of the Chickasaw were drastically reduced. The United States continued to demand more and more land cessions from the Indians to satisfy the hordes of settlers and speculators who poured in, seeking their fortune. The misery and suffering of the noble, trusting Chickasaw, at the hands of the Americans who they initially considered their friends, continued for many years. It finally concluded in the tribe's infamous removal from their beloved domain to lands in the West—the Chickasaw's own tragic Trail of Tears, but that is another story.

HEARTFIRE ROMANCES

SWEET TEXAS NIGHTS (2610, $3.75)
by Vivian Vaughan
Meg Britton grew up on the railroads, working proudly at her father's side. Nothing was going to stop them from setting the rails clear to Silver Creek, Texas—certainly not some crazy prospector. As Meg set out to confront the old coot, she planned her strategy with cool precision. But soon she was speechless with shock. For instead of a harmless geezer, she found a boldly handsome stranger whose determination matched her own.

CAPTIVE DESIRE (2612, $3.75)
by Jane Archer
Victoria Malone fancied herself a great adventuress, but being kidnapped was too much excitement for even Victoria! Especially when her arrogant kidnapper thought she was part of Red Duke's outlaw gang. Trying to convince the overbearing, handsome stranger that she had been an innocent bystander when the stagecoach was robbed, proved futile. But when he thought he could maker her confess by crushing her to his warm, broad chest, by caressing her with his strong, capable hands, Victoria was willing to admit to anything. . . .

LAWLESS ECSTASY (2613, $3.75)
by Susan Sackett
Abra Beaumont could spot a thief a mile away. After all, her father was once one of the best. But he'd been on the right side of the law for years now, and she wasn't about to let a man like Dash Thorne lead him astray with some wild plan for stealing the Tear of Allah, the world's most fabulous ruby. Dash was just the sort of man she most distrusted—sophisticated, handsome, and altogether too sure of his considerable charm. Abra shivered at the devilish gleam in his blue eyes and swore he would need more than smooth kisses and skilled caresses to rob her of her virtue . . . and much more than sweet promises to steal her heart!

Available wherever paperbacks are sold, or order direct from the Publisher. Send cover price plus 50¢ per copy for mailing and handling to Zebra Books, Dept. 3489, 475 Park Avenue South, New York, N.Y. 10016. Residents of New York, New Jersey and Pennsylvania must include sales tax. DO NOT SEND CASH.

FIERY ROMANCE

CALIFORNIA CARESS (2771, $3.75)
by Rebecca Sinclair
Hope Bennett was determined to save her brother's life. And if that meant paying notorious gunslinger Drake Frazier to take his place in a fight, she'd barter her last gold nugget. But Hope soon discovered she'd have to give the handsome rattlesnake more than riches if she wanted his help. His improper demands infuriated her; even as she luxuriated in the tantalizing heat of his embrace, she refused to yield to her desires.

ARIZONA CAPTIVE (2718, $3.75)
by Laree Bryant
Logan Powers had always taken his role as a lady-killer very seriously and no woman was going to change that. Not even the breathtakingly beautiful Callie Nolan with her luxuriant black hair and startling blue eyes. Logan might have considered a lusty romp with her but it was apparent she was a lady, through and through. Hard as he tried, Logan couldn't resist wanting to take her warm slender body in his arms and hold her close to his heart forever.

DECEPTION'S EMBRACE (2720, $3.75)
by Jeanne Hansen
Terrified heiress Katrina Montgomery fled Memphis with what little she could carry and headed west, hiding in a freight car. By the time she reached Kansas City, she was feeling almost safe . . . until the handsomest man she'd ever seen entered the car and swept her into his embrace. She didn't know who he was or why he refused to let her go, but when she gazed into his eyes, she somehow knew she could trust him with her life . . . and her heart.

Available wherever paperbacks are sold, or order direct from the Publisher. Send cover price plus 50¢ per copy for mailing and handling to Zebra Books, Dept. 3489, 475 Park Avenue South, New York, N.Y. 10016. Residents of New York, New Jersey and Pennsylvania must include sales tax. DO NOT SEND CASH.